# My Dad My Dog

## Rebecca Warner

Black Rose Writing | Texas

ISBN: 978-1-68433-588-6
PUBLISHED BY BLACK ROSE WRITING
www.blackrosewriting.com

Printed in the United States of America
Suggested Retail Price (SRP) $19.95

*My Dad My Dog* is printed in Georgia

*As a planet-friendly publisher, Black Rose Writing does its best to eliminate unnecessary waste to reduce paper usage and energy costs, while never compromising the reading experience. As a result, the final word count vs. page count may not meet common expectations.

Cover Design by Johnny King jk@jkingdesign

Praise for
# My Dad My Dog

"Rebecca Warner's unmatched gift for telling a heartwarming story comes through in this touching tale of a woman who becomes caretaker to both her declining father and her beloved dog."

~ Nan Reinhardt, USA Today Bestselling Author
of the *Four Irish Brothers Winery* series

"Rebecca Warner paints a beautiful, timely portrait of unconditional love in her novel about Rachel, who becomes responsible for the care of her elderly dad and dog. No one tops her ability to create hope and triumphs, or characters who feel real. *My Dad My Dog* will linger on as a magnificent achievement from a gifted writer."

~ Jill Vogt, Award-Winning Poet
and Author of *Dancing with Armando*

*For My Dad and My Dog*
*both of whom enriched my life with*
*their sunny dispositions*
*and their brave and loving hearts.*

# My Dad My Dog

1

The knot in my stomach is unraveling with each mile I drive on the Blue Ridge Parkway. I'm nearing my destination, a place of acceptance, though I'd love to reach a state of grace. This is the day I've prepared for, the day that will change my life and my Alzheimer's-afflicted dad's life in ways that are still largely undefined, yet unavoidable. For better or worse, I'm bringing Dad home.

I'm unsettled at the thought of wheeling him out of Crestview Assisted Living for the last time. Once through those doors, the stable and comfortable life Dad has known for the last five years is over, and mine will be altered in ways I'm still trying to envision. He'll need considerable caregiving, and it will be up to me and my husband to provide it.

As I pull Dad's wheelchair van into a parking space at Crestview, I take a deep breath and tell myself it's going to be okay. I may have arrived at a place of acceptance, but now I have to move forward and seek higher ground where we'll all feel safe and happy. Such basic premises, but so vital to our well-being.

Heading toward the entrance, I hit my mental reset button to be present in the now. Inside, they're getting ready for Dad's going-away party, and I want to make it as enjoyable as possible. I can't say it will be memorable for him since his memory is flighty and doesn't stick around, but who knows? He often surprises me with the things he recalls.

My stride into the immaculate, welcoming lobby projects a breeziness I don't genuinely feel because it's tempered by an awareness that this is the last time I'll be here. Even though the administrator assured me they'll "always have a place for Joe," I don't see how we'll ever be able to move him back to this wonderful place. I'm sorry to take him away from this small corner of the world where he's been so content, and am apprehensive about moving him into my own corner of contentment. I quash that thought, push it way down, so that today of all days my anxiety doesn't resurface.

Most of Crestview's residents are already in the dining room. They welcome any change to their routine, and their anticipation of a party has led them here early. Some may remember they're here for Dad's going-away party, though they don't know where he's going or why he's leaving. Others want the simple pleasure of company and cake. As usual, I'm greeted with a chorus of cheery hellos, and I smile and wave in response as I look around the room for my dad.

Ah, there he is, parked at a table in his wheelchair. He's wearing his newest 82$^{nd}$ Airborne cap. Inside or outside, an Airborne cap is a staple of his attire. His favorite CNA, Sissy, is bending down and kissing his cheek. There's a flush of pleasure on his face. Sissy straightens and takes his hand in hers. "I'm sure going to miss you, Joe." Tears are welling in her warm eyes, and her voice is spilling emotion. "I love you, darlin'." She looks at me. "I love him a lot, Rachel."

Well, heck. Right off the bat, the direction of this party is taking a wrong turn. My eyes are welling with tears, too. If there are to be teary goodbyes, I'd hoped they wouldn't happen until we're ready to depart. I blink and nod, then kiss Dad's cheek, taking a moment for my threatening tears to retreat. Dad's gaze is fastened on Sissy, and I suppose he's searching for the right words to respond to her sentimentality.

But hovering over us, taking in every word and nuance, is Grady, a loud, gruff, pencil-thin resident who obsessively hitches his pants, although they're securely belted just slightly south of his armpits and can't get any higher. And just as I anticipated, Grady's booming voice cuts off any words Dad might have been ready to share with Sissy. "Where ya goin', Joe?"

Dad startles, then slowly shifts his body toward Grady. He's redirecting his thoughts from thanking Sissy to answering Grady. I'm tempted to answer for him, but refrain. His dementia hinders an easy flow of words, and I want to give him time to piece together an answer. After only a few more seconds, Dad's blue eyes flash with clarity and he tells Grady, "I'm going home."

For weeks, I've used those words for where he's going, and they seem to have stuck. But does he really understand that he'll be moving into my home, the home I share with my husband and dog?

"Where's home?" asks Della, who is more of a stalker than a hoverer. She's been in unrequited love with Dad since day one at Crestview. She pulls her chair so close to his wheelchair that the arms are touching.

I stay quiet, waiting for Dad's answer. He drops his head and leans away from Della. He plucks at the crease in his pants. "Florida," he mumbles, though he sounds uncertain. He looks up at me for confirmation.

Many of the residents have moved in closer to hear the conversation, but before I can edit Dad's answer, Grady jumps in again. "I thought you was from Tennessee." His tone is pitched between a question and an accusation.

Now I do answer for Dad. "He was born in Tennessee but lived in Florida for many years." And to answer the question of exactly where he *is* going, I add, "He's coming to live in my home, with me and my husband David, here in Asheville."

A chorus of reactions erupts from the circle of people around us, everything from whoops to squeals to amens. While I wanted happiness, these exclamations border on sheer joy. I can't sort out their excitement about Dad's leaving. They've been his companions for five years, after all. I can only attribute it to the novel idea that one of their own is moving into a real home. It's usually the other way around—from home to Crestview.

Crestview is home to mostly mobile adults of all ages who function at an acceptable level but need assistance with everyday living because of diminished mental capacity. And though Dad, at eighty-five, is older than most and his condition more profound, he has fit in well.

Once he moves in with us, his world will become much smaller and these sweet people will not be a part of it, not even occasionally. I don't want to share this reality with Dad or anyone else right now since I've convinced myself that today is about cheerful goodbyes and hopeful new beginnings.

"Does this mean you won't be visiting us anymore, Rachel?" I look over at Celia, a resident of more than twenty years. I've become fond of her, and I'm going to miss her smile, the way it never fails to reach her eyes.

"Dad and I hope to come back and visit, Celia." I clasp her hand and squeeze it. Smiling with relief, she squeezes back.

"I'm gonna miss *you* more than I'll miss Joe!" Ralph, Dad's best buddy, pipes out.

"Ha, Ralph!" I wink at him. "That's only because you'll miss the dollar bills I slip you."

Ralph laughs. Grady hitches his pants.

Dad is poised to say something but is interrupted when the head cook, Mary, pushes through the kitchen's swinging doors with a tray of brightly colored tumblers filled with iced tea. "Hey, Rachel. Today's the big day, huh? You look so pretty. You always do."

Before I can thank Mary, Crestview's oldest resident at ninety-two, James, steps between us and pushes his walker in close. He asks me for what has to be the hundredth time if I'll marry him. I tell him for the hundredth time that if I weren't already happily married, I'd be honored. Gratified, he swings his walker around and ambles off.

Mary has finished setting out the tumblers and is heading back toward the kitchen. Over her shoulder she tells Dad she's bringing his cake out now.

Dad tilts his head. His brow furrows. "Cake?"

"It's your going-away cake, Joe. You'll love it. Yum, yum."

Dad stares after Mary and continues to watch the kitchen door, oblivious to Sissy, who is tying a large bib around his neck. His vigilance is rewarded when Mary swings back through the door, holding the cake high above her head like a ceremonial offering. She sets it on the table next to a vase of spring lilies. Though others comment on it, Dad ignores them. The cake is his focal point. Its inscription, GOODBYE JOE, strikes me as odd in its no-frills frankness; but with deep swirls of chocolate frosting, the cake is something to behold.

"It's beautiful, Mary. It looks luscious."

She leans in and whispers, "I used the sugar substitute like you asked. Hope they don't notice." I nod and mouth my thanks.

Dad's focus is still on the cake. "GOODBYE JOE," he reads the inscription aloud. "Is this for me?" he asks no one in particular.

"It's your goodbye-party cake, Joe," Mary tells him again.

His lips purse and his eyes drift to the right, spotting nothing specific. He's sorting, as I call it, trying to reconcile what's before him with what's been lost to him. Grady's rough voice interrupts the process. "Why're you movin' in with Rachel?"

I'm ready to field this poorly timed question, but Dad's head comes up, and he cranes his neck toward Grady. His voice is uncharacteristically loud and clear when he answers. "Because Rachel and David are broke and can't pay for me to live here anymore."

My mouth drops open, and a hush falls over the room.

*Dear God.* Ask my dad what he had for breakfast and he won't be able to tell you. But ask him what was said in our heart-to-heart talk as I attempted to explain the reason for the move—hoping he'd understand at that moment, even though he'd likely forget in the next—and he's able to not only recall that conversation but to whittle it down to its most salient point: David and I are "broke." *Good Lord.*

It's true that we're having to make adjustments since our income has shrunk and our savings have dwindled, but our situation is not as dire as Dad just made it out to be.

"Is that true, Rachel? You broke?" Glenda, Crestview's bully, asks a little too cheerily. I try to steer clear of her because of her aggressive attitude, which is intensified by her imposing girth. She downright intimidates me, and that's hard to do.

Truth told, I want to tell her to go to hell, but that's unseemly, and I worry my voice will crack. I brush at non-existent lint on my pants and look over at Dad, who is smiling at me. He's pleased he was able to answer Grady's question. Then he looks at me, really looks at me, and his smile disappears. The corners of his mouth turn down and his eyes dull.

He's aware of my distress. His shaky hand reaches for mine. He wouldn't able to describe what I'm feeling, but he senses it. He doesn't think clearly, but he feels deeply; and at this moment, he wants to comfort his daughter. I'm filled with a familiar, soothing warmth, the same warmth I felt as a little girl when he would pick me up and kiss my scraped elbow and tell me I would be okay.

And I realize I *am* okay. This embarrassment is just a scrape that will eventually heal. So what if the secret is out? I'm facing much bigger obstacles. I squeeze Dad's hand and smile to let him know I'm fine, then sit up straighter and glance around.

The staff members stare at the floor. The residents, less inhibited by good manners, are openly surprised. They've witnessed the positive effects of my money on Dad's lifestyle: his lavishly furnished private room, private aides to entertain and engage him, and a married couple who do physical and massage therapy. I've brightened the residents' lives, too, with clothing, toiletries, and many dollar bills used for snacks from the vending machines. Dad's pronouncement likely has them coming to grips with what my being "broke" and not coming here anymore means to them—no more gifts.

Glenda's question hangs over the room like an overinflated balloon ready to pop. I meet her menacing eyes. *Just say it.* "We're not broke, Glenda. We're making adjustments, but we're comfortable enough to have Dad live an easy, good life with us in our home."

"She's got a big mansion, plenty of room for me," Dad declares, pleased to share a glimpse into his new home. *Wow, he's hitting on all cylinders today.*

Before I can refute his grandiose statement, Della asks, "May I come live with you, too?" She looks at Dad with longing.

I'm beyond relieved when Rhonda, an angel of a CNA, steps in. "All right, that's enough. Joe's lucky he gets to live with Rachel and get away from you nosy folks." There's a twitter of laughter. "A chocolate cake is sitting here, ready for eating. Let's give Joe a proper send-off."

Rhonda begins slicing it into generous portions. The confused and melancholy mood dissipates. Someone from the back of the growing gathering asks, "What does it say on that cake?"

"It says GOODBYE JOE," Rhonda blasts so that everyone can hear; otherwise, she'll be repeating it ten more times.

Dora, a resident who lives in the past, circa 1950, has been playing her usual repertoire of melancholy tunes on the piano in a corner of the dining room. Now she executes a wild riff on the keys and starts singing in a wide-open voice. "*Goodbye, Joe, you gotta go. . .*" She bangs the keys as though playing in a Cajun honky-tonk. From the ironic "Try to Remember" to "Jambalaya" in a heartbeat! Wide eyes and surprised laughter tell me I'm not the only one who's astonished at her abrupt turn from melancholy to mania. The residents start dancing where they stand. A few of the livelier ones clog to the tune with surprising agility and gusto. Dad claps his hands, smiling, oblivious to how off the beat he is. The atmosphere has turned festive and fun, taking on the proportions and character of the party scene I'd hoped for.

Besides the excellent care, this is why I've loved having Dad here. These people, despite their confinement to a facility—or maybe because of it—jump on opportunities to entertain themselves, and each other. It's been a good atmosphere for Dad. It certainly won't be as lively in my home.

He loves it here. The staff is excellent, dedicated and kind. No other facility in Asheville would take him in his condition. With his trifecta of Alzheimer's, Parkinson's and diabetes, in addition to the after-effects of a broken hip he'd suffered while still living in Florida, I kept getting directed to nursing homes. But for the right price, Crestview took him in. Homey, safe, spotless Crestview. Yet again, I have to push down the anxiety that's threatening to resurface at the thought of Dad's moving in, upending my comfy life, and depending on me, David and our big black Lab, Nick, to fill his world.

But David and I can't continue subsidizing his civil service pension, VA disability, and Social Security to the hefty tune of three-thousand dollars a month. It's been almost three years since the 2008 real estate market meltdown, and with the Great Recession that followed, we've struggled more each year to subsidize Dad's living here at Crestview. What money we have after liquidating all we could is slated for mortgage payments and living expenses over the next two years. We simply have no choice. *Goodbye, Crestview, we gotta go. . .*

If Dad hadn't broken his hip—and in a hospital, of all places—he could have continued living in the posh assisted living facility in Florida, where he enjoyed a luxurious and activity-filled life. The surgeon's post-surgery prognosis that Dad wouldn't live for more than a year because of his infirmities prompted me to move him up here to North Carolina. I wanted him nearby so I could oversee every aspect of his rehabilitation and medical care. It was an outright effort to defy the surgeon's death sentence. Five years later, Dad's still here—a testament to both our wills.

Now he'll be nearer than I ever imagined. Even as we're enjoying chocolate cake, David and the movers are down the hall emptying Dad's room. I'm taking Dad for lunch and a drive on the Parkway while David gets everything set up at home. At least, that's the plan.

The residents have forsaken dancing for cake. I certainly wouldn't want their afflictions, but I almost envy these people for their ability to live in the moment with no worries about the future. I dare say even their concern about no more gifts has been forgotten. Crumbs decorate their shirts, faces, and the dining room floor, but they're oblivious. Those who have finished start to leave. They're not being rude; they're just being themselves. Everyday life, as they know it, goes on.

It's time for the final farewell. "Well, it's time for us to go home, Dad." I stand and turn to the selfless women who have given my dad five years of loving care. I hug and thank each one, then stand by as they offer Dad hugs and kisses, along with words of love and encouragement.

"I'm really going to miss you two," Sissy says, sniffling, "but I'll come see you and Joe, I promise." She looks past me, noticeably brightening, and adds conspiratorially, "Don't leave just yet. You didn't hear it from me, but they have a little something for Joe." She points to the corridor. "See? Here they come."

The residents are filing back into the dining room. Grace, Crestview's self-appointed spiritual leader who wasn't at the party to pray over the cake, is leading them. She's holding her Bible tight to her bosom, as always. A picture of Mighty Mouse is taped to its back. I never asked.

"I hear you're going home, Joe," she says. She closes her eyes and bows her head. "You're going to a better place."

"Um, he's not going home like that, Gracie," Sissy says.

"His journey home to eternal life." Grace raises a hand high in the air.

"No, not yet," I tell her. "He's coming to my home, to live with me."

I swear she looks disappointed as she hands Dad a sheet of paper. She's written "Psalm 23" at the top, and there are scribbles underneath. Dad thanks her and lays it in his lap. It's her going-away gift, she tells him.

The assortment of odd gifts, including a single brown glove, an empty ring box, and a doorknob, grows in his lap.

Dad thanks each person graciously, until he doesn't, because he's becoming overwhelmed. He's managed to engage each giver as he's accepted the gifts, but that's a lot of sustained activity for his muddled mind and shaky hands. When he folds his hands in his lap, bows his head and closes his eyes—his way of powering down before he's completely drained—I take over in accepting gifts.

Celia gives him the best gift of all—a paper grocery bag with handles.

"You knew just what he needed, Celia, something to carry these gifts."

She hugs me tightly. "Please don't ever forget me," she says.

*Please don't ever forget me.* That's what I silently plead with my dad, each and every day.

## 2

Although he was cognizant beyond recognition at Crestview when he announced that David and I were broke and that he was moving into our "mansion," Dad loses that thread as we ride along the Parkway. I comment on the multicolored wildflowers, blooming bushes and blossoming trees of spring, but Dad stays silent. My anxiety level rises as I exit the Parkway.

"We're almost home, Dad."

"Will Evelyn be there?"

Mother passed away eight years ago, but he still finds her in his dreams. He's related conversations they've had, and I have no desire to dissuade him from the reality of that. Who am I to say what dreams are made of for a man with dementia who still loves his long-departed wife?

"She's always with you," I tell him, "but she doesn't live with us. She lives in heaven." I don't have a clear concept of heaven, but the heaven where you join those you love is a real place to Dad, as it was to Mother. For their sakes, I hope they're right.

He's quiet for a long moment before he says, "I miss her."

I reach over and take his warm hand in mine. "I miss her, too, Dad."

We share a moment of quiet contemplation before Dad surprises me by asking about what is also near and dear to his heart—food. "Who's going to cook?"

I laugh because he's grasped that in living with us, he might not get any more of the good home cooking Crestview provided. *Whoa ho, is he ever right about that.*

"David and I will cook, Dad. I'm turning out to be a good cook." That's a lie. I'm a terrible cook; ergo, I don't cook. But I've been trying out recipes that have fewer than my self-imposed limit of ten ingredients and are healthy for a diabetic. Okay, so maybe he has good reason for concern.

I sense his gaze and glance over. He's not buying it, and I can't blame him. We've all had some awful experiences with my meals.

"You won't go hungry," I assure him. Nevertheless, he looks worried.

The moving truck isn't in our driveway, so I assume the movers have come and gone, and I can only hope that David has had enough time to make Dad's apartment welcoming.

Nick, our big black Lab, greets us with a wagging tail and his goofy smile. He follows the handicapped van into our three-car garage, where I expect to see David, but he's not here. I unbuckle the restraints around Dad's wheelchair, then lower the power ramp, hop out, and give Nick a head rub.

Nick, his tale swishing with eagerness, follows me as I go around to unload Dad. I'm poised to push Dad down the ramp when Nick voices a low and friendly bark.

"Get that dog away from me!" Dad's Parkinson's-diminished voice is surprisingly loud, but it's the harshness in it that catches me off guard.

Nick, no fool of a dog, takes a step back.

"What's the problem, Dad? Don't you like Nick?"

"I don't like any dog," he grunts.

*What fresh dementia hell is this?* I must tread lightly to find out.

"You've never had a problem with Nick before, Dad." There is a photo of the three of us when Dad visited shortly after Mother passed away. He and I were leaning against the deck railing and Nick had his snout in Dad's crotch. It's one of those pictures that makes you wince and laugh at the same time. I always thought Nick's interest in that part of Dad's anatomy, which is common among dogs, was the reason for Dad's grimace.

But faced with this outburst, I see his expression in that photo in a different light. He was nervous and trying not to show it. We had another dog then, our sweet Rottweiler, Rocky, and he was the one that gave people pause. His size and stance were intimidating, though he was a gentle dog.

Nick sits down on the garage floor and waits patiently as I try to sort this out.

Having been a mailman who'd been bitten on more than a few occasions, Dad's dislike of dogs is understandable. He'd steered well clear of Rocky, like most people. But our Nick? Dad always seemed more or less unaffected by Nick. While, in the many times he's been to our home, Dad hasn't shown him any real affection, he hasn't shown any outright animosity, either. Why has this changed?

Before I can ask him that question, Dad grumbles, "If this is my house, I don't want that dog in it."

*His house?* Boy, he's comprehended his reality better than I expected. His outburst threatens my vision of a harmonious home life. Dad has every right to vocalize his opinions and criticisms, and it will be up to me to deal with them. But this is hard going at this early juncture, and my heart drops.

I've learned not to argue with Dad's take on situations. The Alzheimer's is responsible for his outbursts, and any contradictions only increase his agitation. Still, Dad is a fair and kind-hearted man, so I appeal to those qualities. "This is my house, too, and Nick's house. David and I love him. If I promise he won't come into your apartment or be anywhere near you, will that be okay?"

His shoulders relax and he exhales with relief. "Sure, Sugar. He can live here." He pauses, then adds with emphasis, "But he can't come in my room."

"Sugar" has been Dad's pet name for me since I was a little girl. Hearing his endearment touches me. "He won't, I promise. Thanks, Dad."

To prove the point, I tell Nick to go to his bed, which he does. Only then do I roll Dad down the van's ramp.

I wonder again where David is. He should be here to welcome Dad. I'd envisioned David, Nick, and me doing that together, but I'm down by two on the hospitality committee, so there goes that merry image.

The apartment where Dad will live is off the garage. I reassure him Nick won't bother him as I open the door to enter the foyer leading to the apartment's kitchenette, vanity area and bath. A second door leads to a combined bedroom and living area. Designed to be a private apartment for guests, it has accommodated dozens of friends and family members over the years. It also proved to be a sanity-saver when some guests, like David's parents and mine, would stay for a month at a time.

Adding an elevator off the garage was an allowance for Mother's heart condition and her difficulty in climbing stairs. Over the past five years, the elevator has facilitated Dad's many visits, since his wheelchair fits in it with room to spare. But those were for daytime visits. Now that he's an actual resident, I'm more grateful than ever we have it. Otherwise, Dad would be relegated to this ground-floor apartment full time.

A quick visual sweep confirms David has done a wonderful job of getting it set up in such a brief time. I wonder again where he is as I go back out and fetch Dad and push him into his large and sunny apartment. David has opened the Roman shades so that the outside light is pouring in, bathing the space in a welcoming glow.

"This is nice," Dad says. He's stayed in here many times over the years, but now he must be looking at it with the fresh eyes of a resident, rather than a guest.

His gaze creeps from wall to wall, looking for familiar things. He sees those touches of home that have traveled with him from one facility to another. I'm pleased that his memorabilia are on display, and in all the right places.

Dad is beholding the fruits of David's hurried labor, and I'm grateful to my husband for getting everything looking so fine for him.

Photos of Mother and him—from their engagement picture to the last church directory picture taken before her death—rest on the shelves of the same entertainment center he's had since moving into Crestview.

There's the childhood photo of me and my sisters, taken at Christmas when Cindy was six, Kathy was four, and I was two. There are numerous pictures of graduations and weddings and grandchildren, and David has done a great job of putting them in the same spaces they've always occupied on the entertainment center. Planning Dad's space included keeping the things he has lived with every day for years just as they've always been, wherever possible, because familiarity with surroundings is comforting to dementia patients.

His masculine hunter green and navy blue Ralph Lauren comforter is spread over his automated Alzheimer's bed, making it look like a regular twin bed. His other main piece of furniture, a plushy lift chair covered in colorful throws, sits across from the bed. David has moved the small two-person dinette set to a corner across the room, next to the chest of drawers. It all fits nicely.

Hanging on one wall is the large framed collage I'd had made of his Army pictures and medals from his service in the 82nd Airborne during World War Two. Above his bed is a lovely painting of a Florida shore. It was Mother's favorite painting, so hopefully it will serve as a reminder to Dad of the many enjoyable years they lived near the ocean.

Dad stares at the painting for several moments, and I keep quiet as he does. I have no idea if his mind is roiling with memories or processing its current placement in his new dwelling. I don't want to interrupt his processing of thoughts since shifting gears in his brain can bring on frustration and irritation more often than not. That's the last thing I want for him today, so I let him take his time to register what he sees and what it means to him.

He turns his attention to the view outside his windows—majestic trees, a cloudless sky that's bluer than robin's eggs, and rolling mountains that, at 1.8 billion years of age, stand steadfast and serene. On this beautiful spring day in May, the mountains and trees are swathed in variant and glorious shades of green. The distant mountains take on a deep, verdant tone, while the trees outside his windows are caressed by sunlight that tints their leaves an emerald hue. It's an unobstructed and peaceful view, much better than the one he had at Crestview. From here, Dad can enjoy watching the change of seasons. I hope he may have many more seasons ahead of him.

I'm in such a languorous state from soaking up the view that I don't even notice David has come into the apartment until he puts his hands on my shoulders and says, "Sorry I wasn't here when you drove in."

I turn to face him. "Where were you?"

"I was on the phone." In response to my questioning look, he smiles and says, "Could be something good."

He doesn't have to say any more for me to know that, as always, he's working on bringing in income. I smile to let him know . . . well, so much. That I'm happy for him and hope it works out. That I'm grateful for the wonderful job he's done with Dad's apartment. That I'm pleased he's here now. David nods, acknowledging all that my smile conveys.

Dad is still looking out the windows, contemplative and silent. David walks over and gives Dad an affectionate pat on the shoulder. He holds out his hand for a man-to-man shake and says, "Hey, Joe. We're glad you're here. How do you like your new home?"

Dad looks up at David and shakes his hand, then turns his head and looks at me for a long moment. Then his gaze shifts back to the windows and settles on the serene view beyond.

David takes Dad's lack of a verbal response in stride and moves next to me and takes my hand. He's well aware of how anxious I am about Dad's adjustment, and he's signaling that he's here to support me, whichever way the tree falls.

Neither of us says anything. We stand hip to hip in harmony, allowing Dad time to form his thoughts, and perhaps even speak them. A peaceful energy fills the space where we stand. Looking out the windows, I'm mesmerized by the alternating shade and sun rippling across the breeze-stirred leaves of the trees. I take a deep breath and exhale, releasing my fears and tension. I'm keenly aware and deeply appreciative of the fullness of my life. Everything will be fine. I believe I've finally reached that state of grace.

Dad breaks my reverie when he looks up at us, smiling, and says, "This house is full of love." I almost drop to my knees in relief and gratitude.

My dad is home.

# 3

Our previous landscaper's wife, a lovely young woman named Carmen who speaks little English but has a big enough heart to understand what is needed, is our go-to gal in helping with Dad. I've done the math, and after paying for his prescription co-pays, medical supplies, diapers and toiletries, we can afford to pay her forty dollars a day for four hours' work, six days a week. She's agreed to come every morning except Sundays. Thank God she needs the money because I need the help.

Carmen is very pretty, with her high cheekbones and almond-shaped brown eyes, and Dad takes to her and cooperates as she and I work together on this, her first day, to establish his morning routine. The goal is to get her comfortable with handling his toileting, bathing and breakfast, then changing his sheets and freshening his kitchen and bathroom. With her here, all I need to worry about in the mornings are his pills and insulin—well, besides doing loads of laundry and putting together a wholesome lunch.

She's not as quick and efficient as I'd envisioned. Her pace in all she does is unhurried, almost leisurely, and I wonder how she keeps up with her two young children. Oh, well, she may be slow, but Dad likes her. She's also strong and not put off by the toileting requirements. *Good enough.*

The four hours fly by, and when she leaves I find myself facing the next twenty hours of just David and me caring for Dad; and you know, it's downright daunting.

After last night's welcome-home dinner of baked chicken—David's doing, thankfully—we brought Dad down to his apartment and completed all the chores necessary to prepare him for bed. After getting him settled for the night, we'd wearily climbed the stairs and stopped at the top to look at each other in what I would describe as bemused panic. *Writ large.*

We'd burst into laughter—a punchy side effect of our first big dose of reality.

Dad is propped up in bed, no doubt expecting lunch after taking his midday medications. And then the toilet will call. I hope David will be back in time to help me with that. It would be so much easier if Dad would just *let go* in an absorbent diaper, but he's always been adamant about not doing that. So he must be hoisted, transferred and seated. Then the process is reversed. It's a challenging chore to perform by myself.

Then there's dinner, and his evening medications. Then more transferring and toileting and settling him in bed. I'm tired just thinking about the day's demands. A wave of panic swells inside me. I won't allow it. *I won't.*

For certain, I'm no stranger to caregiving, having nursed my mother for six months before she passed away—first for three months in the hospital, where I camped out ten-to-twelve hours a day, and where an overworked staff welcomed me. Near the end of Mother's life, in her and Dad's Florida home, Hospice and a live-in aide had assisted me.

Even with that generous help, the days had been long and draining. I'd thought I had a handle on caregiving, but in this moment of looking at Dad, who's totally under my keep, I recognize my limits and lack of experience as a full-time caregiver.

*Now* I'm having this insight?

I take a deep breath and watch the play of leafy sunlight dance on the wall opposite the window. It is peaceful and pretty in here, even cheery.

With my panic gone and confidence restored, I ask Dad what he would like for lunch. Although pot roast is the only thing on the menu, he will eat whatever I put in front of him, but I want him to think he has a say in the matter.

"What have you got?"

"I cooked a pot roast. Would you like some?"

"I didn't know you cooked." I can't help but laugh at his bewildered expression. Even though we'd been over this yesterday, we're starting over today.

Dad laughs along; he loves to laugh. He's easygoing and charming and funny and sweet, and I think how lucky I am that he is such a congenial man, even with the advancing dementia. His good nature and positivity will make a difference in how we function as a family in the coming years. *Knock wood.*

It's fortunate—if there's anything fortunate about dementia—that both his Alzheimer's and Parkinson's are of the slow-progressing nature. From the time he was diagnosed with dementia, I assembled a progressive group of physicians and therapists to oversee his care, first in Florida and now here in North Carolina. He's not only still alive, but doing rather well, considering his maladies.

If he hadn't broken his hip, he'd be more mobile. But the Parkinson's pushed back against the rehabilitative therapy, despite Dad's hard work.

Because of his dementia, he doesn't grasp his physical limitations, and he believes he'll walk on his own again. I'll never be the one to dissuade him of that notion. I'd sure rather have an optimistic than a pessimistic dad.

Right now, he's optimistic about lunch. "David likes my pot roast, and I bet you will, too."

I hear a scrabbling noise behind me and turn to see Nick hovering in the doorway. He gives a low woof. It's as if he's heard and understands the words "pot roast" and is hoping for his own portion.

I'm ready to shoo Nick out when Dad cries, "Get that dog out of here!"

Poor Nick practically leaps out the door. He's not used to harsh voices or wounded feelings. I want to leap out myself and comfort him, but Dad takes precedence. I hadn't foreseen this chasm—far from it—that ups the ante of caregiving. Keeping Nick out of Dad's way is going to be challenging. Nick has had the run of the house for years. But I've made Dad a promise, and I'll keep it.

"He's gone. I'm sorry he came in. I'll make sure it doesn't happen again."

Dad plucks at his bed covers with tight fingers. "I don't like that dog," he grumbles.

I flinch at his tone and the gloom it inflicts. I'd hoped his anti-dog outburst yesterday was dementia-related and temporary. I'd believed Dad and Nick would become good buddies. I'd thought Nick could help fill a gap and lessen Dad's loneliness if he missed the human companionship at Crestview.

Disappointed and a bit aggravated that he'd hurt Nick's feelings, I'm in no mood to indulge his attitude. "You've made that clear, Dad. Let's move on."

"Let's move on," he repeats. Now he's smiling. His sudden mood swings are not unusual, but they still catch me off guard.

I relinquish my irritation and smile. "Yes, let's move on to lunch."

"What are we having?"

This need for repetition is fairly recent. I shrug it off as another stone to step over. "I'm thinking pot roast. How does that sound?"

"Sounds fine." His brow furrows. "Did you cook it?"

We could go round and round about this all day. "Yes. I followed a delicious recipe."

Dad thinks about it. "Bet it's tough as shoe leather."

We laugh. He isn't criticizing; he simply expects it to be as unsavory as anything else I've ever cooked.

"Tell you what. I'll sprinkle shoe polish on it to give it more flavor."

We share another laugh—a warm and easy moment between us.

"Okay then, I'll get your pills, and we'll do lunch."

Dad sometimes refuses to take his pills, but if there's one pill I hope he'll get down, it's Sinemet. It eases his difficulty in swallowing, which is an unpleasant symptom of Parkinson's. Considering tough-as-leather pot roast is on the menu, we'll need all the help we can get.

I learned from Crestview that a calm and quiet environment facilitates his pill-taking process. It takes ten long minutes of gentle coaxing before he has swallowed all of them. I breathe a sigh of relief as I get up to turn on the TV and tune in to *Judge Judy* to keep him company while I go upstairs to fix his plate.

The judge is administering one of her usual unvarnished verdicts. "She can be real tough," Dad says. "She reminds me of your momma. That's why I like her."

He's right. Judge Judy's no-nonsense demeanor and admonishments are similar to Mother's stern reprimands. She could be tough, but the good side of Mother was very good, and Dad loved her then and loves her still, just as I do.

Nick, looking sad and lonely, is on his bed in the garage. I love him up and soothe his hurt feelings with soft words. He follows me up to the kitchen where I give him a slice of packaged roast beef, thinking it's the next best thing to pot roast.

He follows me back down the stairs but stops outside of Dad's room. "I'll be back," I tell him as I push through the door. Dad is dozing, but I don't hesitate to wake him. The pot roast and peas are hot, and dozing is something he can do anytime. I've cut the roast into small bites, but I don't look forward to the long process of getting the meal into him. Whether he feeds himself or needs help, it's a long and deliberate undertaking.

Dad surprises me when he picks up his fork with agility and makes a successful stab at a piece of roast. "That's good," he mumbles at the first bite. He raises his eyebrows. "Did you really make this?"

"Dad! Of course I made it. It's not applied statistics. I put everything in a Crockpot. David's sister gave me the recipe."

"Well, it's good."

I've never attached any happiness or self-worth to being able to cook, but I'm pleased he likes it.

"Better than those fish sticks," he adds.

"Those fish sticks!" I burst out laughing. Mother had been out of town, tending to her sick father, when I'd made my first attempt at cooking. Heating frozen fish sticks wasn't exactly cooking, but as an uninitiated teenager, anything else was beyond me. I recall serving some doughy frozen hush puppies, too.

I'd forgotten about that until now. "What do you remember about those fish sticks?" I'm curious to see how much he'll recall.

"They were half-cooked. Worst thing I ever ate."

Now I recall something else. "And you let me know that, too. I remember you grumbled, 'What crummy fish sticks these are.' Do you remember what I said to you when you complained?"

He casts his eyes up to the left, searching for a memory that doesn't come. He looks at me and shakes his head.

"I said, 'Daddy! I made those for you and you're going to eat them!'"

"That sounds like something you'd say. You and your momma." He smiles and shakes his head. I wonder if he's thinking about Mother. She wasn't exactly a great cook, either.

"But seriously, that was the worst meal you ever had? Ever?"

"Outside of Army food, yeah, the worst." He barks out a laugh. "I thought you'd never get a husband if you couldn't cook any better than that."

I bark out a laugh of my own. "You never told me that."

"I was wrong. Good thing you're smart and pretty."

"Thanks, that's sweet of you to say. I'll tell you, I think it was your reaction to those fish sticks that helped me decide cooking wasn't something I would bother to learn."

"And you didn't." He eyes his plate. "Until now."

For twenty minutes, I stay beside him, helping him eat. Despite my help, peas roll off his fork and down his bib. The eating process stalls as he reaches down with shaky fingers to pluck cold peas off his chest and laboriously bring them to his mouth. I want to tell him to never mind, but he's intent on the process, and I'm not going anywhere anyway. Still, I chafe at the delay in getting him fed because my back is hurting. I'll have to figure out a better arrangement than this. His bed offers him plenty of comfortable positions, but none for me. I bend over his lap tray from a side angle and shift around, but there is no relaxed angle.

Twice I rewarm the pot roast and peas in the microwave, gaining temporary back relief and sending peppery, meaty aromas out into the kitchenette. This would be easier if I transferred him to a chair at the dinette table in his apartment, but I'm not comfortable doing that alone.

But I am okay with moving him into his wheelchair, and I can just push it up to the table. *Duh.*

Having solved that absurdly simple problem, I focus on helping Dad finish his lunch. Being near his sweet energy gives me pleasure, and I relinquish my dread at getting him fed while worrying about things that could go wrong. Why stack worry upon worry?

Still, I'm relieved when he eats every bite without incident. "Thanks, Sugar, that was nice."

I tell him he's welcome and kiss his forehead, then lift the tray from his lap. He tips his head back and closes his eyes to settle into a nap.

Dad is safe, comfortable and happy—everything I wanted for him when he moved in. I flick a wish out to the universe for many more days of the same.

# 4

David has been invited to play golf at a private club, which means no greens fees for him. He looked so good in his fitted Bonobos golf pants, I almost waylaid him. At six-feet and one-hundred eighty pounds, he's in great shape. He has that lean but muscular athletic build and a confident way of carrying himself that denotes decades of playing sports. His forest-green eyes were enhanced by the emerald green of his polo shirt, and I almost got lost in them. When he took off his golf cap and brushed his hand through his light brown hair and aimed his megawatt white smile at me, I fairly swooned. It's amazing that after twenty-two years of marriage, I'm still smitten with my handsome hubby.

After a sweet kiss, he left with a wish for me to give his best regards to Anna, Dad's "girlfriend." She's not really his girlfriend, but I would never tell Dad that. Fantasy can be a nice place to dwell, and I'm not about to kick him out of there.

Anna is a beautiful, and I mean *beautiful*, CNA whom I hired for daily visits with Dad during a three-week period when times were still good and David and I were in Europe. She's Dad's dream girl. Though she's a knockout, it's her sweet personality and loving nature that have him enthralled. She "loves on him" as he calls it, and several times he has boldly proposed marriage. Yes, he loves Mother still, but he's also just a man, and one with dementia at that. He can't be faulted for his attraction to a beautiful, sweet woman who holds his hand and kisses his cheeks and smooths his hair and tells him how handsome he is.

Anna is more affectionate than most caregivers, but as she has told me so many times, "Joe is just so loveable." She actually has a handsome, long-time boyfriend, but she never mentions him around Dad. She has all the right instincts.

After we returned from Europe, we kept her employed as a part-time companion to Dad. She even became our live-in dog sitter when we traveled to see members of my or David's family, while still spending time with Dad three days a week at Crestview. Anna became an important part of all our lives, and I am sorry I'll never again have the luxury of her own brand of caregiving for my loved ones.

When she drives up, Nick meets her in the driveway and does his doggie dance of greeting before shamelessly throwing himself over and offering up his belly. His eyes roll back in his head and his tongue lolls to the side as Anna obliges. When she stands up, he stands up with her, retrieves a nearby ball, and offers it to her.

I'm the mean mommy when I say, "Not now, Nick," because I know her time is limited. More than that, Dad's eager to see Anna.

Nick looks mighty disheartened as he lets the ball drop from his mouth. I rub his head and give him an apologetic kiss.

He follows Anna and me into the garage but stops at Dad's door. "You can come in here with me, Nick." Anna waves her hand to indicate he should follow her into Dad's apartment. Nick looks at me for permission, but I shake my head and tell him to stay. Another dispirited look. I *hate* being the mean mommy.

I tell Anna why Nick can't go in. She nods in understanding and says, "I hope that changes. They'd be good for each other."

I give her a conspiratorial wink. "Maybe you can whisper that in Dad's ear."

She laughs and tells me she'll work on it. "Joe!" she exclaims as we walk into Dad's apartment. He's sitting in his lift chair, looking dapper, and he knows it. His pretty blue eyes light up at the sight of her. Carmen and I really spiffed him up this morning.

On Carmen's third day, I noticed she was taking a long time to shave Dad, so I told her it was something I wanted to do for him. I take real pleasure in shaving him and combing his freshly-washed hair each day.

But today I took extra care to banish every single whisker, and instead of just combing his thick silver hair, I blow-dried it so it's full and shiny. When I gave him a choice between two of his aftershaves, he pointed to the Armani Code bottle and said confidently, "That's her favorite." He really surprises me at times with the wisps of memory that cling long enough for him to be decisive.

His smile is openhearted, and he stares at Anna like she's a glass of cool water in an arid desert. He lifts his arms for a hug, and as she obliges, his eyes close and a sigh seeps out. She pulls away, but Dad's arms are still outstretched, lonesome in the emptiness of the air that fills the space she vacated. They lower with the semblance of sinking balloons.

Anna doesn't notice because she's crossing the room to grab a chair. She sits next to him and takes his hands in hers. "You're looking so handsome today." Her silky raven hair falls forward as she leans in and subtly inhales his lingering fragrance. "And oh, my, you're wearing my favorite cologne."

Wow, Anna's flirting packs a punch. No wonder he's enraptured.

It's a shame that our financial situation doesn't allow for the luxury of Anna's full-time companionship, because she has a gift for making Dad feel special. I told her most of the truth of our situation, accompanied by apologies that I could no longer employ her. She was sympathetic, but she was also distressed and sad. She has another part-time job as an aide to an elderly woman, but she needed this job, too. I offered to do anything I could to help her, but, being Anna, she found a job the following week on her own.

I so appreciate her being here on a Saturday, her day off, in the capacity of a friend. I can use the break and Dad can use the company.

"You look beautiful, honey. I've missed you." Dad's eyes roam her face, taking in all its fine details. He asks her where she's been.

She glances at me over her shoulder, and I shrug. Let her tell him whatever she thinks is best. She knows him well.

"I got a new job," she says, "and I just can't get the time off to visit every other day like I did before."

*Good answer, Anna.*

Dad looks momentarily deflated, but his interest in her is genuine. "What's your new job?"

"I'm working in a doctor's office," she enthuses, "and I'm making good money and learning new things."

As is so often true, Dad pauses to processes this. Sometimes when I'm waiting for an answer, I get annoyed, but then realize all over again that it's remarkable that he can still process at all. "That's good for you, then."

"It *is* good for me, Joe. The only thing that's bad about it is I can't visit with you as often."

"I understand, honey." He's squeezing her hands, reassuring her it's okay.

"I'm so glad you're here, Anna," I interject. "I made lunch if you have time to stay."

"What do you think, Joe? Do you mind if we have lunch together?"

"You may not want to eat Rachel's cooking," Dad says, grinning at his ongoing joke.

I make a mock protest, then say, "We have deli chicken salad, Anna, so there's no chance of food poisoning."

"Sounds good." Anna looks at Dad. "Does that sound good to you, Joe?" As always, she's solicitous without being patronizing. Another of her charms.

I return bearing a tray with plates of chicken salad on a bed of lettuce, with fresh cantaloupe and grapes on the side. She's already put Dad in his wheelchair and pushed him up to the table. Of course she has. She's an experienced CNA who didn't have to think twice about such efficiency.

As she puts a bib around his neck, she lays soft kisses on the top of his head and whispers words of endearment. Her affection is nutrition for Dad's soul, and he's lapping it up.

The placemats, cutlery and napkins are on the table. She's cutting the cantaloupe into even smaller pieces when she asks me, "You gave him his Sinemet?"

I smile and nod. "Right before you got here." I head into the kitchenette to grab two glasses with ice for their diet colas. I don't mind that she questioned me. She has had to cope with Dad's dysphagia a few times herself. Though she's never given Dad his meds, she cared enough to learn what they were and what they did for him. She's quite intelligent, and it's a shame she could never afford to go to nursing school, as she'd wanted to do.

"I'm going to leave you two to visit. Let me know if you want anything. I have some key lime pie upstairs for dessert. Just call me on the intercom when you're ready for it, and I'll bring it down and join you." It's a sugar-free pie, made with Stevia, from a recipe I found in a diabetic cookbook. I have no idea how it's going to taste, but since I plan to join them for dessert, I'll find out.

But then, it really doesn't matter. Anna has already provided all the sweetness Dad will need today.

# 5

It's been a little over two weeks since Dad came to live with us, and my back has become a persistent sore spot from lifting, positioning and transferring him. Now I wear a back-support belt to protect me from injury, and David often helps, yet the pain persists. It abates with an anti-inflammatory and a heating pad but flares up again each day as I start my chores. Pulling loads of clothes and sheets and towels from the washing machine several days a week, bending over to scrub tubs and mop floors that were previously attended to by a housekeeper, in addition to transferring Dad and positioning him in bed, ensure that it stays sore. I'm also tired, more tired than I can ever remember being. I feel a little bitchy about it all. Okay, a lot bitchy.

Which leads to thoughts about Carmen. I'm grateful to have her, but I'm aggravated that she still needs my help and hasn't become as quick-moving and efficient as I'd hoped. I keep thinking she'll improve, but after two weeks, it's pretty evident that is not going to happen.

I've thought about replacing her, but that isn't easy to do. There aren't home-health agencies on every corner in Asheville; and anyway, to go through an agency would cost eighteen dollars an hour.

I'm in a dark mood until Nick pokes his big black head into the laundry room where I'm doing my third load of the day. Ah, my fur-baby!

His soulful brown eyes silently ask why I'm not out throwing the ball or taking a walk with him, as I did almost every day no matter the weather, before Dad came to live with us.

There is no blame or recrimination in those sweet eyes, only a yearning for more of my attention. He has been so quiet and undemanding these past two weeks, and I've allowed that sweet complacency to overtake my responsibilities to him. Because Nick doesn't need attention, as Dad does, he has received much less of my time and energy.

I miss our time together, though not as much as Nick must. Our walks are always full of joy and discovery, and he rarely leaves my side as we stride through the wooded acreage surrounding our home, toward the creek where he gleefully abandons himself to the flow and fun in the pools of cool water. In the summer, I often take off my hiking boots and wade in with him, getting wet from head to toe from his splashing and shaking, but I enjoy being his playmate.

Sometimes I wonder if I should have gotten Nick a real playmate after Rocky passed away from bone cancer. He was only eight when diagnosed, and it was aggressive. Instead of amputation and chemo, we chose comfort measures until there was no more comfort to be had.

After Rocky passed, David and I spent so much time with Nick that we believed he didn't need anyone but us. We knew we would get another dog—adopt just the right one from the local shelter when the time came. We even added our names to a list at the shelter for a Labrador puppy, thinking Nick would enjoy having a lively playmate, but I've never gotten a call. Now more than a year has passed and I've never given it more than a fleeting thought. It's selfish of me, but after a lengthy grieving period for Rocky, we adjusted to our family of three— Nick, David, and me. The three of us had plenty of time for long hikes, ball throwing, belly rubs and car rides.

All that has changed because of Dad. Nick is feeling lonely and neglected. I try to think of when David or I last threw the ball for him, endlessly, over and over, but I can't recall. David hasn't been spending enough time with Nick, either. In between trying to collect what he's still owed, scrounging for real estate projects that need to be completed, maintaining the yard and house, plus helping me with Dad, he's had little time to spare for Nick.

"Hey there, big boy." Putting down the laundry basket, I kneel and open my arms. "Come here and let me love you up." His gait as he comes to me is not joyful and bounding, as it usually is, but his eyes beam happiness at being summoned into my arms.

I pull him into a hug so I can run my hands through his soft fur. He leans his body into mine. His breath is warm against my cheek, and I snuggle into him for the comfort his solid but yielding body provides. I tell him I love him, then explain why things are as they are. He may not understand the words, but he feels the love and apology within them.

When I release him, he backs up and looks into my eyes. There is a trace of discomfort in those big, brown eyes, and my first instinct is that he's in pain. But is it physical pain, or emotional pain? It was too fleeting to say which. For a second I have the irrational thought of asking him what's bothering him. Okay, now my long-held belief in anthropomorphism where our dogs are concerned may have gone too far. David is equally guilty of assigning human traits to our dogs, but I've always believed Nick is special. And he may well be extra-special, but he can't tell me what's wrong.

My watch shows that more than an hour has passed since I've checked on Dad. Time to give some attention to the other sweet soul under my care.

The large pile of laundry in the basket still needs to be folded. Sighing, I give Nick a kiss on the top of his head and tell him what he's heard so often over the past two weeks. "I'll be back."

I feel a niggling of guilt and look back at Nick. His head is bowed, but his eyes are tilted up, devoid of joy or light, watching me. If ever there were a living characterization of woeful, this is it.

---

When I walk into Dad's room, he barks, "Where have you been?" He's still in his bed, where he asked to stay earlier, but he looks ready to vault out of it. I've stopped in my tracks, stymied by a tone of voice I've rarely heard him use. He's aggravated, and I know why.

"So sorry, Dad, I was doing laundry and time just got away from me. Do you need to go to the bathroom?"

"Been needing to go for a while," he gripes.

I want to remind him he can just let go in his diaper, but that's a waste of breath. Instead I suggest, for the fifth or sixth time, that when he needs me, he should press the red button on the phone. "I get busy, but I'm never too busy for you if you just press the red button and let me know you need me."

Instead of a baby monitor, we had ordered two comically large black phones, reminiscent of the style used in the 1960s, but with huge pushbuttons. I put one phone within easy reach on his bedside table, and the other on the small table next to his lift chair. On each phone, I colored one big button with a red magic marker and covered all others with masking tape. For now, we're keeping a separate phone line in the apartment for just this purpose. Both phones are set on speaker mode, so he doesn't even have to pick up the receiver to press the red button. When and if he ever does press the button, the upstairs phone will ring and caller ID will tell me it's Dad.

"What phone?" His face is scrunched and turning red.

Is he being deliberately difficult, or is this a symptom of Alzheimer's?

"The one right there." I point to it. "And there." I point to the other.

He looks from one to the other and asks, "When did you put them there?"

"The day I knew you were coming here to take up residence in this grand apartment." I smile and spread my arms wide and then move toward him to get him into his wheelchair.

Dad continues to scowl at the bedside phone. Is he trying to recall seeing it before, or is he trying to remember it for the future?

"Let's get you into the bathroom." No need to waste time with a conversation that's going nowhere.

He says nothing else as I raise the head of his bed to its most upright position, move his wheelchair next to it, then lock the wheels. I take a moment to put on my back-support belt and position Dad's gait belt around his waist, preparing to lift and pivot him around into his wheelchair. I swing his legs around so he's in a sitting position on the edge of the bed. Sometimes he's able to assist my lift by using his hands to push up from the bed, fleetingly gathering enough strength in his legs to push up and pivot into the wheelchair as I support and balance him. Other times he's like a sack of flour that has gotten wet and become unyielding and cumbersome. At five-eight and one hundred-forty pounds, I'm not a little thing, but I'm not particularly strong, either. Volleyball and swimming were my sports in high school and college, but the muscles I built from those activities have diminished over time, so any assistance he can offer is appreciated.

"Okay, ready?" I ask.

"Ready." His arms and legs tense as he strains to rise.

Together we execute an up-and-pivot, with a soft landing in the wheelchair. Nice.

We're actually a pretty good team.

# 6

I'm listening to Samuel Barber's "Adagio for Strings" as I pull meat off a deli chicken to add to the salad we're having for dinner. It's about to hit its soul-vibrating crescendo, and I'm in a state of heightened anticipation when David comes through the door carrying grocery bags.

"Hey, babe. What's up with Nick?" He sets the bags down on the large kitchen island and comes over to give me a quick kiss. He looks really worried. Spiritual gratification, a-la-the music, will have to wait.

"What do you mean?"

"He's just lying out in the driveway and didn't even get up when I pulled into the garage."

"Didn't get up? Not even for a treat?"

"Nope. I offered, but he just looked up at me and then put his head down again. Then I went over to pet him, and he wagged his tail but didn't even roll over."

"That sure doesn't sound like Nick. I need to go check on him. Finish washing the lettuce and broccoli, will you?"

Down in the garage, Nick is lapping up water. He stops to look at me and wags his tail. He looks fine. Or does he?

"Hey, Nickaroo," I say soothingly, walking toward him. As he walks to meet me, I see a slight hitch in his gait. Did he hurt his paw? I bend down and rub his head. "What's going on, big boy?"

I sit on the garage floor, and he follows my lead. Something's going on with him, but I have no idea what it is. "Can I see your paws?" I pick up the front right, then the front left, but I see no blood or scrapes.

"Lie down." He does, but slowly. I pick up his back paws one at a time, but they don't seem to be injured either. I take the opportunity to give him a good belly rub.

Satisfied that there's nothing wrong, I summon him to get up. I'll bring him upstairs where he can lie on his kitchen bed and be near David and me while we prepare dinner. But before I do, I'll pop into the apartment and let Dad know we'll be having dinner soon.

As I turn away, I hear the sound of Nick's paws skidding, as if looking for purchase on the garage's concrete floor.

When I turn back around, he's standing up, looking at me with eyes that clearly convey something I've seen only one time before, when he'd run into a barbed-wire fence and gashed his side—pain. Pain and . . . what? Embarrassment?

Forgetting about Dad for the moment, I go back to Nick and ask him, "What's wrong, big boy?" As if he could answer. He just looks at me, willing me to understand.

It's crazy, but I swear it's similar to the look I've seen in Dad's eyes when he can't articulate what's bothering him. There are times when Dad's mind seems to be trying to process the words, but he can't utter them. I sense his frustration when that happens, and I begin the guessing game, running down the litany of things that could be making him uncomfortable or causing him pain or irritation. The list is long: Dry eyes, full bladder, cold feet, bad positioning, thirst, hunger, restlessness, loneliness.

But it goes against Dad's nature to complain about discomfort or pain. Sometimes I go through the entire list and don't get an answer. At other times, his eyes tell me when I've hit upon the right diagnosis.

Of course, Nick can't know what I'm asking nor tell me what he's feeling. I experience the same frustration and helplessness I've had at such times with Dad. I just want to make it better, whatever *it* is, and if I don't know what *it* is, I can't.

Nick is staring at me, and I glean some information from his eyes. He is in pain, but it's not severe.

"Oh, baby boy, let me try to figure this out." I kiss the top of his head before squatting down and exploring his body. I run my hands down his sturdy shoulders and front legs, then move up to his large and muscular chest as I watch his eyes for clues. He looks at me with a mixture of expectation and reluctance. Weird.

He tries to back up, away from more probing, but I ask him to stay, and he does. He starts to sit down but I say, "Up," and he remains standing with cautious rigidity. *What the heck is going on here?*

I scratch his ears to relax him, then gently but firmly run my hands along his sides, but there's no change in his stance or breathing. Not until I get to his hindquarter, and put pressure on both sides of his hip joint, does he flinch. He doesn't whimper, and he doesn't move, other than to tense so hard that his hindquarter is practically vibrating under my hand.

So there it is. The source of his pain. The pain I had failed to notice, even though I had recently wondered at his slowness in coming up the steps. But I gave it no real thought because my thoughts, my energy, my actions are largely tied up in Dad these days. I feel a surge of resentment that he has consumed much of those personal resources, so much so that I don't have time to pay attention to my eleven-year-old dog's needs.

The phone rings, and I pick up the nearby hand-held we keep in the garage. "Rachel?" It's Dad, calling me from twenty feet away. *Well, well, well, he's using the phone.* "Hi, Dad, are you okay?" His only answer is a grunt.

While I'm glad he's with the program, right now I'm not thrilled about being summoned when Nick needs me. I'm pulled between caregiving for these two beings who need my attention. Enough of this. Something's gotta give. I have to get these two together, for their sakes as much as mine. "Let's go, Nick," I say, and we head into Dad's apartment.

# 7

"Where have you been?" Oh, boy, Dad's aggravated.

Since I'm on a mission to foster a friendship for these two, I ignore his question and say, "I need your opinion about Nick, Dad." Turning back toward the doorway, I call my dog.

As Nick slowly approaches, Dad squirms in his chair and draws back. His eyes widen and his breathing quickens. Just what does he think Nick is going to do? I don't understand this fear. Perhaps it's a manifestation of Alzheimer's. I'm not sure it can be alleviated if that's the case, but if I don't try, our home will never have balance and harmony.

But when Dad's eyes become unfocused and he further draws up his legs, practically folding into himself, I wonder if I'm making a terrible mistake. *What's the worst that can happen?* The answer is, I don't know. This is new territory for me, but I have to trust in Nick's friendliness and Dad's innate good heart.

"Dad, I think Nick has a problem with his hips. I'm going to have him walk away and then back toward us. Would you watch him walk and tell me if you think he's in pain?"

His eyebrows draw together, deepening the lines between them. He slants his head and opens his mouth to speak, but no words come out.

"You know what it's like to have hip pain, Dad, so I need your help in deciding if Nick is in pain." Lame, (no pun intended) but I've got nothing else.

Taking Nick's collar, I turn him around and ask Dad to watch him as he walks away at a slow pace, both going and coming. Dad is watching Nick, just as I'd asked him to do, but he's still balled up and looking really uncomfortable. His knuckles are white from gripping the arms of his chair.

"Uh," Dad says.

"Uh *what*, Dad?"

"Uh, can I go to the bathroom first?"

I do a mental smack of my head. Dad needed something and pulled it together well enough to call on the house phone. His sharp greeting of "Where have you been?" always precedes his need to go to the bathroom, and I regret ignoring him when I came in. For heaven's sake, the man has been needing to go to the bathroom and he's been holding his bladder while facing his fear.

Even under these circumstances, when his fear could have caused him to release his bladder, he's holding it in. He hates those diapers so much that he's willing to suffer extreme discomfort.

"Oh, Dad, I'm so sorry." This "I'm sorry" isn't a platitude. It goes much deeper and unsettles my heart because I have made voiding in a toilet an embarrassing issue for him. I've harbored it as my issue, my cross to bear, never considering the effect my attitude is having on him.

We don't talk as we work together to get him into his wheelchair. He's concentrating on holding it in, while I'm contemplative in evaluating my selfish motives.

Through the night, when he sleeps with the aid of a low-dose prescription sleeping pill, he isn't aware of the need to go and his bladder automatically releases. He wakes up with a wet diaper, which embarrasses him. The extra pad I put inside his nighttime diaper keeps the excess moisture away from his skin, but sometimes he's sopping wet. With Carmen or David here to help me first thing in the mornings, we have him shipshape in no time, and he soon forgets about the wet diaper.

But during the day he wants to go to the toilet. Of course he does.

Nick moves out of the way as I push Dad to the bathroom. Dog-and-Dad connection experiment—over. Failed. But where I've truly failed is in giving proper attention to Dad's needs. He closes his eyes and sighs as his bladder releases. I've been in need of a bathroom enough times in my life to empathize with his sigh of relief. Many times I have stood in a long line, thinking I couldn't hold it another second, but I did, because the alternative—letting go—was unfathomable. And so it is with Dad.

My shame deepens as I recall my aggravation at his stubbornness. How many times have I muttered under my breath about how inconvenient or physically exhausting it is to take him to the toilet when he could just use the diaper? And I didn't exactly mutter; I made sure Dad heard. My attempts to guilt him into making my life easier have caused him shame and distress, and no doubt many moments of physical discomfort when he's hesitated to ask because I've made him feel guilty.

Just now he held back his discomfort to appease me. What good can come of my complaining about the one thing he asks of me that maintains his dignity in the sole area he perceives he still has control? He has no control over any other aspect of his life. His diseases have robbed him of that. Having Alzheimer's, which affects cognitive ability, and Parkinson's, which affects motor control, means Dad is fighting a battle on two major fronts. Eventually, the two will join forces to totally vanquish the warrior.

Caregiving isn't just about taking care of physical needs. It's also about uplifting a person who, day by day, is becoming more helpless. Dad's independence, which made him feel anchored and in control and dignified, has been stripped away and replaced with dependence that erodes his self-respect.

He is at the lowest point of his life because he depends on someone else to help keep his pride intact. His most important need, some sense of control over his life, is so much greater than any pill or nutritious meal. Not peeing in his pants is Dad's final control-over-his-life mechanism, and here I've been trying to keep the gears from turning. Shame on me.

Inevitably, the day will come when he won't even know he has to go. Until then, I will do all I can to help him keep his dignity intact.

"I'm sorry my distraction with Nick caused a delay, Dad. Whew, I bet you're feeling a lot better. I know I do when I really have to go and finally sit down on a toilet. That's just the best feeling, isn't it?"

"I was about to burst," Dad laughs.

"I bet you were. Yet you were still willing to be that uncomfortable to help me with Nick. You're just wonderful, you know that?"

Dad lowers his head and remains silent as we finish up. As he settles into his wheelchair, he looks up at me and asks, "You love that dog a lot, don't you?"

"I do."

"Is he in pain?"

"I believe he is, but I needed your opinion. Still do."

"Where is he?"

"Probably up in the kitchen with David. He's fixing dinner."

"Well, let's go see about him." Dad sets his face in determination. He'll overcome his fear of Nick to help me. I almost overlooked another essential element that will make Dad feel vital and valid—to be needed.

---

"Where have you been?" David asks with genuine concern as I push Dad out of the elevator.

*First Dad, now David. Next Nick will bark out the equivalent of, "Where have you been?"*

Pushing Dad toward the living room, I tell David that I was checking Nick out and then took Dad to the toilet. I don't embarrass Dad by mentioning his urgency.

We wheel right past Nick, but Dad ignores him. He's already forgotten his determination to help me diagnose Nick's pain. David helps me get Dad positioned on the sofa, then turns the TV to a sports channel as I head back to the kitchen. My dear husband has not only finished washing the veggies, he's cut them up and has finished deboning the chicken.

After asking Dad if he's comfortable, David joins me in the kitchen. He lowers his voice to say, "You should have called me to help with Joe.

Don't do it by yourself when I'm here. You have to do it by yourself enough when I'm gone."

"It's okay, I've just about got it down pat." I keep my tone light so David won't fret. "And Dad is able to help much of the time, so it's not that bad."

I serve Dad a gin and tonic and an appetizer of Spanish peanuts, and when I return to the kitchen David is mixing the salad. He tilts his head toward Nick, who's lying on his kitchen bed. "So what do you think about Nick?"

"I think he's developing a hip problem." I reach for two wine glasses and fill them pretty darn full.

David accepts my diagnosis along with the glass of wine. "Poor guy. What do you think we should do?"

"I honestly don't know. But I do know I need to take him to the vet, and she'll have to X-ray him. That's two-hundred dollars right there, but it has to be done. Plus, if there's any prescribed treatment or medication, we'll have to bite that bullet, too."

That we would do anything less for Nick, even if it means sacrificing in some other area, is not even a consideration. I can put it on a credit card, even though it won't be paid off as soon as the statement arrives. Knowing we can't pay the balance each month as we've always done, we've talked about using credit cards only in emergencies. Even though Nick's affliction isn't an emergency, the cost of getting it diagnosed and treated is more than we can afford to dole out from the checking account this month.

"I think we're at the point where we need to start buying box wine." We've already moved out of our high-priced wine consumption and into the seven-to-ten-dollar-per-bottle range, and even though we normally only drink a half-bottle a night between us, it's still a pricey indulgence. Box wine was always a joke between us, but now it has become a real possibility.

"We'll figure it out," he says, putting his arm around me and kissing the top of my head. I tilt my head up for a kiss. I can give up a lot of the finer things as long as I have this man's love.

Dad is munching on peanuts and is engrossed is some sports commentary. I wonder if he'll be able to feed himself tonight. He does better feeding himself when he's settled into these happy circumstances, and it brings me joy to have him function at that level of competence. He seems most content when he's with us. While I don't think he has yet developed the fear of being alone, which is often true of Stage 6 Alzheimer's patients, he is definitely more comfortable in the midst of our small family fold.

Nick has always had a place under the table but has been banished since Dad moved in. We've been feeding him downstairs so I can keep my promise to Dad. Normally, one of us would go down and do that while the other finished up dinner, but I decide to feed him in the kitchen tonight, as we did before. Dad needs to get used to his presence if he's ever going to get over his fear.

Again I experience a pang of guilt, along with a swath of sadness, at the thought of Nick's loneliness over these past few weeks. I tell myself Nick has adjusted, but that isn't true. He's a member of the family, and he's been displaced. His sunny personality has begun to fade, although any time he sees my or David's face, he gets that goofy grin and his tail wags in anticipation of whatever we have to offer—a pat on the head, a sweet word, a tasty treat, a belly rub, or—joy of joys!—a ball-throwing session.

"David, while I do Dad's blood check and get his insulin ready, would you please go get Nick's bowls and feed him up here?"

With a conspiratorial smile, he says, "Glad to," before heading down to the garage.

I reach into the refrigerator for Dad's insulin, which we keep both downstairs and upstairs. I prepare the glucose meter and then grab a syringe and the insulin, plus an alcohol pad, and head into the living room.

I swab his finger and stick it with the lancing device on the glucose meter. I hate puncturing his finger to get a blood-sugar reading, but it's vital that I don't give him too little or too much insulin. His reading is in the normal range, so I load the syringe with only four units of insulin, enough to keep his blood sugar level.

When he sees the syringe, he fumbles with his shirt to pull it up over his stomach, where I give the injections. His eyes are glued to the television and he isn't even paying attention as I wipe the area with the alcohol pad and inject him. I learned a long time ago, when I started caring for Mother, that not inserting drama and apologies into must-do medical procedures makes it less anxiety-inducing for everyone.

In the kitchen I pop the used lancet and syringe into the biohazard disposer David drilled into the side of the kitchen cabinet, then set the table.

As I'm plating the salad David comes through the door with Nick's bowl and tells him, "Dinner time." Nick scrambles to his feet and charges toward his dinner.

Dad doesn't even notice. Progress!

# 8

Dad hasn't had many visitors, and his loneliness, as I perceive it, is weighing on me. I'm lonely myself. You'd think I wouldn't have time to be lonely, but I'm missing the company of my girlfriends. Before Dad came to live with us, I would meet them for a cup of coffee or a glass of wine, foregoing costly lunches, but still connecting over beverages two or three times a week. Daytime phone conversations have tapered off since I'm up to my neck in chores, but at least I still have long conversations a couple of evenings a week with my two best friends, Julie, whom I've known since college, and Terri, my best gal-pal from my single days in Miami. My delightful nieces and I catch up each week when they call to speak with their "Papa," and David's sister, Camille, can make me laugh like no one else, so she's high on my list of whom to call when I need to decompress. In the absence of a professional psychologist, these wonderful women keep me centered and sane. David helps with that too, but with my close friends, there's mutual support and encouragement, unconditional acceptance, and a generous amount of nurturing.

Through emails and texts with a number of other friends, I'm able to keep the lifeblood of our friendships pulsing. They never fail to ask how I'm doing, and though I know they're sincerely interested in my well-being, I never air any complaints. And if I do, they're wrapped in humor, because the tone of those friendships is lighter and more social. Besides, I much prefer to learn what's going on in their lives. We always end our emails by sending love and saying we'll get together soon, but we all know my time isn't my own any longer. As a result, my loneliness expands.

On the home front, Dad and Nick are still ignoring each other, but at least they can be in the same room now. I repeated the exercise of having Dad watch Nick walk, but he'd only grunted and said, "He looks okay to me." But come on, what was I expecting?

To help ease loneliness all around, I called my cousin Debra and asked her to come for a visit because she loves Dad and he loves her. Debra is the daughter of Dad's sister, Gladys, who passed away ten years ago. Also, she has worked as a veterinarian tech for years and may be able to tell me more about Nick's condition. Most of all, she's a dear friend, and I am needing her company.

I hug her tightly when she comes through the door. Drinking in her replenishing good energy gives me a much-needed lift.

Debra has always had a deep sense of loyalty and love for family, and she and her husband Charles have been a big part of Dad's life since he moved up here. They live about an hour away in Dad's hometown in Tennessee, and they visited him at least once a month when he was at Crestview.

In the five years Dad has lived in North Carolina, he has never spent a holiday without them. When David and I are home for the holidays, versus visiting his family in Texas, we gather in one or the other of our homes for holiday meals.

Whenever we were out of town for the holidays, Debra and Charles took over and visited with Dad. They always brought one of her delicious homemade meals to Crestview and spent the day with him.

They once drove the sixty-mile distance through one of the worst ice storms in a hundred years to be with Dad on Christmas Day. Debra is just brimming with bright, loving energy, and Charles is as good as they come. They have made my, David's and Dad's lives so much richer.

When we walk into Dad's apartment, Debra sets down the chicken casserole she's brought and dashes over to hug him. His face is flush with happiness when he tells her, "Good to see you, honey. I've missed you."

Dad is still able to recognize everyone he knows, which is rather remarkable. *May it continue*, I silently wish.

"I've missed you, too, Uncle Joe. I'm so sorry I didn't get here sooner, but I've been working overtime." The vet's office leans on her to work extra hours. What started out as a part-time job has morphed into two jobs, a vet tech and part-time office manager. Debra gives Dad another big hug and tells him how great he looks and how beautiful his apartment is. He beams.

I put a big spoonful of the casserole on a small plate for myself and bid them adieu, confident that she knows what needs to be done to help Dad eat. She took care of her mother for a year before she passed away from breast cancer, and her willingness to share the wisdom of her experience in caregiving has helped smooth my way. Like me, she was lucky to have a husband to help; but unless you've had to provide care for more than a day or two, there's no way to fully understand what caregiving demands of you.

It does my heart good to hear them laughing as I close the door behind me. Debra's being here gives me a much-needed break to catch up on emails and paperwork. Nick has already said hello to Debra, one of his favorite people, and is keeping me company in my study. When I finish my busywork, I walk around and stand at my bookshelves, looking for something to get lost in for a while. For love of reading, I majored in English Lit in college, and even taught at South Miami High School for one year for ridiculously low pay. What I learned was that I wasn't cut out to be a teacher. When I shared my disillusionment with my college roommate, Amelia, over happy-hour cocktails, she steered me in what turned out to be the perfect direction. She talked me into getting my real estate license and going to work for her father's real estate company.

My income tripled in just two years, but I hit the real jackpot when I met David. He worked for a major developer who bought decrepit hotels on Miami Beach and turned them into luxury condos. They were a real estate agent's dream come true because they sold like hotcakes.

One day, when I needed an answer to some questions from prospective buyers, I called the developer's office, which was on the first floor of the building, and David answered. He offered to come up and address their questions in person. We had seen each other around, and I always thought he was handsome and had a great, friendly smile. I hoped he would ask me out. After that day, he did, and a year later we were married.

I've missed reading more than any other leisurely activity I've had to give up, though I keep books in Dad's apartment and sometimes read while he's sleeping.

I'm absorbed in my favorite book of nineteenth-century poetry when Debra comes into my study to tell me Dad is napping in his chair, then asks how I'm doing. She also asks Nick how he's doing. In response, he pulls himself up and ambles over to Debra, ready to give and get affection.

"Oh, the poor baby has hip dysplasia," she says as she rubs his ears.

"How do you know?"

She laughs and rolls her eyes and tells me she's seen it a hundred times. She explains that Nick can't stand straight up from a lying-down position. He has to get into a sitting position first, then heave himself forward to stand.

When did Nick start doing this, I wonder? And why haven't I noticed? I've just been thinking he's getting older and therefore slower. We talk about what I should expect in the future, and the course of treatments my veterinarian will likely prescribe, before we move on to talking about Dad's afflictions.

With this kind of agenda, Debra is going to need to be bribed to come back.

It's such a relief to tell her all that's happening with Dad and his care and how it's affecting me, David and Nick. Debra is a great listener. When I pause, thinking I'm saying too much, she gets me to open up even more by asking questions that keep me going. She offers sincere, sympathetic words when I most need to hear them. More than ever, I understand why the social worker I consulted about the decision to move Dad in with us stressed the importance of talking about my emotions with family and friends, or in a support group. I'm not ready for a support group, but Debra is family and friend, a double blessing.

When I speak with my sisters, they want details about how Dad is doing, but they rarely ask, "How are *you* doing, Rachel?" Sometimes I resent that they don't ask, but my parents executed a Living Will and Health Care Surrogate document, naming me, so I've been the parental caregiver since the need first arose. As such, they've gladly abdicated all the responsibility and worry to me. They've said before, "Oh, sorry that's happening, but I know you can handle it."

While the votes of confidence are encouraging, the assumption that I should just handle it, whatever *it* is, without their input or help, aggravates me. Whenever I've tried to get their input on tough decisions, they more or less let me know they trust whatever decisions I make. Why can't they see how much pressure that puts on me? Don't they understand I need to discuss it with them for a reason—that I'm just worn out with making decisions over the years, and I'd appreciate their participation? Sure, they each live in distant states, but that's not a reason for their not contributing in some way or another. If they can't be with me in person, can't they at least be with me in spirit?

The worst part is, I have always had to be strong, decisive and in control. It's a role they'd assigned to me, and I play it well. Yet there have been times when I've felt like breaking down and just weeping a bucket of tears and crying out for help; but then I would look weak, and none of us wants that.

Debra is different. She's a better sister to me than my real sisters because she has experience, understands the challenges, helps me see the realities, and gives advice when I ask for it. And she gives great hugs when I need them most.

Dad and I are both sorry to have her visit end, but she's brought a breath of reinforced resilience into our home, bolstering both of us in different but much-needed ways.

---

Carmen has come and gone and even fed Dad his lunch before leaving. She takes loving care of him, and he enjoys her attentions. I hear them laughing together and wonder what they could be laughing about when neither speaks the other's language well enough to carry on a conversation. I wish I could have her for more than just four hours a day because she's so good for Dad, and for me, despite her slowness in doing chores.

She's gotten him dressed in slacks and a nice shirt, ready for an outing. "We're going for a ride on the Parkway today, Dad." He loves the scenic views.

Instead of agreeing, he asks, "Why did Carmen leave?"

*Where did that come from?* I sigh because I don't want to get into our financial issues with him ever again. "It was time for her to go. She only comes for four hours a day to help us."

"Why don't you let her stay longer?" His tone is challenging.

"That's all the time she can give us, Dad. She has a home and family of her own, and she has to pick up her children from the school bus stop."

Dad takes a long beat to think this over, and then nods.

If I had bothered to explain our financial situation again, what difference would it have made? Why take a chance on raising his anxiety level? He's seen nothing to indicate any change in our living standard. We still have our nice home, and he has three meals a day, so why would he notice?

Dad doesn't hear my and David's conversations, which sometimes go late into the night after he's down for the count. At those times, Nick is in the room with us, enjoying his bed and our company. Things almost seem normal until we start talking about money again.

Our talks are often about how to cut back even more, or about one of us getting a regular job to bring in income. We've both kept our real estate broker licenses current, but there's no brokering going on. A big impediment to looking for work is our commitment to Dad. How will we take proper care of him if either of us has a full-time job?

Over the last few months, I've cleared out my closet and sold designer bags, shoes and dresses. When I first thought of the idea and shared it with David, he'd laughed and said, "There are two kinds of eBayers—buyers and sellers. You're a buyer, Rachel."

I reminded him that a few years before, I'd sold my Barbie clothes that I'd found in Mother's garage and made close to six hundred dollars.

"And what did you do with the money?" It was a rhetorical question, because he knew good and well that I'd donated it to the Children's Food Crisis Fund in Buncombe County.

I enjoyed going through the doll clothes, laying them out and reminiscing as I photographed them, although I felt bad about selling them since Mother had kept them all those years.

But I had not felt bad about selling two Chanel purses, plus two pairs of Louboutins and two pairs of Manolo Blahniks—gently worn because they were cruel shoes—plus five designer dresses. In fact, I'd felt elated when each sale's proceeds landed in my payment account. We used the money to pay the taxes on property we owned but didn't have a chance in hell of selling, and put the remaining amount in savings.

I worried what people thought when they learned of our diminished financial circumstances, which became obvious when we no longer made generous donations to their favorite charities and declined invitations to join them for expensive nights out. They weren't stupid. They knew our business had collapsed.

Even as recently as eight weeks ago, before Dad moved in, we were still getting invitations to dinners and cocktail parties. Although we knew we wouldn't be able to reciprocate, we accepted because we had a residual yearning for our friends' lively company.

Since Dad moved in, we haven't accepted any invitations, so naturally they've stopped. But we can't afford to go out to dinner. Deciding what we can and can't afford is disheartening.

I don't have any more designer goods to sell, so I've been eyeing my jewelry. I've never coveted diamonds, but David has gifted me with some very nice pieces over the years. It's hard to part with them because each one was given as a special gift on a special occasion.

There's mother's wedding band and one-carat diamond ring, but I could never sell those as long as Dad is alive. But maybe her cocktail rings? Or maybe my grandmother's bequeathment to me, two precious Blue Royal Delft hand-painted plates, for which I could get close to five thousand dollars. When I mentioned to David that I could get that amount for them, his mouth dropped open. But then he'd said, "That's all you have from your grandmother. Are you sure you want to do that?"

It pains me a bit to think about parting with them, but we're facing high fuel costs in refilling the thousand-gallon propane tank and heating this huge house through the winter. Plus, it would be reassuring to have some extra money now that Nick is likely to need expensive treatments.

But as I've told David, I don't give a damn about anything but keeping this roof over our heads, taking care of Dad and Nick, and keeping our marriage strong. If we can keep those three balls in the air, I'll consider life as good as it gets.

I used to think exotic travel and our whirlwind social life enhanced our marriage because of the grand fun and exciting adventures we had. When I think back about all of our comings and goings over the years, I wonder why it mattered so much. Sure, I'd love to have another glass of rare and exquisite champagne at Bar Le Dokhan's in Paris. And we like our friends and enjoy their company and conversation over a fine meal. But now . . . well, life is less complicated, despite how complex it has become in other ways. I'm just grateful we had those wonderful times.

Besides, I've found that spending more time with David, since he's working from home, largely fills my need for social companionship. He's my best friend, after all, and we've grown even closer as we've worked together to weather the fallout from the real estate crisis. As bad as losing the house would be, it's far less worrisome than losing what we have as a couple. It's the one real thing I can always count on, and it strengthens my emotional security in this time of financial insecurity.

But it's a beautiful day and Dad's up for a ride on the Blue Ridge Parkway. It is one of the most glorious National Parkways in the country, and it's just a few miles away. I have a full tank of gas and a packed picnic lunch.

I'm grateful for all these things, and so much more. And as Aesop said, "Gratitude turns what we have into enough."

# 9

While Carmen is here this morning, I can take Nick to the vet. David had to go to Weaverville to see about completing a house that another contractor walked away from. He's a great negotiator, and he thinks he can strike a good deal with a client who wants the house finished and has the money to pay for it. Fingers crossed!

The vet couldn't do a morning appointment until today, and in the three days that have passed since I discovered the pain in Nick's right hip, he seems worse. Truth be told, I'm happy to get out of the house and go somewhere with my companionable dog, even if it is just the vet's office. Dad enjoyed our outing yesterday, even thanking me for "a beautiful day" when I kissed him goodnight.

Nick will be happy to get out and go for a ride, although he'll voice his regret when we pull into the vet's parking lot. Who can blame him? His visits almost always involve a needle.

When I tell Nick we're going for a ride, his eyes light up and he does his happy dance, which includes a fast-wagging tail and hip-hopping feet. I open the back door of the old Jeep we use for off-road treks and doggie transport and he springs inside.

That was quite a vigorous move for the old boy. I rethink my vet visit and the cost; but no. His excitement in going for a ride overrode any discomfort. He still needs help.

I lean in to give him a rub on the head. "My good boy." His wagging tail picks up speed.

Dr. Angie Froman is bent down, probing the area where I detected Nick's pain. Nick flinches ever so slightly, but doesn't make a sound.

"From watching him walk," Dr. Froman begins, "and from his response and reaction to my exam, there's definitely some hip pain."

"What do you think is causing it?"

"I could name any one of five things it could be, but I believe it is hip dysplasia, and probably arthritis that's developed because of the dysplasia."

So Debra was right about Nick's hip dysplasia.

"I'll need X-rays to confirm." She looks up from her notes and says, "I'm surprised it's taken him this long to develop these symptoms."

"Why do you say that?"

"He's old, he's large breed—and hip dysplasia is genetic to certain large breeds. In fact, he has likely lived with the condition since he was only a few months old."

"Really? Then why didn't I notice it years ago?"

She tells me he's grown up taking the chronic pain for granted and has learned to live with it. Dogs suffering such pain rarely exhibit acute signs of it until they get to where Nick is now. "Plus, I know you've thrown thousands of tennis balls for him over the years."

"But it's never enough," I laugh.

"Well, I suggest you stop it. It has put a lot of stress on his hip joint over the years, and he can't take that anymore."

"Why didn't you tell me to stop years ago?"

"Would you have?" she asks with a knowing smile. "Or would you have looked at him and thought he looked fine and thrown it anyway since he enjoyed it so much?"

She's right. Whether on land or water, Nick is a retriever, and he retrieves and returns the ball, retrieves and returns, retrieves and returns. It can be as monotonous as it sounds, but he is genetically wired to do it. And then there's the most obvious reason—it's fun for him.

I nod my head in acknowledgment but tell her it will take a lot of fun out of his life.

"He's had years of fun. His remaining years have to be about treatment and comfort."

This makes me sad for Nick. "Will the X-rays show how much the hip joint has disintegrated?"

"They will, but every dog is different. Some X-rays I see, I wonder how the dog is still standing. I'll know more about how we should approach Nick's treatment after I see them."

"Can you do them now?"

"Yes, and I will need your help."

"My help? Sure, what can I do?"

"We get the best results if the owner holds the dog's head. I use a radiolucent tray to provide greater support and stability for the dog during the radiograph. I position the dog's hips, a technician runs the equipment, and you control the head. It's much better than giving him anesthesia just to get X-rays, and I often get better film."

"I like it." Oh, yes, I like she'll get better film, and I also like saving the cost of the anesthesia.

I bend down to pet Nick. "*This* isn't going to hurt," I promise him. His eyes tell me he understands, and that he trusts me. There I go anthropomorphizing again.

But I know I read him right.

## 10

Today is going to be a great day because Dad's favorite former CNAs, Sissy and Rhonda, are coming to visit him.

For the first time since Dad left Crestview, their days off coincide. Since he learned they were coming, he's vacillated between anxiety and cheerfulness. The anxiety is dementia-related, while the cheerfulness is just part of his nature.

I've made a light but sort-of-fancy lunch of quiche Lorraine with garlic-and-lemon marinated asparagus and fruit salad on the side. I'm getting pretty good at this stuff. They'll be able to enjoy lunch with Dad out on the deck on this sunny and clear Carolina summer day.

Dad's in the living room in his wheelchair when they come through the door and squeal with delight when they see him. "Joe! You're looking so handsome, sweetheart!"

"We miss you, Joe!" They hurry to him and hug his neck. He hugs them back with enthusiasm.

"You girls look beautiful," says my always-charming Dad. They are pretty girls, but it's their sweetness and caring that give them a beautiful glow.

Sissy takes over. "Rachel, where's his walker?"

I retrieve it from the kitchen and hand it to her. "It's a pretty day, Joe. Let's take a little walk out to the deck."

Rhonda encourages him further by giving him a big, noisy kiss on the cheek as she unbuckles his seat belt. With efficient, graceful attendance, they have him up and on his feet in seconds. Sissy swings the walker in front of him and waits for him to place his hands on it, which he does with only slight hesitancy. There's no hesitation on the part of Sissy and Rhonda, though. They're ready to walk him right out the door and onto the deck.

This is the kind of attentive tending Dad was used to, and the three of them have moved into the familiar routine so smoothly it's as if it had never been interrupted.

Dad shuffles his feet, yet another symptom of the Parkinson's, until he gets to the stoop of the open door. "Pick up your feet, Joe," Sissy encourages, and I envy her confident demeanor. Dad does as she tells him and makes a smooth transition out onto the deck.

They make it look so easy! If he can move this well with a walker, then David and I can team up to ambulate him more often. It occurs to me that Dad trusts these women in a way he doesn't trust me. He's been used to sure-handed transfers for five years until his well-being was put into the hands of a daughter who treats him as if he's an accident waiting to happen.

I follow them out and see Nick coming up the outside steps to join them. He's a sociable fella, like Dad, and he needs attention, too. I don't shoo him away as both ladies greet him. When Dad says, "Hey, Nick," my heart sparks.

Perhaps he realizes that everyone who comes here likes Nick. Maybe he sees Nick's eagerness for affection. Could he be feeling some friendliness toward Nick? Each time they're brought together, like now, a bit of the barrier comes down.

After they've gotten Dad seated at the table, they take a chair on either side of him and start chatting him up. Nick lies down next to Sissy's chair, and she reaches down to pet him as she engages Dad. "I really miss you, Joe," she says for the third time since she got here.

"I miss you, too." He looks from one to the other. "You girls were always so good to me." He turns his head toward me and adds, "But Rachel's treating me real good."

"We can see that." Rhonda looks up at me and smiles. "He does look good, Rachel. You're taking excellent care of him."

What wonderful words to hear from a master caregiver. "Thanks so much for saying so, Rhonda. And thanks for coming today. Let me bring out your lunches." Sissy offers to help, but I'm happy to be able to tell her, "No, you're our guests. Please let me pamper you today." They wait on others all the time, so it's the least I can do.

I bring out a large tray stacked with three prepared platters and a basket of croissants with butter and peach jam. Dad's bib, along with napkins and silverware, is on the side. With their help, I clear the tray and then dash back in to load it with three glasses and a pitcher of iced tea.

There's a nice breeze, and the table umbrella is providing shade. "You sure have a beautiful view, Rachel," Sissy says as she puts Dad's bib around his neck.

The view from the deck is unobstructed by any residential structure or commercial enterprise. On this clear day, the closer mountains are covered in the greenest-of-green leaves, which are in sharp view. The mountains that rise beyond them seem to unfurl, one mountain range after another, each offering up its own brilliant-to-subdued green hues, becoming less and less defined as they go on for as far as the eye can see. I never tire of this view. It's beautiful in all seasons, but on a summer day like today, it is at its glorious best.

Sissy puts Dad's fork into his hand and helps him take a bite of quiche before taking one herself. I'm gratified by the "oohs" and "ahhs" that issue forth. Their eating is accompanied by chatter orchestrated to make Dad laugh about what's going on with others at Crestview. His laughter is filled with lightness, and he remembers to ask about his buddy, Ralph. When they tell him that Ralph is as ornery as ever, he nods and says, "No reason for him to change." More laughter. It's like a synchronized symphony of happy voices, and I enjoy the harmony of it.

The camaraderie of the atmosphere keeps me rooted in place. When Sissy asks if I'll be joining them, I shake my head. "I'm going to make a few phone calls, so please enjoy your lunch. Call me if you need anything." Dad needs some space from me as well as alone time with friends.

They thank me as I leave, but honestly, I'm the one who's thankful. These three seem like old familiar friends who have missed each other and are delighted to be catching up. They are laughing as I close the deck door behind me, and I laugh, too—for no other reason than I'm happy my dad is happy.

I appreciate their saying I'm taking good care of Dad, but I could never do what they do—take care of strangers. What I do is a labor of love. They, on the other hand, perform the most personal and menial duties for others day in and day out. I've often wondered what makes them choose such a demanding job. It can't be the pay, because I know they only make eight dollars an hour, and there are no job benefits. Being a CNA is one of the most selfless jobs there is because it involves constantly meeting others' needs.

Sometimes I wish Dad could return to Crestview. Yes, I love him and am happy to spend so much time with him, but I wonder if it would be better for all of us if Dad could get the care and companionship he needs and deserves. Short of that, it would be a godsend to have either of these *wunderkind* ladies here with us eight hours a day.

As it is, I have to be satisfied with the four hours Carmen gives us, and take these visits for what they are—gifts to me and Dad.

## 11

While Sissy and Rhonda amuse Dad out on the deck, I enjoy a slice of quiche and check emails on my iPhone. There's one from Remembrance Care, an organization located here in Asheville that focuses on caregivers who have loved ones with memory loss. It's trying to raise funds to expand its facilities because there's a four-month waiting period for its clinical services. The banner on the newsletter asks: "Can you please donate?" I wish I could! It's a wonderful organization that I discovered two years ago through a philanthropic women's group I belonged to when I could still afford the annual dues.

We'd brought in a group of caregivers for a Saturday luncheon at a local restaurant, when spouses, neighbors or children could cover for them. We wanted to ask how we could help. There's no government money nor any compensation, let alone appreciation, for the hard job of being the caregiver for an elderly or ill person.

When I heard those caregivers' stories at that luncheon, I'd felt an odd mixture of discomfort and relief. I was contrite because my dad was in a great facility being well tended to by others. I had thought my daily visits and taking him to the doctor and out to lunch and bringing him to the house for day visits were such *good-daughter* things to be doing.

Alternatively, I was relieved because I wasn't living with the huge challenges those women faced every single day. I'd wondered why there were no men present at the luncheon. David's uncle had taken care of his wife—who suffered from the very worst effects of Alzheimer's—for eight years before she passed away. Was that a unique circumstance? Based on the fact that there were no men there that day, it seemed likely.

The most appalling thing I learned was that these women had little-to-no help with their caregiving, ever. Their husband and children were "lazy," "running around," "mean drunks" or "using drugs."

Many also worked menial jobs and continuously worried about the safety of their disabled loved ones who were at home alone. Feeding and medicating them were major concerns for these caregivers when they couldn't be there to provide those needs.

They wore their fatigue like a cloak with holes that offered little protection from the winds of despair that tore through their lives. Their shoulders were weighed down by labor and despondency.

Lines of worry etched their faces, reflecting the loss of hope that anything would change to make their lives better. Their collective, overriding trait was their desire to do their best by their charges, regardless of their resources, and to keep them comfortable as long as they could. But what a toll it took on them.

The handouts we provided contained grim information, and while we debated whether to include it with the helpful resource and care information, we felt it important that these women learn all the risks—especially to themselves.

Among the many things they learned that day was the shocking fact that Alzheimer's caregivers have a sixty-three percent higher mortality rate than non-caregivers, with forty percent dying from stress-related disorders—before their patient dies.

A medical system that so often failed them, plus grinding poverty, were their biggest obstacles in getting the care their loved ones, and they, needed.

And time. Time is a precious commodity, perhaps the most precious of all commodities, particularly for working caregivers who are also wives and mothers, because there is never enough of it. I had read the excellent book, *The Thirty-Six Hour Day*, which focuses on what can be done to improve the lives of people with dementia and of those caring for them, including how to manage their time. Meeting needs and demands eats up the greatest portion of a caregiver's precious time. A full and good night's sleep was something they couldn't imagine.

It was a vicious cycle that inevitably left the caregiver feeling inadequate or ashamed for not being able to do all that needed doing. More than that, becoming angry, losing their tempers, crying for hours out of the day, and even thoughts of suicide permeated their daily lives.

I remembered bowing my head in gratitude for having the financial means to keep Dad in a facility like Crestview, which did all of these things for him, relieving me of the worries and burdens these women suffered.

These concerns, and many more, were vocalized that day, and it became obvious that these stalwart women hadn't discussed these issues in such depth and so freely with anyone else.

But that day those women were able to talk, to cry, to hug each other, to reach out and generously offer advice and even help for those who seemed even more careworn than they were.

Robin, a member of our group who was a retired social worker and psychologist, had explained to them that everything they felt was normal for a caregiver. She told them that asking for help from family and friends—just having them listen, or sitting with their charge for a few hours—was not just beneficial, but necessary. Otherwise, their frustration, anger, and depression could be misdirected and cause harm, either to their loved ones or themselves.

It was one of our most meaningful meetings, and our women's group had rallied its resources, raised community awareness, solicited donations, and pressed social services to do more, such as liaise with the Capital Assistance Program on behalf of those caregivers whose parents had disabilities and qualified for rehab services.

The president of Remembrance Care of Asheville spoke that day, and it surprised many of us to learn there was such a professional, caring and effective organization right here in Asheville. It is comprised of a team of physicians, nurses, social workers, and volunteers dedicated to one goal—helping individuals with Alzheimer's and other cognitive disorders live as fully as possible for as long as possible at home or in their preferred setting. More to our point that day, we learned it is an organization that focuses on equipping caregivers with the resources *they* need, in addition to providing excellent care to their loved ones.

He encouraged those caregivers in attendance to get in touch with Remembrance Care, and made sure each one had a brochure with contact information in her hand when she left.

Our organization made a large donation to Remembrance Care, confident the money would be well spent. We worked on other ideas, including the initiation of a volunteer program among community church members of all ages and incomes to give caregivers some relief, if only for a few hours a week.

We established a fund earmarked for emergency assistance and administered by a committee. The membership of our community service club stepped up and made a difference.

In the two years following that initiative, we received many thank-you letters that brought tears to our eyes as they were read aloud at our meetings.

I sure could use its help right now, but I'm not going to reach out to Remembrance Care because they're underfunded and understaffed. There are so many caregivers who need assistance from that organization much more than I do.

*I* is a self-aggrandizing word, however, when you have a husband of twenty-two years who is a true partner in everything you do. *We* take care of Dad, and there is a deep layer of comfort in having a partner to share that duty.

Other than David, I can't count on anyone who isn't being paid for help. My sisters have jobs they can't leave for any length of time to come and help out. I understand this, but I also resent it. After all, I have a job, too: Caregiving. It's the toughest job I've ever had because of the emotional element involved and because I've had zero training for it.

I envy my sisters for their full-time jobs that ensure their freedom from caregiving.

## 12

Nick looked perkier this morning when he went outside, and the limp that was developing is gone. He's more adroit at sitting and getting up. The glucosamine chondroitin the vet suggested is really helping.

My breath catches when he trots into Dad's room, where I'm doing a blood sugar check, and sits down next to Dad's chair. His renewed vigor surprises me as much as his trespassing does. I tense up for what's coming next, but instead I'm bowled over when Dad says, "He looks like he's doing a whole lot better."

"He does, doesn't he?"

"What did you do to him?"

"All I'm doing is giving him a supplement called glucosamine chondroitin, which the vet suggested."

"Maybe you should give me some of that," Dad laughs. He gives Nick an appraising look. "I'd like to feel like that again."

Dad already takes that supplement. I have to cut it in half because it's so large. For Nick, scarfing down the pill is no problem. Put it in his food bowl, and it's gone.

For Dad, large pills present problems. Every day he takes twenty-two pills. Well, at least he tries—most of the time, anyway.

He complains about all the pills and sometimes presses his lips together and refuses to take them. I was told there were plenty of occasions at Crestview when this happened, but I'd hoped he wouldn't be as stubborn with me.

"Dad," I coax at those times, "please take these pills. You know they're good for you. They help with your Parkinson's and Alzheimer's and diabetes." I always start with those vital meds. Even if I can't get him to take anything else, I'm relieved to get the most important meds in him.

But there are times when he stares stonily into space, or even puts his head back and closes his eyes—the ultimate refusal. At those times, I concede the battle is lost and get frustrated and even angry. I have to leave the room to calm down because I never want to take my anger out on him.

What's even worse is when he falls asleep and can't be roused to either take his pills or eat. For as long as I can remember, sleep has been Dad's elixir. He told me once that he learned to drop off immediately when he was a soldier, grabbing some shut-eye whenever he could. It's difficult for me to tell if he nods off because it's something he's able to do at will, or whether it's a result of his escalating dementia.

Dad and Nick eye each other, perhaps sizing the other up. As Dad closes his eyes for a nap, Nick lies down next to his chair and closes his eyes, too.

This is a good time to sneak away for some chocolate.

---

Milk and cookies are good for what ails you, and what's ailing me right now is a sense of deep frustration that my sisters aren't more involved and sympathetic about Dad's care or what I'm going through. I'm hunkered down in my study, ready to call one or both of them. It's Saturday, so they'll be home. I can't decide who to call first.

Both had expressed incredulity when I told them about my plans to move Dad in with us. With Cindy, it was my audacity in taking on the job; with Kathy, it was my total inadequacy to do as good a job as Crestview. Her harsh judgment put another brick in the growing wall between us.

But neither sister has offered any help or advice or financial help, which would have been welcomed. Asking for money isn't something I could bring myself to do. If they'd wanted to help, they'd have already offered.

The decision of who to call is made for me when the phone rings and caller ID tells me it's Kathy. She usually calls to speak to Dad, but since he's sleeping, she won't be able to talk to him. Good. It's time for a sister talk.

After I tell her Dad is asleep and can't talk, she asks me how he's doing. I start giving her details, but that's more than she wants to hear because she says, "Okay, enough. I get the picture."

My blood rises to a boil. Oops, it has boiled over.

"Enough? *Okay, enough*?" I mock her. "You can't take a few extra minutes out of your week to listen to everything that's happening with Dad? Things change from week to week with him, not that you'd know that, or care if you did."

"Get off your high horse, Rachel."

"Get off *my* high horse? You've got your nerve, sitting six hundred miles away without a care besides yourself, telling me to get off my high horse. You don't do anything for Dad and you couldn't give a damn about what I'm dealing with. I can't afford to be aloof like you because I'm involved with every aspect of his well-being. I never get a chance to say, 'Enough,' because whatever I do, there's more to be done."

"It was your choice to move him in with you."

"What was the alternative, Kathy? Did you think of anything else? Did you offer to help? Did you offer to take him in? Did you offer any kind of financial help to keep him at Crestview? No!"

"You didn't ask me to, so why should I?"

"Yes, why should you? You've always been self-centered. You have no idea what caregiving involves and no interest in learning. You made that clear the last six months of Mother's life."

Ouch. I know that one's a solid blow below the belt, but she deserves it.

"I came to visit Mother!"

"Visit Mother. Right. You never lifted a finger to do anything to help me or Mother's sweet caregiver, Emmaline, when you were there. You bossed her around like she was your personal servant. You brought up old grievances with Mother and demanded she apologize! You were anything but welcome, Kathy, because you did nothing but create tension and hard feelings, then you'd leave."

"That's not true. Mother loved me and wanted to see me. You always tried to interfere."

"Interfere? How? I left you to visit with her while I ran errands you never offered to run. You'd come over for an hour or two and then take off. You did nothing then, Kathy, and you're doing nothing for Dad now."

"What do you want me to do? You want me to bring him here to live? I can quit my job and take care of him and use his money for our bills. That's fine with me."

Was she out of her mind? Well, yes. She'd had a skewed way of looking at things, and gave opinions without information to validate them *and* without being asked. Kathy picked at things she thought were wrong but offered no solutions or efforts to right them.

"Oh, please. You think you can live off Dad's money? You know that beyond his pension and government benefits, there's nothing there, right? His copay on his medications, and all the non-prescription things you'd have to buy to take care of him, would leave you with less than a thousand dollars a month. I use every bit of that to hire four-hours-a-day of help. So if you think you'll be able to take care of him, knowing all that, I'll drive him straight to your door next week."

I wait for her to explode, but she shocks me when she says, "I didn't realize all that. I didn't know things were that tight. Can I send you two hundred dollars?"

I'm as incredulous as I'd be if the money had suddenly blown into the room. This kindness is so unlike Kathy's usual demeanor that I have to wonder about her motive.

"You'll do that?"

"I offered it, didn't I, Rachel?

To heck with the motive. I'll take the money. And who knows—if I call Cindy and tell her about it, she might also make an offer I won't refuse.

## 13

"It's a pretty day." Dad is looking out the large front window of the van, tilting his head toward the cloudless blue sky.

"It sure is," I agree, taking his hand, which is soft and warm and a source of loving comfort for me.

"Where are we going?"

"We're going to see Dr. Baird to get a prescription for you to get some physical therapy." This is the third time today I've told him this. His memory sure seems to be getting worse.

He doesn't say anything for a few minutes, then surprises me when he asks, "Will Adam do my therapy?"

It confounds me he can't remember what I told him five minutes ago, but he remembers Adam. He and his wonderful wife, Jennie, are both licensed massage and physical therapists. They run the spa at the posh Mystic Mountain Lodge in Asheville during the summer months, and they work at hospitals and rehab facilities throughout the winter. I found them by placing an ad in the paper for a physical therapist to work privately with a patient in assisted living. Physical therapy does Dad a world of good, but Medicare limits the duration of the therapy.

I had decided to keep Dad on physical therapy in between those Medicare-paid sessions, thus the ad in the paper and the joy of Adam and Jennie coming into Dad's life.

Though it was Adam who responded to the ad, he made it clear that he and his wife were a team, and that they would both be working with

Dad. The four of us formed an immediate bond when we met for the first time in Dad's room at Crestview.

Jennie is a kind, easygoing, skilled professional, and with her beautiful smile, big brown eyes and therapeutic touch, she became one of Dad's favorite people. Adam is also all of those things, and he and Dad bonded on a man-to-man level. I once heard Dad say to him, "It's good to have a man around here. There's always so many chicks pecking at me."

I'd never heard Dad refer to women as "chicks," but I knew he meant no offense. Alzheimer's patients could become wildly sexually inappropriate, but there had been no signs of that in Dad, thank goodness. In fact, the way he said it made me laugh because the women who worked at the assisted living were always giving him pecks on his cheek and clucking over him.

Adam and Jennie had split the two-times-a-week sessions with Dad, and it was gratifying to see he ambulated better and moved with more confidence when he was getting therapy. I added a once-a-week full-body massage to the treatment to help with the stiffness related to his Parkinson's, and Dad had some very good months, despite the limited recovery from his broken hip.

In between paying privately, I'd get a new prescription for a Medicare-paid round of therapy allotted every six months, and Adam and Jennie would continue their sessions with Dad, getting paid by Medicare until that benefit ran out. That normally lasted only four-to-six weeks, when he reached the prescribed goals, then I picked up the tab again.

During that Medicare hiatus, if he was in the hospital for three nights or more, his doctor could prescribe another round of Medicare-paid physical therapy. I didn't see that as a great trade-off, since keeping him out of the hospital was priority number one, but I sure took advantage of it.

There has been no therapy since Dad moved in. I'd had to wait until now, six months since his last Medicare-paid therapy, to request another round.

I'd told Adam and Jennie the truth—that we couldn't afford to keep Dad at Crestview any longer, and we couldn't afford private therapy. They'd been sympathetic and understanding. It was a sad and embarrassing moment, but that's in the past. I need to focus on Dad because he's declined since their therapy sessions stopped.

It isn't my imagination that he is stiffening up. David and Carmen have noticed it, too. I want Dr. Baird to increase Dad's dose of Sinemet to help with his rigid muscles and declining mobility.

The enthusiasm in my voice is real when I reassure him. "Adam and Jennie are your personal therapists, so you better believe that's who I'll be calling." I want what they can provide for Dad—not just therapy, but companionship, warmth and love. Many days he is social and amiable, and he delights in telling jokes and war stories. Adam is a World War II enthusiast, and he engages Dad in his war stories by asking questions and listening to the answers.

"Sweet Jennie," Dad mumbles. I look over and see that he's smiling at the thought of her. It's so good that he remembers them both.

"She sure is. It will be good to see them again, won't it?"

"Real good." After a long pause, he says, "I've missed them."

Tears spring to my eyes. I'm failing him by not having him engage with more people. But who? He has Carmen, Anna, and Debra, plus Sissy and Rhonda. But their visits are infrequent and relatively short. If Dad would just latch on to Nick. Nick could be at his side every day, providing the comforting company that only dogs can provide in their undemanding way. But even canine company can't measure up to all the good that comes from Adam and Jennie's sessions with him.

I have to face the fact that Dad is lonely. Whenever he asks if his "friends" have called, I lie. I tell him yes, but they called when he was asleep. "Wake me up and let me talk to them next time they call," he'll say, with a touch of wistfulness in his voice. "I'll drive and meet them somewhere." I'm not even sure which friends he's referring to, but I assure him I will wake him when they call.

Dad misses driving, and he wants me to believe he's capable of it. About every other time we go out, he offers to drive. He wants me to hand him the keys and say, "Sure, Dad, here you go." The thing is, he really believes he can do it.

My inevitable response is, "Not today, Dad," as I try to come up with a reasonable excuse such as, "I'll need you to drive next time we go to Tennessee since you know those roads so well."

It's all an attempt to appease him, but I don't like doing it. I'm guilty of lying and treating him like a kid asking for ice cream and having to respond with the equivalent of, "Not today, but we'll go to Dairy Queen soon." Delaying, deflecting, and hoping he'll forget.

Which makes me realize I tend to pick and choose what he remembers, and what he doesn't. It's like I'm using his cognitive impairment for my own purposes when I want him to stop obsessing about something. On the other hand, I'm hoping he'll remember things that will make my life easier, like how to use a fork. It's confusing and convoluted reasoning, but I don't have an abundance of tools in my toolbox.

But the wistfulness in his voice, his desire to see those who had given him so much loving attention, stymies my response at times. He is secluded, and the few of us in his life, compared to the many at the assisted living facility, are not enough to alleviate that.

I'm failing Nick in that respect, too. What time I give him isn't enough to offset the long, lonely stretches when David and I are busy with Dad or unending chores. I envision Nick standing in the driveway a few minutes ago with his head lowered and his posture heavy with disappointment. Before Dad, he hopped into our vehicles and accompanied us on our errands.

We use the old Jeep to transport him to the vet or for hikes that guarantee we'll all end up muddy, but we also put a specially-made, textured cover on the leather back seat of the Tahoe so he can join us and enjoy the ride without having to dig into the leather when we round corners or make quick stops. Since I go so few places these days, with David running most of our errands and doing the grocery shopping while he's out, Nick gets fewer rides.

David has taken Nick on trips to see about surveying portions of land parcels we own, hoping to sell smaller parcels to raise some money, even if it's at a big loss. He knows Nick enjoys exploring fresh sights and scents as he walks along with David and the surveyor, but even with the glucosamine, our buoyant boy isn't able to hop into the tall Tahoe any longer without help.

David has helped Nick by lifting his haunches while Nick gains purchase on the back floor of the Tahoe before getting up onto the seat. It's awkward, and Nick seems confused and embarrassed, but David is great with him. He acts as if helping Nick is the most natural thing in the world, not saying anything and closing the door without a glance. Business as usual is David's message, and Nick buys into it.

It's funny how dogs and people can delude themselves in different but similar ways. Dad thinks he can drive; Nick thinks he's getting in the Tahoe by himself.

Both can also find joy in the simplest things. Dad is happy at the prospect of driving "next time." Nick is happy to be along for the ride. Dad enjoys tilting his head and look up at the blue skies and sunshine. Nick enjoys sticking his head out the window and feeling the wind on his face.

Even as their bodies are giving out, their joys in everyday living are not.

Today, Nick could have walked up the ramp of Dad's van to join us. The deep bench seat in the back of it would have been a perfect place for him to ride. But that was out of the question since Dad is still largely ignoring him, even if he is tolerating him.

So once again, Nick is left behind and left alone. I wish there were a way to reconcile the needs of both, but being physically and emotionally pulled between my dad and my dog is causing internal conflict that dampens my own mood. I believe I'm failing both of them, despite my efforts to give each the time and attention they want and need.

And then there is my put-upon husband. He does so much, but as there is so much to do, it doesn't seem to be enough. Our lovemaking, which has always been frequent and enjoyable, has waned amid the worries and fatigue. Those evenings of drinking wine and watching a movie or reading a book, and then going to bed where we took our time with sweet lovemaking, are in the past.

I miss our physical closeness, and so does David. We've talked about it, acted on it when we could, and promised each other to "get back to like it was before."

But nothing will ever be like it was before. Our carefree life as we have known it, is over.

*Oh, woe, woe, woe,* I silently admonish myself. "Get over yourself," I say aloud.

"Get over yourself," Dad mimics. Parkinson's patter, I call it. Just repeating the last thing said.

My thoughts return to the women who work at hard, low-paying jobs while they care for husbands, children, and parents, which forces me to adjust my gratitude meter and put things in their proper perspective.

David and I are together, healthy, and in love; we are making it work financially; and Dad and Nick are safe and well-tended, if not exactly healthy.

Our life, just as it is, has value, meaning and purpose. More than that, I can't ask for.

Well, maybe I could get a milkshake while we're out today.

---

I hug Candy, Dr. Baird's nurse, as we're leaving the office. She's one of those healthcare workers whose capacity for caring and efficiency has long made my life, and Dad's life, so much better over the years.

"Thanks, Candy, for everything, as always," I say as I pull back from the hug.

"You're welcome. He's doing good." She pats Dad's shoulder with genuine affection. "I know it's not easy, but you're doing a good job with him, Rachel."

It's wonderful to hear those words from Candy, since one of the most insecure things about being a caregiver is you don't have a measuring device of any sort to determine how well you're doing.

Infused with renewed energy by a new prescription for a round of physical therapy, plus Candy's heartening words, I push Dad at a brisk pace through the parking lot toward the van.

After securing his wheelchair, I give him a hug and kiss his cheek. "So the doctor says you're doing great, Dad."

"Another good report!" I'm surprised at the excitement in his voice, and realize I don't hear it much anymore. Being around others who praised him, asked him questions and joked with him has lifted his spirits.

I hope Adam and Jennie will take on his therapy, giving him another outlet for his effusive nature and—when his mind is at its clearest—a chance to come up with one-liners that crack everyone up.

We could sure use some levity in our lives right now.

# 14

We've had a fine day since returning from the doctor's office. Dad has been in a great mood since waking from his afternoon nap, and he was funny and engaged this evening at dinner.

I reached Adam earlier, and he was happy to hear from me. He said he had a cancellation at the spa tomorrow and would be here at five o'clock. I hadn't expected him to come so soon, but I couldn't be happier. Adam knows where we live because he'd been here many times to give David and me massages, back when things were rolling merrily along.

I could sure use a massage now. Not going to happen. Five o'clock tomorrow is a perfect time since it's after Dad's nap and before dinner. But Adam could have said midnight and I would have agreed.

As I drift off to sleep, I have peace of mind in knowing that Dad and I both have something to look forward to. I've just fallen asleep when the phone rings. Caller ID shows me it's coming from Dad's phone. I grab the phone and say, "Dad?"

He's wailing Mother's name. "Evelyn? Evelyn?"

"I'm coming!" I shout into the phone, then spring from bed and race downstairs.

My heart takes a hit when I see Dad on the floor with the phone in his hand, still calling for his late wife. "Evelyn? Evelyn?"

It's impossible for Dad to get hurt even if he falls out of bed. One great thing about the Alzheimer's bed is that it lowers to six inches from the floor. Every night I put a four-by-eight-foot, four-inch-thick pad beside it. Since one side of the bed is against the wall, the only way he can roll out is on the side where the pad lays, and it's only a two-inch drop. The assisted living facility had done the same from the day he'd moved in, and there was never a worry about a broken bone or serious injury with this system in place. I had been told that sometimes they found him on the pad during the night, calling for "Evelyn," but this is the first time it's happened since he came to live with us.

Still, it alarms me to see him on the floor, pleading into the phone he has dragged down with him, and looking so lost, sad and scared. David comes up behind me, with Nick on his heels. I don't think to tell Nick to stop as I rush toward Dad. But Nick does stop, and watches as David and I get on either side of Dad and lift him onto his bed while reassuring him that all is fine, that he'll be fine.

Breathing hard from fear and exertion, I sit down beside him on the bed and take his hand. "Evelyn?" he asks again as he looks right into my face, and I know his mind is elsewhere, that he's disoriented and can't comprehend what's happening—and that he's confusing me with my mother.

This is a new and disturbing turn of events, and I wonder if he is moving further into Stage 6 Alzheimer's.

He moans, then reaches out to gently touch my face with trembling fingers, while making an "oohing" sound, over and over. He is looking at me with lonesome longing, and it's obvious he thinks I'm his wife.

I can't help it. I slip to the mat on the floor, put my face in my hands, and start bawling. I have never cried in front of Dad since he moved in. Sure, I've shed my share of tears of frustration, but always in private. Now I cry for Dad's loss and loneliness; I cry for all that has happened, and all that is coming. I cry because whatever I do, however much I try, the Alzheimer's will steal him away from me.

Wiping my eyes on the sleeve of my pajamas, I look up at Dad. He's back, and he looks alarmed, as does David. Dad says, "Don't cry, honey. I love you."

Whether he is talking to me or Mother, I can't distinguish. But I pull myself up off the floor and sit on the bed next to him. I take his hand and put my heart into my reply, "I love you, too, Dad. So, so much."

David and I work together to reassure Dad and get him settled again. Our feet sink into the pad, and we're clumsy as we position him on his bed. I cover Dad and tuck his comforter around him.

I'm startled to see that Nick is standing next to me, on the pad, wanting to offer his own sweet brand of comfort to whoever needs it. But Dad doesn't even notice Nick, though his eyes are wide open. I follow his upward gaze. The ceiling isn't an impediment to what he's seeing, because he's seeing beyond this room. Now he looks serene, and I wonder if he's imagining Mother.

David and I look at each other, acknowledging we've had the same thought. Dad closes his eyes and falls into a breathing pattern that tells us he's gone back to sleep. We're relieved but still shaken.

David takes my hand, makes a motion to Nick, and leads us both out the door.

He stops and puts his arms around me, and I am comforted by the outpouring of his emotions and love when he says, "I'm sorry, baby. I'm so sorry."

Nick is leaning against my legs, and with one arm still wrapped around David, I reach down to rub Nick's head. My family. My strength. My source of comfort. My heart. My David. My dog.

And yes, my dad.

## 15

After such a tumultuous night, and a day when Dad has vacillated between sleep, anxiety, and expectancy, it is a joyful moment when Adam walks through our door. I greet him with a warm hug, which he returns.

Dad is in his wheelchair in the sunroom, where David and I have cleared wide paths for ambulation. It's a big room, and with the furniture pushed against the walls and the large area rug rolled up, it should be perfect for physical therapy.

As Adam rounds the corner with me, I look at Dad's face and see his eager expression and wide, welcoming smile. It reminds me of Nick when he knows he's going to get a special treat. I can practically read Dad's mind (*my buddy Adam is here!*) Excitement is spread across his features.

"Joe, my friend, how're you doing?" Adam's voice is friendly and enthusiastic.

He extends his hand to Dad, who takes it and says, dignified and man to man, "Good to see you, Adam."

He's delightfully clear at this moment. Despite his confusion last night and his ups and downs today, he's taken all of his pills and eaten all of his food. He reminds me of a kid at Christmas, doing all the right things just before Santa is due to arrive. A visit from someone he likes so much, but hasn't seen in months, has inspired such clear thoughts and determined actions. Interesting. I mentally catalogue it.

Going beyond the handshake, Adam bends down to Dad and gives him a one-armed hug. Dad hugs him back, and their embrace lasts for several tender seconds before Adam pulls away. "You're looking fine, sir!" Adam says.

Dad smiles at Adam and sits up a little straighter in his wheelchair. He told me earlier today that he's looking forward to getting strong and walking on his own again. Although that's not going to happen, I tell him I'm sure he can do it if he works hard with Adam. After Sissy and Rhonda's visit, when he ambulated so easily with just his walker and their support, David and I worked together to accomplish the same thing. Dad didn't respond well. He would droop so quickly that we had to catch him and haul him upright. At those times, we were bearing his entire weight and putting him in danger of falling.

Maybe we can work with Adam on that. But right now, Dad needs encouragement, and no one is better at providing that than Adam.

He tells Adam that he's glad he's here so he can get back on his feet once and for all. The conviction in his voice is meant to impart to Adam that he is determined and capable. It's almost as if he's willing Adam to tell him this expected outcome will come to pass. It's a man thing, and I admire Dad for taking the opportunity to flex his will.

"That's why I'm here, Joe. Let's get you in fighting shape." Kind, encouraging, optimistic. *Thank you, Adam.*

"Thanks for working Dad into your schedule, Adam." Adam and Jennie are busy running their spa, and he is giving up valuable time in driving here. I'll give him extra money for that time.

We now have the money to do so. I sold my grandmother's Blue Royal Delft hand-painted plates for forty-two hundred dollars the very day I put them up for sale on a china auction site. That cushion of cash will help with many extra things.

"I'm glad to be here with Joe, Rachel." Adam's smile is like a splash of sunshine across the room. "And it's good to see you, too. How's David?"

"He's fine, considering everything." David is gone, but he hopes to be back before Adam leaves.

Adam and Jennie have come to mean a great deal to us over the years. Adam can be so funny, and he makes Dad laugh. But he can also have meaningful conversations with Dad when he's clear and articulate, and mundane conversations that don't challenge Dad when he isn't. Adam adapts. I was so grateful to him and Jennie for making special visits to Dad the two times he's been in the hospital.

Jennie would bring homemade sugar-free cookies she baked just for Dad, and Adam would do light massage and physical therapy for Dad in his hospital bed, with no doctor's order and no expectation of payment.

Such kind people are a source of relief and gratitude when you're caring for a parent in the hospital. Those hospital-room chairs for guests are torturous, no doubt made that way to discourage long visits, but you want to maintain a constant vigil to ensure that nothing goes wrong. You interact with everyone from doctors to nurses to CNAs to ensure the best care and outcome.

After myriad mistakes were made with Mother in a hospital in Florida, on top of all the infections she contracted that led to a three-month hospital stay, I became very protective of Dad. Both times Dad was in the hospital, I hired CNAs to relieve me when I was exhausted or craving decent food. I wouldn't have that luxury now.

But I do have the luxury of Adam being here now to help Dad. He is holding out his hands to grasp Dad's to help him to his feet. "I am so glad he's able to live here with you and David," Adam tells me. To Dad he says, "I bet you like being here a lot better than at Crestview, don't you, Joe?"

Dad's only response is a nod. He's concentrating on his balance.

"We like having him here, Adam."

I need to leave them alone so they can get down to business. "Okay, I'll let you two get started. Could you please stop early so we can have fifteen or so minutes together down in Dad's room? He's still getting used to things."

"Sounds good." Adam turns his full attention to Dad.

Dad scowls at me, as if I'm intruding on his time with Adam. Sheesh, it's only been five minutes. But five minutes to him is different than five minutes to me.

"Have fun, guys." Even though I have a million things to do, I need some time with my sweet dog, and he needs some time with me.

Nick is in our bedroom, where I left him with the door closed so he couldn't hear Adam's voice when he arrived. He likes Adam, but he can visit with him when therapy is finished.

Nick gets up from his comfy corner bed as soon as he sees me. He makes an extra effort to stand, although the bed is new and doesn't have so much give that he should get bogged down in it. He's declining again and needs something stronger than glucosamine chondroitin. *Well, hell.*

"Hey, Nickaroo," I coo, acting as if I don't notice his exertion. Now he's off the bed and coming toward me, and I put my arms around his neck and burrow my face into his soft fur. He leans into me, affirming how much he loves to be loved.

"How would you like to go for a *walk*?" He knows the word and the tone, and he wags his tail, tongue lolling as he smiles his goofy smile, and I share his joyful anticipation as I say, "Let's go!"

He saunters by me and heads to the door leading down to the garage, where I will put on my hiking boots and get my water pack and hiking stick. He's waiting for me to open the door, his tail wagging and eyes bright, ready to tear down the steps, when he goes still and his ears perk up at the sound of Adam's voice.

He switches gears and trots toward the sunroom. I follow, and watch him come to a halt at the entrance to the room. His tail is hanging low and wagging slowly, indicating his hesitancy. He seems to be assessing the situation. I step behind him and take in the scene. Adam's back is to us, and his body is blocking Dad's view. They don't know we're here. Nick remedies that when he *woofs* a single sharp bark. Adam looks around and smiles, but Dad jerks and then freezes. *Uh oh.*

"Hey, Nick!" Adam's tone holds an unmistakable invitation for Nick to join them. Nick takes tentative steps farther into the room. His tail wags like mad.

Although Dad is clutching his walker, Adam holds Dad's gait belt in one hand and reaches toward Nick with the other. "Come here, Nick."

Nick breaks into a full trot at Adam's invitation. He nuzzles Adam's extended hand.

"How are you, big boy? You doing okay?" Nick squirms with welcoming happiness as Adam pets him.

Dad looks down at Nick and says, "You need therapy, too, Nick?" Nick whines with pleasure at the attention he's getting.

I get goosebumps at the surge of pleasure that runs through me. Dad is acknowledging Nick without fear! "He probably does, Dad, but we're going for a walk. He heard Adam's voice and had to say hello."

"It's good to see him. He's a beautiful dog." Adam turns back to Dad. "Okay, Joe, you and I have some work to do. Ready?"

When I call Nick, he trots back to me, happy upon happy. Happy for the attention from an old friend, and a new friend. Happy he's going for a walk.

"See you downstairs in about forty-five," I say as we leave.

As I go around the corner I hear Adam say, "You got a good buddy there, Joe. Nick's one of the sweetest, best-behaved dogs I've ever known." I want to hear how Dad responds, but time is dwindling for a decent walk before therapy ends. Nonetheless, I sure am curious about it.

# 16

The elevator is descending when I return from my walk with Nick, who heads straight to his water bowl.

When the door opens, Adam pushes Dad out and I reach in to grab his walker.

Nick is still lapping up water, and as Adam maneuvers Dad past Nick, with a three-foot clearance, Dad eyes Nick but doesn't react.

Adam greets Nick again, but I give him a hand signal that tells him to stay. I don't want to push things too far, too fast.

Dad's apartment is nice and fresh from the thorough cleaning I gave it this morning while Carmen tended to him.

"This is a beautiful place you've got here, Joe."

Dad's eyes rove his apartment and settle on the view. He smiles. "It is, isn't it?"

"Sure is. Much better view than you had at Crestview. Bigger room, too."

Dad looks a little confused and somewhat disconcerted. But why? Sometimes it's hard to read his expression because the Parkinson's mask—the loss of some control of the face and head muscles that creates a stare-like feature—is becoming more pronounced. I've been denying the change, but now in the late-afternoon light that illuminates Dad's face, the reality is evident.

With every escalation of symptoms, my instinct is to find medicine or therapy to reverse the effects. But that's a fruitless pursuit. Regardless of how much therapy Dad has or what medicines are used to fight his Parkinson's and Alzheimer's, the battle will be lost, but maybe we can slow the onslaught. Adam's therapy and mobility exercises give me hope that we'll delay balance, muscle, and stiffness problems. Transferring Dad from a wheelchair to a bed or chair isn't enough.

Dad says he needs to go to the bathroom, and Adam offers to help.

Adam pulls Dad into a standing position, and using his walker, Dad shuffles toward the bathroom with confidence. I realize Carmen, David and I should be ambulating Dad to the bathroom, instead of using his wheelchair. That would be good for all of us. Adam takes the opportunity to show me easier transfer and toileting methods using the handicap bar next to the toilet.

We walk Dad back to his bed, which he drops onto with a heavy sigh. "I'm tired."

As I help him lie back, I tell him that's understandable since he's worked so hard today, and ask him if he'd like to have dinner in bed.

"I don't like to eat alone." He looks embarrassed to admit this.

"How about on the days you have therapy, I bring my dinner down here and eat with you? Then as you get stronger, you won't be as tired after a session with Adam, and you can sit at the table with David and me."

"That sounds good, Sugar." He closes his eyes and is sound asleep within seconds.

Adam's kind look tempts me to blurt out that I'm not equipped to handle everything that comes my way. I want to voice my fears and frustrations to this empathetic man who would understand. But I can't show weakness or self-doubt in front of anyone, even Adam. If I crack, I may break.

With Dad resting, we agree to go upstairs to talk about plans for his therapy.

Nick is waiting for us, tail wagging, outside Dad's door. I know he's there for Adam more than me. Adam is a fresh source of love and attention, and Nick is going to take advantage of it while he can.

"Hey, Nick." Adam reaches down to pet him.

"What's the story with him and Joe? I thought they would be good buddies, but Joe pretty much ignores him."

I tell him about Dad's reaction to Nick the very first day, and how it's likely due to his experiences with biting dogs when he was a mailman.

"He'll get over it, and then he'll realize how good a friend Nick can be to him."

"You helped today, you know. Maybe bringing Nick into the room when you're doing Dad's therapy will move things along. What do you think? We just regret there isn't enough time to give both of them the attention they need. I think their being together more often could help alleviate some of their loneliness."

"I agree with you, Rachel, and I'll do what I can to help when I'm here." He glances around at Nick, who's coming up the stairs behind us. "Nick has a hip problem?" I don't question how a physical therapist as astute as Adam would know that.

"Yes, poor guy. I've taken him to the vet, and she suggested glucosamine chondroitin for now. She doesn't want to put him on arthritis or anti-inflammatory medicine yet because it can be tough on his stomach and liver. But I think the effectiveness of the glucosamine is wearing off. He was better for a while, but he seems to be stiffening up again."

Dad's stiffening up. Nick's stiffening up. The therapy can alleviate Dad's stiffness to some degree. But Nick? I sigh, knowing we're moving toward prescription drugs for him, and I worry about the side effects. Dr. Froman mentioned Rimadyl, an anti-inflammatory. I tell Adam about this, and also about an alternate treatment of Adequan that requires two intramuscular injections a week for four weeks, then one injection every two weeks for maintenance.

"I'd go with the injections," Adam suggests. "The anti-inflammatories can be hard on a dog, even one as big and strong as Nick."

We're in the kitchen now. "Thanks for that advice, Adam. I better get him started on it sooner rather than later, I suppose."

Changing the subject, I ask him if I can get him anything—water, juice, a glass of wine?

"Water would be good, thanks. But give me a few minutes with Nick first."

Nick is licking his empty food bowl. Hope springs eternal that a morsel may magically appear or might have been left behind. Since he empties his bowl in about thirty seconds at each twice-daily feeding, it sits empty each day for twenty-three hours and fifty-nine minutes. Nevertheless, to our gluttonous Lab, it's a worthy pursuit.

Adam has a natural affinity and empathy for all living things. He merely holds out his hand, and Nick is standing in front of him, anticipating and trusting.

As Adam leans over him and puts his sure hands on Nick's hindquarters and speaks to him in a soothing voice as he moves his hands around Nick's hips, getting a sense of the hurt. His touch is light, and Nick's eyes close as relief takes hold. He's taking in whatever energy Adam is giving, as dogs do. There's no resistance, only gratification for the touch and its positive effect.

Adam sits on the floor behind Nick, massaging his hips. I watch his technique so that maybe I can help Nick in the same way. After a few minutes, Adam finishes and praises Nick. "You're such a good boy, Nick, such a good boy." Nick seems much more relaxed, and tears spring to my eyes in gratitude for this kindness shown to my dog. Nick's demeanor reminds me of Dad's when his pain pill begins to take effect. His face and features soften as the pain subsides. It occurs to me that Adam could help Nick more than any medicine, but that's not a realistic consideration, for so many reasons—money being the main one. But I can massage Nick's hips myself.

"Look at him. He looks so much better. I didn't know how stressed by the pain he was until now. Thank you so much for doing that for him. Maybe next time you're here, you can show me what you do."

"You got it." Adam smiles as I turn to open the refrigerator, remembering my offer of water. I take the opportunity to bring my emotions under control. *Jeez, get a grip. You've been ready to burst into tears all day.*

Nick is now on his bed in a far corner of the kitchen, his breathing soft and easy as he rests more comfortably than I've seen in a while.

I look at the clock. "Oh, Adam, you've been here almost two hours! I'm sorry, I didn't realize."

"No problem, but I better get going."

"I wonder where David is. He was hoping to see you." I'm prattling now, taking up even more of Adam's valuable time.

"I'm sure I'll see him soon." Adam takes a swig from the water bottle as I reach for my purse on the kitchen island and pull out my checkbook.

"You don't have to pay me, Rachel. I'm billing this to Medicare."

"I know, but you only get to bill in units, and Medicare doesn't cover your travel time. And it and certainly doesn't cover doggie therapy."

We both laugh, but Adam shakes his head and says, "Not necessary, Rachel. Really."

My emotions get all liquid again, and it's all I can do to hold back my tears. "I know it's not necessary, Adam, but I'd feel much better if you'd let me pay you for an hour of your time, outside of what you can bill Medicare. Please let me do this. We can afford it."

I'm so grateful to be able to say those words and know they're true. I say a little prayer of thanks for Grandmother's china.

"You know, Rachel, there was a time there when we were really up against it. It was winter, and we weren't as established with the hospital and rehab centers as we are now. I used to bill you up to a thousand a month for Joe's therapy, and you never blinked."

"But you and Jennie did the work. You earned that money."

"Yes, we did, but I can't tell you how grateful we were to have it during that time. I'll never forget seeing that ad you put in the paper, and saying to Jennie, 'This could be an answer to our prayers.' We were praying for something to come along. Then when I called you, and I learned what you wanted and how much you were willing to do for your dad, I knew our prayers had been answered."

I remember so well the relief I felt at finding someone who could help Dad when he needed it most. He was still rehabbing from the broken hip when the benefits ran out, and I was desperate to keep him moving and progressing.

When I'd added massage therapy to his regimen, Adam provided a massage table to leave in Dad's room. Two physical therapy sessions and what turned into two massage sessions per week, at sixty dollars a session, had added up. I felt I had gotten a bargain, but until this moment, I didn't know how much that money meant to Adam and Jennie.

"You and Jennie have given Dad and me much more than I could ever pay you for. Dad wouldn't be nearly as well as he is today without you. He'd be bedridden without that therapy. And I'll never forget your kindness and help when he was in the hospital those two times."

Adam nods. "We've said the same thing to each other about you. God led us to you and your dad. So we helped each other when we needed it."

Before I can respond, I hear the garage door open. "David's here."

My tears begin to flow just as David comes through the door. At first he looks startled, then he takes in the scene, and smiles.

He walks over and offers Adam his hand. "Good to see you, Adam. Good to see you."

# 17

David and I are enjoying dinner with Dad in his apartment. After Adam left, I felt drained and didn't want to cook, and David didn't feel like cooking either. He's had a stressful and disappointing day. He didn't get the job for finishing the house because he just couldn't underbid the other contractor.

Taking an easy way out for both of us, I've baked a frozen pizza and made a salad. Dad loves pizza, and he's in a great mood while we're having dinner. His favorite big band music is playing, and he hums along, off-key and out of tempo, as he chews his pizza. It's taking him a very long time to eat, and most of his salad has ended up in his covered lap, but we are all happy just being together in his cozy apartment. By unspoken agreement, we put David's disappointment aside during dinner and focused on conversation with Dad. But soon enough, worry lines settle on my husband's handsome face.

Dad, exhausted from therapy, falls asleep with his plate in his lap. David insists on doing Dad's toileting and bed-readying. I'm grateful he's willing and able to do it alone. He can handle Dad much better than I simply by virtue of his strength, especially when Dad has already nodded off and needs to be awakened.

As I wash the dishes in Dad's kitchenette, my conversation with Adam plays through my mind before my thoughts turn to the memory of a birthday card Jennie gave me two years ago. She had written it on behalf of Dad, and even though I can't recall what it said, I can recall the profound effect it had on me. I intend to look for it after I go up.

Upstairs, I give Nick some much-needed attention. When David comes up he reports, "All taken care of. He's asleep." I hug him and thank him for his help.

He yawns. "I'm bushed. Let's have a glass of wine and watch a movie. I may fall asleep, though."

"Why don't you put on a baseball game and stretch out on the sofa? I want to go up to my study and look for something, and it could take a while. I'll be down soon and we'll go to bed."

"Sounds good," he says through another yawn.

The file cabinet in my study contains hundreds of cards I've received over the years. Most are from David, but I've kept every birthday card I've received as an adult, for as far back as I can remember. I've been lucky to have so many good friends who never forget my birthday. While I can clean out my closets and cabinets and get rid of many things without a qualm, greeting cards—and the words written upon them—have a special place in my life, and I can't part with them. In the past, when leisure time existed, I would occasionally grab a handful to read again.

Lord, that's good for the soul.

Now I'm in search of the card Jennie gave me. I don't remember what it looks like, so I have to open each card to check. I'm almost at the bottom of the first stack when I find it. The front of the card doesn't even say HAPPY BIRTHDAY. It's a cute, generic card that says, WARNING DON'T CROSS THIS FIELD UNLESS YOU CAN RUN IT IN 9.9 SECONDS. OUR BULL CAN DO IT IN 10 FLAT. I smile as I open it to read the rest of the message. AGE HASN'T SLOWED YOU DOWN ONE BIT . . . IT'S JUST THAT, THESE DAYS, YOU NEED A LITTLE MORE INCENTIVE TO GET MOVIN'! HAPPY BIRTHDAY.

I drop down on the sofa in my study and start to read the words she wrote on it.

*Dear Rachel,*

*Today is a special day because 49 years ago, you were created in God's image and grown into the compassionate, energetic, generous, and intelligent daughter you are today. Knowing that Joe has some challenges with communication, we decided to help him express what is in his heart concerning you. My beautiful Rachel, you are an angel who always watches over me, making sure that I have the best of loving care. You do so much for me and with a cheerful heart. I can't always tell you what I'm feeling inside, but it seems like you're an expert at reading my mind. So read it now and know how much I love, appreciate, and call for you. The smallest things in life are some of the most important. Thank you for investing your time in making me such a big part of your life. I love it when you read to me, hold my hand, rub my forehead, kiss my cheek and surprise me with a beer and a hamburger. It makes me feel young again! From combing my hair, buying me new clothes, taking me out to eat and to my appointments, I have so much to be thankful for. You don't just meet my basic needs, but see that I have more than enough to help me live an abundant life. I thank God for my little girl. Happy Birthday to my precious daughter! Rachel, you are my hero, and I love you,* (and here, Jennie had drawn a heart and signed it) *Daddy.*

At the bottom she had added, *"Give thanks in everything, for this is the will of God for you." 1 Thessalonians 5:18.*

I lean my head back and let the tears flow again. It has been an emotional day, and rereading this beautiful tribute is a perfect way to end it.

No, there's a better way to end it.

Filled with love and gratitude, I go downstairs to find David sacked out on the sofa, with a baseball game playing on TV. It's a large sofa, with plenty of room for us to lie down together.

I snuggle up next to him, and he wakes up and pulls me into his arms and gives me a slow, passionate kiss.

"Let's go to bed and make love," I say, as I catch my breath.

And we do. My cup runneth over.

# 18

With Carmen in residence four hours a day, six days a week, my Spanish is improving slowly while her English is improving rapidly.

"I want to talk to Mr. Joe," she told me, "and I want him to *unnerstan*."

The language barrier has kept me from getting to know her as well as I would have liked, and these two months of trying to communicate have been frustrating for me, even with the app on my phone that translates our words. But somehow Dad understands much of what she says. It isn't the words; it's more her tone and her actions. Her touch is gentle, but firm and reassuring. Her tone isn't condescending, but patient. Her smile evidences the goodness is in her heart. She has come to care about Dad, as he has her.

Dad sometimes makes jokes, and even though it isn't possible that Carmen fully understands the jokes, let alone the nuances, she laughs. Dad appreciates nothing more than being able to make someone laugh.

She's become more efficient, as I'd hoped she would, and her being here six mornings a week gives me the time I need to clean my house, do laundry, maintain our banking and finance records, and keep up with emails and phone calls from friends and family. It isn't always enough time to get everything done, but it affords me a measure of freedom I treasure.

So this morning when Carmen tells me her mother is sick and will no longer be able to take care of her children while she comes to my home to tend to Dad, my heart sinks. When I had hired her back in May, school had been in session and she had a routine of seeing her children, Emil and Lucy, ten and eight years of age, get on the bus at seven-fifteen, before driving to my home to arrive by seven-thirty. She wastes no time in getting started with Dad, and she never slacks in the four hours she's here. At eleven-thirty she leaves to tend to her own chores at home before her children return on the bus.

When school let out for the summer, there had been no change in routine, except that she now comes at eight instead of seven-thirty so she can prepare her children's breakfast and have a little more time with them in the morning. Her mother, Isabel, who lives with them, has been watching Carmen's children during these summer months, but now she won't be able to.

"Oh, Carmen, I'm so sorry your mother's ill. I hope it's nothing serious?"

*"Corazón,"* she answers. "Hurt." I know *corazón* means heart, but I don't know if she's saying "heart" or "hurt" in her response. Using the language conversion app, I type in "her heart hurts?" and when the translated words appear I ask, *"Le duele el corazón?"*

*"Si,* she go to hospital. She no have strength now to take care of Emil and Lucy."

I wish she had told me about this problem that has been plaguing her. If she had, I might have anticipated her leaving and could have started looking for someone else.

"Who's taking care of your mother and children now?"

*"Mi hermana."* Her sister. She gestures for my phone. *"Por favor."*

I switch the setting on the app so that her typed-in Spanish will translate to English and hand her my phone. Her nimble thumbs type out a number of characters. When she hands it back to me, I learn that her sister is newly employed and no longer available to take care of Carmen's family. Carmen hadn't told me because everything had been okay. She ends with, "Now not okay."

*No shit.*

Well, if there's a reason for cussing, this is it.

She has tears in her eyes. She hadn't expected to have to leave this job. I embrace her when tears turn to sobs. She pulls back with a string of apologies until I hold up my hand and say, *"No es necesario."*

Dad has been watching our rapid half-English, half-Spanish exchange without the benefit of knowing what's being translated. He can understand the mood and tone. His eyebrows are furrowed in concentration and his eyes are going back and forth between us, trying to decipher the conversation.

Taking his hand, I explain what's going on. His eyes drop and the corners of his mouth pull down. "I . . . I'm sorry, Carmen." His voice is infused with sadness, but I don't know if it is for her situation, or that she's leaving. Perhaps both.

Carmen bends over to hug Dad in his easy chair. "Oh, I so sorry, Mr. Joe. I will miss you." He sinks into his chair and his shoulders slump. He doesn't seem to be able to muster the energy to respond.

I hurt for Carmen, for her distress about her mother's illness. I've been there. My mother had heart problems, too. Carmen *should* be with her mother and children, taking care of them instead of my dad.

I also hurt for Dad. Carmen has been a source of comfort and caring in his life, someone he could count on seeing regularly, who has expanded his small world. I'm concerned for Dad and the emotional splintering her leaving will cause, but I'm also concerned about the extra work this will mean for me and David.

After Carmen leaves each day, I fix lunch. I often give Dad a choice of where he wants to eat—his apartment, upstairs, or outside on the deck. After lunch, there's toileting before he settles in for his afternoon of watching TV or listening to music and napping. It has become a comfortable and convenient routine, which changes only if I've planned an outing or he has an appointment.

In the afternoon, he's content to be in his chair. Much of that afternoon time is spent alone because I need to spend some time with Nick, and David if he's home. Plus, there are always more chores to tackle, phone calls to make and emails to answer.

In between, I come down to Dad's room to check on him. I enjoy spending time with him. We watch TV or put on music, and when he's in the mood, I read to him or play some memory games designed for dementia patients. There are many afternoons we enjoy sitting on the deck and taking in the view. Nick often joins us, as does David when he's home. Dad gets mesmerized watching the hummingbirds drink from the feeders we've put up around the deck, and often nods off in the warm afternoon sun. Then there's toileting, another nap, dinner and bedtime preparations.

My days seem full to the brim, but now, I realize, they will be overflowing.

But Carmen has served notice and will *adios* the job in a matter of minutes. I'm somewhat stunned by the reality that David and I will be taking care of Dad full time until . . . well, who knows when?

With a mixture of anxiety and resentment, softened by sympathy and gratitude, I watch her bend down to give Dad another big hug. He raises his stiff arms which, I notice for the first time, are thinner, and puts them around her shoulders, which are shaking with her sobs.

"Oh, Mr. Joe. I love you." She is still embracing him.

"I love you." Dad's voice is trembling with sadness.

She has been such a big help, and her efficiency has increased quite a lot, so much so that I've barely had to help her over the last month. She's freed me up to get so many other things done and saved a lot of wear and tear on my body. But that's now over, and I'll just have to accept it, and help Dad do the same.

Carmen wouldn't be leaving unless it was necessary because she needs the money. Her husband already lost his job taking care of our lawn when we had to cut expenses. Though she told me he was very busy and earning money, I wonder how they will make it with only one income. And in the winter, when grass doesn't need to be cut, their income will drop substantially. From the worn-out car she drives to the worn-out clothes she wears, I know they are living on the edge.

I have the uplifting thought that maybe Carmen could come back when school starts again in a few weeks. Perhaps her mother will be better by then?

I ask her.

"No, so sorry Miss Rachel, but now I help *mi madre* like I help Mr. Joe. She weak."

Carmen's situation is even worse than she has let on. She is taking on full-time caregiving duties for her mother. She has children to care for, too. I think again about the unfairness that there is no compensation for family members who take on the role of caregiver.

I do a quick mental calculation of the money we have in Dad's account to see if there is extra to give her. I'm thinking along generous lines, like maybe an entire week's pay since it will take me at least that long to replace her. But I check that generous impulse and decide instead to reach into the therapy fund and give her a hundred dollars. Even with the cushion from the sale of grandmother's china, we have to watch our dollars because there's still no source of income—and we have no idea how long that will be the case.

If a parent can't qualify for Medicaid, or if there is no money for private care, the entire financial burden will fall on the family caregiver's shoulders. We're saving the government tens of thousands of dollars a year because it doesn't have to pay out Medicaid benefits to warehouse Dad in a nursing home. Not that I would do that, but shouldn't caregivers, who are doing the job the government would pay for if laws and circumstances allowed it, be paid something for taking that burden off the tax system?

I read in a brochure in Dad's neurologist's office that an estimated 15.9 million Americans annually provide 18.2 billion hours of unpaid assistance to relatives with Alzheimer's and other forms of dementia. It's ludicrous that it isn't compensated in some way because it's the very definition of labor: work, especially hard physical work. Carmen can attest to that.

Shoving down my rising resentment yet again, I come back to the painful situation before me. "Carmen, can you wait while I go upstairs to get something?" When she looks at me quizzically, I say, "*Un minuto, por favor.*"

When I come back with my checkbook, she looks startled and says, "No, no Miss Rachel, no!"

"*Solo un poco algo.*" Just a little something.

Dad, watching what is unfolding, says, "Give me my wallet. I'll pay her." Dad's wallet in the chest of drawers has only twenty-five dollars in it. I keep it in there because every so often, he wants his wallet. The first time I had given it to him empty of any bills, he'd gotten agitated. He even accused me of taking his money, which did not offend me because I understood why he would think so. A wallet represents cash and security to Dad, and that had been taken away the first time he looked in his wallet and found it empty except for his expired Florida driver's license.

Dad can no longer count money. He recognizes the different denominations, but he can't add them together. So when I had put a ten, a five, and ten ones in his wallet, it was filled out and seemed abundant to him. He's assuming he has money in his wallet, and he wants to share it with Carmen.

I take his wallet out of the bureau's top drawer and hand it to him. Carmen starts crying again and says, "Oh no, Mr. Joe. No es necesaria!" Dad ignores her as he unfolds the wallet and shakily pulls out the entire wad of bills. He holds them out to her. "Here's a thousand dollars," he says. "You take it."

Carmen looks at me, and I nod my head. I'll replace it later. But for now, Dad is giving because that's what his heart tells him to do.

Carmen surprises me by saying, "Oy! A thousand dollars! Oh, Mr. Joe, is so much, gracias, gracias!" Her role-playing rings with sincerity. I want to hug her again.

"You're welcome," Dad says with a tinge of pride in his voice and a satisfied smile on his face. I will add my hundred-dollar check to that, but wish it could be more because, even in her last moments with us, she has given Dad something else he needs—a sense of worth in being able to help someone who needs it.

# 19

Happiness and relief in a single package walks through the door two days later, and her name is Jennie.

Adam had texted me to say that Jennie had no late-afternoon appointments, so she would be coming with him. When I told Dad, he'd paused, and I could see him shuffling through the tattered index cards in his mind. He was trying to put a face to the name, though only days ago he'd commented on how sweet she is. It took a bit, but then his face lit up in that extraordinary way it does when he's able to recall something or someone. He'd said, "I can't wait to see that angel again."

When she comes through the door, we squeal and hug and laugh before I relinquish her to Dad's arms. Many sweet hugs and words ensue, and I wonder at the light and goodness this woman emanates. Her presence alone would be a healing balm to anyone who's hurting. Add to that her incredible professional skills, and she's worth ten times her tiny weight in gold.

The other half of the dynamic duo comes through the door, with Nick following him. Together Adam and Jennie are a formidable team of healing and good energy. Their presence re-energizes my waning vitality.

Adam greets Dad and then looks at me with concern. "What's going on with you, Rachel?"

Do I look that haggard? That distressed? Do I look as run-down as I feel after just two full days of caregiving for Dad? What will I look like in a week? To my surprise, I find I'm slightly offended. I've washed my hair, put on a little makeup, and donned a nice pair of slacks and a pretty top. But this is silly. He means no offense. Besides, I've already had a pity party just this morning, so it is with dry eyes and a strong voice that I tell Adam and Jennie why I look so worn-down.

"I'm tired, truth be told, but fine overall. Just overwhelmed right now because the aide I had coming in six mornings a week had to quit suddenly, so David and I are handling everything ourselves."

Their shoulders sag in sympathy.

Dad pipes in, "They take good care of me."

I thank him for saying so.

"I'm sure they do, Joe," Jennie says kindly. She takes Dad's hand and squeezes it, then looks at me. "You poor thing. Are you going to hire someone else?"

"If I can find someone. I put an online and print ad in the newspaper, but it's only been a day and so far nobody's responded. Anyway, I don't expect to have a replacement anytime soon." I could go on and on, but instead, I take a deep breath and say, "We'll be all right either way." I don't want their focus on me; I want it on Dad.

"I may have someone for you," Jennie says.

"What? Really? *Who*?"

"Marcy, who cleans part-time on the afternoon shift at the hospital. She's not a CNA, but she's a hard worker and she's strong, so she may be able to help."

"Is she looking for more work?" I ask, my hopes rising.

"She asked me if I knew anyone who was looking for someone to clean because she needed to make more money. That was a couple of weeks ago, though. She gave me her number in case I learned of someone. You want to call her?"

*Did I!* "Yes, thanks, Jennie—that would be great."

She takes out her phone and thumbs through it, then asks, "You want to write this down?"

I grab paper and pen and jot down the number. "Do you know her last name?"

"No, sorry, but just tell her I gave you her number."

"I will. Thank you so much!" Could I be lucky enough to find someone to replace Carmen so quickly?

"I'll call her while you're working with Dad." I can see he's getting antsy and is eager to start therapy. He wants so much to "get better," as he says, and he believes the therapy will do that for him. It's the best kind of motivation.

David comes through the door at the top of the stairs. He's been out cutting the grass and is covered with a green patina and sweat. I have to assume he and Adam and Jennie have already said hello because David merely nods at them and says, "Going to get in the shower."

Nick has planted himself beside Jennie and is getting some righteous petting, while Dad is getting anxious.

"Are you all finished yakking yet?" Dad's voice is gruff and impatient.

Adam and Jennie look startled. Dad is usually all sugar and spice with them. I start laughing. I can't help it. "He's all yours," I say through my laughter. It's the fatigue turned to hysteria that's driving the laughter. They're both staring at me, and I wonder if they worry I'm losing it.

"Go on, go on," I say, letting my laughter die out and waving toward Dad. "I'm going to go call Marcy."

They nod in tandem, and Jennie pushes Dad's wheelchair toward the sunroom. Adam follows, but then stops and turns back to Nick and me. He gives me a conspiratorial wink and then says, "C'mon, Nick."

Nick doesn't hesitate to follow the three of them into the therapy room, as we've started calling it.

When I hear Dad say, "You giving that dog therapy, too?" I can't help bursting into another fit of laughter. I laugh so hard that I grab my sides and squat to the floor.

I don't care if they hear me. If I am indeed losing it, well, so what? It feels *good*.

## 20

Sometimes the angels just smile down on you. After leaving Adam and Jennie, I went into the bathroom to smooch a bit with my naked, freshly showered husband, and to give him the good news that we may soon have a replacement for Carmen.

Whispering a simple prayer of, "Please," I called Marcy. She was not only still available, but thrilled to be offered the job. I'm gratified to learn she helped care for her grandmother for several years before her passing. Because she works at the hospital from noon until eight P.M., the morning timing will work out perfectly. When I asked if she had any conflicts because of children, husband or perhaps with her own parents' care, she assured me she didn't. At the age of forty-five—something she had volunteered—her kids were grown, her husband was long gone, and her parents were fine.

We agreed on a wage of ten dollars an hour, which is more than she makes working at the hospital, something else she readily volunteered. Maybe I could have gotten her for less, but the fact that she will be able to start tomorrow morning adds considerably to her value. Besides, it's what I paid Carmen, and it seems only fair to pay Marcy the same.

Adam and Jennie's therapy time with Dad is almost up. David is in his study, talking with Lily, his mom. Lily is definitely a talker, so it will be a while before he comes down. He speaks with his parents, brother and sister at least once a week. They are a close family. I know he misses them, and they miss him. Before Dad lived with us, we traveled to their

Texas home each July and also visited during one of the major holidays. This past July, I urged David to go without me, to put the airfare on a credit card that we'd worry about later; but he refused, knowing I'd be overwhelmed without him.

Besides, Lily and Artie are often cruising in their Class C Motorhome. In their early eighties, their health and stamina are remarkable—so different from my parents'. Artie's hip replacement two years ago barely slowed him down, with much of his speedy recovery attributable to his daughter Camille's dedicated nursing and therapy. Should they ever need care similar to Dad's, she'd provide it. I'd help as much as I could, paying forward David's goodness to my parents.

I walk into the sunroom to see Nick walking next to Dad, keeping the same slow pace as he ambulates with Adam's support. Jennie is trailing the trio. It's such an unexpected and comical scene that I almost burst out laughing again, but I rein myself in to avoid embarrassing all of us.

"Almost finished here," Jennie says. "I want to give Joe a shoulder massage."

Adam guides him into the seat of his wheelchair, and Dad sighs in relief. Nick plops down next to the wheelchair and echoes Dad's sigh. Dad looks down at him and says, "What you got to be tired about?" Nick just looks up at him and pants. When Dad gives Nick a crooked grin, my heart does a backflip.

Adam tells me, "Joe's a hard worker. He did great today, didn't you, Joe?"

Dad is flushed, probably from exertion as well as the compliment. No matter. He looks pleased, even if he does look tired.

"You're a killer," Dad grunts, pretending to be put out with his taskmaster.

"Nothing you can't handle, you Devil in Baggy Pants," Adam chides, referring to the nickname Dad's unit had been given by the Germans in World War II.

I so appreciate that Adam has taken an interest in Dad's military service. During all the years I was growing up, Dad hadn't spoken about it. Mother never wanted to hear his war stories, and it wasn't until I visited my grandmother—his mother—during a summer break from college that I learned the extent of his service.

Grandmother had taken me up to her attic to show me a box of his Army memorabilia. I had been stunned to see the number of local newspaper articles that had been written about Dad. The first one I picked up had a caption under his handsome photo that said, WIRE MAN.

*Wire Man?* I read the article with a sense of apprehension mixed with incredulity as I learned that my mild-mannered father had parachuted behind German lines and garroted German soldiers with piano wire. *My* dad? My sweet, easy-going Dad?

Another article talked about his being wounded at Anzio. I knew Dad had a deep scar on his right shin that was from the war, but I didn't know the extent of the horror of the battle that had resulted in his injury. With the exception of Dad, his entire platoon had been killed. I hadn't even known how many men were in a platoon, but I had felt an odd sense of gratitude, mixed with wonder, that Dad had not been killed also. Grandmother then showed me the Western Union telegram she and Granddaddy had received, telling them their son was seriously wounded in action in Italy, and they would let them know when reports were updated.

I had asked her how she felt when she received the telegram, and she said that she had "gone all to pieces."

When I next saw Dad, I asked him about his service and told him what I had learned. He was reluctant to talk about it, but he opened up when he sensed my interest was genuine. Soon after that, he sought out other 82nd Airborne veterans and began attending reunions and events until he broke his hip. Fortunately, I had been able to attend several reunions at Fort Bragg with him.

When I told him we wouldn't be able to go that first year after the hip break, he was as disappointed as I had ever seen him. Not being able to bask in the glory that was afforded him by the young soldiers at Fort Bragg diminished his spirits for weeks.

I understood, or at least thought I did. It was just something else that had been taken away from him, another loss to be endured. Those reunions had meant so much to him, and even more so after Mother died. Loss of wife, loss of independence, loss of mobility, loss of memory, loss of friends, loss of glorification . . . Loss took a bite out of you one painful chomp at a time until you were nothing more than a mere morsel of your former self.

How can I ever hope to fill the void left in Dad's life by all those losses? Meeting his physical needs just isn't enough to make him whole again. He needs more love and companionship in his life, but where will it come from?

I've never deeply regretted that David and I weren't able to have children, but at this moment I think how wonderful it would be to have children who could help fill the hollow holes in Dad's long days. But I have two loving nieces who over the years visited their Papa as often as college breaks and time off from jobs allowed. Both have plans to visit at Thanksgiving, and Dad is looking forward to their visit as much as I am.

But that's more than three months away. I envision Dad and Nick's friendship growing during those months. I believe he's beginning to realize that dogs can be affectionate, undemanding companions; and for that, there is no better dog than Nick.

David and I didn't know the joy of living with dogs until we moved to North Carolina. In Miami, we lived in a high-rise condominium on Brickell Avenue, and we worked such long and erratic hours—David, with his real estate development projects and me, selling high-end ocean-front condos—that having a dog didn't make sense. But after moving to the mountains, it made all the sense in the world. From our first dog, Stormy, then Rocky and Nick, plus the dogs we fostered through the years, we learned how fulfilling it was to give and get doggie love. I want Dad to know that kind of love, too.

I share the good news with Adam and Jennie that Marcy will start tomorrow morning, and thank Jennie again for the reference. They're genuinely happy for everyone involved.

"You two always bring a touch of magic into my life. I've gone from being on the brink of utter doom to utter relief." They laugh and then assure me they'll always be here to help in any way they can.

Nick nuzzles both of their hands, one after the other. "Aw, he's thanking us for making his mommy happy," Jennie says, and I agree. As Nick and I walk Adam and Jennie to the door, I rub his ears and tell him what a good boy he is.

Maybe Dad is beginning to understand just how good a dog Nick is. Maybe you *can* teach an old dog new tricks—with Dad being the old dog in this case.

## 21

Marcy McKinney is large and loud, with a ready laugh and a deep accent that is redolent of the heritage of the Mountains. She's a bit opinionated and quick to take offense at suggestions. Her bright blue eyes are probing and challenging, but in a non-threatening way. She, as Carmen did, calls me Miss Rachel, even though I told her, as I told Carmen, to just call me Rachel. I can't figure out why they both think the "Miss" is necessary. But she can call me anything, as long as she stays. She is a caregiver *extraordinaire*.

I'm in my study, sipping coffee, reading a book and relaxing—something I haven't done in months. She grabbed control of the situation the first morning she stepped through the door. There's nothing tentative about her. Her boisterous personality is not in accord with Dad's low-key demeanor, but she makes him laugh and encourages him to help himself when he can, and she does it with kindness. There's actual mental and physical improvement in Dad this first week.

There's been no need to train her. It's obvious she's very adept at taking care of an incapacitated person.

The only real conflict we've had is the administration of Dad's insulin shots and medications. She considers that part of her job, but I don't want anyone besides David or me to touch those things.

A number of medication mistakes were made when Dad first moved into the assisted living facility in Florida, with some alarming side effects. Crestview always got it right, and I intend to keep it that way.

She'd argued her point. "I gave my grandmaw her pills and diabetes shots for years. You ain't never gonna be able to leave him for long if you don't trust somebody else to take care of him all the way around, includin' givin' him his medicine."

"I never need to be away from him so long that it's an issue," I'd countered. "And besides, if I'm not here, David can do it."

"What about you and your husband takin' a few days away? How are you going to do that if you can't trust nobody else? I could get some time off from the hospital and stay with him."

I had laughed out loud and set the record straight. "A few days off? Marcy, I can't take a few days off. I can't afford to go anywhere, and I can't afford to pay you to take care of him for that long."

Marcy's eyes widened as she looked around at the expensive furnishings of my home. "Miss Rachel," she had said, "I don't know about affordin' it or not, but you look plumb worn out. You could use a few days off."

Now, recalling Marcy's remark that came on the heels of Adam and Jennie's similar observation, I think, *Hell, did everyone have to comment on my haggard appearance?* And what's so bad about it? I shower every day, and I put on a little makeup and fix my hair. My clothes aren't designer clothes, but neither are they tattered or mismatched. In other words, I'm not rags and bones. I believe I'm holding it together pretty well, all things considered, and David certainly hasn't complained.

I'd responded, "I am *plumb worn out*, Marcy, but that doesn't mean I'll be able to take any time off. There are still twenty hours left in the day when you're not here. Believe me, those hours are full, and much of it relates to caring for Dad."

"I hear that," she'd said with a note of commiseration in her voice, and I was glad the argument was closed. One thing about Carmen, she didn't speak enough English to chastise me or argue with me.

Getting used to Marcy's sass is going to take some time and patience . . . but didn't just about everything these days?

I decided that staying out of her way was the best thing I could do during those four hours she's with Dad. Sometimes she comes upstairs to find me and ask me a question, but other than that, she's devoted to caring for Dad.

It's the beginning of her second week on the job, and I'm going down to ask Dad if he wants to come up on the deck for lunch today. It's such a pretty day, and I'd like to eat outside myself.

Despite wanting to stay out of Marcy's way, I find excuses to go down there once or twice each morning because I want to get a better sense of how they're getting along. This morning I find them in the bathroom. Before I can ask Dad about going outside for lunch, Marcy asks, "What's the story with Joe and that dog? He don't like that dog, huh?"

I don't like it when people talk about Dad as if he isn't there, but I'm not going to get into that with her right now. I tell her about Dad's bad experiences with dogs and ask him, "You're still getting to know Nick, aren't you Dad?"

It shocks me when Marcy *harrumphs*, looks Dad in the eyes and says, "Why, that's foolish. What's to get to know about a sweet dog like that, Mr. Joe? He ain't gonna bite you."

"Marcy, please don't talk to Dad like that." There's strong reproach in my tone. No one can speak to Dad like that, and I have to make that clear. I would rather have her walk out the door and leave me stranded than have her think she can do so.

Well, maybe not; but still, she's being rude.

"I'm sorry, I didn't mean nothin' by it, Miss Rachel." She turns back to Dad. "You ain't foolish, Mr. Joe, you just got an old worry that don't make much sense anymore. When was the last time you was bit by a dog?"

Dad is in a vulnerable state. He's having his butt wiped by a woman who has just called him foolish. His teeth are clenched and he won't look at Marcy. I'm so proud of him when he takes a deep breath and turns to face her. "Been a long time. Doesn't mean I'm likely to forget it, though." *Well said, Dad!*

Marcy nods, then finishes up with Dad without saying another word. I don't care if she's offended by either Dad or me. She has to learn there are boundaries that can't be crossed. And disrespecting my dad is something I will not tolerate.

But I've never had that much exposure to someone who was born in the more rural mountain areas and who has different ideas about what constitutes foolish and what doesn't. Survival through the generations has required mountain people like her to get past their fears. I suppose she does think it foolish that Dad would be afraid of such a docile dog. But why had she even asked the question?

"What made you ask that, Marcy? Did something happen between Dad and Nick?"

"No, I just wondered why Nick don't come in here. Just seems natural he would now and then. I figured it had to be 'cause one of 'em didn't like the other."

"I like him well enough." Dad says, and I have to clamp my jaw tight before it drops.

"He likes you, too, Dad."

"He does?"

"Sure. Why do you think he stays right beside you during therapy?"

"Huh."

"And he always lies next to your chair when we're out on the deck. Speaking of which, would you like to go up on the deck for a while, get some fresh air? It's so nice today. There's just a hint of fall in the air." Even though it's only August, there has been a refreshing change that promises autumn is coming.

Autumn is Dad's favorite season, and I can see he's taken with the idea. "Marcy, would you mind taking Dad up on the deck? I'll make us some sandwiches. It's a bit early for lunch, but that way you'll get to eat before you have to go to the hospital."

"That sounds good, Miss Rachel. How's that sound to you, Mr. Joe?" Marcy is being solicitous now.

"Good," Dad grunts. I think he's still upset with Marcy, but it will pass soon enough.

"What do you want on your sandwich, Dad?"

"Dog meat," he deadpans.

## 22

Adam is working with Dad in the sunroom, and I'm happy to see Nick joining in. He's walking so close to Dad's legs I fear he'll bump into them. But Nick is a graceful fellow for such a big dog, and he doesn't make a single false step.

As he did after that first day of therapy with Dad, Adam sticks around for a while after Dad's session to give Nick some relief. I've been giving Nick massages as well. Even though Adam had suggested I treat Nick with Adequan injections, the vet had different ideas. She convinced me that Rimadyl, an anti-inflammatory, was the next step. I'm relieved that Nick doesn't seem to be affected. No upset stomach, no diarrhea, and a still-hearty appetite. The change in his energy and ease of movement has been remarkable, and he's enjoying taking more strenuous hikes with David or me again.

Unless we can do it when Marcy is here, David and I rarely hike together any more. It's usually one or the other hiking with Nick. But we all need to be outdoors, to stretch our legs, to breathe in the invigorating air and the fertile earth. We need the soul-refreshing tonic that the mountain outdoors provides in abundance.

Plus, my tush is getting bigger. I don't understand it, because I seem to be in motion every waking hour of the day. David and I split the cleaning chores for the most part, and my part entails lots of squatting and swabbing, plus going up and down stairs. Shouldn't that provide plenty of calorie-burning exercise in itself? But I guess eating those Oreos on cleaning days offsets the calorie-burning effects.

Hey, I deserve to treat myself, right? When I'm the one who goes to the grocery store, I buy a package (or two) and then hide it under the sheets in the linen closet. Then I sneak a few on the days I clean.

It's silly that I hide them. David wouldn't care, but I care that he knows because, to me, they signal a weakness. I should be able to resist the temptation, but they seem to fill a hole I didn't know was there. They lift my spirits; it's as simple as that.

On an intellectual level, I know it's the sugar high that brings about the lifted spirits, but on a more primal level, those cookies feed a need. There is a sinister gratification baked into every chocolatey, creamy one of them.

I'm not going to beat myself up over it, but I *will* be a little stingier with them. Yesterday, when I was sneaking a couple, I was surprised how few were left in the package. For a fleeting moment, I'd wondered if David, or maybe Marcy, was stealing my cookies. But that had been a ridiculous thought, and when I gave it some real consideration, I realized I was dipping my hand into that pseudo-cookie jar a little more often than I had in the beginning. Okay, a lot more often.

So the hikes we take are good on many levels, and it's a pleasure to be able to take the more challenging hikes with Nick again. Though I don't know which is more responsible for it—the healing hands of Adam or the pricey Rimadyl—I do know that my dog moves with more ease.

Dad has also rallied because of the sure-handed care he receives from Marcy and the therapy from Adam and Jennie. The quality of our family life depends so much on the quality of life for Dad and Nick. Right now, their quality of life is good.

But Adam has told me that Dad is close to meeting the goals of the allowed therapy threshold and that he will have to report that, thus ending the Medicare-paid physical therapy.

We had agreed, on that first day, that I would pay Adam thirty dollars for each visit. It was less than half of the Medicare fee he would collect for a session, but enough to offset the cost of travel. I had been anticipating paying at least fifty or even sixty dollars, but Adam wouldn't take a penny more than the thirty. As a result, the therapy fund has not diminished as quickly as I anticipated, and I'm contemplating asking Adam to continue private therapy after the Medicare benefit stops.

However, we'll need to fill our big propane tank in the next couple of months. It fuels our house if the power goes off, and feeds into our indoor fireplaces, which we use to offset the high cost of electricity. We did that even when the good times were rolling.

That's always more than a thousand dollars, and I calculate the number of therapy sessions I could get for that. I've had to do a lot of such calculations over the past six months.

David wasn't able to sell any more of our land holdings over the summer, which is normally the peak season. Plus, although there are signs that new construction in the mountains is emerging, David hasn't found any opportunities to build and earn income. Besides, his crew is scattered and scrounging for construction jobs around the state and across state lines, so they wouldn't be immediately available even if David did get a contracting job.

Having to lay off his crew had cut David to his core. We've had a lot of quiet nights at home to talk about our feelings, but we seem to skirt around the embarrassment and insecurities that have crept into our lives because of our diminished financial capacity, as he calls it.

We wake up each day facing the same financial challenges, despite his hard work in trying to somehow turn things around, and we have to adjust our perspectives and come to a place of acceptance if we hope to weather this downturn and come out whole. And we would come out of it whole, I was certain of that. It was the *when* that dragged on us.

Quite a few who had second homes here in the mountains walked away from them, letting the banks foreclose. Some whom we thought were really well off were affected, and we've come to realize our scaled-back lifestyle isn't as unique as we'd originally believed.

We haven't had time to worry about others because we're scrambling to keep the roof over our heads. Those who walked away from their second homes had another home to live in, usually in Florida, but this is our only home and we will do all we can to keep it.

We do love our home. It's situated on five acres in one of the most beautiful areas of Asheville. David and I worked together designing our house. We were there for the "first cut" when the backhoe displaced earth in preparation for pouring the foundation. We watched as the three-story house was framed and closed in. We were fascinated as our plans took definitive shape when the soaring two-story glass windows were installed in the front of the house. Like excited children, we held hands and marveled at the expanse of them, and at the unobstructed view of rising and sloping mountain ranges beyond those windows.

Just as we had been in total agreement about the design of our home, we were in complete accord with the decorating. Together we picked out the natural Brazilian cherry hardwood flooring and the large area rugs that complemented it. We had fun shopping for the granite kitchen and bathroom countertops and top-of-the-line stainless steel appliances. We readily agreed on the shade of taupe wall paint and style of window treatments.

The master bedroom and bathroom are a combined five-hundred square feet of comfort and convenience. The bedroom is large enough for a king bed, a divan and a sitting area for reading, with two comfy chairs and a small table.

The master bathroom is my favorite room in the house, with its private water closet, an oversized double shower, a Jacuzzi tub and a sauna.

We had it to spend then. Shortly after we married, we began escaping the heat of Miami summers and spending time in the cool mountains of North Carolina. With our considerable combined savings, we began buying property in and around Asheville. At first it was just for investment purposes, but the more time we spent in these mountains, the more certain we were we wanted to live here full time. We took our time in finding the perfect land for the home we envisioned building. After moving up here, we acquired our North Carolina real estate sales licenses, then our broker licenses, and David procured a general contractor's license, which allowed him to go into business for himself.

We rode the real estate crest, with me selling and David building, and made a good deal of money. Home prices and land values were soaring, and we bought land in all areas of Western North Carolina, believing real estate values would continue to rise. We also used our earnings—combined with a conventional mortgage—to build our home. How often we've wished we had pulled back on investment property and instead built a mortgage-free home. With the sharp drop in home values, we're underwater, since the value of our home is now less than the original mortgage principal. Because we didn't pull back, we're living in a luxurious home that owns us, instead of the other way around.

I didn't grow up with such luxury, not by a long stretch, and I have to pinch myself at times to stay awake to the reality that this is our home. Lovingly conceived and tenderly nurtured throughout its development, it retains the imprint and energy of the love that created it. Some might say it filled a hole that opened when we found out we couldn't have children. Metaphorically, they might be right, because we're determined our house will never be, ahem, *adopted* by anyone else.

But right now, that large, luxurious shower needs to be cleaned, and I'm not feeling so kindly toward it.

I head to the linen closet for the chocolate fuel I'll need to tackle the job.

# 23

The weather has changed, and so has the atmosphere in our home. Nick and Dad are often in the same room, and I'm more comfortable going upstairs to work in my study when Nick is with Dad.

Since the therapy sessions ended, there has been a void without Adam and Jennie, but Dad and Nick seemed to adjust by keeping each other company—from a comfortable distance. Their joint-therapy sessions created a bond, and in the absence of their therapists, they've settled into a companionship that doesn't include words or contact, just togetherness. Dad has yet to actually touch Nick, and until that happens, they'll never become close. But for now, it's enough.

Despite my optimism that we would be able to continue Dad's therapy, we made the hard decision not to do so when the Medicare benefit ran out. The positive effects from therapy are diminishing now and it's getting harder for me to accommodate his stiffening limbs and the heaviness of his weight collapsing upon itself.

Every day is different. Some days Dad can rally and offer assistance, but most days he wavers. I just take whatever comes.

There's still no money coming in, and we continue to use our savings for the mortgage payment, health insurance, auto insurance, and food and utilities. With autumn closing in, we're coming face to face with a different kind of distress about what the future holds.

We've cut back everywhere we can, including scaling back cable TV to the most basic plan, which thankfully still includes Dad's favorite channels. But we still need the two phone lines and the Internet, the cost of which seems to go up with every other bill.

The home equity line we opened two years before the real estate market crash is still available, and although we've long expected the bank to close it, considering the diminished value of our home, it is still available if worse comes to worst. But we have no income to service debt, and we'd end up pulling down more equity to make the payments, which would lead to a vicious cycle.

The consequence of all this angst and uncertainty has rendered my dear husband, for the first time since I met him, depressed. I occasionally see him staring out over mountains, deep in thought, his shoulders slumped. He doesn't laugh as often as he used to, and he's much more tired than I've ever seen him. Normally the promise of autumn energizes him, but this year it seems to drain him. Sometimes he takes long naps in the middle of the day, which he never used to do, and I'm beginning to think there might be something physically wrong with him.

I'm fighting my own dampened spirits and growing insecurity. I find it hard going at times, and so must David. We need to be together in this fight against our despondency. *Strength to strength* has always been our personal motto, and we're losing sight of it.

Dad's lethargy isn't entirely due to his lack of therapy. Subconsciously, he's picking up the anxious and melancholy vibes around here. He's not trying as hard at anything, from eating by himself to responding to attempted conversation from any of us, including Marcy. On top of that, he's sleeping more than ever.

Even Nick seems sad. His eyes are not as bright, and he no longer does his happy dance at the prospect of a hike or a doggie treat. He is a willing companion on hikes, albeit a bit slower, and his appetite hasn't diminished, but the joy of those simple activities is no longer evident. His light has dimmed.

We have to get ahold of ourselves.

I come upstairs after watching *Bonanza* with Dad and getting him settled into bed for the night. Thank goodness basic cable still includes Nickelodeon. Dad has seen every episode of *Bonanza* at least a hundred times, but he never gets tired of that show. Watching Ben Cartwright and sons together gives us an opportunity to enjoy the quiet comfort of being in each other's company, without having to think too hard about the plot.

I've started moving a dinette chair next to his bed and holding his hand while we watch TV. It's contact that I believe every human needs, and Dad more than most. I have my husband to cuddle with each night, giving me that sweet interaction that fosters comfort and security. I can love up on Nick any time, and get a dose of warm affection. Dad has little physical contact and touch outside of us and Marcy, and though he never says anything, I know he must miss it.

Debra has come to see him twice in the last three weeks, and Anna came to see him yesterday and even took him to Burger King in the van.

In an attempt to cheer him up, I took him to Crestview on Monday of last week, and he was greeted with such warmth and friendship that he didn't want to leave.

He reveled in the attention from his friends and the staff. I hadn't seen him laugh so much in months. He even smiled at Dora and told her she looked pretty.

Celia hugged me and said, "I was beginning to think you forgot me," and never left my side. Sissy told me how much she missed Dad and promised to visit again soon. Three days later she did, and we shared a glass of wine with Dad out on the deck. When he'd napped off in the warm sun, she asked me whether I would consider moving him back to Crestview if "things got good again."

I hadn't considered it until she asked, and surprised myself with my first thought being that David and I could reclaim our previous life. With Marcy in our home six mornings a week and Dad's needs being on standby twenty-four hours a day, we had lost the luxury of time and privacy we always coveted. We'd adjusted, as people do, but we hadn't embraced our new lifestyle. Not by a long shot.

So when Sissy added that Dad seemed to miss his friends at Crestview, I made up my mind. If—and it was a big if—we could ever afford to move Dad back into Crestview, we would. We would all be better off. The prospect of alleviating his loneliness was a big factor in reaching that decision, but the allure of not being his primary caregiver cemented it.

If Dad returns to Crestview, his friends will drop by his room throughout the day to keep him company. The CNAs will fuss over him and take extra time and care with grooming. When they cut his nails, shave him and comb his soft, silver hair, they will make it a pleasant interaction. Marcy and I don't do that. We don't rush, but we allot a certain amount of time for grooming and approach it as a chore to be checked off the list.

But something has grown between Dad and me that compensates for my lack of things like lavish grooming. When he lived at Crestview, we were not just father and daughter, but also amiable companions. Because I wasn't involved with his intimate personal care, we maintained a cushioned barrier that allowed our friendship to flourish.

We crashed through that barrier on the first day Dad moved in. Preparing him for bed that first night was awkward for all of us. I recall my and David's stunned realization of what was in store for us. We had burst into laughter, which was the sanest way to come to terms with it.

Now we've seen every private part of Dad, and while it was unsettling at first, it actually morphed into something I take pride in—caring for every need of my surviving parent. On my part, it's the desire I have to stay tethered to my childhood. I had a typical, mostly happy childhood, mainly because I always felt loved and protected by parents who were solid and present. His presence still comforts me, and I would surely miss that.

But the thought of not hopping out of bed early every morning and hitting the ground running appeals to me. The prospect of visiting him at Crestview, and then leaving him in their capable care without having to be intimately involved, entices me.

When Sissy left, I started reshaping our lives in my mind. If our financial situation improved, Dad would move back to Crestview, and we could go back to our comfortable and unencumbered life. I pictured the guest apartment as it had been before Dad moved in.

Funny thing . . . it didn't look as warm and attractive as it does with Dad living there.

# 24

I've just kissed Dad goodnight and am at peace when I walk into the living room where David and Nick lie side by side on the sofa, watching TV. I don't know where the contentment came from, but I want to share it with my husband, spread it around so that David can be uplifted as well. But how to do that?

"Ready to put Joe to bed?" he asks, starting to rise. I put a hand on his shoulder to keep him where he is. "All done."

"Rachel," he starts to admonish me for doing it myself, but I stop him when I bend down and give him a kiss. I then give Nick a vigorous rub and shower his sweet head with kisses. David is smiling when I look over at him, and he reaches up with his arm, inviting me to join him and Nick on the buttery-soft leather sofa.

I share my thoughts about moving Dad back to Crestview, stating my belief that things will get better for us and we may not have to be his caregivers to the end of his life. Before David can say anything, I let out a little moan and say, "But I would miss him."

"You know, babe, if we're ever in that position—*when* we're in that position—we'll decide together, all three of us, what's best. Right now, it's not worth thinking about because I don't see things turning around anytime soon. Joe may very well live out his days here."

He's right. It could be months or even years before something changed for us financially. "Do you resent it, David? At all? Be honest."

"This has been tough, Rachel. Every once in a while I've resented the time and energy you use taking care of him. But I'm thinking of you, not me, when I start to resent it. I just wish it hadn't come down to this.

"But there's still a lot to be grateful for." David pulls me closer, surprising me with his positivity.

"I agree, honey. What are you grateful for right now? Right this minute?" Maybe this is the time to start talking about things we've been avoiding.

"Right this minute?" He winks at me. "Okay. Well, the fact that we're keeping this roof over our heads and we're able to take care of Joe and Nick and each other, to start."

He pauses and then says, "Look, I'm trying to stay positive, but I guess you've noticed I've been down, huh?"

"Sure, I've noticed, but I don't know how to help you with what you're feeling because you don't talk about it."

"You've got enough to deal with, without worrying about me."

"But that's the thing, David. I do worry about you. If you'd talk to me about why you're feeling this way, you'd feel better and I could understand, and maybe help you."

He stays quiet for a few moments, and I know he's thinking about how to tell me what he's feeling. Although he's good at telling me how he feels about me, he's bad about sharing his feelings about himself. Yeah, I know, it's a man thing, but he's my man and I want him to share his vulnerability with me.

"For the first time in my life, I feel like a failure," he admits.

*Whoa.* Where do I go with this?

Do I reiterate the obvious, that while the real estate market was booming, it was being fueled by greed and corruption, and we made lots of money, but then when it crashed, we lost most of that money? Do I remind him we were luckier than many in being able to hold on to our home?

But he knows all of this. He knows he couldn't have seen it coming, but when he did recognize the slowdown and the shifting markets, he made some smart moves and honorably did all he could to fulfill his obligations. He took on wind-down projects, managed property, and did appraisals for bank foreclosures, keeping us solvent in those first two years after the collapse.

Yes, he knows all of this, so why does he think he's a failure? I ask him.

"I should have made better investments. I shouldn't have bought so much land. I could have put more away. I just didn't plan well enough." He empties his wine glass with one large gulp.

"Oh, bullshit! What's with the 'I'? *We* made those decisions together, and based on everything we knew from our education and experience, there was no reason not to make those decisions. We couldn't know about the evil forces behind the scenes that were scheming and getting richer even though they knew it would crash the economy. If that's what you're basing your feeling of being a failure on, you are just going to have to get real and get over it, because millions and millions of people were just as affected as we were, and through no fault of their own."

Well, wasn't that a sweet way for me to show sympathy and understanding? He may clam up forever now.

Thankfully, he doesn't.

"Okay, okay, I get it. And I hear what you're saying. But I missed some opportunities, and made some risky land investments. If I hadn't, we'd be out of this by now. Nothing I do is bettering our situation, and that's making me feel like a failure more than anything."

"So a part of it is you think you have no control over your life—our life—right?"

He pulls away from me to pour more wine. Nick grumbles at being jostled, but settles back down when David does.

"That's basically it. I've always been able to make things work, to control the outcomes. I can't do that anymore, and I don't know how to deal with the loss of that control." He takes a deep breath. "Or the insecurity it brings up in me."

"I understand, David, I do. You've worked since you were in high school and all through college. You set goals and you succeeded. You gave us a great lifestyle and helped others by paying a good wage and giving them steady work. You've either built or sold people their dream homes. Now you're unanchored, and it has to be a terrible feeling for you to live with."

"That's exactly it. It is a terrible feeling, but I'll be all right." David doesn't look at me as he says this.

"I know you'll be all right, but you're not all right now. But we will be. Even though the old life is gone, we've got this still-wonderful life. We're healthy and have a beautiful marriage. That's what we have to focus on."

"You're right." He reaches for the wine bottle again, and I'm rather startled to see he's finished the last glass so quickly.

"David, we just have to start being more grateful. We talk about all that we're grateful for, but then we grouse about all we've lost and life's imperfections. We need to be fulfilled again, despite the fact that we have less."

"God, you're right. I do appreciate that you're fulfilled in a way I'm not. I see the positive effect this has on you."

"You do? How do you mean?"

"Well, to start, you've always been confident and capable, but you stumbled for a while after our financial crash, and again when Joe moved in."

I tense up. David pulls me closer. "That's not a criticism. You know it's not. It's just the way it was. But you've shouldered the burden of our financial problems and your dad, and you've only gotten stronger. Seeing you rise to each challenge makes me stronger."

"It does?"

"Sure. Yeah, I get down, but it would be a lot worse if I didn't see you rallying like you do. It makes me want to rally, too. I spend a lot of time making phone calls, swallowing my pride, trying to rustle up business or sell something because I think, if Rachel isn't giving up, then neither am I."

I wonder if he is giving me too much credit. There are still moments when I'm overcome with despair, although they come less often and pass more quickly.

"You know, honey, maybe knowing Dad doesn't have that much time left makes me more appreciative of my life—our life. I mean, I hope he has many years left, but still, what's happening to him can't be cured. We still have the health and ability to make our lives better. He doesn't have that, and I've come to realize the value of those things. And time. Especially time. We can make the most of it, or we can squander it. We've both always made the most of life, so why shouldn't we do the same now?"

He nods. "I've let time become my enemy. These long days with nothing to do make me think of it that way. But I can change that by filling my time with more productive things."

"Like what?" I reach up and brush his hair from his forehead, and our eyes meet and hold.

"For one, doing more to help you with Joe." I start to protest, but he shakes his head to let me know he has more to say. "Yes, I can be doing more to help you. I've been selfish because you just handle it all, and I've let you."

"You've been a tremendous help, David. I won't let you think otherwise."

"Thanks, but I can still do more. Second, I can do more with Nick. We're all he's got, and he's getting older, too. I know you spend as much time with him as you can, but I also know you believe it isn't enough."

"I think I've said that a time or two." *Or a hundred.*

"Yes, and I always think you're wrong. You give him a lot of attention, considering, but if you don't think so, then I need to do something about it. Instead of sitting in my office when things aren't going well, obsessing about it, I can get up and go outside and take him for walks. It would be good for me, too."

I'm happy David is realizing this. I've often thought if he would just get out of the house and do something physical outside—other than tending the lawn—he'd feel better. He was invited to play golf with friends at private clubs a few times over the summer, but since he couldn't afford to reciprocate, he stopped accepting invitations. God, how dismal for him.

When we first moved here, we spent much of our free time outdoors. We'd hiked our land with Rocky and Nick daily, whatever the weather. We'd made donations to a land conservancy, which allowed us to attend its special outdoor events and take amazing hikes to places not open to the public. David had played golf at least once a week. We'd picnicked at state parks where dogs were allowed. We got out and enjoyed nature.

Yet there were too many days this summer when we made excuses not to hike—days we'll never get back. This summer passed so quickly, and we didn't take advantage of the long, sunny days to give ourselves and our dog much-needed exercise on our land, or anywhere else.

"It would be good for you to get outside more. I need to get out, too. Not just for hikes, but I need to see my girlfriends. I miss them." I've avoided telling him about the number of times I've turned down invitations to lunch. Not enough time, not enough money. But a group lunch with several friends once a month would be wonderful. In fact, Jessica had called just today about several of them taking me to lunch for my birthday next week. I'd hedged and said I'd get back to her. I'll call her tomorrow and accept. But if I'm going to put my plans for a richer social life into action, I'll have to take David up on his offer to get more involved. He'll have to do some of the things I've been doing.

"You could watch *Judge Judy* with Dad now and then. You could get him out of this house and take him for a burger. Bring him up on the deck and just have some man-to-man time with him. And that's a great opportunity to bring him and Nick together. I swear, if Dad and Nick would spend more time together, I wouldn't stress so much about their being neglected and lonely."

"They tolerate each other pretty well these days."

"There's a big difference between tolerance and friendship. They need each other, but they don't realize it yet."

David nods in agreement.

"But you need to spend even more time with Dad than just that. When he doesn't want to come up here, you can go down and watch TV with him, and not just *Judge Judy*. He's good company, even when he doesn't say much. I should know; I've spent hundreds of hours with him in that cozy apartment. And take Nick along when you do."

"Right. And if I spend time with Joe doing those things, you would have more time to yourself and time to do things with friends?"

"Well, yes!"

We laugh, and then hold each other more tightly, letting our emotional healing have its head. I actually *feel* the oppressive air around my husband dissipate; and as a result, I feel lighter, too.

Nick moved to the other sofa earlier and has been napping, but he opens his eyes, raises his head, and looks directly at us. Is it my imagination, or do his eyes seem brighter?

But I know my big boy well enough to know it's not my imagination.

# 25

The very air we breathe has changed. No doubt it's augured by the invigorating autumn breeze that sweeps through our home now that we keep the windows open, but the magic in it is that it continually refreshes our recently-lightened souls. Our sense of well-being is restored, and we drink it in until we are intoxicated with the gratitude of living.

On this fine day in late September, right after Marcy leaves, I head down to Dad's apartment to bring him up to the deck for lunch. The air is crisp, the sun is shining, and the leaves are vibrant with their oncoming change of color. I want to spend as much time as possible outdoors with him before winter comes.

His eyes are squeezed shut and his hands are clenched. He's in pain. "What's wrong, Dad?" He shakes his head from side to side but doesn't answer.

I look closer and see tears seeping out from beneath his eyelids. "You have soap in your eyes, don't you?"

He nods, and I hurry into the bathroom and run warm water over a washcloth until it's sopping wet and grab a towel to catch the drip. It is all so natural now just to do what needs doing, without any hesitancy or alarm.

I peel back one eyelid and squeeze plenty of water from the washcloth into his eye, then dab it with the towel. I do the other eye, then repeat the process until he opens his eyes, blinks a few times, and lets out a relieved, satisfied sigh.

His eyes are still red, so I put in some hydrating eye drops and catch them with the towel as they spill out from the corners of his eyes. I'm put out to think Marcy had gotten soap in his eyes and hadn't even noticed his discomfort. In her defense, Dad rarely complains. *But still.*

It makes me wonder what would have happened if he had been at Crestview and had soap in his eyes. Would someone have noticed? Would they have done something about it? They took good care of him, but they also took care of dozens of other patients, and this was something that could have easily been misconstrued as just sleeping.

These are the most gratifying times—the times I know I'm taking care of him as well as possible, and maybe even better than the workers at Crestview. Comfort is such a simple premise, but it is a basic human need, and in Dad's case, the absence of comfort exacerbates his anxiousness. I have tuned into Dad, and I know which dials to turn when something needs tweaking. I have become more intuitive and am trusting that intuition more and more.

"Are you okay now, Dad?"

He blinks several times and says, "Thanks, Sugar. That feels a lot better."

"Good. Let's go up on the deck now and have some lunch with David."

"What are we having?"

"Let's go find out."

In the kitchen we find David making grilled cheese sandwiches. Nick stands close by, on high alert, no doubt hoping that David will notice him and slip him some cheese, or that something will hit the floor and it will be *his.* Either way, Nick believes his vigilance will pay off.

Though Dad and Nick are now comfortable being in the same room, they still haven't formed any kind of bond. They're still in a state of détente.

David has already set the table on the deck. Nice. He's plating the sandwiches, so I grab a bag of chips and the pitcher of iced tea and head out the door. I leave Dad sitting in the kitchen, and Nick isn't following me because there is still a human with a plate of food, and that requires all his attention.

David's phone rings, and he doesn't bother to put the plate of sandwiches down before reaching into his pocket. I'm coming back through the door just in time to hear his phone ring and witness the commotion that follows.

With his phone in one hand and the plate in the other, David is distracted, and when he makes a slight turn, he knocks into Nick and pitches forward. The plate bobbles, and there is no way it isn't going to hit the floor.

When it does, it makes a loud clatter, but because it's melamine, it doesn't break. I hear Dad yell, "Hey, hey, he's eating our lunch!" while at the same time I hear David exclaim, "Sorry, I'll have to call you back!"

Nick is indeed wolfing down our lunch. I start to yell at him to stop, but I know it's useless. He's involved, *really* involved, in making the five grilled cheese sandwiches disappear as quickly as possible, knowing that if he hesitates, one or two sandwiches might get snatched away. You simply cannot stop a Labrador from vacuuming up food once that switch is turned on.

David and I look at each other and start to laugh. When Dad joins in, our laughter escalates until we are all doubled over. Nick is now scouring for crumbs, oblivious to our hysterics.

"I've never seen anything like that," Dad says, still laughing. "That dog cleaned the floor in ten seconds flat!"

We all burst into laughter again, and now Nick does look up. He looks from David to me, and then he looks at Dad. And I swear, I swear, he's laughing with us. I know it's so when Dad says, "Look at him! Look at him! He's laughing too, that rascal!"

David starts over in making sandwiches, and to fend off Dad's hunger I give him the bag of the chips I've retrieved from outside. Nick is lying contentedly on his bed in the kitchen, only a few feet from Dad.

The wheelchair is turned at an angle so Dad can watch Nick from the corner of his eye. He munches the potato chips, seemingly happy to be in the midst of the activity. I'm responding to a couple of emails on my iPhone, so it is by sheer happenstance that I glance up to see Dad toss a potato chip toward Nick. I start to ask him not to do that, to tell him that Nick has had plenty to eat already, but I'm curious to see how this will play out. Could food be the glue that ultimately bonds them?

David's back is to us, but I don't want to say or do anything that might alter what happens next, so I keep quiet—although I wish he could see this.

Nick's head comes up and his eyes zero in on the potato chip. I'm sure it's only because he is full beyond full that he doesn't gobble it down immediately, but I also think he's confused. He looks up at Dad, and sure enough, I can see the question in his eyes.

Dad chuckles low and whispers to Nick, "Go ahead."

Nick doesn't have to be told twice. When the chip is gone, he looks at Dad again. I know Dad will shift his eyes to me to see if I'm watching, so I make a point of seeming involved with my phone. Because Dad moves slowly in all things, I know it will take him a moment to fish out another chip for Nick.

This time, when a chip lands right at his nose, Nick doesn't hesitate. In fact, the chip disappears so quickly that I could have missed it if I'd looked away for even a second. Now I know Nick's eyes will light on me, so again, I study the screen of my phone. My hair hides my face from them at this angle, so they can't see that my eyes are upturned and that I'm watching this whole unbelievable scenario.

It's hard to describe the jolt of incredulity that shoots through me when I realize that these two are conspiring against David and me. Dad seems to be indicating to Nick to keep a lookout, even as he turns his head slightly to look at me out of the corner of his eye. Believing that I'm not paying attention, the two of them eye each other. I can't see Dad's expression, because his face is turned toward Nick, but I can see Nick's expression, and I see happiness, which I choose to believe has more to do with having a new friend and a new source of food, than with the food itself.

David plates the last sandwich and holds it out to me. "You take these, please. I don't trust anyone else in this room." He turns and points the spatula, first at Dad, then at Nick. "I've never seen so much food flying around this kitchen," he admonishes them, and then he bursts into laughter again.

*Caught!*

Seems while I was paying so much attention to my phone and the food action, I had missed the fact that David was also aware of what was happening.

I'm laughing now, too. Nick has the good grace to look chagrined, but Dad loves that he's gotten away with something. A sly smile curls his lips, and I see a gleam in his eye that has been missing for a long while.

---

Nick lies by Dad's chair the entire time we are eating outside. He often lies by Dad's chair when we're out here, and I wonder if it's because he knows Dad is the one most likely to drop food, or if the real bonding process has begun.

All of us are in high spirits, and it's rewarding to realize just how much the maudlin mood that had hovered throughout our home has lifted. When you live together in such close proximity, despite the size of the house, there is no way to avoid the effects of the other occupants' moods.

Communication isn't confined to speech, especially in our household. We are attuned to the others' thoughts, feelings and moods without having to discuss them.

David and I agree that Nick reads our thoughts and moods and reacts accordingly. Everyone knows that dogs watch their people for cues, but in our estimation, Nick's attention and intuition go beyond that.

Yesterday, when he approached a wounded bird with the intention of finishing it off, he sensed my strong displeasure without my having said a word. He looked at me and backed away.

So it only makes sense that when David and I were down in the dumps, Nick naturally absorbed those vibes and responded in kind.

Why should Dad be any different?

I think again about the glee Dad had felt in believing he'd gotten away with feeding Nick. Dad has always been a prankster, just one more thing that was a subset of his sense of humor, but I had seen little evidence of it since he had come to live with us.

But David and I have cleared the cobwebs that had been blocking the light around us. Nick has established a buddy-bond with the other person in the house and is much more relaxed. Dad's sense of humor and tendency toward mischief has been revived.

Contentment flows over me, and I'm feeling more peaceful than I've felt in, well, years. I only hope it will last.

# 26

It has been raining for a week, and we've all tried not to let the gray skies and relentless rain dampen our recently-brightened spirits.

Since Nick can roam freely now, we keep Dad upstairs with us most of the time. How different the atmosphere is when we're all together. We're complete.

Dad is happy to sit on the end of the sofa that turns into a lounger with the pull of a lever and watch his favorite TV shows. I normally keep the radio on the intercom on the classical music station, but I've turned it off now that the TV is going all day long. At first, I was annoyed by the constant talk on the television, but I've learned to block it out as I go about my chores.

In deference to the chill the rain brought, we've turned on the gas log fireplace in the living room. Nick lies on the rug in front of it, behind the sofa. Dad's aware Nick is there, just a few feet away, but he's largely ignoring him.

Dad is stuffing little cheese crackers into his mouth while a game show drones on. I know he shouldn't have so many carbs, but he loves to snack, and I can't keep trying to tempt him with carrot sticks and hummus.

"Rabbit food," he'd mumbled the first time I brought it to him. Then his eyes had lit up a bit as he thought of a joke, one he'd told countless times before.

"Carrots are good for your eyes, you know," he would start. "You've never seen a rabbit wearing glasses, have you?"

And the thing is, I always find his same old, silly jokes funny. So does he. Dad simply enjoys a good joke, whether it's his own or someone else's. I cherish his humorous nature because I know that just the opposite could be true.

Alzheimer's patients can be verbally abusive and also physically abusive if still strong. While this is often due to an aggravation or discomfort they can't articulate, something as basic as organic changes in the brain, like damage to nerve cells, can bring it on as well.

It had chilled me to hear, in the meeting my women's group had with the caregivers, that they'd experienced behaviors such as cursing, hitting, grabbing, kicking, pushing, throwing things, scratching, screaming, biting, and making strange noises.

One woman had cried because her husband, after seeing the bruises and scratches on her after an episode with her father, had insisted they "tie him down" so he couldn't hurt her again. That had made her father even angrier, and he became impossible to take care of.

Fortunately, she was one we had connected with an appropriate social worker who found a bed for him at a nursing home in the next county. While wracked with guilt at first, the vast improvement in her life and that of her family eventually outweighed the guilt. Hers was one of the thank-you letters we'd received. It was a long letter, rich in detail and emotion, and I knew as I'd read it that she was telling her story and by doing so, pardoning herself.

Caregivers have to learn to pardon themselves or they can never be truly effective. Even I had needed to learn to do that. No one is a perfect caregiver. Mistakes are made. Indecision and doubts haunt us. Negative consequences from our actions, no matter how well intended, weigh upon us.

If we let each perceived failure penetrate our psyche, we became useless, because we doubt everything we do, and therefore fail to act. We miss important signals as we obsess about unnecessary details.

In those first few days Dad lived with us, I hovered too much, studied his reactions too intensely, asked too many unnecessary questions, and generally fussed over him, making him more anxious. But I knew that a change of residence could bring about aggressive behavior, so I was hyper-vigilant.

After I started relaxing, so did Dad. Mercifully, he still knew who we were and that he was in our house, and that was, no doubt, a factor in his docility. If and when the time comes that his recognition of us and his surroundings changes, I'll have some serious adjustments to make.

It had been a reverse action that could have had bad consequences for all of us from the very beginning. Normally, people transition their Alzheimer's parent out of the home and into a facility. We'd done just the opposite.

The social worker I'd met with to discuss the changes, and what I could expect to experience, had covered a lot of ground and answered many of my questions. Other than the one time when I had found Dad on the floor calling for Mother, he hadn't experienced too much disorientation, which was something she had warned me about.

There are still many times I can't get Dad to articulate what's bothering him, and I have to go through a checklist to see if I can pinpoint it. Not everything is as simple as noticing he has soap in his eyes.

But at times like these, when peace permeates, I experience a sense of well-being that is worth every adjustment I've had to make.

"Can I get you anything, Dad?" I call from the kitchen.

"A beer."

"Too early in the day. Plus, it will make you have to go to the bathroom all afternoon."

I hear him grumble, but I'm not going to put myself, or him, through the effects of a beer so early in the afternoon.

I wait to see if he says anything else, but when he doesn't, I go back to peeling potatoes.

"Hey, Dad, remember what you told me about how I peeled potatoes?"

There's no response, so I walk into the living room, holding a peeled potato. He won't look at me. Is he being petulant over a beer? How aggravating. I want to just turn around and go back into the kitchen, but I don't want his mood to descend any further.

So I cajole him. "You used to say I peeled them so much, they looked like marbles when I got through with them. Remember that?"

Still no response.

Standing directly in front of him, I show him the potato. "Now look at this one. If you hadn't shown me how to peel a potato, we'd be eating marbles for dinner."

There's a long pause before he responds. "I peeled enough of them in the Army."

"And you learned to peel them perfectly. Thanks for passing that on to me."

Mollified, he starts digging into the box of crackers again.

"You never did learn to cook," he says with more humor in his voice, which is muffled because of the crackers in his mouth. *Never did learn to cook.* What does he think I've been doing these last few months when I'm stirring pots on the stove or taking things out of the oven? Gee, thanks so much, Dad. But that's not worth getting into. This is about getting Dad reset.

"I always hated cooking. Still do. But at least I've learned a few things, thanks to you."

"She didn't like to cook either." Of course, he's talking about Mother.

"No, but she still put three meals a day on the table, bless her heart."

"Fried chicken."

"It was the best thing she cooked."

"Can you fry chicken like that?"

"Not a chance—but I can try. Do you remember anything about how she cooked it, so you could help me?"

Dad casts his eyes up and to the right, which tells me he's trying to recall something about the chicken. "She used corn meal in with the flour."

What clear recall he has about that. "You think that was her secret?"

"Yeah."

"Okay, I'll try to fix Evelyn's fried chicken tomorrow night for dinner."

"What are we having tonight?"

"Hamburger steak and mashed potatoes and broccoli. How does that sound?"

"Good. Sounds good."

I'm relieved that Dad is engaged in the conversation now. Most often when we converse, there are pauses between questions and responses, but he is fairly quick and sure in this moment.

Nick watches our exchange with interest. Or is it the potato in my hand that has his attention?

"I think Nick wants this potato."

"Give it to him."

"Dad, I'm not going to give Nick a raw potato. Or any potato. Dogs don't eat potatoes."

"Where is he?"

Dad knows where Nick is, but I answer anyway. "Lying behind you, by the fireplace."

He cranes his neck to look behind him, not quite succeeding, and says, "Nick, come here."

Nick gets up and comes to stand beside Dad.

Dad digs into the box and asks Nick, "You want a cracker?"

Nick knows the names of lots of foods. His mouth lolls open, his eyes light up and his tail starts wagging, so that no one could mistake his response as anything but a big, happy *Yes!*

Dad tosses it onto the floor, and it's scarfed up in a millisecond. I want to ask Dad not to throw crackers or anything else onto the floor, but what the hell does it matter? I have to mop the wood floors sometime this week anyway.

"Well, he sure seemed happy to get that cracker, Dad."

"He did, didn't he?" Nick is watching Dad's hand, hyper-aware that the hand is the real giver of treats.

Dad digs another cracker out of the box and says to Nick, "Last one. You're going to ruin your dinner." He chuckles and then he tosses the cracker.

I chuckle along with him, appreciating his humor.

"He's a good eater, like me."

"He sure is, Dad. You two are a lot alike in your love of food."

Dad looks over at Nick, who is still vigilant.

"I told you, that was the last one." Dad wags a shaky finger at Nick.

Nick does the equivalent of a doggie shrug and returns to his spot in front of the fireplace.

"He understood me!" Dad exclaims in wonder.

"Of course he did. He's smart, and he wants to please you."

Dad smiles as he puts his head back and closes his eyes, ready to fall into one of his afternoon naps.

I won't swear to it, but I'm pretty sure I hear Dad mumble, "Good dog," right before he starts snoring.

# 27

David calls me from the basement intercom to ask me to come down. When I get there, he's standing in the doorway of the garage with his hands on his hips, surveying the lawn and landscaping.

"Last time you have to mow this season, huh?"

"Yeah, last time. But you know, I kind of like it. I sure did enough of it growing up. It's nice to see the immediate results of hard work."

"Unlike with building homes."

"Yeah, those results aren't immediate. I usually have to wait a year to appreciate my hard work. But this . . ." he pauses as he looked around, "this is immediate gratification."

He points to the boxwoods, and then to the garden of plants and shrubs, and asks, "What do you think?"

He's trimmed the boxwoods and weeded the garden area, and the landscaping looks perfect. I tell him so, then give him a quick smack on the lips, even though he's sweaty.

"Okay, let me put this stuff away and I'll come in and shower."

"Good, and then I'll tell you about Dad and Nick connecting over food again."

His eyes light up. "They did?"

"Yes. But I wonder if that's the only connection they'll ever have."

"It's an honest one," David says, shaking his head.

The hand-knotted Persian Tabriz carpet under the dining room table has taken a beating since Dad became a regular at our table.

Even though I put a bib around his neck and a towel on his lap when we eat, he still gets a fair amount of food on the rug. I sit right beside him to cut his food and help him with eating. He either allows my help or insists on feeding himself, using specially designed utensils. They have a unique angle with a large grip to make them easy to hold, perfect for people like Dad whose hand can't completely close around normal cutlery. They also help to align his hand to prevent food from tumbling off before reaching his mouth.

Even using these utensils, there's more of a mess to clean up when he goes it alone. When I help him, I usually manage to get most everything into his mouth, but sometimes he jerks before I get the food all the way in, and it tumbles off the utensil and down his bib. Sometimes he reaches down with his stiff and shaky fingers and tries to retrieve something. I don't stop him; I just wait until I have his attention again so I can give him the next bite.

I'm happy Nick has taken up his position under the table again, diligently vacuuming the rug with his tongue, saving me the work. When Dad drops a piece of hamburger for the lurking Lab, I keep quiet. But that doesn't mean I'm happy about my carpet being deliberately soiled. As if reading my mind, David reaches over and squeezes my hand. "It's just a rug."

*Yes, it's just a rug.* Even though it had cost ten thousand dollars when we bought it, it has no value now except to make the place we gather for dinner more inviting. That is its purpose. I nod in agreement.

Out of the blue, Dad speaks up and says, "The way to a dog's heart is through his stomach."

We all laugh and agree; but even as I laugh, my eyes tear up. Dad's just told us he is trying to win Nick's heart.

# 28

"Let me help you get Joe ready for bed," David says.

"Thanks, I'd appreciate it." My back hurts and I'm really tired. I fantasize about spending just one whole day in bed with a heating pad, knowing that my body needs it.

"Dad, hey, Dad." My mouth is close to his ear, and I speak softly so he won't startle. When he's startled awake, he's more confused.

His eyes open halfway and he murmurs, "Yeah?"

"Time to get ready for bed."

He grunts and closes his eyes. I wish there were a way to leave him here on the sofa just for tonight, but I know that isn't feasible. He needs the familiarity and safety of his own bed in his own room.

Nick has gotten up from his bed, and it looks like he wants to follow us. This is a first. Is he getting to *like* Dad's company?

"Stay here, big boy." He stands there and looks at me, as if asking if that's what I really mean.

"Stay here," I repeat, and he returns to his bed.

Dad has woken up enough for us to toilet him, get his teeth brushed, his pajamas on, and his sleeping pill and pain pill downed. After settling Dad into bed, David asks me if I'm tired.

"Not too tired," I fudge. "Got something in mind?"

"Let's take some wine out on the deck and look at the stars."

I thought he was going to say he had lovemaking in mind, which would have been welcomed, but I love this idea. The rain stopped earlier in the afternoon, and the sun came out long enough to dry things out. It's perfect for some "us time" on this clear and chilly evening.

"I'd love that."

We put on robes and I slip my feet into some warm Uggs before we carry our glasses of box wine out onto the deck. After the first couple of tart sips, I can't tell that much difference from better wine. In the beginning, however, it gave me an unpleasant jolt. David was watching me when I took that first sip of tart, fruity wine, and he'd laughed and said, "Shivered your timbers, eh?" Indeed it did.

Nick is next to the deck loungers where we've settled. We are blanketed by the inky-black sky that's ornamented with luminous stars. I pick an especially bright one and make a wish. I promise myself I'll never be too jaded or too hopeless to wish upon a star.

This is our nirvana, our divine place, out here on the deck under a sky resplendent with stars. I've missed this. We need to do it more often. It settles our souls. We sip our wine in companionable silence. I'm filled with contentment and appreciation. I take David's hand.

"Name something you're grateful for," I say, beginning our game that we haven't played in way too long.

"Your great legs," David answers.

I like that.

"Now you," he says.

"Our beautiful lawn, thanks to your efforts."

"These warm robes."

"Your kisses."

"Your laughter."

"Rug cleaner."

We laugh.

"College football."

"Uggs."

"These stars."

"This night."

"Box wine."

We laugh.

"Dad."

"Nick."

"Dad and Nick."

"Joe and Nick."

"Pending lovemaking." My final volley.

"Oh, yeah."

# 29

Now that autumn is upon us in its full splendor, I want to be outside every minute to revel in it. Apparently, so do Dad and Nick.

They've taken to sitting out on the top of the bank beside the house to watch the sunset. I got the idea when Dad and I went on a Parkway picnic. At one of the turnoffs is a partially-paved area with a picnic table and a bench from which to enjoy one of the most spectacular views in North Carolina. It was the last day in September, when the leaves were beginning to turn in earnest and the air was crisp and mildly cool. After eating lunch at the picnic table, I transferred Dad to the bench to relieve him of being in the wheelchair. "Beautiful," he sighed as he settled back, removed his hat, and lifted his face to the soft sunlight streaking through the pale-yellow clouds. I joined him and held his hand, and together we beheld the panorama in silent contentment. A welcome peacefulness took hold, and Dad nodded off. I let him sleep for twenty minutes before getting his wheelchair and loading him into the van.

"That was real restful," he said. "Can we do it again tomorrow?" Well, no, but we could do the next best thing, which was overlooking the mountains right from our home. Though not as incredible as the view on the Blue Ridge Parkway, our view is still breathtaking. An arbor covered in ivy leads to a cobble-stoned sitting area where there's a wrought-iron table and two cushioned wicker chairs. David and I have watched hundreds of sunsets there, sipping wine and remarking upon the varying beauty of seasonal sunsets.

The setting sun takes its time here in the mountains, and in autumn it regales us with its remaining tendrils of light, foisting a glint of gold on the yellow leaves, teasing the red leaves until they blush scarlet, and firing up the orange ones until they look like burnt sienna. The fading rays play hide and seek with the remaining leaves on the trees, shadowing some while kissing others, then shifting in the blink of an eye, until the colors fade amid early-evening shadows. For its finale, the sun folds back unto itself, takes a bow, and descends behind the sheltering mountains.

The days are getting shorter and chillier, so I cover Dad with a thick, soft throw. After locking his wheelchair, I hand him a gin and tonic and set a bowl of Spanish peanuts on the table within easy reach. I give Nick a doggie treat and then give both a kiss before going inside.

Initially I would watch them from the living room windows to make sure the arrangements were safe. Even if, by some absurdly random accident, Dad were to unlock the wheels, there's no slope to facilitate a roll, and there's an eight-inch oak bumper separating the top of the bank from the steep hillside, so there is no way he can go over. Assured of his safety, I'm not as vigilant, but I still watch him and Nick now and then because it's such a peaceful tableau to observe.

Nick most often stands or sits close to Dad, remarkably free from distraction as he looks out over the mountains. I wonder what Nick sees, since he can't see the same colors as Dad, nor intuit the shifts of shape and shades. His gaze is steady, and I wonder if he understands that another day of his life is coming to an end, foretold by the shadows that usher in the dusk. Before sitting there with Dad, he never paid attention to the oncoming night. Now, he watches the shadows moonwalk across the mountains until his world is bathed in twilight. I wish he could tell me what he's thinking.

Dad's ability to verbalize the sunset's effect on him is hardly better than Nick's. I had once asked him what he thought of the sunsets. "Beautiful," was all he said. But it was enough.

At these times, he is quiet and appears introspective, and I try to imagine where his thoughts are drifting. Is he wishing Mother were here to watch this with him? Is he remembering the times of his life, good and bad, full and empty, peaceful and violent? Is he thinking about the men in his platoon, who all, save him, were gone too soon? Is he wishing for something he can never again have, like mobility, clarity, youth . . . health?

As I've watched over the last two weeks, I've recognized their growing bond—not only with each other, but with the earth and the sky, whose constant adherence to the march of time marks their days on earth.

Rustling leaves and wind chimes alert me that a strong breeze has kicked up. I walk to the window just in time to see Dad's favorite 82nd Airborne cap blow off his head and somersault down into the valley. Dad speaks to Nick, and for a skinny minute I envision Nick tearing off down the steep bank to retrieve it. But no. Now if it had been a ball, Nick would have charged to hell and back to get it. But he can't know the significance of that particular cap. I do.

I hurry down to where they are, tell Dad I saw his hat fly away, and that I'll go look for it later.

"When?"

"In the morning, after Marcy gets here," I tell him.

"It could be gone by then."

"Okay, Dad, as soon as David gets home, I'll go down and look for it." I can't leave Dad alone to go look for his cap.

"When's he coming home?"

Dad is even more attached to the hat than I thought. "I'm not sure, but it will be soon."

"It's gonna get dark. You won't find it."

Wow, he's really anxious about it.

"Tell you what, Dad. Let's get in the van and drive down the driveway and look for it together." It's the only way I can keep an eye on him and look for the cap at the same time.

Despite hurrying to put my plan in motion, it's twilight by the time I start the search in the valley. Nick is by my side, but he doesn't know what I'm looking for, so he's no help. Dad is watching us from the van. His window is rolled down, and he's giving me instructions I can't hear.

I can't find it anywhere. I have to give up for the evening, but tell him I'll look again in the morning when there's more light. He's disappointed, and he doesn't try to hide it.

"I promise, I'll look really hard in the morning, Dad, and David can help me. We'll find it."

Dad has several more 82nd Airborne caps I've had specially made for him over the years. If we can't find his cap, he'll have to pick a new favorite.

---

We had no luck finding Dad's hat, so I put another on his head this morning as we prepare to venture out. When he looks at himself in the mirror, he seems pleased. "AIRBORNE ALL THE WAY" he says, reading the insignia on the hat. I give him a little punch in the arm and whoop, "Hell, yeah!" I'm hoping the other one will be completely forgotten.

It's the last week in October, and today it is pleasantly cool, clear and sunny, so I'm taking Dad for what is likely to be his last ride of the season on the Parkway because soon, parts of it will be shut down for the winter.

David has gone to Burnsville, where he's meeting with developers he sold property to several years ago. Their project has been on hold, but now they're ready to move forward. When he told me about it, David expressed amazement that they had chosen this time to do so. After all, the real estate market in the area is still stagnant; and even though David hears rumors of start-up projects, it may be years before it comes back. Nevertheless, I hope they can somehow use David's expertise in moving forward—and pay him for it.

I'm securing Dad in the van for our outing when Nick ambles over and pokes his head inside. He's never ridden in it before, so here's another test of the trust that's forming between him and Dad.

When Dad doesn't notice him, Nick barks. It's a soft bark, a woof of greeting, certainly not one that could ever intimidate Dad.

"What's he want?"

"Don't know for sure, but I think he wants to go with us today."

"Can he?"

"It's fine with me, but it's up to you, Dad."

He thinks this over for a bit. "I guess it would be okay. Where are we going to stop to eat? Will he be able to eat there, too?"

I reflect on Dad's thoughtfulness while also considering the importance that food has had in connecting these two.

"Well, we can pick up some roast beef sandwiches and drinks, and have a picnic at our special spot on the Parkway. How does that sound?"

"That sounds real good, Sugar." Dad is twisting his head around now to see Nick. "You wanna go have roast beef sandwiches with us, Nick?"

Nick knows "roast beef," and he recognizes an invitation when he receives one. He climbs up the wheelchair ramp that leads into the van and steps up next to Dad. To my surprise, and Dad's shock, Nick licks the side of Dad's face. Nick has been taught not to lick since most people don't appreciate a wet tongue that's been who knows where; but despite his training, he's laid a big one on Dad. I stifle a laugh.

"Aww, I don't want that dog slobbering on me!" Dad protests, but I think he secretly likes the warm wet tongue and the affection behind it. He's half-smiling. "Get back there," he tells Nick, though Nick doesn't know where "back there" is in this vehicle, so he looks at me.

There's a long bench seat in the very back of the van. I point and say, "There, big boy." He dutifully pads back, jumps on the seat, and settles in with a big smile and a wag of his tail.

I fasten my seatbelt and start the van. "And we're off!" My voice is pitched high with happiness.

"We're off!" Dad repeats, excitement in his voice.

Nick stays quiet. I look in the rearview mirror and see he's sitting up on the bench seat, looking out the back window. His tail is swishing back and forth at a rapid rate.

We each have our own ways of expressing our joy for being out, *together*, on such a splendid autumn day.

---

"It's the craziest thing, Rachel," David remarks as we sit down to eat dinner.

He's ready to tell me about meeting with the developers, and I can see he's excited, even though he's holding it in check.

"What's so crazy about it?"

"Well, I sold the land to these guys right before the market started to collapse. Apparently, they spent the next couple of years just talking about what they wanted to do."

"What's been the problem, money?"

"No, you would think so, but no. More like they've been victims of analysis paralysis. They talked and talked about how they would approach the project, but never did anything until last year, when they realized they needed to do more than draw pictures on the back of napkins. They contracted with a very expensive planning and design company that came up with a grand plan for developing the land."

"You saw the plans?"

"I did, and it's something else, this development. As nice as anything in Asheville."

"So these developers have a lot of money."

David nods. "Deep pockets. A master engineering firm validated the design company's plan, and the zoning board approved it. So now they're ready to move forward with the infrastructure. They met with Frank and Mark Gelding, whose family has been involved with the Appalia Way Electric Cooperative for generations."

"I know Frank and Mark. They're nice guys." I had met them at some point or another, and I remembered they were down-to-earth local men who did a lot of good in the community.

"Yes, they are, and they didn't take to the developers too well."

"Why not?"

David sighs, and I can tell he's trying to decide how much he should share. I'm hoping he'll give me the entire scoop, and I encourage it by saying, "Oh, just tell me."

"Okay. These developers are from South Florida. They fly in and out on a private jet and have developed a local reputation for being, well, assholes."

Dad bursts out laughing just as I'm putting a forkful of meatloaf into his mouth. Food goes flying.

Dad starts coughing, and I thump his back until the coughing subsides.

"You okay, Dad?" He's winded from the coughing spell, but when he nods his head, I can see he is indeed okay.

"Maybe we should talk about this later," I say to David.

David is cleaning up the food that flew out of Dad's mouth. "Sure, no problem."

"Don't wait 'til later on my account," Dad squeaks out.

David gives me a questioning look, and I nod my head as I help Dad drink some water.

"Okay, then. The rest isn't so funny, but it is interesting. I think you should hear this, Joe."

I'm so gratified that David is never condescending to Dad. He may not follow the entire conversation, but at least he'll feel included.

"So anyway," David continues, "they flew in last Friday. They had a meeting set up with Frank and Mark for five-thirty. Cocktail hour. To hear them tell it, those 'bible thumpers' wouldn't join them in a drink, and things went downhill from there."

Dad laughs again, and so do I. "Did they really call them bible thumpers?" I ask, still laughing.

"I don't know if they said it to their faces, but that's what they said to me."

"Who are these men? I mean, are they full-time developers? Is that where they get all their money for private jets and upscale developments?"

David shakes his head. "No, I keep calling them developers, but they're three lawyers who still practice and have big bank accounts. They want to build a beautiful development up here, and the shitty real estate market isn't going to deter them."

"Shitty market," Dad repeats, as if he's thinking about it, but I think he just likes to say a cuss word now and then.

"It is shitty, Dad, which is why David and I are in this mess." I realize I've said too much. Dad seems to have forgotten about our being broke, and I don't want to remind him.

"What mess?" He turns and looks at me with genuine concern.

David saves the day. "We've got a lot of property that we're having reappraised, and it's a mess sorting it all out."

Dad looks closely at David, then nods his head, satisfied with the explanation.

David continues. "So their side of the story is, they were trying to assure Frank and Mark that they're ready to spend whatever it takes to get the infrastructure work done. They asked them if they knew the property, and they said they did. So after a few cocktails, these Florida guys are feeling pretty good, and they tell Frank and Mark to name their price."

I think I see where this is going. I smile, encouraging David to continue. He pauses to eat some meatloaf and mashed potatoes, then takes a sip of water before he continues.

"Frank and Mark quoted them five hundred thousand dollars."

I can see David's waiting for me to say, "No way!" but I really don't know enough about the issue to comment.

"So, is that like, a really high number?"

Dad says, "That's a half-million dollars."

*Good for Dad!*

"Yes, that's a half-million dollars, Joe, and I can tell you for a fact that's about three times what it should be for the job. When these guys sobered up the next day, they realized it was an unrealistically big number, too." David says this to Dad, continuing to involve him in the conversation. I love my husband.

"Okaaay," I say, indicating I want more. "What's the rest of the story?"

David shakes his head. "I don't know the whole story yet, but I'm meeting with Frank and Mark on Thursday to get it. The developers asked me to talk to them to see if there's any chance of making a better deal."

"And you're going to do that? You'll get involved?"

"Hey, Frank and Mark are good guys. My thinking is, they didn't like these assholes," and here he looks at Dad and winks. "And so they jacked up the price because they don't want to work for them. I'll see if I can soften the situation."

"Assholes," Dad says.

What's up with him? I can't help myself—I laugh, and so do Dad and David. Then I say what I can't help thinking.

"Imagine being able to do that," I sigh. "To have enough money to tell someone to go f—" . . . I catch myself before I say the f-word, and continue, "to go to hell if you don't like them." I've never used the f-word in front of Dad, even when I felt it was really warranted, which in my mind has been plenty of times, but I'm not about to start now.

"Like I said, that's just my thinking, but I won't know for sure until I talk to them." David concentrates on his food, and I know it's cold by now, so I ask him if I can pop it in the microwave.

"Nah, I'm almost finished. This is really good meatloaf, Rachel."

"It was good," Dad says. I've finished feeding him, and now he's picking bits of meatloaf and errant peas off his bib and tossing them onto the floor for Nick.

"Thanks. I'm glad you both liked it." My first few attempts at meatloaf had been grim, and while there had been no vocalized complaints, there had been plenty left on the plates.

"And what do you get out of this?" I'm not challenging him. I'm just wondering why he's agreed to get involved.

"I don't know if I'll get anything out of it, but it's the right thing to do. At the very least, if we can get the project moving, there will be jobs to be had in the area. Plus, who knows, maybe some sort of money-making opportunity can come out of it."

"That would be great, honey." I'm not going to question David any further about his motives. He's brilliant, he's a people person, and he knows how to get things done. He's on good footing with every businessperson in the county. He's well respected. It will be good for him to put those attributes to work. Besides, he's not doing anything now that's financially productive, so why not do a good deed and see if any opportunities arise?

"I'll do the dishes while you get Joe set up to watch TV," David volunteers.

I look over at Dad, and though it's early, he looks really tired.

"Want to watch TV up here with us, Dad?"

His head droops as his eyes close, and he doesn't answer. I look at David. "He's tired. Let's get him into his own bed, then I'll help you with the dishes."

We used to transfer Dad from his wheelchair to a dining room chair, but now we just leave him in the wheelchair. It occurs to me that we started doing this because it took more out of Dad than it did us. One day he said, "I'll just stay in my chair," and that's been the case ever since.

His energy is on the wane, and that's even more evident tonight, when he's ready to fall asleep at seven o'clock.

David rolls Dad to the elevator, and Nick crawls out from under the table and follows me downstairs. Nick's moving like he's more tired also. I wonder if he's pacing his energy to Dad's, but dismiss that thought. And then it hits me: They're both getting older. It's as simple as that. In the five months Dad has lived with us, he's aged. It has been so gradual that I hadn't really noticed. And of course Nick, at eleven—almost twelve—is aging too.

I don't want to think too much about what all this means.

After getting Dad into bed, we start to leave to go upstairs to clean the kitchen. Nick would normally be right behind us, but tonight he's standing at the foot of Dad's bed. His shoulders are stooped, and he's panting.

"Come on, big boy," I whisper, not wanting to wake Dad.

Nick doesn't move. Instead, much to my surprise, he lies down. This just won't work, because he'll need to go out later to use the bathroom. And what if Dad wakes up and sees him there? Will he be disoriented, and maybe even scared?

"Come on, Nick." I've put more assertiveness into my voice.

Nick raises his head to look at me, and I can see he's about to obey when Dad quietly says, "He can stay here."

David and I look at each other, and I can only imagine that my own quizzical expression matches his.

I hesitate. "He'll have to use the bathroom later. Let's leave door open so Nick can use the doggie door in the garage."

"Good idea."

Nick is lying on the carpet, outside the perimeter of the thick pad beside Dad's bed. He's forgoing his own comfy bed, but he seems content.

"Think we'll have to move one of his dog beds in here?" David asks.

I smile at that thought. "I hope so."

---

Back upstairs, I clear the table as David rinses the dishes and loads the dishwasher.

"I'm worried about Dad."

"Me, too."

"What do you think is going on with him?"

David shrugs. "Do you think it's just because he's getting older?"

That's exactly what I think, and I say so.

Somehow I've expected Dad to maintain the status quo. He's been doing well, and he's had no infections or hospitalizations. I wonder if old-people time is like dog time, in terms of aging. Do they start aging faster as they get older? The question doesn't make sense, but it takes root.

I need to take Dad to the neurologist soon and get some answers. An unexpected melancholy comes over me. I suspect I already know the answers.

# 30

David has learned that, sure enough, Frank and Mark had decided on the spot they didn't want to work with "them Floridiots" so they "shot 'em a high price to scare 'em off."

I burst out laughing, and congratulate him on being right. "So what did you say?"

"I asked them what they would charge me personally to do the same job. They said a hundred and fifty thousand."

My jaw drops. "Are you kidding me? That's a huge difference!"

"They're in a position to do what they want. They'd be doing it as a personal favor to me, they say."

I'm astounded, but I'm getting all tingly-optimistic, too. "So what's next?"

"They said if I'd run interference between them and the 'Floridiots,' they'd do the job for that amount."

"The hundred and fifty thousand? They'll do it for that if you run interference?"

"Yep, and now I'll parlay saving those guys three hundred and fifty thousand dollars into a consulting job. I'm going to offer to run interference for them with all the local companies."

I whoop, and throw my arms around David's neck and kiss him. *Hard.*

"Do you think they'll hire you?"

"I'm pretty sure they will." Hope shines in his beautiful green eyes. And there's something else in his eyes . . . a teasing gleam I can't interpret. But I love this confidence in my husband, and I love the idea of his having a job again. Then it hits me. "You'll be a consultant, though. Are you going to be okay with that, after being your own boss?"

"Babe, I can do anything if it means bringing in money."

"You can work with those Floridiots?"

We laugh, and he assures me he can. My relief is immense at the thought of having money coming in, instead of savings going out. "Thank you, honey."

"Don't thank me yet, I don't have the job. Whatever happens, we'll still be okay."

"I want to believe that, David."

"Well, maybe this will help." He reaches into his back pocket and pulls out his wallet.

"What's going on?"

He removes what looks like a folded check, then hands it to me with a big grin.

I unfold the check. I scream.

"Oh, David!" I throw myself into his arms. "Is this for real?"

"It's for real, all right."

"And you're just now telling me about this?" Now I understand the gleam in his eyes.

"I wanted to shout it out the minute I came through the door. But you were busy with Joe, then there was dinner to put on the table, then getting Joe to bed—"

"Okay, I get it, but really? You'd wait three hours to let me know you had a check for thirty-five thousand dollars?"

He starts to answer, but I say, "Oh, forget it! What matters is we have thirty-five thousand dollars we didn't have when you left here this morning!"

"Yes, ten percent of what I saved them." We laugh and reach for each other again, sharing a long, joy-filled hug.

"I kept wanting to tell you, but I also wanted to wait until we were alone so we could celebrate properly."

"Oh, we're going to celebrate, all right! Let's open that bottle of Veuve Clicquot we've been saving for Thanksgiving. This definitely calls for champagne."

"I swear, that's just what I was thinking. I'll go get it."

David heads down to the garage to get the champagne out of the wine refrigerator. It may be the last bottle of anything in there. I imagine refilling it with some nice Pinot Noirs and Cabernets, crisp Vouvrays and Chardonnays and . . . and I catch myself.

No, this money is going to be used where it can do the most good right now.

I'm thinking about Dad going back to Crestview when David comes up behind me and pops the cork. I jump about three feet, then turn around and grab the bottle, both of us laughing as I pull it out of his hands. "You're so bad!"

After I've poured the champagne, we pause and look into each other's eyes.

"What shall we toast?"

"Better days ahead?"

I nod and clink my glass against his. "Better days ahead, for all of us."

We take a sip, holding each other's eyes. I take his hand and lead him outside, to the deck. Without speaking, we put our arms around each other's waists and look up at the stars. I think about the wish I made the other night. I put my head on his shoulder and whisper a prayer of thanks. "Thank you for this great blessing."

"Yes, thank you for this great blessing."

I share what I was thinking before he popped the cork. "David, I know we said when we had the money, we would move Dad back to Crestview."

David nods. "If that's what you want to do—"

"I don't know what I want to do."

"Nothing wrong with that. We have time to decide."

But did we? Are we compromising Dad's health and happiness by keeping him here and cloistered with just us? Would he be better off at Crestview?

"We don't have to decide tonight, Rachel." He kisses the top of my head.

We didn't have to decide tonight, that was true; but I want to talk about it. "If we kept him here, we could hire more help, and maybe a companion, you know?"

"Sure we could. We have choices now."

"Would we be doing the right thing for Dad?"

"That's hard to say."

"Do you think it would do any good to discuss it with him?"

"We could try. I don't know how much he'd understand. But there's a bigger factor to consider here, Rachel. What do *you* want to do?"

What do I want to do? I close my eyes and picture Dad downstairs, alone for hours at a time despite how much I try to fill up his days. Then I picture the apartment without him, in the same pristine condition it was before he moved in. I see the apartment restored with the elegant décor that has been sitting in our storage unit. I picture it devoid of the clutter of pill bottles and toiletries and packages of diapers and his wheelchair and walker. And devoid of Dad.

I mentally step into the room, sans all of those things, and feel the cold emptiness that would exist if Dad weren't there.

For a flicker of a moment, I imagine reclaiming my life—our life, and the freedom that would mean for David and me.

"David, do you miss our former life?"

"I do."

I wait for him to say more, but he remains silent, watching me.

"I miss it, too. But I think I would miss Dad more than I could ever miss our old life."

"I'd miss Joe, too."

"You would?"

"Sure I would."

"So, you're okay with him staying here?"

"Of course I am, Rachel. But I really want you to hire more help. I won't be here as much to help you if I do start working with the developers."

"When will you know for sure?"

"Probably next week. If we can come to an agreement, I'll start right away."

"That soon, huh?"

"Yes, so you better start looking for more help."

More help. I let go of the tension I didn't know I was holding. More help. A wave of relief washes over me, and through me. I take a deep breath and wipe my eyes.

"I will. Thanks, honey." I hug him tighter. "Now, where's that champagne?"

"Let's go in and pour some more."

I flick the switch to ignite the fireplace and then turn off the lights. We snuggle on the sofa and clink our glasses again.

"To us," David says.

"To all of us."

*To all of us.* We are an *us,* to the end, whenever it comes, and whatever that entails. Me, my husband, my dad, my dog.

# 31

Marcy is getting Dad settled into his comfy lift chair when I come downstairs. She'll leave soon, and I'll give Dad lunch. It's my third trip down this morning because I'm worried about him. He's been really lethargic. In fact, he's fast asleep.

"How's he doing?" I ask Marcy.

"He seems awful tired this morning." She lets out a big sigh. "It was tough to get him in and out of the bath, 'cause he wasn't cooperatin' at all."

"I'm sorry, Marcy. Please, call me down to help anytime. I don't want you or Dad getting injured."

"I will, don't you worry. But right now I'd say he might have a UTI comin' on. My grandma got them about every other month."

"That's right, you said she was a diabetic."

"Yeah, she was. Why?"

"Diabetics are more prone to UTIs."

"They are?"

I'm surprised that she's never heard this from a doctor.

"Women much more so than men. Dad has had his share of them before, but I've worked hard to make sure he doesn't get them the usual ways, like not emptying his bladder. I make sure he stays on the toilet until he's gone all he can."

Marcy nods her head. "I do that, too."

I think about Dad's asking to go to the bathroom more frequently, even though he's drinking less and less water. That's another symptom, feeling like you have to urinate even when you don't. I chastise myself for the few times I've said, "But Dad, you just went. Can you hold it a little longer?" It is a chore that never gets any easier.

I should have been more on top of this, seen the signs earlier. I don't share my shortcomings with Marcy.

"Or it could happen because of a high blood glucose level, though it's been within target range since he came here."

"I think it's 'cause he holds it in until he gets to a toilet. He don't never have a wet diaper."

"That's a good thought, Marcy. If he holds it in, or doesn't go completely, the urine stays in the bladder and becomes a breeding ground for bacteria." Now I'm becoming really worried. "Did his urine have a strong odor this morning?"

"It's coming on. That's what made me think of it."

"I'll go call his doctor. Maybe I can get him in today. Thanks, Marcy."

She gives Dad a kiss on his forehead and pulls a blanket over him. "He seems chilled, too. He was real cold in the bath, even with the heater in there running. I got him out quick."

Now I know I *have* to get Dad in to see Dr. Baird today.

---

"I'd like to admit him to the hospital," Dr. Baird says.

I'm crestfallen. "You don't think a round of antibiotics will cure it?"

"Joe's got a lot going on anyway, and I want to keep an eye on this UTI." He hesitates before he continues. "Mortality from a UTI is five times higher in patients aged sixty-five and older who have diabetes. I don't want this to get out of control. I want to start him on a drip with antibiotics. I also want to get him fully hydrated.

"Right now," he continues, "It looks like a lower UTI, and I want to keep it and kill it there. It's just affecting the bladder. But the infection can spread as the bacteria move up from the bladder through the ureters. If they reach the kidney, they can cause a kidney infection, which can become a very serious condition. If it gets to that point, it can be deadly for someone like Joe. If he's in the hospital, I can keep a close eye on him."

After that explanation, any arguments I might have put forth are fruitless. I already knew all of this, because I had been through it with him before. Dad's going to have to be admitted. He's vulnerable, since he's already had a TURP procedure for an enlarged prostate. That almost killed him because the catheter that had been inserted a week before the surgery had created both a lower and upper UTI, and the surgeon didn't bother to get a urine sample before surgery. The operation had caused the bacteria to enter his bloodstream, and it was the closest Dad had come to dying since he was wounded at Anzio.

I recall sitting by his hospital bed in Florida when his granddaughter, my niece, called. I handed him the phone and he said to her, "Pray for Papa. I'm real sick, honey."

Dad was the very definition of stoic. Such an admittance shook me from my complacency in believing he'd be just fine, and drove me to take action.

I'd had his general practitioner call in a specialist, and it was just in time. It was touch and go for a couple of days, but Dad recovered.

I can't take a chance that he could get that sick again because I'm not sure he could survive. He's six years older now, and his health is much more precarious.

"Then let's get him admitted and started on the antibiotic drip," I say, with a mixture of conviction and dread.

# 32

Nick follows me up the stairs from the garage, bumping my hand a few times as a reminder to pet him. I set my purse on the counter and kick off my shoes and wonder where David is. The house seems different without Dad in it. He has been fused into our house vibe, and it has a different tenor when he's not here.

Yet there's a softening of the knot in my stomach that I didn't know was there. Just being responsible for another person's health and well-being every hour of the day brings on a low-simmering sense of anxiety, even when there are no specific problems or issues. There's a subconscious awareness of pending health issues, and the always right-below-the-surface worries of *What can happen?* And *Am I doing enough?*

But that knot has been replaced by anxiety of a different kind because I've put Dad's health in the hands of others. I know from experience, from medication errors and infections and even septic seizures, that a hospital can be a dangerous place for anyone, but especially for a sick and elderly patient with a compromised immune system.

David comes down from his study, gives me a hug and asks how I am. My one-word answer sums up how I am. "Exhausted." I've just returned from getting Dad settled in for the night at the hospital, and it's almost ten o'clock. The admittance, and all that goes into that process, was time-consuming and stressful. Then I had to spend a lot of time feeding Dad his dinner while reassuring him he was where he needed to be. Despite being disoriented, Dad knew full well where he was, and he was pretty darn unhappy about it.

It was difficult to explain to Dad why he needed to stay in the hospital. I used all the right words, although I tempered Dr. Baird's dire prognosis of the worst-case basis if he didn't stay there. Nothing I said mattered. Dad argued he was better and ready to go home.

Of course, he would say that, and he honestly believed he could convince me. He's the parent, after all.

Convincing him to do what's best for him is part of my caregiving job, but it's hard. I just want to be a daughter who makes her dad happy. I hate having to be the enforcer, and I could see Dad getting more and more agitated—which is another symptom of the combination of Alzheimer's and UTIs. Had this gone on another day without medical intervention, he would have moved into the deeply disoriented stage.

Finally I reminded him, without going into full details, of the time he had been so very sick because of a similar UTI. I swear I saw some of his agitation dissipate as he processed that memory.

I'm telling all of this to David while he gives me a foot rub. Bless this man. I continue the saga. "So I said to him, 'Dad, the sooner they get you well, the sooner you can come home. Just let them do what they do best, and then you'll feel so much better. I bet you feel rotten, don't you?'

"He didn't answer, so then I said, 'You want to be well when Laura and Sarah come for Thanksgiving, don't you?' I mean, that's still a month away, but I had to use something. I felt like I was bribing a child with a treat, like if he behaves, he'll get to see his granddaughters. Is that terrible?"

David shakes his head. "No, it's not terrible, Rachel. You did what you had to do."

"Well, anyway, it worked. He stopped fighting me about it."

He takes my other foot in his hands and starts his healing ministrations. "What did Joe finally say?"

"He just said, 'Okay,' and then he turned his head away from me and, just like that, he fell into a deep sleep."

Now I'm tired of talking. I'm just tired, period. David's foot rub is about to put me in la-la land. I haven't eaten all day, but I'm too tired to eat a thing.

"What did the doctor say caused it?"

Though I'm tired of talking, I go over most of the things Dr. Baird and I had discussed, including Dad's need to be hydrated.

David looks thoughtful. "It's tough to get him to drink water, I know that. We'll have to find a way to do better."

"I can't think how. It's hard to get his pills down him."

David nods. "And sometimes he chokes on them."

"Right."

The first time that had happened, David hit the house phone button on Dad's big phone, and when I'd answered, he'd yelled "Help!" I'd flown down the stairs and given him a hands-on demonstration of how to use the heel of his hand between Dad's shoulder blades to relieve the obstruction.

"It's been getting worse, too," I say. "The thing is, I think every day that it will be a better day for him taking his pills, and that he'll get them all down with no problem. I feel guilty when I skip pills because he refuses to take them."

David and I keep a log each day of the pills Dad's taken, beginning with the vital ones. If there is a chance to get Dad to swallow vitamins and supplements, we jump on it. It's pills on top of pills. I wouldn't want to take that many, even under the best of circumstances.

Medication and meals are taking longer to accomplish. I guess I haven't noticed until now; or, if I were being honest with myself, I guess I didn't want to think that it's getting harder. The occasional day when he takes his pills and eats without discomfort lures me into thinking he's over the hump, whatever that hump was. But then it happens again.

"His dysphagia is worse, David. I've been in denial. The increased dosage of Sinemet hasn't helped like I thought it would. I should discuss it with Dr. Baird and ask him to order speech therapy."

David agrees. I glance at Nick lying on the rug in front of the fire, listening to our conversation. He gets up slowly and comes over and puts his head in my lap. As I rub his head and coo loving words, I notice that he seems more lethargic than usual.

"Does Nick seem okay to you?"

David gives me a sort of startled look, which I can't read and am too tired to contemplate. "Maybe he just misses your Dad." He's joking, but I'm also too tired to laugh.

"I need sleep. Marcy's going to cover Dad at the hospital tomorrow morning for those regular four hours, but I'll be there the rest of the day."

"Would some good news help?"

"What? You have some? Does it even exist?"

"Babe, we'll have money coming in now. I'll get my first check on Monday. Ten thousand dollars."

I go from exhaustion to exhilaration in a split second and spring to my knees, whooping, "Whoo hoo! Whoo hoo!" I settle on his lap and wrap my arms around his neck. "So they hired you?"

"They hired me. Ten thousand a month. Can you believe it?"

"Yes, I can, because you're amazing! Congratulations, baby!"

We hug and kiss. Then we do it again.

"So with that," he says, "and the other thirty-five thousand, we can afford someone to be with him around the clock if that's what you want. You don't have to do it all by yourself." He's grinning at me, and I can see he's been eager to share the good news, but has held off in deference to Dad's overriding issues. That's how he does things: unselfishly, patiently.

"Yes, since we have the money now, we can pay for extra help, both at the hospital and here. Oh my God, David, that's so wonderful."

David heaves a happy sigh. "It's a big relief, isn't it?"

"To say the least! We can hire Adam and Jennie for extra sessions."

I feel a lightening of my spirit. It's an odd feeling, sort of like when a leg cramp releases and you feel the relief, with just a tinge of residual pain left behind. Regardless, it's a welcome sensation—so very welcome.

I scoot off David's lap and stand up and stretch. My mind starts whirling. "I'll call Adam tomorrow. Maybe he can go to the hospital and give Dad a massage."

"That's a great idea."

I'm getting an upbeat mood, but then I remember I'm supposed to call my sisters, and exhaustion overtakes me again. "I have to call Cindy and Kathy and let them know what's happening with Dad."

"They know he's in the hospital, right?"

"Yes, but that's all they know. I got both of their voicemails when I called them earlier. They've both texted me since, asking me to call again and let them know everything that's going on. I dread their questions. Maybe I'll do a three-way call."

"They both love Joe very much. They visit when they can."

"Yes, they do, but as you well know Cindy lives in Washington and Kathy lives in Florida and their jobs are demanding, so they haven't come lately. They say they can only get away once or twice a year."

They do call him every weekend, however, and there is lots of laughter and upbeat chatter from Dad's end when he's doing well. At times, I've seen him mumble and nod off. But he's always so happy to talk to them, and I'm pleased he has another outlet for his thoughts and ramblings. It puts a sparkle in his eyes.

It dampens my spirits when Dad asks them, "When are you coming to see me?" I never hear their answers, but Dad's responses of, "That's okay, honey," or "Sure, I understand," give me the gist. But his voice, to my ears anyway, betrays his sadness and his longing to see them.

I continue, "Just the thought of having Kathy's daughters here for Thanksgiving has cheered him up. I only hope he'll be completely better by then. I'll do all I can to make sure of it, anyway."

Maybe it's time to press the point of visiting. If anything bad happened to Dad, my sisters would feel so much worse for not visiting more often. Heck, they haven't seen him since last Christmas. And frankly, it would be nice to have their help with his social and emotional needs now and then. No hired help compares to a daughter's help. But nothing bad will happen anytime soon. Dad will get over this just as he's gotten over everything else.

David starts massaging my tired shoulders. "They're too comfortable with the situation, knowing you're taking such great care of him."

"That *we're* taking such great care of him," I remind him.

"Yeah, okay, but you need to insist they get here sooner rather than later."

"Why are you saying that? Are you thinking something bad will happen?"

"No, but it would be nice if they spent some time with him, because he's not getting any younger or better. You know that."

"Yes, I do. I've already decided I'm going to press them on it. Maybe at least Kathy and Tom can come at Thanksgiving, too. They'd get to be with Dad *and* their daughters."

David stops the massage and sits forward, clasping his hands together. "Suggest it. Strongly. It's time." He's is in his protective mode— of me. He knows I need family support. I need my sisters and nieces.

"Yes, it's time. Maybe Dad has years left, maybe not, but whatever time he has left, he needs to see his other daughters. Like you said, sooner rather than later."

But I don't have the energy for those conversations now. I'll just text them, fill them in, and phone them tomorrow.

To fend off replies, I keep it short: *Exhausted. Dad okay, fighting hard. Asked about you both. Misses you. Hopes to see you at Thanksgiving. Full update tomorrow. Good night.*

Okay, so I embellished. But I want to lay the groundwork for getting them to come for Thanksgiving. A shovelful of guilt is a good way to start.

# 33

It's odd to wake up and realize I don't have to jump out of bed to go check on Dad and greet Marcy, who has her own key to Dad's outside door. I'm tempted to lie in bed for a while and fantasize about David bringing me a cup of coffee, as he often did before Dad came.

And now here he is, coming through the door with coffee for me—a vision I conjured up, come to life. How does he know? I don't care how he knows, I'm simply elated. Coffee in bed! I thank him as he bends to kiss me and say, "You read my mind, honey."

"I've missed bringing you coffee in bed. I love to see that smile on your face first thing in the morning."

I take a long sip. Ah, perfect. I tell him so.

"By the way, I haven't seen Nick around this morning." He looks worried.

I'm not particularly concerned, because Nick has two doggie doors to use, one upstairs and one in the garage. He's probably just exploring the nearby woods. I sip my coffee and tell David this, then mention that I have to call the hospital to check on Dad's status.

But first, the coffee has triggered a full bladder and a dire necessity.

I head to the bathroom, telling David, "Please go outside and look for Nick."

David comes into the bathroom as I'm getting in the shower.

"He's in Joe's room." We smile at each other, sharing our happy thoughts about what that means.

I call the hospital and learn that Dad did well through the night and that Marcy had been there for more than an hour and had fed him breakfast. I'm relieved because it frees me up to get some neglected chores done. My house could use a good cleaning, but I reject that idea almost as soon as it surfaces. *I'll be damned if I'm going to spend the first day I've had to myself in six months doing house cleaning.*

*I'll be damned.* I'm using that a lot these days. I don't usually curse this much. Rebellion is rising in me, rebellion against the responsibilities that encircle my life.

I expect to see Nick in the kitchen when I go in to get another cup of coffee, but he's not here. Not only is he not here, but his bowl of food hasn't been touched. After telling me he filled Nick's bowl, David had taken off for a meeting in Burnsville with the developers.

I wonder if David absentmindedly closed the door to Dad's room and trapped Nick in there. That could be one explanation for Nick not having eaten.

But he's not in Dad's apartment. I turn to leave, and call for him. "Nick? Nick? Where are you, big boy?"

I find him in the garage and am surprised to see him just standing there, facing his doggie door. Why didn't he come when I called? He doesn't act as if he's even aware of my presence. I think he's deciding whether to go out when he does something I've never seen him do. He turns sideways, raises his leg, and *lets go* on the doggie door. The strong odor of his urine causes me to reel back, even though I'm ten feet away. I'm dumbfounded as I try to reconcile what I've just witnessed. Not only is this bizarre behavior from my well-trained dog, but the strong smell of his urine is all too familiar. My dog has a UTI.

*Holy crap, what's happening?*

"UTIs are not contagious," Dr. Froman tells me matter-of-factly. She's confirmed the infection and is writing on Nick's chart. She's trying to decide which antibiotic she wants to give him. It will take two days for the culture results, when she can pinpoint the exact bacteria to target, but she wants to get him started on something now. She'll change it if she has to when the culture results come back.

We discuss how he might have gotten it. I recalled that, during a hike with David the week before, Nick had come upon a dead snake and, according to David's description, had gleefully rolled around in the remains, attaching the horrible stench to his flesh and fur. It wasn't the first time, and it wouldn't be the last.

The first time it happened, David Googled *Why do dogs roll around in dead smelly stuff?* We learned they are most likely camouflaging their own scent, making it easier to sneak up on prey animals. It's a wolf instinct that has carried through generations to domestic pets, even though they don't hunt for food.

Wearing a mask and gloves, I'd given him two rounds with the doggie shampoo. When even that didn't eradicate the stench, I spritzed him with some old Chanel No 5. Nick sneezed twice, then tossed me an injured look. It was all I could do not to burst out laughing.

I concede to Dr. Froman that maybe that's the cause of the UTI, but I'm not ready to give up on my contrived theory that things are catching. "But Nick's never had one before, so don't you think it's weird that both my dad and my dog have a UTI at the same time?"

She's still writing on his chart when she says, "I've seen weirder things."

My curiosity is piqued. "Like what?"

Dr. Froman hesitates before she answers. "I had a situation where the dog owner and the dog were getting chemo treatments at the same time." She shakes her head. "I don't think I've ever seen anything as sad."

"It sure sounds like a sad situation," I commiserate, hoping she'll tell me more—and she does.

"He lived alone except for his dog. A month after he was diagnosed with cancer, I diagnosed his dog with cancer. They were both so sick during treatments, and I worried about them. But they were both so stoic," and here she sniffs, as if she's holding back tears. "Kind of rooting each other on, is the only way to describe it."

Tears prick at my eyes. What a bond they must have had. I don't want to ask, but I have to. "Did they both make it?"

She looks at me with tear-filled eyes and shakes her head. "No. He was here when I put his dog down, and I read in the paper two weeks later that he died." She turns away from me to grab a tissue, and hands me one, too.

"That is just so sad," I say, my tears flowing freely now.

"It was one of the hardest cases I've ever had. *But,* that cancer wasn't any more catching than a UTI." She's back to being Dr. Froman, and she's made her point.

I think about the symmetry of the man and dog's lives, and also about how wretchedly miserable the last two weeks of his life must have been without his beloved dog. My heart aches for that stranger, and I know I'm projecting the future of both Dad's and Nick's passing.

Nick has been lying on the floor with his head on his paws, disinterested in us. But at the sound of my sniffling, he raises his head and meets my eyes. His eyes hold a question. In answer, I bend down and pet his head and tell him, "I'm okay, big boy, I'm okay. Now we're going to get you better."

---

By the time Dad comes home from the hospital, Nick is well on the road to recovery. The laboratory results revealed that his kidney function had decreased, which also could have contributed to the UTI. Dr. Froman wasn't willing to directly link the Rimadyl that she had prescribed a few months earlier to the change in kidney function, but she thought it best to take him off it for a while, and try Tramadol, a simple pain reliever.

Dad takes Tramadol. He had been taking Darvocet for years for his related hip pain, but when it was pulled off the market, I asked Dr. Baird for another pain reliever, and he had given me a prescription for Tramadol.

So when Dr. Froman suggested Tramadol for Nick, I was perplexed. "My dad takes Tramadol twice a day. Can dogs and people take the same pain medicine?" I'd asked.

"In this case, yes," she'd replied.

I give Dad one in the morning to help him get through the day, and another in the evening, along with his sleeping pill, to help him sleep through the night. If I can't get him to take those pills, his pain will flare up and become harder to control. Keeping a small but steady amount of pain medication in his system means he won't experience sudden bursts of pain. One of his physicians told me it was better to stay ahead of pain, to prevent it from grabbing hold. Nick will be on the same two-a-day regimen as Dad.

Today Dad is doing well. He has lost weight, evidenced by his protruding hip bones and pronounced ribs, but his color is good and his spirits are high because he's home again. Marcy has propped him up in his bed, and he is telling her how much he's missed sleeping in his own bed.

"You're home now, Dad." The tray I'm carrying holds a huge bowl of chicken noodle soup and French bread slathered with butter. He said he was hungry, and I'm going to take advantage of that to put some weight back on him. In the hospital, he'd eaten one-quarter to three-quarters of his daily meals, no matter how much I'd tried to persuade him to eat more. Even Anna's and Marcy's honeyed coaxing hadn't worked. Since he was on the hospital's unappealing diabetic diet—no bread, sweets, pasta, hamburgers—I'd put his reluctance to eat down to that.

Well, maybe this tasty soup and warm French bread will do the trick. I set the tray on the dinette table and go hug his neck. It's not enough. I sit down on his bed and give him a big, warm, needy hug. I want him to feel the love I have for him, and I need to feel his love for me in return. And I do. He has his arms wrapped around me, and though he's weak, he holds me tightly.

"I've missed you so much. I'm so glad you're back."

"I've missed you, too, Sugar."

Sated with love, I tease, "Ready for your master-chef daughter's delicious soup?"

"I can give it to him, Miss Rachel." Marcy has been across the room, putting away Dad's clean pajamas and underwear, respectfully giving us the space and time we needed.

"Thanks, Marcy, but I'd like to do this."

She nods and says, "Why don't I go on up and start cleaning the house, then?"

Wonder of wonders, blessing of blessings, Marcy resigned from her part-time cleaning job at the hospital to work for us eight hours each day, except Sunday. It was she who offered to add housecleaning to her chores, and I gratefully accepted. I'm also entrusting her with Dad's meds and insulin. She's earned that trust. With this welcome change, it won't be necessary to hire anyone else—at least for now.

Continuing to count my blessings, I add to them the fact that Dad's three-night hospital stay qualifies him for Medicare-paid therapy. Dr. Baird agreed speech therapy would also be good for Dad, but not immediately. He felt Dad didn't need the stress of speech therapy after what he'd been through, and suggested an appointment with Dad's neurologist to get a prescription for that. Dad's chart showed that he had "refused" much of his medication while in the hospital, along with food. Dr. Baird had chalked both up to dysphagia, and not merely stubbornness.

Adam had made it to the hospital twice over the weekend to give Dad a bed massage and some light therapy, which gave me an opportunity to share the good news about David's newfound employment. We shared a happy hug and made plans to start physical therapy for Dad again. He agreed that he and Jennie could start three-times-a-week therapy sessions now that Mystic Lodge had closed for the season, and we reached a financial arrangement.

But now that Medicare will pay for a good part of that, at least for a few weeks, I can augment those payments and save that money. Even with our recent good fortune, I still don't feel we have money to throw around.

Our previous unbridled spending brought us to the point where we had to move Dad out of Crestview. How that had changed our lives! Now, after doing without and realizing I hadn't really given up much,

I'm much more cognizant of the value of money—and how quickly it can slip through your fingers.

I'll never take anything for granted again. All those wasted years of thinking fine dining and golf club memberships were *necessities*, that annual trips to Europe were *enriching*, that facials and manicures and pedicures were *essential*. Such vapid, misplaced values. What *is* essential is having more help with Dad and housekeeping if I'm going to give him the best possible care for the rest of his life.

As I hold up the first spoonful of soup for Dad, I'm all glowy inside at having him with me right here, right now, and I promise myself that I'll never again lose sight of what truly makes life not only valuable, but rich.

I hear a noise in the doorway and look up to see Nick poking his head in, wearing his goofy smile. Dad notices him right away, and returns his smile. "Hey, big boy," he says in greeting. "Come on in."

Nick happily accepts Dad's invitation to join us.

# 34

Dad and I are watching *Wheel of Fortune* in his room, where we're enjoying eating dinner together. David is out tonight with one of the developers, so I've opted for the simplicity of turkey and cheese sandwiches and coleslaw.

Dad is propped up in his bed with a tray across his lap. Nick is lying nearby on the floor, keeping an eye out. He's feeding himself, holding the sandwich in both hands and taking small bites. I'm encouraged on so many levels.

"Where'd you get that dog?"

His question takes me by surprise. I finish the last bite of my sandwich and mute the TV. Dad doesn't notice. He's looking at me, waiting for an answer.

"It's kind of a sad story, but it has a happy ending, obviously." I look over at Nick and smile.

"One day I was getting my hair done, and the woman who owned the boutique next door came into the salon and asked if anyone wanted a black Labrador retriever. I certainly didn't, so I didn't say anything. We already had a dog, Rocky—do you remember him?"

Dad and Mother had visited twice a year for several years before she became too sick to travel, and Rocky had been with us then. They both had given Rocky a wide berth because, with his massive head and large jaws, he looked intimidating.

"Sorta. Scary dog," Dad mumbles, and I can see the memory makes him uncomfortable. Well, at least he remembers.

Though Rocky the Rottweiler looked scary, he had been a sweet and gentle bundle of a love, and he was so smart. I had kept Rocky away from Mom and Dad then, sensing their anxiety, though I had no idea of the extent of it in Dad's case. But Dad hadn't been as sick and afflicted back then, so he'd hidden his fear of Rocky much better.

"Yes, Rocky looked scary, but he was a sweetheart. Anyway, this woman started talking about how they wanted to put a pool in their backyard, but the dog lived there in a pen, and they needed to tear it down to put the pool in.

"I remember thinking how terrible it was that a dog lived in a pen in a backyard, but I still wasn't interested until she said, 'I guess we'll have to have him put down.'"

Dad is listening intently, and it seems Nick is, too.

"I don't know why I spoke up, but I did, and I said I'd like to meet him to see if he'd be a good fit with our current dog. She jumped at my offer, said she was headed home, and asked if I could come over as soon as I was finished. Then she gave me her address and left."

I pause to reflect on Nick's sorry state upon our first meeting. It makes me sad.

"He lived in an eight-by-eight pen with no grass, just dirt. He had a doghouse in there, and I didn't see him at first because he was in the doghouse. She had to call him several times before he slinked out."

"Slinked out?" Dad asks, as if he doesn't understand. He has a hard time pronouncing *slinked.*

"Yes, slinked out. And Dad, he was the skinniest, dirtiest dog I'd ever seen. His head and shoulders were so bowed I thought he had something wrong with his spine. He went to his water bowl, but it was dry. I was so mad, I could have spit nails!"

I take a sip of my iced tea, followed by a deep breath, and continue.

"But I wasn't going to get nasty. Instead, I would get him out of there. Even if I decided not to keep him, I would find him a better home."

Dad nods, and his intense gaze tells me he's fully engaged in the story.

"I asked her if I could go into the pen and pet him. She looked at me like I was a little crazy, but she opened the latch and I went in. There were piles of poop all around the pen, and I had to be careful to step over them to get to him.

"He didn't even look at me, but I bent down and started talking to him. Then he startled me when he barked really loud and moved his head toward me like he was going to bite me."

Dad's eyes get big and he asks, "Did he bite you?"

I shake my head, recalling the scene. "No. I understood him perfectly at that moment. In fact, I don't think I even flinched. I just saw this pitiful-looking, lonely creature who lived a miserable life, and I understood he hadn't had enough human touch, or loving. I had invaded his space, and he was letting me know it. But I'll tell you, if he had wanted to take my face off, he could have done it. He was just warning me."

"About what?"

"I can't say for sure. I believe it was because he didn't trust people, and I had gotten too close.

"The woman started apologizing, but I told her not to worry, that I'd just invaded his space and he was letting me know. She looked at me like I was a weirdo, and I can tell you I wanted to smack her face. But she was twice my size, so I thought better of it.

"I told her I'd have to talk to my husband, but I was pretty sure he'd make a great companion to our dog. I said I'd call her that afternoon with my decision.

"But I'll tell you, Dad, even if David had said no, I would have still gone and gotten him and kept him until I found him a better home. I wasn't sure how he and Rocky would get along, and I wasn't sure if David would want another dog, especially one who looked as scruffy as Nick."

"But you got him," Dad says.

"Yes, the next day. I hated to wait even that long, but it was the sensible thing to do. Now here's the really good part of the story. When I went back to get him, he was standing up in his pen, looking like he knew I was coming for him."

"How did he know?"

"I can't tell you that, Dad. But when we looked at each other, I saw relief in his eyes. I know that sounds crazy, but it was almost like he was thinking, *There she is. She's coming for me.*"

Dad looks over at Nick, seeming to reappraise him.

"I had brought one of Rocky's leashes, but Nick didn't even have a collar to hook the leash to. So I just opened the pen, with that woman standing there watching me, and I said, 'Let's go, Nick.'

"He walked right out of that pen, came right up to me, and stood still, just looking up at me. I said again, 'Let's go,' and walked toward the Jeep. I didn't even say anything to that woman. I've never seen her again, and I hope I never do.

"Anyway, he was walking beside me, like he'd been with me all his life. I opened the back door of the old Jeep, and he jumped right in. From that very moment, I believed he was supposed to be with us, and I really think he did, too.

"He smelled awful, so I rolled the back windows down as soon as I pulled out of her driveway, and he stuck his head out. I'll never forget the way he closed his eyes and took in the fresh scent of the air. I was looking at him in the rearview mirror, and it was like he sensed it. His eyes met mine in the mirror, and I just felt this overwhelming connection with him. I believe he felt it, too. And what was really remarkable, Dad, is that his eyes were just full of joy. In a matter of minutes, he went from being one of the saddest dogs I've ever seen to one of the happiest. Labs have a gift for happiness, you know."

Dad looks over at Nick and nods. "He is a happy dog."

"Well, he put his head out the window again and kept it there the entire ride home. When we got home, I felt a little anxious about him meeting Rocky. Here were two male dogs, one who was the established alpha, the other coming into his territory. Plus, Nick wasn't neutered at the time, so I was concerned he would be aggressive. Believe me, I'd already had a horrible vision of the two of them tearing into each other, but I chose to believe they would get along.

"When I got out of the car, Rocky ran up to me but stopped when he saw Nick in the Jeep. Nick was impatient to get out, but I didn't know if it was because he was going to attack Rocky, or if he wanted to meet him. But he looked friendly, and so did Rocky."

"How could you tell?"

"Because Rocky's tail started to wag, and so did Nick's."

I stop to catch myself before I start sniffling at the happy memory of that moment.

"What happened?"

"I took a deep breath, said a little prayer, and let Nick out of the Jeep. At first there was kind of a standoff, but I just decided to act like it was the most natural thing in the world for Nick to be there. I petted Rocky, then petted Nick, said a few words, and the next thing I knew, they were sniffing each other's butts."

Dad laughs.

"Then Rocky picked up one of his toys and tossed it at Nick's feet. Nick seemed confused at first, but then he picked it up and ran off. Rocky ran after him, and they began playing tug-of-war with it. I remember being so happy that they fit together. Nick had found his home, and Rocky had found a playmate."

Dad doesn't say anything for a long moment. Then he looks over at Nick, cocks a shaky finger at him and says, "You lucky dog."

Nick gets up and comes over to Dad, then puts his head in Dad's lap—something he's never done before.

I'd say we're all lucky.

# 35

Both Dad's and Nick's health hold, and we're all looking forward to the arrival of our family for Thanksgiving. Not only are my nieces Laura and Sarah coming, but so are their parents—my sister Kathy and her husband Tom.

And joy of joys, so is my other sister, Cindy. She's living a fulfilled life in Washington State as the director of a public relations firm that promotes the concept of "green" on behalf of solar energy industries, wind farms, and companies that collect, clean and distribute water. Her long-time boyfriend Jay won't be coming with her, and we're sorry that's the case. We were hoping her son Daniel would accompany her instead, but he had to fly to China for business. It's too bad, because David and I like him very much, and Dad hasn't seen him in at least two years.

We're just happy everyone else is making the effort to come. I'm looking forward to seeing everyone, although Kathy and Tom can be challenging. Cindy, on the other hand, is a gentle soul who can calm the rough waters that tend to swell when Kathy and Tom are in the mix.

It isn't as if they aren't good people. They just have a tendency to rub both David and me the wrong way with their passive-aggressive barbs, uninformed opinions, and unwelcome suggestions—which often seem more like criticisms.

Their daughters, on the other hand, are delightful young women. They're educated, well-traveled, and employed in jobs they love. Neither is married, but they're still young and more interested in pursuing their careers. I adore them.

So does Dad. He loves his family with a wide-open heart, and that heart is near bursting in anticipation of having them with him again.

Today David has gone to the airport to pick them up. Flights were coordinated to arrive within hours of each other, and I'm glad the big Tahoe has plenty of seating, plus room for luggage. Dad keeps asking me how much longer before they get here. I don't pacify him with, "Soon," but rather tell him it will be a few more hours. The Charlotte airport is two hours away, and the drive, along with the wait for staggered arrivals, means David will be gone for at least eight hours.

The days are shorter, and darkness is upon us when I see the Tahoe's headlights coming down the lane. I've been watching for them so I can get Dad down to the garage in time to greet them when they pull in.

David drives in, and the gals tumble out like a small army of ants, all of them descending on Dad with loving pincers, hungry to hug him.

David moves much more slowly in getting out of the Tahoe, and I burst out laughing when I see his hair has telltale signs of having been raked with nervous fingers. He looks shell-shocked, and I can only imagine what he's had to listen to in the close confines of the vehicle over the last two hours.

The volume of their excited voices is amped so high that Nick, who's waiting in vain to be acknowledged, trots into Dad's apartment to escape it.

"Let me stand up, let me stand up," Dad says, trying to rise against the seat belt on his wheelchair. I unfasten it and lock the chair in place, then watch in amazement as he begins to push up from the seat, leveraging his weight on the arms of the wheelchair. He's determined to give and receive proper hugs.

Cindy and I have exchanged hugs and are now on either side of Dad, gently supporting his back, giving him a little assistance as he rises, until he's taken from us and enfolded into the warm holds of my nieces and their mother.

As David and Tom unload the luggage, we women get Dad resettled in his wheelchair and aim it toward his apartment so we can gather together to fully embrace the blessing that is family.

After having our chicken-surprise dinner—an untried recipe at that—we women take Dad to his apartment. David and Tom are wordlessly delegated the job of cleanup. Nick stays upstairs with the guys, and I can understand why. Our happy voices that dissolved into laughter time and again over dinner, rising in volume as two bottles of wine were emptied, convinced him it was the only safe and sane thing to do.

An hour later I give my sisters brief but thorough instructions about what they need to do to get Dad ready for bed. I'm happy to relinquish that responsibility and spend time with my nieces. We head upstairs to the room they will share. They unpack as we talk, and about a half hour later, Kathy and Cindy join us. They're both so pretty, but right now they look downright haggard. I hold in my smug smile. It's good for them to get a taste of what goes into getting Dad ready for bed. Admittedly, they've done this on top of a long day of travel, so their deep fatigue is understandable.

Kathy plops down in a chair, and Cindy throws herself back on one of the twin beds and says, "I need another glass of wine." Laura and Sarah and I have already had a glass, but there is still enough in the bottle for a generous pour for my sis.

"I'll go get another bottle of wine," Sarah volunteers. Yeah, that's the ticket, let's all get tipsy and spill our souls. I can see the evening unfolding before us . . . and I smile.

Marcy has come in for a few hours this morning to help with Dad before going home to prepare the Thanksgiving meal for her family. Everyone likes her well enough not to take offense when she says, in her spectacularly frank fashion, "You ladies need to get here more often. Rachel here's been killin' herself taking care of your dad. And it don't hurt your dad none to see ya, neither. He's in a fine frame of mind this morning, happier than I've ever seen him."

They're a bit shocked at being talked to like this, and therefore momentarily speechless, which gives Marcy a chance to hit them between the eyes with one last barb. "And he ain't gonna live all that much longer, so ya gotta make peace with yourselves before it's too late."

Now I'm the one who's shocked, but mostly because the phrase "ain't gonna live all that much longer" has taken root. Cindy says, "The family's lucky to have you, Marcy. You're right. Rachel's been doing everything and we haven't even been here to visit, let alone help. Thank you for your honesty." Always the diplomat.

Kathy, Laura and Sarah vocalize their agreement, and the next thing you know, we are all in a group hug, with Marcy sandwiched in the middle.

We say our goodbyes, wishing her a Happy Thanksgiving, and head upstairs with Dad to have a quick continental breakfast before we begin preparing the Thanksgiving meal.

We're all tired and hungover, and after Marcy's admonishments, we're subdued during breakfast. But the atmosphere becomes festive and lively as we five women start working together. We're all speaking loudly so we can be heard over each other. Unlike me, my sisters are capable in the kitchen and have everything under control, so if I play my cards right, I'll only have to deal with garnishes and drinks.

Laura and Sarah are setting the table, going back and forth to the china room to root out all they need to make it festive. Their chatty questions and suggestions, along with my sisters' friendly disagreements that often turn into laughter, have kept Dad, David, and Tom out of the kitchen. Even Nick, who knows many hands flying around can often produce tasty tidbits, has left us to join the males. They're watching the pre-game shows, and I wonder how they can even hear the TV over our loud voices.

The volume rises to an "11" when Cousin Debra walks into the kitchen. I hadn't even heard her knock, but apparently David had. Her husband Charles, trailing behind her, staggers back from the cacophony of happy squeals that greet Debra. Whatever Debra has in the food-warming bag she's holding is in peril of being knocked out of her hands, so I hurry to rescue it and set it on the counter.

Charles moves into the mix, holding a bottle of wine in one hand and returning hugs with his free arm. Behind his wire-rim glasses his eyes are large and round with a hint of shocked desperation. He seeks out David in the living room, almost as if he's looking for a touchstone of testosterone to counter the decidedly female dominance in the kitchen.

Tom stands rooted in his spot and raises a hand in greeting, keeping his distance from the teeming throng. David is coming our way, pushing Dad's wheelchair, with Nick on his heels. Another round of hugging and kissing ensues. Kathy, Cindy, Laura and Sarah have been effusively loving on Dad all morning, as if they can't get enough of him. Charles extracts a quick handshake from Dad before getting bumped from the circle.

Dad is beginning to show wear from all the demonstrations of affection. His hair is tousled and his sweater is askew. Six different colors of lipstick pockmark his face and the top of his head in a dozen places. He's handling it well, even cheerfully, but he startles when Kathy, our family's loud and effervescent cheerleader of yore, bends down and cries, very close to his ear, "Debra's here!" in a voice that has enough robustness behind it to push David, Charles, and Nick out of the kitchen and into the recessed safety of the living room.

<hr />

The third bottle of wine bites the dust as we wind down our eating. I splurged on a case of decent mixed wines, and I must admit there is definitely a difference between good bottled wine and box wine.

The turkey has been slain for a second time, and the table, which looked so elegant just an hour before, is strewn with bits of food and blots of stains. Dad added color when he set his wine glass on the rim of his plate instead of on the table, and it toppled over. Fortunately, his wine glass was plastic; but, not so fortunately, my best tablecloth is ruined.

I find it oddly comforting that I couldn't care less. A dish towel had sopped up the worst of it, and the dinner din had resumed with barely a blip.

With nine pairs of legs occupying so much space, there is no room for Nick under the table, so he keeps to the edge of the rug, quietly mincing about, sorting out which hands are most generous.

After two rounds, he stops by Dad's chair and sits down. Dad's hand reaches over and rests on top of Nick's head. Nick doesn't move, though I see him register the touch. His eyes close, and he lets out a soft, happy puff of breath. Despite their growing amount of time spent together, it's the first time Dad has shown physical affection for the big boy.

No one else notices, but there's the equivalent of a seismic shift under my feet at this development. When Dad removes his hand, he reaches for the soggy remains of a roll but doesn't drop it on the floor. Instead, he holds it between his thumb and forefinger with atypical agility and waits for Nick to take it from him.

Nick's tongue slips out and gently gathers it in. It's the most delicately I've ever seen Nick treat food, and I realize his delicacy is rendered on Dad's behalf.

Tears sting my eyes, and I'm sorry David didn't witness the touching transference of so much more than food. It would have been nice to have that shared moment to start off each subsequent telling of the time when total trust between two reticent beings was finally, irrevocably, established.

# 36

The first snowfall of the season has Dad mesmerized. He's been staring at it for half an hour. I've stayed quiet and let him enjoy it.

Though November was cold, no snow fell, but now, two weeks from Christmas, we're being treated to a blanketing of white enchantment that is quickly covering everything in sight.

We've rearranged the furniture to accommodate the Christmas tree. Dad is on the sofa, facing the large floor-to-ceiling windows offering an unobstructed view of the snow-topped mountain peaks. Since the sofa is now turned away from the TV, we've been watching less of it and listening to Christmas music. Dad's very favorite Christmas song is "A Christmas Prayer," by Marty Robbins. He's delighted to learn that I can, with the push of a button, play that song any time he wants to hear it. Which is a lot.

I'm sitting on the other end of the sofa, reading a book, and Nick lies between Dad and me. David is in the kitchen chopping vegetables for a soup he's putting together for our dinner. Though he's staying busy with his new job, he's finding reasons to stay home with us more often, rather than making the trip to the office the developers provided in one of their buildings.

Things are slowing down with the infrastructure phase of the development now that the earth is frozen. From what he tells me, the hardest and most important part of the work has been done, and things should quickly move to completion once spring arrives.

He's lining up subcontractors for the other jobs that will be required, and he's happy to be using his real estate knowledge and negotiating skills to move the project forward. What makes him happiest is the promise that the project will create much-needed jobs in the area.

Christmas carols playing, Dad watching the snow come down, Nick lying in between me and Dad, my husband cooking an aromatic dinner . . . I'm feeling mighty blessed. On top of that, we're looking forward to going to Debra and Charles's home for Christmas.

Dad dozes off—his favorite pastime on days like this. Come to think of it, he's been dozing a lot more, and for longer periods. I think back to when I first noticed this, and recall it was the week after Thanksgiving. I put it down to exhaustion from the hectic activities of that long holiday weekend. But it's been more than two weeks now, and he should have recovered.

*Wait, wait, wait.* Why do I always expect him to recover to a previous state of energy and health? He's on the decline—constantly and unabatedly, every single day. Why do I find it so hard to reconcile myself to that reality?

After the long, hard days and nights of taking care of Mother for the last six months of her life, I felt I had aged a few years, and wondered if I'd ever return to the place I was before. Yet I did. It took a while, but I got caught up on my rest at some point. I'm thinking Dad should be doing the same.

I look at the gentle rise and fall of his chest and have a desire to reach out and grab onto every breath he exhales and stuff it back into him for recycling, so that his life is prolonged. Every breath that escapes is one less breath he will draw in the future. That's true for all of us, but it is more meaningful for an old person with serious afflictions.

In the meantime, Nick has found further relief for his arthritic hip with the Adequan injections I'm now giving him. It's only been six months since he first showed symptoms of pain and started on the glucosamine. Poor Nick has been on quite a journey to find relief—from glucosamine to Rimadyl to Tramadol, and now Adequan. Tramadol in itself just wasn't enough to control his pain, since it's not an anti-inflammatory. But with the addition of Adequan, which stimulates cartilage repair processes and diminishes joint damage while reducing the pain caused by osteoarthritis, we seem to have found the magic combination.

When I asked Dr. Froman why she didn't prescribe it earlier, she told me Adequan was the last effective treatment for what Nick has. She wanted to give the others a try, because once we began the Adequan injections, there was no further treatment.

She gave him the first two injections, but now I'm giving them to him. It saves time and money, and Dr. Froman was kind enough to give me a prescription for the Adequan and a lesson in giving the intramuscular injection.

I've given Nick two injections this week, for a total of four now, and I can already see an encouraging change in his comfort level. I've also replaced his beds with new and better-quality memory foam beds. The main one in the kitchen even has a heating pad built in. Although Dr. Froman told me it would take at least a month to see improvement with the Adequan, I think all of these things have helped already. He's definitely moving around with more ease.

But he's sleeping more these days also. I think about what I've learned in researching symptoms and treatments: A dog who sleeps and *doesn't* move around and eat is very sick. A dog who sleeps a lot and still eats and seems social is aging.

That pretty much describes both my dog and my dad.

# 37

Dad has slept this entire trip to Debra and Charles's home. He's been really lethargic ever since breakfast. He took his most important pills, and ate his oatmeal with banana, but he was more sluggish than usual as he opened his mouth for feeding.

A little later he opened one of his presents, which seemed to take forever, and seemed pleased with yet another sweater. In the short time it took for me to turn around and retrieve another gift from under the tree for him to open, he had closed his eyes and was unresponsive to my gentle prodding to wake up.

Since Marcy has the day off, it was up to David and me to get him ready for this trip, and it sure wasn't easy. Despite his weight loss, which hasn't been reversed, Dad still weighs about a hundred and sixty-five, and when he goes limp, he's dead weight. Even with the two of us working together, it was a harder chore than usual. By the time we got him bathed and dressed, we were both short of breath. We left him lying fully clothed on his bed while we went upstairs to get ready ourselves.

It took all of our combined strength to hoist him from the bed into his wheelchair. Now I'm wondering why we didn't call Debra and let her know the situation and just beg off. I keep thinking he'll come around, but we're halfway there, and that's looking less likely by the mile.

I sure hope he's not coming down with another UTI; but something is causing him to be this lackluster, and I need to get to the bottom of it.

This is such a bad week for any possible health problems because Dr. Baird's office hours are shorter between Christmas and New Year.

David is driving, and I'm on the back-bench seat, where I've been observing Dad's flopping head.

"David, please pull over somewhere. I want to put Dad's neck pillow on him, or he's going to have a sore neck." I don't know why I didn't do this before we started out. Sometimes I let my worries drown out lucid thoughts. I need to step up my game.

Even though there's a light covering of snow on the ground, the roads are clear and the tires are new, making it safe for David to pull over. With his help, I lift Dad's head and position the pillow around his neck. Now, no matter which way his head tilts, his neck muscles will be supported.

"He sure is out of it today," David comments as he pulls back onto the highway.

"Yes, and I'm getting worried about him. I just hope he wakes up and is able to enjoy himself."

David chuckles. "He'll be upset if he wakes up only in time for dessert and realizes he's missed Debra's honey baked ham and sweet potato casserole."

I know David's just having fun, but I'm too troubled about just how sluggish Dad is to appreciate it. Even if he wakes up, it's going to be tough to get food and pills into him. I start to get a headache at the thought of what all of that can mean, and my back is hurting like crazy from the heavy lifting this morning. I tumble into a foul mood.

I try to keep the petulance out of my voice as I call Debra and ask her to put on a pot of coffee, explaining that the trip has put him to sleep, and I can't keep him awake. What else am I going to say? That he went practically comatose this morning, but we decided to drag him across the mountains anyway?

Just as we're turning into Debra's driveway, Dad mumbles, "Where are we?" I'm excited to think he has come around, but by the time Debra, Charles, and their son Brad come out to greet us, Dad's head is dipping in sleepy torpor again.

David rolls him down the van's ramp onto their driveway. Debra, Charles and Brad hail Dad with hearty Merry Christmas greetings, accompanied by hugs, pats, and kisses—but he doesn't move so much as an eyelash.

We all contemplate Dad for a moment, and a sense of dismay descends on our group until I say, "Let's get him inside and get some coffee into him." The hint of optimism in my voice must be motivational, because everyone starts moving.

Debra assures me in a confident voice that she has a fresh pot at the ready, and further assures me it will help. I love my cousin's positivity. She sets off at a brisk pace to get inside the house, no doubt to ready a cup of coffee for the medicinal purposes we've assigned to it. As we all come to a rolling stop inside the foyer, Debra comes out of the kitchen with a plastic coffee mug with a sippy top. Smart.

Having done their duty to get Dad hauled up the outside steps and safely inside, the guys relax, shake hands and slap each other's backs. They unanimously agree a glass of Scotch would hit the spot, and Brad catches David up on football scores as they round the corner, their voices fading away from us. They're leaving the revival to Debra and me.

"What's wrong with him today?" She looks seriously worried, and rightfully so. She extends her arm and holds the sippy mug under his nose, hoping the stimulating aroma will bring him around.

There is still no response from Dad as I confess, "I don't know, but he's been like this since this morning after breakfast. It was tough to get him ready."

"Do you think he has another UTI?" From taking care of her mother, she knows this kind of lethargy is one of the symptoms. Her mother was able to vocalize the discomfort, whereas Dad, like so many patients with dementia, is not.

"That's what I'm worried about."

Debra sets the cup on a table in the foyer while I remove the neck pillow. We struggle with Dad's stiffened limbs to get him out of his heavy jacket, and then I reposition the pillow. The bottom of his face has more or less disappeared into it and he seems to descend into an even deeper slumber.

Debra gently unfurls his fisted right hand and wraps each finger around the coffee cup. It has a serious tilt to it and looks precarious to me, but it's plastic and has the spill-proof top, so it shouldn't cause any damage if he drops it. I have to wonder why she'd put it into his hand when the bottom half of his face, including his mouth, is buried in the neck pillow. I see no coffee-drinking action forthcoming. But hey, it's there if he wakes up and decides he wants a sip of revitalizing coffee.

We study him for an anxious moment, then Debra tries the old magic-kiss cure. She takes his face in both of her hands and raises his head. She plants a big kiss on the top of his head and says, "Merry Christmas, Uncle Joe!" She has used her best and most robust holiday-cheer voice. However, when a plausible amount of allowed time elapses without a response—not even a crack of the eyelids—she looks at me and says, "Oh, boy."

Indeed.

Christmas dinner happens around Dad. He's at the head of the table, with Debra and me on either side of him, trying to wake him and encourage him with enticing smells. We go so far as to hold forks and spoons laden with different foods under his nose, using food as an equivalent to smelling salts in hopes of reviving him. At one point he moans, but we don't know if it's with appreciation or in aggravation, so we abandon our efforts.

Charles suggests we sing Christmas carols, reminding us that Dad loves them and loves to sing along with them. We all hail the idea, so he changes out the classical renditions of Christmas carols currently playing and puts on a lively CD of various artists.

We all sing along with gusto. I'm particularly good at singing along with Brenda Lee when she's belting out, "Rockin' Around the Christmas Tree." No one can put more emphasis on the word "deck" than I can when Brenda gets to the line, **Deck** *the halls with boughs of holly!* I give it my best today, in a voice that's been known to startle people to the point of dropping things or jumping a half-foot in place.

Too bad Christmas music only comes around once a year.

I direct my song at Dad with real intent. His eyes pop open, but they are bleary and disengaged until they land on Charles. Then they focus and widen, and we all watch with anticipation, thinking *this is it, he's coming around.* But he only gives Charles an oddly accusatory look, then nods off again.

Mild-mannered Charles looks confused, and a little injured. "What did I do?" he asks us.

Brad's girlfriend Paula, who arrived a few minutes after we did, shyly suggests, "Maybe the music is too loud?"

Charles looks like any wrongfully accused man at a holiday table would look, but he doesn't reply.

Just then, in a startling moment that catches us off-guard, Dad emits a loud grunt and his eyes pop open again. With his head still resting to the side on his pillow, he takes a slow-roving inventory of his surroundings. He straightens his head and looks directly at Charles. We all watch as he raises his arm in slow motion. His gaze doesn't falter as he points an unsteady finger at Charles, and says in a tone of accusatory mirth, "You're an *instigator,* you know that?"

We all burst into laughter, and Dad smiles his devilish smile, then states he's hungry. It's like a switch has turned on, activating his mind and his body. He becomes animated and takes pleasure in each and every bite of food Debra and I offer.

As I watch him, I think about how, over the years, we've received invitations to parties with a little maxim which said: NO GIFTS, PLEASE. YOUR PRESENCE IS OUR PRESENT.

Until now, I always thought that was kind of hokey, even if it was well intentioned. But it's perfectly applicable to this day of celebration.

Dad's presence is the best Christmas present I'll receive this year.

# 38

Dad continued to be present and aware during the week following Christmas, though he was quiet and slept more than usual. Then, the day before yesterday, he went back into a sleepy funk.

On this third morning of the New Year 2011, a six-inch snowfall has blanketed our world in a whiteness so complete it distorts my perception.

Even though I'm concerned about Dad, I stop to appreciate the beauty before me. Yes, it's beautiful, but it's inconvenient today because I was able to get Dr. Carter's nurse practitioner to work Dad in at eleven o'clock this morning. I want the neurologist's opinion because Dad's sluggishness and sleepiness, along with his seeming reluctance to talk, have me more than a little concerned.

I want Dr. Carter to do an evaluation and perhaps determine if these periods where he sleeps for hours or days at a time are symptoms of the progression of dementia. I've researched it online, and it might be related, or it might not. There are certain symptoms that are universal with Alzheimer's, but each patient does have different behaviors since they can be related to environmental factors. But nothing about the environment in our house has changed, so I'm leaning toward its being something physical. But what do I know? Every time I think I have a handle on what's happening to Dad, something changes. Like Dad's reluctance to talk—that's different.

But there's no way I can take Dad to his appointment in this snowy weather. Even if the roads are safe for driving, unloading him from the van and pushing his wheelchair across the parking lot and into the doctor's office will subject him to the cold and snow for too long a time. Dad doesn't need pneumonia on top of everything else.

Because I saw not just normal sleepiness, but the same total non-responsiveness we'd dealt with on Christmas Day, I'd called Dr. Carter's answering service on Saturday and asked for a call back from him. His nurse practitioner, Mimi, called me instead. I'd described Dad's condition, and after asking a few questions she'd told me he was probably okay, but if I was really worried, I should take him to the emergency room. I told her I would if things got worse.

He'd slept all the rest of that day, and all day yesterday, too. Though I was in a constant state of worry, nothing seemed to be hurting him, and his vitals remained normal, so I'd refrained all weekend from taking him to the ER.

Mimi had made today's appointment during that call, and I told her I would call first thing this morning to cancel if he was admitted. That event was averted because there didn't seem to be anything that was causing Dad pain or distress. But there was surely something going on, even if it weren't dire enough to qualify as an emergency.

David comes up behind me with a cup of coffee. "Here, babe."

I turn to accept the coffee and give him a quick kiss. I don't have to vocalize my concerns; he knows them.

"If Joe takes a bad turn, we'll call an ambulance."

David knows me well enough to know what I'm thinking. "Don't beat yourself up for not taking him to the emergency room." He puts a reassuring arm around my waist. "You checked his vitals, and everything was normal. They would have done the same thing there and sent him home."

I sigh, appreciating his reasoning but not letting myself off the hook. "I know, but what if he gets even worse because I don't have him where he can get immediate treatment if things do turn bad?"

"You checked his vitals at least a half dozen times yesterday and last night. I'm sure they'll be fine this morning, too. He's just in the same place he was on Christmas Day, and he came out of that."

"Yes, but that was for less than a full day. He's been sleeping around the clock for two days now. *And*, he's not talking."

"I can't argue with that, but as I said, we can always call an ambulance if he gets worse. Now let's go down and check on him."

"In a minute," I tell him. It's early, only six A.M. and still dark, but my concern for Dad caused me a restless night of waking up off and on. Twice I went to check on him, but his breathing was normal and he wasn't in distress.

When I awoke at five forty-five, I knew I wouldn't go back to sleep, so I rolled over to hug David and ask him to get up with me. He got out of bed and put on a pot of coffee, while I made my way to the bathroom and then toward the stairs. But I'd gotten waylaid by the beautiful snow, and so here I stand, in a kind of stupor, drinking coffee and making no move to go down to Dad's room.

Normally Dad doesn't wake up until around seven, when Marcy arrives. It's rather remarkable he sleeps through the night, when many Alzheimer's patients are awake and restless. I always let him sleep until Marcy gets here, knowing she will do the heavy lifting to get him going for the day.

With his being so out of it, he hasn't been able to eat or take his meds for the past two days, and that worries me the most. Yesterday, David and I had propped him up and brought him around enough to get some chicken broth and a cup of hot tea with sugar and lemon into him. He wasn't interested in water, but getting any liquid into him was important. His blood sugar spiked with the sugared tea, so I'd had to increase his dose of insulin. It's so difficult to balance the effects of my decisions.

Marcy will be back today, and we can sure use her help. She'd taken Christmas Day and the day after off, as well as New Year's Day. When she left around one o'clock on Friday, New Year's Eve, Dad had been his usual self, so she isn't aware of his condition. I wonder if she'll have any thoughts or suggestions, based on her experiences with her grandmother.

"Okay, I'm ready." As we start down the stairs together, the phone rings. It's Marcy.

"Miss Rachel, I'm not gonna be able to get down my driveway to get there today."

I almost moan aloud, but catch myself. I turn to David and put my hand over the handset and whisper, "Marcy's not coming."

His look is more panicked than pissed, and I know just how he feels. Another difficult day for the two of us in taking care of Dad by ourselves.

I might have to call an ambulance for *us*.

"I understand, Marcy. This is a heavy snowfall."

"I shoulda parked at the bottom of the driveway, then I could of got there. Maybe if the sun comes out and burns some of it off, I can get down my driveway."

"I appreciate that, but don't put yourself in any danger." I would hate for her to take any chances, even if it would make our day worlds better.

"How's he doing?"

"Not so good. He's been very sleepy over the last two days." Now she's going to feel even worse about not coming, so I quickly change the tone of the conversation. "I'm sure he'll be fine. How was your New Year's?"

"I had a date."

Hmmm, she hadn't told me that before she left on Friday. "Was it a good New Year's Eve for you, then?" I can't believe I'm having this banal conversation, but I'm happy she had a date. She's been lonely and hoping to meet someone.

"It was, and I think I'm gonna be seeing him again."

"That's so nice to hear, Marcy." David is looking at me as if I've lost my mind. I'm chatting about Marcy's social life when Dad's care looms before us.

"Okay, Marcy, I'm going to go. David and I were just about to check on Dad."

"I'm sorry I can't help ya today unless the sun comes out this morning and burns this off. Then I'll call ya."

"Thanks, Marcy. We'll manage until you get here." No need to make her feel bad for something she can't help.

"I'll at least get my car down to the bottom of the hill so I can get there tomorrow. I was just caught by surprise with all this snow."

"You and me both. Take care."

I hang up and look at David and shrug my shoulders.

"Where's Nick?" I ask, realizing he hasn't found us to say good morning. Since he's started sleeping in Dad's room, we keep the door at the top of the stairs open so he can go back and forth.

"Probably in with Joe. Let's go see."

Dad's still sleeping, no surprise there; but the real surprise is that Nick is on Dad's bed, lying right next to him. He must have come down after I checked on Dad the second time. It's strange to see him stretched out beside Dad, instead of curled up, which is how he sleeps on his own bed. It looks mighty crowded in that twin-sized bed, with Dad smooshed against the wall and Nick's body next to his.

Nick gives us a guilty look, but he doesn't get down from the bed to greet us.

"Well, what do you think of that?" David asks, smiling.

"I'm not so sure it's the best thing for Dad, but it doesn't seem to affect his ability to sleep."

*But then that's a worry in itself, isn't it?*

Nick looks at us, waiting for his cue about what to do next. Neither of us has the heart to fuss at him. In fact, we're glad he's here with Dad. But on the bed with him? This is a first, and David and I are taking time to absorb it.

Dad moans.

"Oh, good, he's still alive!" David teases.

I laugh and elbow him in the stomach. "Yeah, but is he *live-lee?*"

Now Nick jumps down from the bed, almost as if he's absconding before Dad realizes he's there.

He trots past us, not even slowing for some love-love, so I know he has a full bladder and is heading toward his doggie door.

Wait until he tries to push through it and can't because of the snow, which is undoubtedly piled up against it. He'll be perplexed, just as he is every time a large snowfall blocks either of his doggie doors.

"David, will you go open the garage door for Nick?"

"Sure." He heads into the garage. I hear him call Nick's name and tell him he won't be able to use his doggie door. The garage door goes up, and then I hear a loud, "Whoa!" I close the apartment door to keep out the cold air, and then walk toward Dad's bed. His eyes are open now, and he smiles when he sees me approaching. My heart melts.

"Hi, Sugar." I'm so very glad to hear him say those sweet words to me.

"Good morning, Dad. I love you." I bend over to push his soft hair off his forehead and give him a kiss on his warm cheek. "How are you feeling this morning?"

Dad thinks about it, then declares, "Rested."

"Well, that's good. You've been sleeping a lot over the last two days. Do you feel okay?"

He takes time to consider this question, too. "I have go bathroom."

*Have go bathroom?*

"All right, then, let's get you up and into the bathroom." Hallelujah! He's been incontinent in his sleep over the last two days, and David and I have had to change his diapers in bed. It's a hard chore because he has to be cleaned and dried thoroughly between changes. We've checked him every few hours, except through the night, when we put an extra pad inside the diaper for additional absorbency.

It's so important Dad doesn't stay so wet that his skin starts to break down. We've also turned him each time, repositioning him, and rearranging pillows between his knees and against his back for comfort so he doesn't get bedsores.

I've gotten him in position to transfer to his wheelchair. As long as he's able, I vow to myself, I'll welcome his wanting to use the toilet. It's good that he does because any movement is good, plus voiding his bladder in the toilet keeps the acidic moisture away from his skin.

This is another shift in my awareness. These shifts come at the most unexpected times, but when you are caring for someone you love, someone who is dependent on you for his entire well-being, you embrace the new mindfulness.

Before I can move Dad into his wheelchair, I feel the cold air flow through as David comes back in. He sees Dad is wide awake, and smiles. "Morning, Joe! How are you doing this morning, buddy?"

"Good," Dad answers with a little smile of his own. "But I have go bathroom."

David flicks me a quizzical look, but then says, "Yes, sir, let's go then." His voice conveys kindness and respect, as always.

As we move Dad into his wheelchair, I ask David about Nick's reaction to the snow.

"Like always, a little taken aback, but then he hustled out to do his business. I waited a minute after to see if he wanted to come back in, but he took off up the hill."

"Is the doggie door blocked?"

"Yeah, I'll get it cleared up a little later." I realize he didn't take the time to do it now because he knew I needed help with Dad.

"Good, but let's not leave him out there too long. Do you know if we have towels by the door?"

"There are a couple there." He takes control of Dad's wheelchair. "Let's get you into the bathroom, Joe, and then I'll go let Nick back in. He'll get chilled fast in this snow."

"It snowed? It doesn't snow in Florida." Dad thinks he's in Florida?

"It snowed big time here in North Carolina." I say. "We'll open the shades so you can see it when we come back."

As we wheel him into the bathroom, Dad asks, "Where's Nick?"

David and I look at each other, a little perplexed, because Dad just heard David say Nick is outside. But David doesn't let much time elapse before saying, "Just running the snowy hills. He's okay."

After Dad is situated, David tells me, "I'll check the bed and then go let Nick back in." I know he's going to strip the bed and put the sheets in the washing machine. That will give me a few minutes alone with Dad to try to find out if he knew Nick had shared his bed.

"How'd you sleep, Dad? Did you wake up during the night?"

"We went for a walk," he answers.

I don't contradict him. "Where did you go?" I ask, keeping my voice nonchalant.

"Your momma and I went for a walk on the beach." Ah, maybe that's why he thought he was in Florida. When I don't answer right away, he repeats it, with emphasis, then adds, "She was right there next to me. Where is she now?"

"She's not here, Dad. I know she was with you last night, but that's because you two met at the beach. She's back in heaven this morning."

Dad's eyes close, and I grasp that his being with Mother was, in some way, a factor in bringing him back around this morning. I wonder if he thinks Nick's warm body was Mother's body. This is warped thinking, but I believe I always have to try to make sense out of these things. I long to understand his thought processes, even when there's no reality or rationale involved.

"Did she stay with you last night after you walked on the beach?"

"She stayed all night. Why did she leave?"

How am I supposed to answer that? What tale am I supposed to spin? What truth am I obligated to share? I sometimes feel so lost, so inept, in answering such questions.

"Because she came down from heaven to be with you. She misses you. But she had to go back this morning." It's the best I can do.

"I want to go with her."

My heart hurts. "You will, Dad. Just not yet. But you'll be with her again, and in the meantime, she'll continue to visit you."

Somehow I believe my words have a ring of truth to them, and I have to wonder if loved ones do indeed come down from heaven or wherever and make their presence felt. It makes as much sense as anything else in this mysterious world.

"I miss her." Dad lowers his head and takes a shallow, shuddering breath.

"I know. I miss her, too."

I give him a quiet moment to finish his business and gather himself. By then, David is back.

"Joe, do you want to go back to bed?" David asks him.

"No, I'm good and rested," Dad answers. He grins at David and asks, "What's for breakfast?"

This day has started out so much better than I imagined it would. Dad would get strong again. He's just been going through a stage of being extra tired.

I so want to believe it.

# 39

While David is starting breakfast, I do a quick check of Dad's vitals, which are all within the normal range. As I freshen him up a bit, the delicious aromas of coffee and bacon beckon us. Dad comments on how good it smells.

"Which smells better to you, Dad, the coffee or the bacon?"

"Coffee. Really use cub."

What's with the abridged talk? And did he say *cub* instead of *cup*? Then it hits me. Alzheimer's patients become less articulate as they move into later stages. My mind sifts through the files of all I've learned over the years. Could Dad's sleeping so much be a transitioning into a later stage of the disease? Are his mind and body going through a shift that will lead to nonsensical speech and babbling, or worse, not speaking at all?

I'm left breathless as the punch of that possibility hits me.

Bouncing information and ideas around my brain at warp speed, I'm at a loss for answers and more certain than ever I have to get him to the neurologist today, whatever it takes. David can go with us. It's time for some answers, so I'll ask Dr. Carter to order more in-depth testing. I need to know what to expect if I'm going to keep up with the oncoming changes and the level of care he'll be needing. I feel sick to my stomach.

As I'm pushing Dad into the elevator, he asks, "Where's Nick?"

"I don't know, Dad. I think I heard David let him back in a little while ago. My guess is he's in the kitchen, hoping to get some of that bacon."

"He's waiting me gib it him," Dad chuckles.

More abridged talk. Ignoring it, I say, "Yes, and I know you will."

When we enter the kitchen, we see Nick standing by the stove where a plate of bacon is sitting on the warming burner. He's very attentive, but when he sees Dad, he comes over and sits down in front of him, waiting for acknowledgment. Dad extends his arm until his hand reaches Nick's head. His fingers contract and expand, contract and expand, achingly slow. He's doing his best to scratch Nick's head.

It's seven o'clock, so I have two hours to decide whether or not to call the doctor's office to cancel Dad's appointment. I desperately want Dad to get checked today, but it's still snowing and the sun hasn't come out. Maybe I can get them to move the appointment to a later time, when I know the roads have been cleared. I'll call Tony, the young man we always hire to clear our driveway, to see if he can get here this morning. I have to get Dad to the doctor. I just *have to.*

"Scrambling some eggs now," David says as he pours the yellow liquid into the hot skillet. Dad continues to rub Nick's head and asks him how he's doing today.

Nick puts his head in Dad's lap and looks up into his face. The two look at each other for a long moment while some secretive communication takes place. Dad gives a short nod, at which point Nick turns and trots back over to the stove. How odd that Nick didn't even acknowledge me. But I don't take offense. In fact, it gives me an opportunity to reinforce their connection.

"Wow, Dad, he completely ignored me. Seems he just wants you."

"He's my buddy." There is pride and pleasure in his voice.

"He sure is. What do you think about him sleeping in your apartment every night now?"

"He does?"

"Well, most of the time. You didn't notice?"

"No. He's real quiet."

"You've been quiet these last couple of days, too, Dad. You slept a lot. Do you remember feeling sick or anything?"

I have Dad pushed up against the table now and am putting a bib around his neck.

He seems perplexed by the question, and then gets distracted when Nick appears at his side.

"Where's the bacon, David?" Dad doesn't want to keep Nick waiting. I've been listening closely to his words. He's speaking normally again.

"Coming up right now, Joe." David passes the plate of bacon across the divider to me. He grabs the platter of scrambled eggs and a breadbasket of toast, then comes into the dining room.

I set the bacon in front of Dad and start counting. One thousand one, one thousand two, one thousand . . .

An entire slice of bacon has hit the rug and been devoured by Nick in less than three seconds.

Despite my worry, I'm delighted we're back to our routine and that Dad is acting just as he did before the big sleep.

He starts to toss another slice, but I ask him to wait until we people have had what we want first.

David chooses not to get involved in the exchange as he fills our plates with food.

Dad gives me a pointed look. "He's hungry, too, you know."

"Yes, he is, but like us, he has to be polite and share—right?"

Dad looks down at Nick. "Just like her momma, always so bossy."

Nick, who watched Dad's hand hover over the plate of bacon, only to be withdrawn, gives me a look that says he tends to agree.

---

David and I get Dad bathed, shaved and dressed, and put him in his chair to watch TV, as he'd asked. Nick decided to hang with Dad again, and I feel better about leaving him alone, because he's not lonely with Nick by his chair.

After loading the dishwasher and wiping down the kitchen counters, I pour another cup of coffee and check my phone for emails and messages. At nine o'clock I call Dr. Carter's office to see about moving Dad's appointment to this afternoon, but I get a recording saying that, due to the weather, the office will be closed for the day. I leave a message to please call me to reschedule. I'm relieved in one way, anxious in another.

David comes to get more coffee. "What's going on, Rachel?"

"The doctor's office is closed today. I asked them to call to reschedule."

"It's okay, babe. Joe seems fine now."

I have to agree Dad seems fine, but I'm still unsettled. I can't change a thing about where this day is going. Marcy's not coming. The doctor's office is closed. Might as well make the best of it. It's a good day for some phone time with my girlfriends.

"I'm going to run down and check on Dad, then I'm going to make some phone calls. What's on your agenda today?"

"Paperwork I need to get done before a conference call with Marcus and Andy." It turns out David gets along very well with the developers. He's assured me they are not Floridiots, but good businessmen who are treating the people involved with respect. David mentioned having a friendly talk with them about local cultural expectations, and it seems to have worked.

After checking on Dad I head up to my study and call my best-listener friend Terri. Next I call fun-friend Jessica, and she makes me laugh until my sides hurt with stories about the stray cat she took in and the different ways it intimidates Max, her German shepherd. It's almost noon when we hang up, and I'm refreshed and uplifted from my conversations.

Dad, looking perkier and in good spirits, eats most of the leftover beef stew I warmed for lunch. David and I settle him on the living room sofa. Nick comes in from doing his business, and I greet him at the doggie door with a warm towel to dry him off. He does a big shake, then goes over to the sofa to join Dad. Looks like more nap time for those fellas.

Over the next couple of hours I do laundry and mop the kitchen floor. There are other chores I could do, but I can't muster the energy. I think I have post-holiday blues, exacerbated by a bad night's sleep.

We took down the Christmas tree yesterday, tossing it over the deck railing for our neighbor's son to haul away for ten dollars. He planned to come today, but I doubt we'll see him. I miss the Christmas tree, but it's nice to have the living room restored to its usual arrangement.

Dad is watching *Family Feud*, a show that drives me crazy, but he's as alert as I've seen him in a while, so I figure it's a good time to take advantage of his acuity and get out a game. It's good to occupy him with something requiring concentration and hand dexterity.

The art ball has twenty multicolored interconnected spheres that can be scrunched, turned and twisted into an endless array of creative configurations. It's colorful and engaging, and I can sit with him and admire his creations.

Marcy calls to say she's able to get down her driveway now and asks if I want her to come. Since it's almost three o'clock and she would only be here for a couple of hours, I thank her for offering but tell her to please just come tomorrow.

I bet she's worried about another day without pay. Though I don't have to, I'll pay her for today. If not for the snow, she would have been here. How nice that there's no worry involved in the decision to pay her.

David's bonus and paychecks have put us back on our feet and restored our sense of security. We were happy to catch up on our donations to charities, but there's been no splurging. We've decided that as long as we can continue to take care of Dad and Nick, make our mortgage payment, keep the lights on, and eat three healthy meals a day, that's enough.

Enough is a blessed way to live. Anything more than enough is excess, and as I learned the very hard way, that's a perilous way to live.

Dad is getting tired of the art ball activity, but in a healthy way. Sometimes his interest wanes after only a few minutes. At other times, he can get obsessive until he hits a wall, and then he goes into an exhausted stupor. Best to stop the activity before that happens.

"How about some hot chocolate, Dad?"

"Good." He releases the ball and I retrieve it from his lap.

"Do you want anything to eat?" No response. "Dad, do you want anything to eat?"

He closes his eyes, which is a way he avoids answering questions—particularly questions that call for a decision. Perhaps he's forming a thought, but he can't articulate it. This is a common occurrence in patients with Alzheimer's. Some get angry and yell or lash out physically because of the frustration. I'm fortunate Dad just closes his eyes and doesn't even try to answer. It's his way of coping with the inability to express himself or make a decision, and I never push him.

He doesn't get angry, and I don't get exasperated. We rely on trust and love to convey all that we wish to say but can't. I wonder how long that can continue.

His eyes are still closed, but he's not sleeping. His face goes soft and doughy when he is. So I know he can hear me when I pat his hand and say, "Okay, good, I'll bring you some banana bread then." I say it as if we've decided together.

In our own way, born out of necessity, we have.

# 40

Dr. Carter's office called first thing this morning to reschedule Dad's appointment for this afternoon.

Marcy got here with no problem, though she said it was "kinda tough" getting up our driveway because it was "a little icy." Even though it has stopped snowing, the temperature has dropped and it is bitter cold. The lane and our driveway are still covered in snow, and with the lower temperatures, they are going to get even icier.

Tony wasn't able to get here yesterday to clear them but called this morning to say he would be here soon. No doubt the main roads have been cleared, but getting to them in the van may be a problem because of potential underlying ice. The van isn't four-wheel drive, and I shudder at the thought of our setting off, only to get stuck.

"Marcy," I call out as I'm coming into Dad's apartment.

"In here," she says, and I follow her voice to his bathroom. She's cleaning the tub in preparation for giving him a bath.

"Do you think we can get Dad in the Tahoe and get him to the doctor? That heavy four-wheel-drive SUV in low gear is pretty reliable under all road conditions."

"Sure, I guess so. But does he really need to go? He did good eating his breakfast this morning."

I hesitate before answering because she might have a point. "Let me go check on him." I head into his bedroom. Déjà vu. He's back to limp-necking it in his wheelchair. I wonder how she'll even be able to bathe him. In the interest of safety, I resign myself to staying and helping. But his recurring lethargy helps me make up my mind.

"He needs to go to the doctor," I tell Marcy, and explain that although he had a good day yesterday and ate his breakfast this morning, he has sunk right back into a stupor and remains there.

"That fast?" she asks. "He was fine ten minutes ago."

"Even more reason to get him to the doctor." I tell her it's good for Dr. Carter to see his state of sluggishness rather than have me describe it. I'm doing more to convince myself than her, but she's giving me her full attention, which means she sees my distress.

"Well then, don't you worry, I'll get him ready to go."

"Let's not bother bathing him, Marcy. We'll put him on the bed and give him a sponge bath. David and I bathed him yesterday, so a sponge bath today should be good enough."

I just want him to get stronger, to get better, and to return to his "old self." To that end, I also want a prescription for speech therapy. Dr. Baird had suggested I get it from Dr. Carter anyway. Plus, his six-month Medicare-eligibility for physical therapy is coming up, and I want to get a prescription so Medicare pays for Adam and Jennie for a while.

With our bank account now replete, I've been paying them to keep the sessions going. They haven't been able to see Dad over the last week and a half because the Mystic Mountain Lodge closes at the end of October, but reopens for the last two weeks in December. There are a plenty of holiday travelers looking for a posh place to enjoy a white Christmas, and part of Mystic Mountain's allure is the spa that Adam and Jennie run there.

Since the hotel has one hundred percent occupancy during those two weeks, Adam and Jennie have been booked from morning to night. Now that the holidays are behind us, I'm hopeful they'll be able to resume his three-times-a-week therapy schedule. I'm desperate to keep Dad moving, since I—and they—associate ambulation with health.

During these winter months they spend more time doing therapy with hospital and rehab patients. They're a hard-working couple, putting their special skills to good use in several ways. They weren't able to have children, though they wanted them very much. Adam once told me that having a successful business was no substitute for not having children, but they were able to devote more time and energy to growing their practice. It's grown enough to keep them busy year-round.

Adam and Jennie have been on a waiting list for an adoption for almost five years. They're both in their mid-thirties, and the last time I saw Jennie, she confided that she and Adam are worried if they don't adopt soon, they'll age out of the ideal range for adopting a baby. As she said to me, an adoption clock can be every bit as nerve-racking as a biological clock for those who want to start a family before it's too late.

On the other end of that family cycle is the biological clock that counts down to the final minutes of one's life here on Earth. Family is what teaches us about love, from the very beginning to the very end of life. I desperately want to hold on to the earthly bond of love that is my dad. He may need me, but I need him more.

I'll fight for every moment I can have with him. It's self-serving of me, I know, but it's part of the love gene I inherited, and I won't deny its power over me.

***

It's slow going on the snowy roads to Dr. Carter's office. I look over and see Dad is fast asleep, his chin bobbing against his neck pillow. This is why I'm hell-bent on getting him to the neurologist today. His sleeping so much throughout the day is bound to have an effect on his sleeping pattern, and may cause him to lose his ability to sleep through the night.

For years, Dad has been subjected to annual dementia evaluations. His first evaluation was shortly after Mother passed away, when he became uncommunicative and disoriented. Grief no doubt played a part in that, but I still felt he needed a mental status checkup.

Dad had been diagnosed with Parkinson's three months before Mother passed. We were sitting by her hospital bed when I first noticed he was doing something odd with his fingers. He seemed to be rolling a pill or another small object between his thumb and index finger. I didn't call his attention to it, but I asked one of Mother's nurses what it could mean. She told me it was a "pill-rolling tremor," and that it was an early symptom of Parkinson's disease.

I remember my heart rate speeding up and my mind reeling with thoughts of what this was going to mean for me and my family. As complicated as my world was with keeping Mother alive, it was about to get even more complex as I managed Dad's healthcare.

I took him to a highly regarded neurologist in Florida, Dr. Monica Bass, who confirmed he had Parkinson's. It could not be cured, but it could be eased with Carbidopa/Levodopa, a combination medicine used to treat symptoms of Parkinson's disease. She started Dad on a low dosage and gradually raised it until his symptoms improved.

Soon after Mother's passing, Dad became subdued and had trouble expressing thoughts. He also became more forgetful, and while much of that might be attributed to losing the love of his life, I had learned Parkinson's could also cause dementia. *If it's not one thing, it's another.*

When I described these new, worrisome symptoms to Dr. Bass, she began diagnostic cognitive testing. She gave Dad the Mini-Mental State Exam to determine if he was aware of his symptoms and if he could remember a short list or words and instructions. That test also measured the strength and range of his everyday mental skills.

Next was the Mini-Cog test, a very brief test in which Dr. Bass named three words and asked Dad to repeat them back. Then she had Dad draw a clock. Then she asked Dad to repeat back the named three words.

Based on his medical history and performance in these tests and others, Dr. Bass assigned him a clinical dementia rate of one. With a score of zero being normal, and a score of three indicating severe dementia, Dad fell into the mild range.

As Dr. Bass explained to me that day, dementia and Alzheimer's disease are not the same. Dementia is an overall term used to describe symptoms that impact memory, performance of daily activities, and communication. Alzheimer's disease is the most common *type* of dementia. Alzheimer's is responsible for about fifty to seventy percent of dementia. She specifically diagnosed Dad with Alzheimer's disease because she believed his symptoms would get worse over time, affecting his memory, language and thought.

*Alzheimer's disease* are two words you never want to hear when it applies to you or a loved one, and nothing can prepare you for the impact of those words. You know your loved one's quality and length of life are on a downhill course, and there is no stopping it, no curing it. There's only the possibility of slowing it through management of its symptoms with drugs and various therapies. If you're a person who likes to be in control and who believes she can manipulate things to her liking, as I am, it's a painful reality to realize just how much control has been taken from you.

The next phase of my being a health care surrogate began with that diagnosis. I thoroughly researched treatments and medications that might ward off further decline. Keeping his Parkinson's and Alzheimer's symptoms under control required frequent doctors' visits to tweak the type and dosage of medications. At that time, his diabetes was still managed with Glyburide, an oral medication. Carbidopa/Levodopa helped control his Parkinson's symptoms, and Exelon seemed to yield the most positive results for his Alzheimer's.

I accepted Exelon as sufficient until a friend told me about a German drug called Namenda. It had shown promising results in Europe but had not yet been approved by the FDA for use in the United States. When it was approved in 2003, it was only for use in treating advanced stages of Alzheimer's. The FDA rejected the manufacturer's application to expand approval to include mild Alzheimer's.

Nevertheless, I was in Dr. Bass's office the day after FDA approval. She agreed it was worth a try and prescribed it for "off-label usage." It's legal for doctors to prescribe drugs for unapproved uses, and I was grateful she was willing to treat Dad's Alzheimer's aggressively.

To this day, I believe adding Namenda to the Exelon slowed the progress of Dad's Alzheimer's. I've taken him for annual testing, and not until 2009 was his clinical dementia rate raised from one—mild dementia—to two, moderate dementia.

Now I'm worried Dad is moving toward severe dementia. If that's the case, he may lose all ability to communicate. When he's awake, he still has control of his bladder and bowels, but with severe dementia, that will change. He may even lose his ability to sit up in his wheelchair or hold his head up.

What a cruel disease this is! It steals everything from every corner of the body. Sometimes it's stealthy and slow developing. Other times it's like a bulldozer, plowing through the body with determined destruction.

But always, whatever its method and pace, it ends up stealing everything, right down to that precious last breath.

If I'm going to thwart its progress, I need to be armed with facts and get some direction. I hope whatever Dr. Carter has to offer in today's visit includes access to a cache of both offensive and defensive weapons.

We won't win the war with Alzheimer's, but Dad and I can continue to fight for small victories along the way.

# 41

After dinner, we move Dad to the sofa and turn on the TV. Nick jumps up next to him and puts his snout on Dad's leg. "Hey there, buddy." Dad puts his hand on top of Nick's head.

Both doze off in a matter of moments. Nick is sleeping more, too, and I wonder if it's a companionship thing or a biological thing. I recall Dr. Carter's diagnosis earlier today, and what this kind of sleep means for Dad. I can't help but wonder if the same could be true for my aging dog.

"Let's go into the bedroom where we can talk," I tell David. We replenish our wine glasses and settle into the reading corner, where there are two chairs with footstools, and a table with a lamp. I turn it on and lower the setting so the light is dim.

David has been waiting to hear what Dr. Carter had to say. From my solemn mood, he knows it isn't good. "So, tell me, honey."

"Here's the thing," I begin. "Alzheimer's patients don't die from having Alzheimer's. That sounds strange, I know, but it's usually something else that causes their death, like pneumonia, or a stroke. Dr. Carter actually said the words, 'Pneumonia is the old person's friend.' I understood what he was saying. Without something specific happening, people with Alzheimer's just shut down a little at a time. Their bodies wear out, and it can be a long and painful process as organs start to fail."

David nods, encouraging me to go on. "This extra sleeping is one of the first indications that, that . . ." I pause because I don't want to say the words.

"That his body is failing?" David finishes for me.

I nod. "I asked him what stage of the shutdown process Dad was in. He said it's been happening all along, since he was diagnosed, but now it's escalating."

"Oh, babe, I'm sorry."

I nod again, acknowledging David's sympathy. I know he is sorry for me, sorry that I must witness my dad's decline moment by moment, day by day, as we've talked about before. But that seemed years off. Now . . .

"The good news is, he still has an appetite. As long as he eats and drinks, he has nourishment for his body to keep going. It's part of the will to survive. But if he gets to where he can't swallow, then we move into a more serious stage. For now, Dr. Carter agreed we should switch him from oral Namenda and Exelon to patches. I filled the prescriptions today."

"So that's good, right? That's two fewer pills he has to swallow twice a day."

"Yes, thank goodness."

"You researched all this before you went today, didn't you?"

"I've been researching for years, but I never thought to research alternative methods of delivery until a few months ago. I mentioned the patches to Dr. Baird the last time we saw him, but he said I should talk to Dr. Carter about it since he's the neurologist and he prescribes the Alzheimer's medications."

"Here's the thing, honey—and it's what I discussed with the doctor. I've noticed Dad doesn't speak as distinctly as he used to, but I can still understand him. You've also noticed his abridged speech, but he's starting to speak more softly, too. So between those two things, it's getting harder to understand what he's saying."

"That's true. I have to ask him a lot more often to repeat himself." David pauses. "Usually, he isn't able to."

"That's right. See, we've both been doing that, yet neither of us thought too much about it. But there's a name for that kind of 'speech disturbance.' It's called *dysarthria*. A speech therapist can help with that, so I'll call the agency tomorrow and see how soon they can assign one to him. There's more to it, but I can't remember everything off the top of my head. I'm going to check on Dad and I'll grab my notes from today."

"Let me check on him while you get them."

"Thanks, honey." I take off upstairs to my study.

"How's he doing?" I ask when we resume. David has refilled our wine glasses. *Good man.*

"Sleeping, with Nick matching him snore for snore."

I laugh at his description. "We need to get him to bed soon, so let me finish going over this with you. It will help me lay out a strategy, too."

"I'm ready." David reaches over and gently squeezes my knee.

"Okay, so a speech therapist might involve a specialist who'll use procedures to visualize Dad's swallowing technique. One procedure is fluoroscopy, which uses X-rays, and the other is an endoscopy, which uses a tiny video camera. This helps her determine Dad's swallowing technique so she can better target the kind of muscle therapy he needs."

"Isn't it great there are people who learn these things and can make such a difference in people's lives?" David asks.

"It is. I admire people who choose professions that are all about helping people. That's true of physical and massage therapists, too."

"Speaking of that, what about physical therapy?" David knows how much stock I put in the magic ministrations of Adam and Jennie.

"He gave me a prescription for that, too. I'm sorry Dad hasn't had his regular three-times-a-week sessions through the holidays, but now that the resort is closed until April, they're going to resume his therapy."

"It's good they'll be able to work with him again." David hesitates before he adds, "And you know, Rachel, there are other physical therapists in this city who can do it when they can't."

He's right, but I'm so attached to Adam and Jennie, as is Dad, that I haven't wanted to hire anyone else.

"I know, honey; but back to the speech therapy. We both just admitted we've noticed the difference in Dad's speech and he's having more trouble swallowing his pills, and we've just chalked that up to being a temporary thing."

David agrees. "I guess I just keep thinking everything is temporary, and he'll get back to normal."

"I do the same thing! There is no *normal* for him anymore though, is there?"

David shakes his head. "I guess we'll just have to accept that every change is the new normal for Joe. Until that changes again. Does that make any sense?"

"Perfect sense. If Dad has a good day, we think all is well again, and we expect the same in the future. It gets to where we look for the good days to justify our thinking that he's functioning the same as always."

David takes another sip of wine and nods his head in agreement. "I've noticed we have to wait longer in between for the good days. It used to be that Joe would sustain those good days for longer periods of time, but now they come less often and don't last as long. So you're right, we have to be more aware. Maybe we should keep a diary, and not just of the meds he takes each day. If we go back through that, maybe we'll be able to pick out a pattern."

"That's a great idea. Can you start on that? Maybe do an Excel spreadsheet?"

"I'll get on it tomorrow. No, wait. I have to meet with someone at the Planning Board office. But I should be back by early afternoon, and I'll tackle it then."

"Thanks, honey." I sigh and set down my still half-full glass of wine. I'm getting tired. "Let's get Dad into bed, and then I want some us time."

"Sounds good to me."

Dad wakes up enough to help with the transfer to his wheelchair. Nick has been lying beside him on the sofa, but now that we're here, he trots across the room and slips out his doggie door. It occurs to me that

Nick has assigned himself the job of Dad's watcher when we aren't in the room, and I've subconsciously accepted Nick in that role.

Just as we're settling Dad into bed, Nick comes to the door of Dad's room with fresh snow on his paws. At least he's standing on the tile floor in the kitchenette and isn't tracking the snow onto the carpeting. We've trained him to bark to let us know he's back inside and needs drying off, but he finished outside and just walked into Dad's apartment with snowy paws and a wet coat. How could he forget to follow the routine?

I snap my fingers and say, "Nick, *out*." He turns and trots into the garage.

"That's weird," David says as he settles the thick pad beside Dad's bed.

"Isn't it? He always barks and then waits until we dry him off."

"Maybe he's cold and wants to jump into bed with Joe to warm up." We share a little laugh at the thought of that.

"I hope he's not sleeping in Dad's bed every night. I don't think that's healthy for either of them. Which reminds me, I want to get a camera so we can see what's going on down here through the night."

"That's a good idea. I'll get one tomorrow while I'm out."

I smile at my sweet husband. He indulges me in so many ways. "I'll wipe up those wet spots in the kitchenette, then go dry Nick and let him back in here. You go upstairs and turn our electric blanket on, will you?"

After wiping the wet floor, I head into the garage where Nick will be waiting by the doggie door to be dried off. The garage is heated—another extravagance—so at least Nick won't be cold.

But he's not there, and as I'm wondering where he is, I hear David saying, "Nick, what are you doing up here?"

"He's up there?" I call from the bottom of the stairs.

"Wet paws and all."

"Honey, grab a towel and get him dried off." Now I see his wet paw prints on the carpet. "And then throw it down here so I can dry the carpet."

When those are blotted up, I call for Nick. He doesn't come right away, so I call out to David, "Where's Nick?"

"I thought he went down," David calls back.

Enough of this back and forth. I'm going to find my dog.

---

I find Nick curled up on his bed in the corner of our bedroom. It's been several weeks since he's slept here. He has four beds around the house, including the one in Dad's room. Until I started cleaning the house myself, I didn't realize how much hair accumulated on and around those beds. I haven't had to vacuum the one in our bedroom for a long time. I wonder why he's choosing to sleep here tonight.

Ah, well, I'm happy to see him here. I rub his ears and scratch his head, and ask him how he's doing. I'm making chatter, telling him I'm glad he'll be sleeping in our room tonight, when David comes out of the bathroom.

"There he is. Did you bring him in here for the night?"

"No, this is where I found him. It's odd, don't you think?"

"Not so much." David shrugs.

"Well, when you put this on top of padding on wet paws all over the house, I think it is."

"Let's not worry about it, Rachel. I thought we were going to spend some romantic time together tonight."

I get up to go hug David's neck, and I smell Hermes cologne on him. It has the desired effect. I give him a kiss that lets him know I'm looking forward to our romantic time.

"Go ahead and get in bed, honey, I'll be there in a few minutes." I head to the bathroom to wash my face and brush my teeth.

When I slide into bed, David opens his arms and enfolds me, then starts kissing me. Pulling back for an instant, he says, "Nick is going to be a witness to this, you know."

"Won't be the first time." I shut down any more conversation by covering David's lips with mine.

# 42

With Adam and Jennie coming three times a week, and the speech therapist planning to see him twice a week, Dad's schedule will be full. I'm hopeful their visits will give me more time to do something I've been negligent about, and that's calling, writing, and emailing friends.

I've managed to get birthday cards off to friends, and I even mailed off almost a hundred Christmas cards in mid-December. I didn't have time to write personal notes in each, as I normally do, but at least friends and family knew David and I were thinking about them. I let everyone know, via an enclosed picture of David, Dad, Nick, and me, that Dad is living with us. Marcy took the photo of us in front of the Christmas tree, and it represented us pretty darn well—a happy family that includes a big black dog who looked extra handsome with a red bow around his neck.

Those who received it would think all is well, and that Dad is well. We'd propped him up between us by putting our arms around his waist. He leaned slightly forward to support his weight on his walker. Nick sat in front of Dad, hiding his legs. Maybe it was a false picture of reality, but I wanted Dad to be represented in the best light. The forest green sweater and pleasant smile he wore contributed to the illusion of wellness.

I click on that picture in my photos file and study it. It was taken a little more than a month ago, but I can see a marked difference in Dad from then to now. True, the picture was taken on one of his "good days," in between his post-Thanksgiving drowsiness and before his out-for-the-count sleepiness on Christmas Day. His color was much better and his eyes wider and brighter.

I look at the spreadsheet David prepared to analyze Dad's medication intake. It revealed Dad was indeed taking fewer pills in the last two months. When we studied it and realized we were allowing him to skip Exelon and Namenda, two very important drugs for his dementia, we felt we had contributed to his declining cognitive function. That was also the period in which Dad had days of heavy sleeping. But we assuage our guilt by acknowledging that he's getting the proper dosage now with the patches Dr. Carter prescribed.

We'd also started the other log we talked about—what and how much Dad ate. We didn't have the historical information on that and relied only on our memories in deciding that, in simplest terms, Dad used to clean his plate, but now he doesn't.

I thought it might be the fatigue and boredom in the effort of eating, which was now taking an hour or more. David pointed out that the slower Dad ate, the more likely he was to feel fuller, faster, and so he just quit eating because he'd had enough.

But really, who could say? Dad still hasn't regained the weight he lost in the hospital, but at least he isn't losing more.

David and I accept that everything we will ever do in the future, every effort we make, will not cause Dad to become better or stronger. Even the physical therapy and speech therapy won't accomplish that. The best we can hope is to keep further deterioration and decline at bay for as long as possible.

It's an insight steeped in sorrow.

Looking at the Christmas picture once more, then forming a mental picture of Dad as he looked this morning after he was dressed and put into his chair to wait for Jennie, I concede his life energy has waned. He has had no illnesses, no cold or flu, yet his eyes are red-rimmed and his Parkinson's mask is more pronounced than ever.

The speech therapist is coming back for a second evaluation this afternoon. Two therapies in a day might be physically exhausting for Dad, but difficulties with staggered scheduling have made it necessary to double up. I don't have to worry about his getting a good nap after his PT session with Jennie and before the speech therapist comes at four o'clock, because he naps every day after lunch. He's not as interested in being upstairs with us as he was, and more often than not says he wants to nap in his own bed.

Nick always keeps him company. I think it's because they enjoy that peaceful time together, without the hubbub of the household noise. I put on his big band music at a low volume now, instead of the TV, and as he drifts off, I wonder if he envisions himself and Mother dancing to the music.

I decide to send Cindy an email and tell her these things. She hasn't been able to speak with Dad the last two times she's called because he's been deep in sleep and doesn't want, or isn't able, to come out of it.

Once she asked that I put the phone to his ear and just let her talk to him. Dad's eyes were closed, but from the small smile that appeared on his face during the one-way conversation, I believed he heard the loving words from his daughter.

Kathy calls also, although it's been a while now. Last time she called, Dad was asleep. She insisted I wake him up, so I tried, but it was useless. She started grilling me about why he was sleeping every time she called, what was going on with his health, and what I was doing about it.

It's so easy for a child who isn't involved in any aspect of a parent's care to fire off questions, demand answers, make judgments, and proffer unwanted and unhelpful suggestions.

It's not so easy, however, for me to keep my temper with her. "Tell you what, Kathy," I'd said. "You come and pick him up and take him home with you for a while. Then you'll be able to instruct me how to take better care of him."

"That's just like you," she'd snapped. "Trying to make excuses and pawn him off on someone else."

I'd just hung up on her after that comment.

Pawn him off? *Pawn him off?* How did she view Dad, I had to wonder, to have said something like that? Then I remembered she had accused me of pawning him off when I first moved him into the beautiful assisted living facility in Florida. When I'd asked her if she'd rather he live with her, she'd retorted that I was his Power of Attorney and Health Care Surrogate, and if anyone should take him in, it was me.

Hanging up on her was not my finest moment, but I didn't have the patience or energy to continue a conversation that could only widen the chasm that already exists between us. We haven't talked since that phone call. When I see her number come up on Caller ID, I let it go to voicemail or ask David to field the call and put Dad on the phone. I must say it's a relief to not have to defend and justify every decision I make regarding Dad.

So while I'm more than happy to let Cindy know the details of what is happening with Dad, I will keep Kathy out of the loop because I don't want any of the negative feedback she'll inevitably offer.

Cindy has mailed Dad sweet cards, called him on a regular basis, and been there to listen when I needed to vent. She has sent me cute ecards, some that make me laugh and some that offer encouragement, and she never judges me. In fact, in every communication, whether verbal or written, she thanks me for honoring our father by taking such good care of him. She always lifts my spirits.

"Hello, hello, Rachel, are you here?" It's Jennie calling out from downstairs. I look at the clock and see she's fifteen minutes early. That's unusual.

"Coming, Jennie."

She's at the bottom of the stairs, with her smiling face turned up in greeting, and she looks absolutely radiant.

I have a flash of what that might be about, but I don't say anything. She's bursting with news she wants to share.

"What is it, Jennie? What's going on?" My voice carries a current of excitement.

"Oh, Rachel, we just got a call from the adoption agency! They have a baby boy for us!"

I let out a whoop and fly the rest of the way down the stairs and embrace her. We squeal and hold each other tightly.

"Oh, Jennie, I'm thrilled for you and Adam!"

She nods and whispers, in a voice filled with wonder, "God has answered our prayers."

"Never did anyone's prayers so deserve to be answered. Come, sit down, and tell me everything." I motion her over to the sofa.

"I want to, Rachel, but can we bring Joe up now? I want to tell him, too."

"Of course! I'll have Marcy bring him up."

"No, let me go get him. I need to give him a big hug right now."

Sharing the joy; with family, of family. "He'll like that."

I watch Jennie as she does arm rotation and leg exercises with Dad. She tells us about the unwed seventeen-year-old girl in Louisiana who is eight months pregnant and will deliver mid-February.

She has decided to give up her son for adoption to a loving Christian couple. She's a very good student who has a scholarship to Louisiana State University and wants to pursue her degree. Her family offered to help raise him, but it would be hard going, considering their low wages from manual labor jobs that come and go. That's not the kind of upbringing she wants for her son.

"We have to leave the day after tomorrow to fly down there and meet her and her family. They know all about us from the agency and have chosen us to adopt him (and here she lets out a little squeal). I'm really nervous about it."

"I bet you are, but you shouldn't be. They'll be bowled over by you and Adam. They'll love you just like everyone who knows you loves you."

"Thank you, Rachel. That means so much to me." Jennie tells me Adam is rescheduling their appointments and making travel arrangements. They won't be able to see Dad for the rest of the week, and maybe even the following week, depending on how things go. "But we know another therapist, Sherri Stark, who's just great. Would it be okay if she fills in for us until we get back?"

"That's fine, Jennie. Thank you for thinking of it."

Dad has been listening, and now he joins the conversation. "What you going name him?" His voice is low, and his words choppy, but he's interested and engaged, which is great.

"We want to name him Lucas," she effuses. "What do you think, Joe?"

"Good name. Strong name."

Jennie beams. "It was Adam's grandfather's name."

Dad gives a single approving nod. "Even better."

"Lucas Anthony Reynolds." She's loving the sound of the full name.

"That's a beautiful name, Jennie."

"Beautiful name," Dad mumbles in agreement.

"Thank you, Rachel. Thank you, Joe." She kisses Dad on the top of his head, prompting a smile from him.

Jennie's hand is on Dad's right arm, and he shakily reaches over and puts his left hand over hers. She looks into his face, knowing he wants to say something to her.

"He's a lucky baby boy," Dad says, slowly and carefully, enunciating each word.

Jennie throws her arms around Dad and puts her head on his shoulder. Her petite body is shaking with tearful happiness. Dad's arms come up and encircle her, and I slip off the sofa and join them in a hug of overjoyed celebration.

# 43

The speech therapist has been working with Dad for the last hour, and I expect her to come looking for me soon so we can discuss Dad's prognosis and his prospects for successful speech therapy.

I've just baked chocolate chip cookies and made some hot chocolate. It's a cold January day, and this seems like the perfect comfort-food snack.

"Smells good in here," Brittany says as she comes through the door.

"Cookies and hot chocolate." I smile at her. "I thought we could indulge a bit as we talk."

She pulls out a chair, drops her backpack onto the floor, and sits down with a sigh. "Sounds real good to me."

After a few minutes of snacking and small talk, we're both fortified for whatever she has to tell me.

"I wish I had gotten to Joe a few months ago," she begins. I nod for her to go on.

"His dysarthria is progressing pretty quickly. I'm sure you know it's due to neurological injury of the motor component of the motor-speech system."

"Yes, I've read up on it. I know he drops certain words when he's trying to speak a whole sentence, but I haven't noticed him mispronouncing words very often."

"Maybe because he speaks so softly, you're not picking up on it?"

She takes a book of pictures out of her backpack and puts it on the counter between us. I pull it toward me and open it. There's a picture of a baseball bat on the first page. I look up at her with a question in my eyes.

She nods and says, "He calls it a 'bad.'"

Okay, yes, I have heard Dad mispronounce words, like using 'cub' for 'cup.' And there are his incomplete sentences. But that's only been a few times. But she's right—if Dad said 'bad' instead of 'bat,' I might not be able to distinguish the difference because he does speak so softly. I hear what I expect to hear. What I want to hear.

I look up from the book. "I'm in denial about this, I think."

She nods. "Pretty common. Some family and friends pick up on it, but many don't. They don't realize it because they've adjusted to the changes in speech as they go along, which can be subtle, and so they tend to overlook slips like this."

She takes a deep breath. "This is only going to get worse, Rachel, no matter what I do, because it's organic."

I'm dismayed to hear this. She's an ASHA-certified speech-language pathologist. I thought she'd be able to work with Dad to get him back to his previous levels of speaking and swallowing.

"I gave you the bad news first. There's good news, too."

I feel a slight sense of relief and nod for her to go on.

"There are things we can do that will help Joe." She hands me a folder. "I'll leave these reports for you to read. They include my initial assessment, which establishes the baseline data necessary for evaluating expected habilitation or rehabilitation potential, setting functional goals, and measuring communication status at periodic intervals."

Big words, but I follow her. "I've outlined a speech-language pathology goal for Joe. I may be able to get ahead of further deterioration if I can sufficiently address the apraxia—that's motor disorder caused by damage to the brain. It won't be restorative treatment, because the function can't be improved or repaired. I'm opting for compensatory treatment, which aims at compensating for deficits not responsive to retraining.

"There are several treatment options for it, and I want to speak with my supervisor about which one will be best for Joe. I may need to use a combination of treatments, but I won't know which ones until I see how he responds to them. My goal is for Joe to be able to continue to initiate short intelligible phrases with a minimum of errors."

I hold up my hand for her to stop. "I'm feeling overwhelmed," I tell her, "and I need some time to process this."

"Sure you do. In fact, that's all I'm going to cover with you today. I would appreciate it if you could read everything I've given you. Your input and participation will be key in this since I can't be here every day."

"Whatever work I do with Joe, you'll have to be a part of it. You need to understand it so you can use it—often, every day, with him. As the saying goes, if you don't use it, you lose it. I can get the wheels moving, but if we don't keep them oiled, he'll regress."

"Will this help with his swallowing difficulty as well?"

"Yes, the therapy helps with both. With your permission, I'd like to set up a fluoroscopy and an endoscopy for him." I believe she's willing to pull out all the stops to help Dad, and I'm grateful. I tell her this and promise to be as involved as she needs me to be.

"That's great, Rachel. I knew you would feel that way and would want to be involved in his treatment. Not everyone does, but I can tell Joe is loved and well cared for."

"Do you really think he can be helped?"

"I do, or I wouldn't be making these recommendations."

"God, I so admire you for what you're able to do."

"I love what I do. There's a lot of gratification in it."

"I'm thankful you're the one who's going to be working with Dad."

She points at me and smiles. "And you."

"Yes, I get that. I'll be involved in every session so I can learn all you can teach me about helping him. Thanks for taking the time to go over all of this, Brittany. I promise to read every word before you come back. Can you give me a schedule so I can plan my days?"

She taps on the folder. "It's in there."

I offer her the last cookie on the plate, which she eagerly accepts.

She has a real sweet tooth, too. I like her. A lot. Enough to go to my hiding place in the linen closet.

"Hey, Brittany, do you like Oreos?"

"They're my favorite. I like dunking them in milk, coffee . . ." She looks down at her cup and smiles. "But especially in hot chocolate."

Yep, I really like her.

# 44

Sheri Stark, the fill-in for Jennie, is here today, but it's a bad day for her to be introduced to Dad because he's sluggish. After trying several times to roust him and get him to cooperate in his therapy, she says to me, "I don't think I'm going to be able to help him today." She looks distressed. That makes two of us.

I'm not blaming Sheri. I can tell she's competent, but what do you do with a patient who won't even open his eyes?

Nick gets up from his corner in the sunroom and walks over to nudge Dad's hand. Nothing. He sighs, then goes back to his corner and lays his heads on his paws, watching us.

Sherry has watched him walk back to his spot. "Handsome dog. He has some hip problems, huh?"

"Yes, he does. He's been getting treatment for about seven months now, but I'm not sure if there's anything more we can do if the Adequan stops being effective."

"That's good stuff for hip dysplasia. Still, I can tell by the way he lies on his side and licks himself that he's uncomfortable."

I can't get into Nick's problems right now. "I know. I'm doing what I can for Nick. But back to Dad. I have to apologize. I should have called you and told you he's been sluggish, but I was hoping he'd perk up by the time you got here."

"He ain't gonna perk up today." It's Marcy, speaking from the kitchen where she's mopping. And eavesdropping.

I want to roll my eyes, but Marcy knows Dad too well for me to dismiss her remark. It's just not what I want to hear at this moment.

"Can you come in here for a minute please, Marcy?"

She and Sheri have already introduced themselves, so I skip to the reason I asked her to come in. "Did you notice anything different about Dad this morning?"

"Just what I told you earlier. He didn't want to wake up at all, but I got some coffee down him and he perked up long enough to take his Sinemet and eat a coupla' bites of eggs. Then he went all Wynken, Blynken, and Nod on me again."

Sheri laughs, then apologizes.

"No need to apologize," Marcy tells her. "Things just pop outta me sometimes. I'm used to people gettin' a kick out of me."

"So what makes you think he won't perk up again?" I ask her.

After thinking about this for a moment, she says, "He goes into a different kinda sleep than just usual sleep. It's not just napping, when I can talk to him and get him to open his eyes. It's more like he goes way down and don't respond to nothing."

A good description. I know just what she's talking about.

"Well, if that's the case, I'm afraid I won't be able to help him today." Sheri looks so disappointed.

"Can you do some isometric exercises?" I ask her.

"What's that?" Marcy is always eager to learn.

Sheri tells her, "It's strength training. Physical exercises that make your muscles stronger by pushing your arms or other parts of your body against each other or against something." She puts her hands together, elbows out, and pushes one hand against the other to demonstrate. Muscles in her forearms and hands bulge. "Isometrics can help maintain muscle strength."

Marcy imitates Sheri. "Oh, yeah, I get it. Well, that's good then, right?"

Sheri looks at Dad. "Yes, under the circumstances, it's good."

"I'll be glad to help," Marcy volunteers. "What can I do?" As usual, she's enthusiastic about doing anything to help Dad.

"Let's get him downstairs and onto his bed, where I can show you."

I'm relieved Dad's going to get something out of Sheri's visit. "Anything will help, I'm sure," I tell them.

"And if his muscles is stiff, can you do a little bit of massage?" Marcy asks Sheri.

I'd had that same thought but didn't want to ask. I smile at Marcy to let her know I'm glad she did.

"Sure. But I'll need you to help me move him around, okay?"

"Ain't nothing I ain't used to doing," Marcy says, and I can tell she's happy to be able to help.

Hell, I'm happy she's the one who's going to be doing the helping, too.

---

"You know, I watched Sheri real close, and I think I can help Joe with those isomecric exercises," Marcy tells me.

I don't bother to correct her pronunciation. She's too dear to ever embarrass. She enjoyed helping Sheri today, and before she left, Sheri complimented Marcy on her "natural affinity for physical therapy."

Marcy was so pleased with the compliment that she blushed— something I'd never seen her do.

"I think that would be wonderful, Marcy. I can't think of anything better you could do for Dad, although you already do so much for him— and for me."

"Just my job." She blushes a second time.

"You know, Marcy, I think you deserve a raise. You've been working for ten dollars an hour, but I think fifteen dollars an hour would be more appropriate for all you do."

Like anyone working hard and scraping by, she's not about to turn down a raise. She gives me a hug as she thanks me. Marcy isn't a hugger, and I'm taken aback. What has her so effusive these days?

Ah, ha! The New Year's Eve date. Has he become her boyfriend?

"Hey, Marcy, let's have a cup of coffee and talk about the new man in your life."

She looks surprised, but then smiles and dips her head. "His name's Joshua."

---

Sheri comes for two more physical therapy sessions with Dad, and they go well. Dad's confused about who she is, and even after explaining to him three times that she's filling in for Adam and Jennie, he still doesn't understand why she's demanding things from him that, until now, only they have had the right to do. But to his credit, he leans into the therapy and smiles when Sheri praises him.

In between, Brittany and I have been working with Dad, and while I notice some small improvement in his speech, I can't tell a difference in his ability to swallow. He takes his pills at will, with no more difficulty than always, but I no longer obsess about it. Marcy and I have been vigilant for quite some time about cutting his food into tiny pieces and giving him plenty of time to chew and swallow. She feeds him breakfast and lunch, and I spend at least an hour each evening with him at the dinner table.

David usually reheats Dad's food in the microwave at least twice during that time. I love that he stays at the table with us, never minding the time it takes Dad to finish. Lately, he's begun reading to us from a book of lovely short stories. Many are reminiscent of times past, the so-called simple life, with caring neighbors, one-room schoolhouses, and loyal dogs. More than a few of the stories have made me cry, which brings Nick into the fold when he comes out from under the table and puts his head in my lap.

This is our sweetest family time, and I grab onto every moment of it.

# 45

"I can't get him woke up," Marcy says to me when I come into Dad's apartment to greet her and check on Dad this morning.

I raise his bed as high as it will go and touch his forehead to see if it's hot. It feels normal. I run through the vitals routine, and other than slightly lower blood pressure, everything checks out.

"Let's change him here in bed and let him sleep, then."

After we finish getting him and his bed clean and dry, she asks how we're going to get him to take his Sinemet and then get him to eat. I have no answers. He had already gone through the two-day, deep-sleep period at the beginning of January, and he had pulled out of that just fine. As I'd learned from Dr. Carter, Dad would continue to go through periods of prolonged and deep sleep, with nothing that could be pinpointed as the cause other than the progression of his Alzheimer's and Parkinson's.

I tell Marcy we'll just let him sleep and keep checking his vitals, and if he seems to take a turn for the worse, we'll have to call an ambulance. I can always have Dr. Baird meet me at the hospital.

Nick *woofs* from the doorway, and I can tell from the wet shimmer of his coat that he's been outside. He's making wet paw tracks again.

"Was Nick in here when you came in this morning?" I ask Marcy.

"Yes, ma'am, and he trotted right out as soon as I come in."

I look at the clock on the wall. That must have been about fifteen minutes ago.

Nick wants to come in and keep Dad company. I'll have to dry him off first, and I tell him this. He turns back toward the garage.

"That dog understands everything you say to him," Marcy marvels.

"He knows a lot of words, but he also knows by my tone what I'm saying. He's a smart dog, and eager to please, which makes it easier. I'll bring him in here when I'm finished so he can spend some time with Dad."

"You want me to stay here with Mr. Joe, or go up and get started on housework?" she asks.

I want to be with Dad, so I tell her to go upstairs. I know David is up and doesn't like having her in his space first thing in the morning, but laundry is piled up and the kitchen needs cleaning.

"Please tell David what's going on with Dad," I say as I head out to the garage to dry Nick off.

Nick is lying on his bed, which has absorbed much of the moisture he carried in with him. I tell him how much I love him as I dry him, then tell him he can go into Dad's apartment if he wants to.

He hauls himself up with some difficulty and heads that way.

I decide I need another cup of coffee, and as I head upstairs, I hear Marcy's voice. "You want me to cook you some breakfast, Mr. David?"

"No thanks, Marcy, I'm just going to get some coffee for now."

When I enter the kitchen, David turns to greet me with a quick kiss. Marcy looks a little embarrassed as she heads to the laundry room.

"So Joe's gone into another of his funks, huh?"

"It seems so. I hope he wakes up because he has a speech therapy session this morning at eleven."

"Do you think all this therapy is wearing him down?"

I've wondered the same thing, but I tell David I'm reluctant to stop it because I've seen incremental improvement in his speech and swallowing.

"Well, what about cutting back on the physical therapy?"

"I'll talk to Adam about it. He's in the best position to make that kind of assessment."

Adam emailed me last night that he and Jennie were back from Louisiana and would be resuming Dad's therapy starting tomorrow. He also said he was excited to share all the details of the trip with me.

We talk about David's plans for the day, which include his going to Hendersonville to talk to one of the subcontractors for the development.

"Nick's downstairs with Dad. Would you please feed him while I go shower?" Even after a second cup of coffee, I'm still slow-moving and need a hot shower to energize me.

Just then we hear a loud and distressed *woof* from downstairs.

If the laptop had been on the kitchen island where it normally is, instead of in my study where I took it to update some notes about Dad, we could have looked at the feed from the camera David installed in Dad's room. Instead, David and I rush down to Dad's apartment. What we see startles us, though Dad's in no danger.

I had forgotten to lower his bed before both Marcy and I left his apartment. Even if he'd fallen from that height, he wouldn't have gotten hurt because of the thick pad beside the bed, but it was still careless of me.

Dad is flailing at the edge of the bed, but Nick has his body pressed up against Dad's, keeping him on the bed. Dad lands a couple of unintended blows on Nick's shoulder and head, but Nick doesn't flinch.

We both rush over to get Dad settled down and properly situated on his bed. Nick is in our way, but we work around him. He's not moving until he knows Dad is safe.

I thank Nick and motion him away, but he basically only steps out of our way and stays nearby. David has lowered the bed and is reassuring Dad, who's wide awake but looking frightened and disoriented.

I sit down next to him, take his hand, and tell him we think it's a good morning for pancakes and bacon. I ask him what he thinks.

I'm trying to normalize conversation and get him centered. He stares at me for a long moment, and I realize he doesn't recognize me. He's staring at me as if I'm a stranger, and his eyes are filled with confusion and fright.

Though I'm rocked to my core at this new turn, I continue my modulated, one-sided conversation.

"David said to me, 'Rachel, let's make Joe some pancakes this morning,' and I thought that sounded great. Are you hungry for pancakes, Dad?"

I'm hoping that by using our names, Dad will reconnect. I repeat what I just said, and after looking from David to me for about thirty seconds, I see his eyes change. There is recognition in them, but he still doesn't speak.

Nick pads over and puts his face right in Dad's face. I start to wave him away again, thinking Dad will be startled anew.

But my anxiety melts away when instead Dad says, "Morning, big boy."

I made a big deal of serving Dad breakfast in bed, pronouncing him "King for a Day" and getting him to laugh. The pancakes have been cut into tiny pieces and covered in butter and sugar-free syrup.

Dad tries to eat them by himself and is doing a pretty good job, although his fingers have become so sticky that they're stuck to the fork, and his bib is showered with crumbs. Many have found their way to the bed covers, and help arrives in the form of a big black dog.

Nick starts cleaning Dad's bib with his tongue, and I don't have the will to stop him. Dad is laughing and encouraging him, so what's the point? I'm beginning to think all the regimentation in Dad's life is detracting from the joy.

Up at seven A.M. The constants: toileting; pills; blood check; insulin; breakfast; bath; lunch; nap; pills; blood check; insulin; dinner; toileting; pills; bed.

The variables: doctor appointment; speech therapy; physical therapy; being read to; watching TV; listening to music; memory games; extra-long naps.

It makes for long days for all of us. I've refrained from hiring extra help now that Marcy's here eight hours a day, but it may be time.

When Brittany arrives, we stay in Dad's apartment for the speech therapy. He cooperates, for the most part, in the exercises she's specifically designed for him based on what she learned from the results of the fluoroscopy and endoscopy.

"I can tell you're working with him in between our sessions," Brittany says afterward. "It's really helping."

I thank her as she heads out the door. "See you Thursday," she says with a wave and a smile.

I'm weary of all the work I'm involved with every day, and of all the time I spend within these four walls.

Other than the fabulous birthday lunch Jessica put together for me at the Grove Park Inn, I haven't been out and haven't seen any of my friends. My days, and the walls, are closing in on me, and I'm resenting it.

David gets out a lot more often because of the development project; and although he's working hard and making money, I'm beginning to envy his freedom in coming and going.

My resentment at being an unpaid caregiver flares up again, and I'm developing a very bad mood. I don't know where to stuff my frustration and anger. I could call someone and vent, but I don't want to subject anyone to my foul disposition.

Exercise. I need some exercise and fresh air. It's freezing cold outside, but I don't care.

Since Dad was nodding off when Brittany and I walked out, I decide to take Nick for a walk. Dad will be okay for whatever time we'll be gone since Marcy's here to keep an eye on him.

"Marcy," I call over the intercom. "Brittany has left, and Nick and I are going for a walk. Can you please come down and check on Dad in a little bit?"

"Sure will, Miss Rachel."

I have all the winter gear I need to suit up right here in the garage. Before putting on my snow boots, I pop into Dad's room and say to Nick, "Let's go for a walk."

His hesitation is more obvious than ever, but he hoists himself off his bed and comes toward me. Am I being mean, expecting him to get out in this cold weather with me? He's obviously slowed down even more, and even with his medications, I know he's in pain.

I'm going to ask Adam if he can give Nick a good massage when he comes tomorrow. But for now, I can't subject my dog to the harsh effect the cold weather will have on him. He needs to stay inside and indulge his aging body.

Dad and Nick have both slowed down this winter, in similar and telling ways. Just like now, Nick has been reluctant to go for walks for weeks.

I realize I've been doing the same thing with Nick as I have with Dad. *Exactly the same thing.* I've been ignoring the signs, thinking the meds, or Adam's brief massages, or his new orthopedic beds will set him right as rain again. In actuality, when we go for walks, he doesn't want to go as far, nor for as long a time. I've put it down to his not tolerating the cold as well as he had in the past, and at those times I choose to think he'll be livelier on our walks when the weather turns warm in the spring.

I can relate to his reluctance. Even bundled up in cumbersome winter wear, I don't have as much tolerance for the cold as I've had in the past. And I don't have chronic pain from achy hips like big boy does.

In past winters, Nick took much pleasure in being outside. He loved digging in the snow or taking off to chase a critter that had unexpectedly come out of its burrow. He hasn't been doing that on our hikes, and that has to take some of the joy out of them.

The routine in wet or snowy weather is that he goes out to do his business, explores for a while, then comes back in and barks so I can dry him off. If I'm delayed, he'll lie down on his bed in the garage and wait. Sometimes he barks a second time, and it has an impatient pitch to it.

But this winter he's been making shorter and shorter jaunts outside. He just doesn't enjoy the outdoors like he used to.

"Go back to your bed, Nick. I'll see you soon." He returns to his bed and lies down with an audible *humph.*

I still need exercise, and I'm going to get it. But I'm sure going to miss the big boy's company.

# 46

Because Dad is listless today and was irritated at the prospect of physical therapy, Adam is just giving him a massage and doing some range-of-motion exercises in Dad's apartment. He has agreed to spend some time with Nick afterwards, even though it means he will have to cut Dad's therapy short. I'm torn about this, but Nick needs help almost as much as Dad does.

Dad has succumbed to Adam's skillful hands and is peacefully dozing while being massaged. I'd sure like to trade places with him, but I'm enjoying hearing about the trip to Louisiana to meet the adoptive mother and her family. Adam is full of excitement and joy that he and Jennie were given the family's blessing in adopting the baby.

"Of course you would have their blessing. Who could possibly be more wonderful parents than you two? When will she deliver?" I ask.

"February 15th is the expected date. Only three weeks from now."

"Three weeks? That's so soon, Adam."

He nods. "We have a lot to do to get ready, and we're going back for the birth. We're expected to be there, but we really want to be, anyway. He'll be put into our arms immediately."

He describes the family, but he doesn't share any names, not even the mother's. It's part of the agreement.

"And here's the coolest thing, Rachel. Her grandfather's name was Lucas."

My mouth falls open. I get goosebumps. "Wow! Of all the names in the world . . ."

"That's what we said. And apparently he passed away when she was still a little girl, but she's grown up hearing about him and feels close to him."

"That is so amazing, Adam. Just another sign Lucas is supposed to be your baby."

"We said the same thing, and then we all prayed about it. It was powerful."

Adam lowers his head and takes a deep breath, apparently recalling those powerful emotions and the effect they had on him.

"I'm so happy for you and Jennie, and I can't wait to meet Lucas!"

I sit back and absorb the wonder of it all. How life changes so quickly. Until ten days ago, Adam and Jennie had no idea there was a baby who was meant to be theirs. Three weeks from now, that will become a reality.

As T.S. Elliott said, "Sometimes things become possible if we want them bad enough."

*Sometimes.*

---

Post-massage, Dad is settled into his chair and watching TV. Adam and I go upstairs, with Nick trailing us. Poor boy is having a harder time with the steps. While we wait for him, I pour Adam a glass of iced tea. He downs it in one long drink, then starts working on Nick. I settle on the living room sofa so we can talk.

Since this is the first time Adam has seen Dad in ten days, he doesn't know about the change in the amount of time Dad's sleeping. I tell him about the longer sleep pattern and what Dr. Carter had to say about it.

I share my worry that so much physical therapy and speech therapy is wearing Dad out and ask him if he thinks we should cut back. To best illustrate my point, I walk over and show him two pictures I've printed: The one taken in mid-December, and the one taken in mid-January—

just last week, in fact. He looks at the pictures for a long moment, and his shoulders rise and fall with the deep breath he takes and releases.

"What is it, Adam?"

"I'm a strong believer in keeping somebody moving as long as they can move. Ambulation is good for Joe since he sits so much. His hip flexors get tight, and I like to work with him on elongating those. When Joe sits for hours, he has contractures."

"Oh, yes, contractures. Shortening and hardening of muscles and tendons that can lead to deformity and rigidity of joints."

Adam nods and says, "Which is why it's hard for him to get on his feet for therapy, and why it's hard for you to transfer him. We're working against every destructive and aging mechanism there is with Joe." Adam looks sad as he says this, and the sadness is contagious.

Sometimes I feel I have taken blow after blow in caring for my parents, and I'm feeling pretty battered right now. Death has its own agenda, and it doesn't stop working until it has met that agenda. It can be thwarted temporarily through medical interventions, but it will fulfill its agenda in the end. This I know to be true, yet I want to fight back and deny its tenacity.

From previous conversations I know Adam doesn't think Dad has brain damage, per se, but he does know Alzheimer's hollows the brain out so it eventually looks like Swiss cheese. Losing portions of the brain is in itself brain damage, as far as I'm concerned. And that's what's happening with Dad.

I want to be alone. I need time to process everything we've talked about, and I don't want to lay sadness on top of Adam's happiness about the adoption.

"Well," I say, presenting a stalwart façade, "let's see how Dad does with the next session. I hope he's awake enough to participate so you can evaluate if we should continue or not."

The look on Adam's face tells me he sees through me, sees my sadness, but he allows me to hold onto my poise by not pushing the conversation any further or in any other direction.

"Sounds like a plan, Rachel."

Nick stays where he is, basking in the good feelings that Adam's hands have delivered. As I hand Adam a check, I say, "Give Jennie my love, would you? And please tell her I'm thrilled it all worked out so well. In three weeks, you'll be parents of a beautiful baby boy!"

The irony of the situation doesn't escape me. One life is being ushered out, another life is being welcomed in, and all I can hope for is they have a chance to meet before they begin their separate journeys down the forked road of life.

# 47

David comes home to find me soaking in the Jacuzzi tub with tears running down my face. Marcy is with Dad, and I had asked her to give me a couple of hours to myself.

Now David is intruding on my time and space, and I have no desire to share what I'm feeling. I need to wallow in my gloominess all by myself.

So when he asks me what's wrong, I hold up a bubble-covered hand and say, "Out. Please, just get out. Close the door behind you. I'll find you later."

He looks dejected, but that's his problem. I don't want to deal with anyone's feelings but my own.

I'm so weary of being responsible for others' well-being. Dad, Nick, and even David are consuming me, morsel by morsel, even though it's through no real fault of their own. I just feel sliced and diced and want to get back to being whole. I don't know how or where to start, and I worry about not being able to put myself back together.

Oh, yes, I'm luckier than so many others, as I've often told myself. But I'm tired of being strong, of looking on the bright side, of holding on to hope, of pushing others to do their part in my plan for . . . for what?

Exactly what is my plan? Is it keeping Dad well and alive? He's not well, and he won't live. No matter what I do, no matter how much effort I put into it, that plan will fail. I will fail.

When I moved Dad here, I was so sure he had years left to enjoy being with us. He'd come so far. *We'd* come so far. We fought together to defy the one-year death sentence the surgeon had given after his broken-hip surgery. Dad never learned about that prognosis, and he believed, always believed, he was getting better. And for a while, he did. Or so it seemed. He had thrived and been happy at Crestview.

He's been well tended here, with only the one UTI, which was quickly resolved. He has never had bed sores or skin breakdowns. He's been fed and watered and medicated as well as possible. He's gotten plenty of sunshine and had fun excursions. He's enjoyed the company of family and friends and personal aides. He's had physical therapy that benefited him and gave him the hope he could get "back to normal."

Like David said, there is always going to be a new normal for Dad— and subsequently for us. But did it have to be so rapid and multi-faceted in its onslaught?

I add more hot water to the tub and reach for the glass of lovely Chardonnay I'd brought in with me. Along with the bubbly, herbal-scented hot water, it has a soothing effect on my wounded spirit. But none of these transitory luxuries is providing the emotional relief I hoped for. One afternoon of indulgence isn't enough. I need a vacation, dammit. But that's not possible.

I can take a day off though, have a full day to myself. And I'm going to do it.

⸻

Invigorated after my therapeutic bath, I find David in the kitchen. His back is to me when I say, "I need you to take tomorrow off from everything you have planned and take full responsibility for Dad for the entire day."

He turns around quickly, startled by both my demand and my tone. "What's wrong?"

"What's wrong is I'm worn out. I'm tired of thinking, worrying, and making decisions. I'm tired of being responsible for everyone who trods the floors of this house, whether it be on two legs, four legs, or in a wheelchair." I'm wound up, and words of anger and frustration are flying, unfiltered. "Everyone always asks me what to do, how to do it, when to do it, whatever *it* is. I schedule, I manage, and I participate in every aspect of Dad's care."

David starts to speak, but I hold up my hand. "Please just let me finish," I say, softening my demeanor a bit.

He crosses his arms over his chest and nods.

"I just need a day off. I need a day away from my responsibilities. I need you to take full control of everything for one full day, from morning until night."

"Rachel, you don't have to talk to me like that. You could have just asked me if I'd do what you're asking instead of coming in here and jumping down my throat."

He's right. I take a deep and steadying breath. "I guess I envy you for getting to leave here for hours at a time. Sometimes for the whole day."

"I'm working, Rachel."

"I understand that. But tell me you haven't driven out of this driveway and been glad to be making an escape?"

"I don't look at it like that. I look at it like I'm busting my butt to keep a lot of balls in the air so we can maintain this lifestyle and still put some money away."

I start crying. It's the last outlet I have for my pent-up frustrations. I can't take them all out on David. I need to talk to a professional. I need a support group, maybe one of those online groups I've joined just for mining information from the discussions. I need to express myself in a healthy way, not a harmful way.

David wraps me in his arms. He just holds me.

"I'm going to go get dressed." I give him a quick kiss before pulling away. "So, will you please take total responsibility for Dad tomorrow?"

"Of course I will."

"Thank you."

And while I don't doubt I would have gotten that same response if I'd approached him in a more diplomatic way, I have to say I feel better for having vented.

After all, *for better or worse* includes venting, doesn't it?

# 48

I've reached out to the staff psychologist at Remembrance Care, who agreed to meet me for lunch, my treat.

I'd met Clare that day at our women's group meeting with the caregivers and had enjoyed talking with her. I had meant to call her about having lunch to get to know her better, but I never followed up on it.

I called her first thing this morning to give her a brief description of what was going on in my life and ask for a recommendation for a professional I could talk to.

"Let's start with me," she offered. I counter-offered with lunch, and so here we sit at a lovely bistro enjoying a delicious lunch. I'm refreshed and revived because I've just had a manicure and pedicure for the first time in forever. I'd forgotten how uplifting pampered grooming can be.

"I'd like to ask you a question I ask every child who's a caregiver for their parent." I nod, and she asks, "How did you become the designated caregiver?"

I've asked and answered this same question for myself. "I had long been there for Mother through a number of illnesses, hospitalizations, and surgeries. Then David and I encouraged my parents to get a Living Will and Designation of Health Care Surrogate drawn up. I thought they'd want my oldest sister, Cindy, to be their health care surrogate, so I was surprised when they named me, with David as secondary. I had no idea how much responsibility it would entail until I had to start making hard decisions on their behalf. So, I was the official decision maker, and that led to my becoming the official caregiver."

I take a sip of water and gather my thoughts before continuing. "I believe for most caregivers it comes down to other members of the family looking around and asking: 'Who in the family is most able to take care of the parents? Who has the most time? An extra bed? The stamina? The inability to say no? Or, in some cases, who drew the short straw?'"

We laugh at this, but Clare agrees there's some truth in all of those cases, even the last one.

"I mean," I continue, "I'm the third and last child. My parents were good to me and certainly showed me they loved me in many ways, but it wasn't like either was partial to me or spoiled me or did so many amazing things for me that I owed them all the loyalty in the world. I think being their designated health care surrogate had to do with how they perceived my capability, more than anything. I went from being a kind of overseer of their health care to taking ownership of it. It was only natural that I'd move Dad into my home when it became necessary."

Clare takes a sip of wine and asks, "Do you resent it?"

"Ah, that's a tricky question, Clare. Resent it? I think it's more that I resent I have to do it without much family support, except for David. I don't resent taking care of Dad. Do I get frustrated, aggravated, despondent, and angry about it at times? Sure, but I don't direct any of that toward Dad. It's my own shortcomings in being a caregiver that create those emotions."

"That's not unusual for caregivers," she says. "Many don't feel what they do is adequate."

"Oh, what I do is adequate, it's just not always up to my own self-imposed standards."

"And thus your desire to talk to a professional about reconciling the two."

She's nailed it. It's such a relief to talk to a professional who has so much experience with this issue.

"So you've finally reached the point where you admit you can't keep going the way you've been going," she says matter-of-factly, but with empathy.

"You've summed it all up very nicely."

Clare smiles and nods. "Sometimes you have to have a breakdown to have a breakthrough."

I let her words sink in. How apt. How assuring. "Thank you, Clare."

"No need to thank me. That's why Remembrance Care exists, Rachel. We offer support for people who are going through the most difficult time they're ever likely to experience. I wish you had sought me out sooner, but there's still hope for you."

I burst out laughing, and it's like opening a pressure valve. My relief at being heard and understood is enormous.

We talk about options and make plans that include her coming to our home to evaluate the situation and see what comfort measures Remembrance Care can offer Dad—and me.

I feel like a weight has been lifted as we part company, but I still have a long and unencumbered afternoon ahead of me, so I head to Asheville's beautiful Biltmore Village.

At my favorite bookstore there, Beckett's Books and Nooks, I spend an hour curled up in a comfortable chair reading about the fascinating lives of bees. I sip a delicious cup of cappuccino to fortify me for my next planned activity of trying on one beautiful outfit after another in the shops around the Village.

In former times I would have bought something. But I leave the shops empty-handed and find I'm just as satisfied in buying a real-chocolate cup of hot chocolate and a big chocolate croissant at a nearby cozy bakery.

I've made plans to meet Jessica, Patti and Carole for dinner, none of whom I've seen since my birthday lunch at the Grove Park Inn. Although I'm not hungry after lunch, coffee, and a late-afternoon treat, I wouldn't miss the opportunity to spend an evening with them for all the croissants in Paris. Even better, I can afford to treat them to dinner!

I'm feeding my soul, after all, and I'm being gluttonous about it. It is so very satisfying.

It's five minutes after ten when I call David to tell him I'm on my way home. Before I can ask, he says, "Joe's had a good day, and he's tucked in for the night."

"Thank you, David."

"You're welcome. See you soon, babe."

---

Remembrance Care has a lot of resources, and I've started using them.

I was surprised to learn that caregivers affiliate with Remembrance Care *years* before their loved one is at the end stage of dementia. During that time, they receive resources, information, and guidance to help them cope.

I've been attending support group meetings where I've learned so much. While dementia manifests at a different pace and by different degrees in each person, its course is set. Every patient goes down the same road, and their caregivers take the journey with them. The best we can do is walk beside them, hold their hand, catch them when they stumble, and cradle them as they finally succumb.

After our talk about whether or not to continue physical therapy, Adam determined he should keep working with Dad until his body says a clear and unmistakable, "No more." A physical therapist with Remembrance Care evaluated Dad as well, and he agreed with Adam's assessment.

"One day his body will just stop moving. As long as it's able to move, it will. Movement's always good, until it isn't. You'll know when that time comes. When it does make itself obvious, don't fight it," he'd told David and me.

---

February is an eventful month that brings some changes into our lives. It starts with Nick, who has seemingly overnight become perplexed about stepping over the thresholds of all doors that lead outside. The doggie doors are forgotten altogether, and now I wake up even earlier to rush down to Dad's room to lead him outside. It's so cold that his pee steams.

Nick won't sleep anywhere but in Dad's room. Via the camera feed, we see he has even forsaken his bed, preferring to sleep on the mat next to Dad's bed, which can't be as comfortable as his orthopedic bed.

One morning before I went down, I looked at the feed on the laptop and saw he had his head on Dad's bed, with his snout very close to Dad's face. Dad's face was turned toward Nick so I couldn't see his expression—or even tell if he was awake—but Nick was looking at Dad as if he were listening to him. It was so intense that I woke David and asked him to watch. "Sure looks like he's listening to Joe, doesn't it?" he'd said, confirming what I was thinking.

Dad's ability to swallow has improved slightly, but his speech is not getting markedly better, and he speaks less and less. But was he talking to Nick?

Every day I use the techniques Brittany taught me with Dad, but I can tell it's hard work for him. At times he just stops, puts his head back, and goes to sleep. His original enthusiasm has waned, as has his energy. Despite the stalled progress I'm experiencing with Dad, Brittany says it's a good sign that his speech isn't deteriorating further. In fact, she got authorization for four more weeks of therapy, which means she still sees room for improvement.

I'll leave it to her to determine if he should continue after those additional four weeks. I just worry that it's exhausting him, and I'm at the same point of questioning the benefits of speech therapy as I had physical therapy.

Sheri has been filling in again for Adam and Jennie since they've been so busy with preparation for the arrival of their son. They are now in Louisiana to be with the mother during birth, then they'll be bringing Lucas home.

Sheri is sweet, patient and capable, and when Dad refuses to participate in physical therapy for any meaningful length of time, she and Marcy put him on his bed and do exercises that will lengthen his hip flexors. She isn't Adam or Jennie, but she's special, too.

I spend every moment I can spare with Dad, and that's mostly in his room now. Nick is always with us, and when I'm reading to Dad or watching a movie with him, I expect them both to nod off. It doesn't matter. The Zen is in our being together.

A week after they return from Louisiana, Adam and Jennie host a receiving party for Lucas at their house. David and I are delighted to join their friends and family in welcoming their beautiful baby boy into their loving home. I put together a huge basket of baby goodies, so huge that David can't see around it as we mount the steps to their home. He complains, but I tell him I'll catch him if he falls. He isn't reassured.

We're sorry we couldn't bring Dad, but he'll get to meet Lucas soon enough, since Jennie has promised to bring him over for a private introduction to Dad and Nick.

But I do wish Dad could see just how jubilant Adam and Jennie are. They are glowing like two young people who are falling in love—and they are, with Lucas. It's a different kind of love that's bringing about the glow, it's true, but it is just as enchanting.

Despite being new parents, they have professional obligations and they need to make money, now more than ever. One or the other will continue therapy sessions with Dad twice a week for the remainder of February. With each visit, they share the wonder and joy they experience every day in parenting Lucas.

We are feeling the blessing of the ten thousand dollars that's coming in each month, so we insist on giving them a substantial raise. But no amount of money can compensate these two wonderful people for all their selfless giving in keeping Dad going.

# 49

Today is March 5th, Dad's eighty-sixth birthday. We're having a party and I'm really hopeful Dad will be awake enough to enjoy it. Debra, Charles, Brad, Anna, Sissy, Rhonda, Carmen, and Marcy will all be here to help us celebrate. I'm especially excited Adam and Jennie will be bringing baby Lucas.

I'm also delighted the guest list includes Dad's first cousin, Will, who still lives in their hometown, where Debra and Charles also live. It was Debra's suggestion to invite him, and I'm looking forward to getting to know him. We moved to Florida when I was a teenager, and although I'd met Will at some time before we moved away, I don't remember him. I'm just hoping Dad recognizes him. It will be nice to have additional family with us today.

Nick is in the kitchen with me, waiting for a slice of turkey or roast beef to hit the floor as I prepare a party platter. I'm not sure I would have acknowledged just how far along Nick was on his own road of demise without Remembrance Care's intervention. They didn't diagnose Nick, of course, but the things they made me more aware of in terms of changes in personality and behavior became evident in Nick, who never could have told me himself.

Around the same time he stopped going over thresholds, I found him in the corner of the sunroom, the same corner where he lay while watching Dad do his therapy. But he was standing up and facing the corner when I found him, and he seemed to be stuck. He must have heard my footsteps, but he didn't turn. His body was trembling slightly, and it wasn't until I laid my hands on him and whispered his name that he relaxed. Even at that, I had to physically take his collar and turn him around so he was facing out again.

He had looked at me with an odd expression, sort of a mix of embarrassment and perplexity. He seemed normal the rest of the day, but I wasn't about to fall into that trap again. There was no normal for Nick any longer, just as there was no normal for Dad.

Since then, we've found him in that same corner three times. The same scenario as the first time plays out, but now he seems scared, as if he's lost and doesn't know how to get back to where he needs or wants to be.

He stays in close physical proximity to either Dad or David or me, and I believe he's afraid of getting lost.

After finding a mess in the utility room, David and I have to remember every couple of hours to ask him if he wants to go outside. Nick is fastidious and proud. For him to have had an accident inside means his mental and physical functions are moving beyond his control.

Last month, Nick was following me up the steps when I heard what could only be his falling down them. *Tha-tha-thump-thump.* I cried out, and ran down, expecting to find him in pain.

Instead, he smiled at me, his tongue lolling out of his mouth, and pretended to be playing. He was acting as if he meant to fall, and even as he struggled to stand, he kept up the pretense. I helped him keep his dignity by going along with his farce and talking to him in a playful voice as I helped him get to his feet.

"You silly doggie, what are you doing? Are you wanting a belly rub? Are you being silly?" His tail wagged as I led him back down the steps and around to the elevator.

I grabbed a treat and threw it into the elevator. Nick didn't hesitate to follow it in. He had no problem grasping where he was when I opened the elevator door on the second floor, and I've come to believe he enjoys the ride because now he steps into the elevator without hesitation, even without a treat for enticement.

I learned in a visit to Dr. Froman a couple of days ago that the hip joint has suffered further degradation, and the cartilage repair, which is a slow process even with the aid of the Adequan, has not kept up. She thought the medication was still keeping the pain at bay, but also thought we should increase his dosage of Tramadol. After doing a milligram and weight calculation, she told me I could give him a third pill at midday.

Nick was one hundred and five pounds at one point. That's when we started calling him big boy. During a regular vet visit, Dr. Froman told us that for his own good, he needed to lose at least twenty-five pounds.

We worked hard to get that weight off him over a period of six months. The hardest part wasn't the longer hikes; it was cutting back on his food and treats. Whether it's your dad or your dog, it's difficult to deny someone you love what he enjoys, even if it's for his own good. But he lost the twenty-five pounds and has stayed at eighty pounds for what is now four years. Dr. Froman told me back then we were doing him a great favor by taking the extra weight and stress off his hips. Now, however, age and genetics have taken over, and there's nothing we can do except try to keep him as pain-free as possible.

So as I look down at his eager and expectant face, I can't decide if I should accidentally drop some turkey or roast beef for him, considering the need to keep any extra weight off his achy hips, or whether I should ignore him. I compromise and accidentally drop a half-slice of turkey.

---

The birthday party was planned back in January, which gave everyone time to work it into their schedules. It's funny to think that at that time Adam and Jennie didn't even know they would be adopting a baby, but now he will be joining the celebration.

I'm so thankful Dad's gotten to the age of eighty-six, in spite of his many afflictions. We're now almost six years past the time he broke his hip. I don't know if we will be celebrating his birthday next year, so I want to make this one as wonderful as it can be. I had hoped Kathy and Cindy would make it, but neither one could manage the time off, even with two months of lead time. I hope Dad won't notice. I told them he had declined a bit, and I was worried this could be his last birthday. I don't think either believed me. Kathy said Dad had looked great at Thanksgiving and wondered how there could be any meaningful decline in less than four months.

I have no doubt that if she or Cindy saw him now, they would recognize the obvious decline. I'll send pictures from the party; it's the best I can do. Maybe they'll make time to visit in the next couple of months when they see he doesn't look nearly as well as he did at Thanksgiving.

I'm just sad for Dad that they won't be with him on what may be his last birthday.

# 50

There's much joy and festivity around Dad, and he's absolutely beaming at the attention, the laughter, the food, the wine, and the kisses from all the gals who love him.

Dad doesn't recognize everyone, however. He gives Carmen a blank stare and pulls back from Sissy's touch, which has to hurt her feelings. He looks at Brad with suspicion. So it's rather miraculous when he looks at his cousin and says, "Will, how are you?" There's cheeriness in Dad's voice, and the fact that he recognized Will after decades of not seeing him only adds to the mystery of dementia's manifestations.

He and Dad are now engaged in swapping memories. Will is patient with Dad's halting speech. I'm happy Dad is having such clear memories that are prompting moments of laughter for the two of them. Everyone's busy eating, drinking, talking, and laughing, and beautiful baby Lucas is getting much of the attention that might otherwise be on Dad. Jennie is comfortable with his being passed around, even though he's only three weeks old. He sure is a sweet baby.

It's a festive yet relaxed and calm atmosphere. The party I threw for Dad at Crestview seems so long ago.

"I want to give you my present, Joe." Anna hands him a colorfully wrapped box and kisses his cheek. After thanking her, Dad pulls off the bow, but his hands are holding the package clumsily, and he can't find the seams. At this pace, opening his gifts will take hours.

Anna and I exchange a look and a nod. "Lord, look at all the tape I put on that, Joe! What was I thinking? Let me get that tape off there first."

It's a beautifully framed photo of the two of them I had taken some time ago. It is a great picture, and Dad is tickled with it. "That's our engagement picture," he says with a crooked smile and a gleam in his eye, and we all laugh with him at his joke.

With guests taking turns helping him, Dad opens fourteen gifts, including some from Kathy and Cindy. He hasn't even asked where they are.

He's being bombarded, and at times he's confused about who the people are who are handing him gifts. He's innately gracious, so it isn't readily evident. He seems to understand his required participation in the festivities.

Now that all the others' lovely and thoughtful gifts have been opened, I hand him the one from David and me. It was a challenge to come up with something unique for his birthday. Though he loves handsome sweaters, he has a plenty, and another one just wouldn't do.

So I combed every corner of eBay and the Internet to find every badge and insignia that is relevant to his Army unit, the 82nd Airborne Division, 504th Parachute Infantry Regiment, Company C. I've sewed them or pinned them onto a lightweight fleece vest.

The vest elicits the biggest smile I've seen from him today. I've snapped pictures all afternoon and looked at each one the very moment I took it. In some, his eyes are glazed, his Parkinson's mask is pronounced, and he's looking off to the side. In others, he looks removed from what's happening around him, despite his noble efforts to stay alert and participate.

But he's fully present for this gift, and the picture I take of his open expression of wonderment is one I'll cherish forever. I snap another, and in this one, he's studying the patches and insignias. His expression is oddly proud and humble at the same time. Although he was part of an elite unit and was awarded a Bronze Star and a Purple Heart, among several other medals, he's never bragged about them.

Anna and Debra slip his arms through the vest. As everyone is admiring the effect, Adam says, "Hey, Joe, remember what you told me when I asked you why they called your unit *'Those Devils in Baggy Pants?'*"

Dad looks at Adam and grins. "I remember."

There's light laughter and questions of, "Those *what*?"

"Devils in Baggy Pants." Adam repeats. "There've been lots of books written about Joe's unit, so I asked him why they were called that.

"He said, 'Well, Adam, as a paratrooper being dropped behind enemy lines, you have no supply line. What firepower you had on you was it, so paratroopers had the pants with big pockets and they could carry twice the firepower of normal foot soldiers. We could really make our presence known.'"

"That's right," Dad confirms.

"There's something else I would like to say about you, Joe. Something you taught me," Adam continues.

Dad looks a little wary, but then he nods his head, giving Adam the go-ahead.

"Joe, you've taught me to have a good attitude no matter what happens. You told me that even though you were injured in the midst of hell, it probably saved your life. Now if you could look at a serious war injury like that and put that kind of positive spin on it, I figure I can handle just about anything that comes my way, too. You're a true American hero, Joe. That's what I think of you."

Dad has been looking at Adam as he spoke, but now he looks down and begins fingering the vest. "I'm not a hero," he mumbles.

Unexpectedly, Will speaks up. "You are a hero, Joe."

Dad looks up at Will, but there's no recognition there now. Will seems to realize this but handles it well by forging ahead.

"Do you remember when you used to come into my office and sit on my desk and eat crackers, Joe?"

Dad shifts his eyes to the right, a sign that he's trying to remember. He shakes his head slowly. He doesn't remember.

"Well, you did. You got crumbs everywhere."

"He still does," says Marcy. We laugh, but quieten to a hush, waiting for what's coming.

"One day you asked me if you could tell me something about the war. You seemed to be weighed down by whatever it was, so I wanted you to go ahead and tell it." Will pauses and waits to see if Dad has anything to say, but he stays silent, just staring at Will, who continues.

"For those of you who don't know, Joe was seriously injured in Anzio, Italy. His platoon was out on patrol and hiding in a barn when a shell hit it. His leg was busted up from hot shrapnel."

I don't interrupt Will to tell him everyone in the room has heard the story and knows Dad was the only survivor, and spent many months in the hospital in Italy. After all, this is something I'm grateful for (else I wouldn't be here). I don't allow much time to pass in between someone's meeting Dad and my telling that story about him.

From the nods he sees around him, Will realizes everyone's heard the story.

"You told me that day, Joe, that there was one other man still alive."

Wait. I haven't heard this part of the story. What is Will talking about?

"And you told me you threw him over your shoulder and walked five miles back to the front line to get help."

Now I'm truly astonished. I've questioned Dad about the incident. I've asked him how he survived when everyone else died. He'd told me he was sitting behind several other men, and they had absorbed all the shrapnel before it got to him. But he'd had his leg cocked out to the side, so that a piece had hit his lower leg—the only part of him that was exposed.

Dad's forehead furrows into an agonized frown and he drops his head. Maybe it's emotional pain being dredged up at the memory. I want to stop Will, but I also want to learn what he knows.

"I don't think you ever told me that part, Joe," Adam says. "What happened?"

Dad doesn't answer for a long moment. "He was dead by the time I got there." His voice is barely audible, but we all hear. The air seems to go out of the room.

"But you carried him five miles on your back to save him," Will says. "Five miles with a busted leg. If that's not a hero, I don't know what one is."

Dad hunches his shoulders and averts his gaze. Perhaps he's reliving the harrowing truth of it. I'd long suspected he had "survivor's guilt" in being the only man in his platoon to survive, and I've often wondered how deeply that affected him throughout his post-war years.

But to learn he had tried to save another man's life, and failed, on top of losing every other man in his platoon . . .

Even as my heart swells with pride for his heroism, it also aches for him. Talk about Post-Traumatic Stress Disorder. Where has he put that all these years? My eyes meet David's. He's as affected by this news as I am.

Everyone's quiet. Even baby Lucas had ceased his happy gurgling. Now I'm ticked at Will for throwing a wet blanket on what was a joyous occasion.

Debra puts her arms around Dad's neck from behind him. "You *are* a hero, Uncle Joe," she says. "I'm so proud of you." She kisses him on his cheek, adding another layer of color to his face.

Everyone crowds around Dad and praises him for his valor. What an incredible group of good and caring people. Their love and admiration seem to pull Dad up from the depths of sadness, but he doesn't come back to us with the same level of engagement as before. The empty stare in his eyes tells me he has disconnected from his surroundings. *Well, hell.*

"I'm sorry, Rachel," Will leans over and says to me. "I never intended—"

I interrupt him. "I know, Will. You were just trying to point out he was a hero, and why."

"I was, but I guess it was the wrong time to do it."

"Yes, it was, but what's done is done. Will, this is the first time I've heard about him carrying a wounded man over his shoulder. He's never told me that part of the story, so I'm in a bit of a stupor right now."

"From the way he told it, I think he's always felt guilty he didn't save the man's life."

That makes sense, but I also believe there's another part of Dad that kept him from telling anyone, aside from Will, about his act of valor and the devastating outcome. He did what a soldier should do. He carried out his duty with a badly-wounded leg and earned a Purple Heart. I realize now that heroic feat is probably what also earned him a Bronze Star. When I'd asked him what he'd done to earn it, he'd been vague. He'd said something about taking out a nest of snipers, but now I believe it was because he tried to save another man's life under the toughest of circumstances.

Pieces of conflicting, puzzling information fall into place. My irritation with Will turns to gratitude. I've learned something about my dad that makes me admire him even more, and I didn't think that was possible. Will has given me a gift on this day of gift giving. I tell him so.

"But I tell you what, Will. I'm going to let you cut the cake and pass around the plates, and you'd better do it with the intent of getting this party back on track."

He looks surprised, but then bursts out laughing. "Easy penance. Thanks."

After hiding from the commotion, Nick has appeared next to Dad. He puts his head on Dad's hand and awaits a response. When Dad says, "Good boy," Nick's tail wags. He stays where he is, looking into Dad's face, waiting for more.

I bend down in front of Dad and tell him, "You Devils in Baggy Pants gave those Germans hell! You're all heroes."

"All heroes," he repeats, looking into my eyes. His face smooths out as the fog lifts. Then he delights me by reaching out for a hug, and we hold each other for a minute. Happy and uplifting conversation is once again humming around us. Dad asks, "What kind of cake did you burn for me, Rachel?"

There are more than a few laughs in acknowledgment of my lack of baking skills.

"Dad!" I pretend to be indignant, but then I laugh along. "It's your favorite, red velvet, and it's only burned around the edges."

"*Black* velvet cake, then," David teases.

There's another titter of laughter, and then Jennie starts singing, "Happy Birthday to You." Everyone enthusiastically joins in.

Dad's spirits are revived. He takes the slice of cake proffered by Will, sets it on his lap, and cuts into the first bite with steady determination.

He carefully guides it into his mouth and says, "Mmm, that's good. Happy Birthday to me!"

Being the generous soul that he is, Dad holds the plate out to his buddy. Nick licks it clean.

## 51

Two days after Dad's birthday we get a snowfall of six inches, followed by another four inches. We're stuck inside, but no one's complaining because we're warm, safe, and content to be in each other's company.

Dad occasionally stays upstairs with us after dinner until bedtime, though now he falls asleep very shortly after we settle him on the sofa.

Nick has become too incapacitated to jump up next to Dad, so we bought some ingenious foam stairs sturdily constructed to provide support for weight distribution. At first, Nick didn't understand what they were. When I attached a leash to his collar, gave it a gentle tug, and told him to "step up," he did. He didn't need to be told again as he stepped onto the sofa. *Success!* We all praised him, especially Dad, who'd watched with genuine interest. Dad puts his hand on Nick's head. "We're a couple of old fellas, aren't we?"

It's painful for me to look at Nick's now-deformed hips. He can still use his hind legs, thanks to the Adequan and Tramadol that keep the pain under control, but his hips are bony and protruding. I'd talked to Dr. Froman about a total hip replacement, and even though the cost would be close to four thousand dollars, we would spend that amount or more if it would put our big boy right again. But the prognosis wasn't good enough to outweigh the sheer misery Nick would be subjected to through surgery and recovery. And so we decided that with Nick, as with Dad, what time we have together should be about comfort, and comforting.

I've taken Dad to see his neurologist because of extreme lethargy and further diminished mobility. It's becoming nearly impossible for Dad to stand or walk for physical therapy, and even Adam is admitting we may be coming to a point where that is no longer an option. He and Jennie continue with the massages and range-of-motion exercises twice a week.

Because it is hard on Dad to do four transfers—bed to wheelchair, wheelchair to toilet, then the reverse—I've put a porta potty next to his bed.

Nick also needs extra help him to relieve himself. We slip a dog harness through his back legs and around his hips so we can lift his back end. It's a well-designed device that has put an end to David's back strain.

Dad and Nick's additional care is wearing on all of us, and I think it's time to hire another person to help. I call Remembrance Care to ask what level of caregiver is needed at this point.

A lovely nurse named Marilyn comes to assess the situation. When her evaluation is finished, we sit down to talk over a cup of coffee and crullers. I always believe comfort food diminishes the angst of *necessary* conversations.

Too bad I've run out of Oreos. I'd toss them right into the middle of the table and gobble them up in front of David and God and anyone else at this point.

Marilyn doesn't pull any punches. "I must tell you, I'm surprised you haven't called in hospice."

I rock back in my chair with such a thump that I hurt myself. David asks if I'm okay. I shake my head. *No, no, no, I'm not okay.*

She continues, "I see you last consulted with us in January. I wish you had allowed us to stay involved."

"But Dad was doing well until just this week," I counter defensively.

With a kind smile she says, "It may have seemed that way, but he's declined quite a bit since January."

"He's had a lot of good days since then. He had a birthday just two weeks ago, and we had a party for him. He was good for hours."

"And since then?"

"Well, he has been more tired, and as you saw, he can't stand at all."

"You've done a great thing by keeping the physical therapy going," she continues, "but he can't participate any longer. Even his porta potty is going to become impossible in a short time."

"Why impossible?" David asks. "We can hire extra help."

"His brain and his legs are not communicating any longer. You won't be able to put him on the porta potty unless you lift him by his arms and legs and set him there. Extra help could assist you, but it's putting him through unnecessary effort."

At my dazed silence, she says, "You've read the hospice pamphlet for end-of-life signs and behaviors, I assume?"

I think, *but we're not there yet.* "I have it on his bedside table. I've read it many times but I'm not seeing the signs it says to look for."

David takes my hand. With sympathy in his eyes, he tells me, "I have."

"Like what?" My voice is a whisper.

"The physical changes, mostly. Plus, he hasn't been speaking much, barely at all. And he rarely responds to my questions. Or Marcy's. Or yours."

"But he's just tired." I hear the pleading in my voice.

"Yes, he is. He's tired, Rachel." Marilyn's words carry so much meaning, and so much weight.

"And you know he's not eating or drinking as much." David's eyes are willing me to acknowledge what these changes mean.

While I've been denying, David has been noticing. I'm sure he's relieved there's an objective professional in our midst.

I repeat something I heard in a Remembrance Care support group meeting. "You start out in denial and work your way down to acceptance."

I look at my hand in David's, and have another thought. "His hands are always so cold now, too." As a person gets closer to death, his blood pressure lowers and there's decreased blood flow to the feet and hands.

"Your father's blood pressure today was eighty-nine over forty-eight. It's time to call in hospice, Rachel," Marilyn's voice is filled with compassion. "You're going to need their help now. They can make him more comfortable, which is the most important thing."

I want to tell her we keep him comfortable, but I know she's talking about comfort medications like morphine. I know because I had to give it to Mother during her last week.

And here I am again. I've worked my way down to acceptance.

Tears stream down my face. When David takes me in his arms, I sob into his shoulder.

As Marilyn hands me a tissue, I tell her, "Thank you. I'll call and get the order from his doctor today."

She looks relieved. "He can fax it directly to Buncombe County Hospice, and I'll follow up with them. They're very responsive and have a great team of nurses and caregivers." She pauses before she adds, "And chaplains."

"All will be welcome," I tell her. "But I'd still like a recommendation from Remembrance Care for a private, top-notch caregiver. Even a nurse. Hospice only comes in two or three times a week, and I want someone here full time. A live-in, so that Dad has the best care until the very last moment of his life."

"I understand, and agree you could use more help. But, Rachel, your presence is what he will need most." She looks at David, "And you need to be there for your wife."

Before David can say anything, I tell her, "He is. He will be. He's always been there for me, and for Dad."

She nods her head. "You're lucky, both of you. I can tell you're a strong team and that you've given Joe amazing care. But I have to ask you if you would consider moving Joe to a hospice facility? They're excellent in handling his needs at this stage, and you can be with him the entire time, if you wish."

Both David and I say at the same time, "Absolutely not." We squeeze each other's hand in unity.

Marilyn respects our decision. "Okay, then. I think a good CNA is your best bet, instead of a nurse. You're sure you want a live-in?"

I nod emphatically, and she says, "I'll make arrangements to get someone over here by late this afternoon, then."

And this is why I need Remembrance Care's help. They have resources and referrals at their fingertips. I wouldn't have known where to start, other than calling health care agencies. I'm confident whoever Marilyn finds will be the right person—for all of us.

## 52

Janet McGregor moved in that evening. She fed Dad his dinner of pureed vegetables and beef. Then she gave him a sponge bath, took care of his needs, and got him settled in for the night. Even though I offered her a private bedroom with an en-suite bathroom, she said she'd rather sleep in the lift chair beside Dad's bed. I give her two nights before she crawls into that comfy guest bed. I've spent many an hour in that lift chair, and it isn't conducive to a restful night's sleep.

I gave Marcy the next two days off with pay so she will be rested for what's to come. She didn't argue, but implored me to call her if anything changes, or if I need her.

With Janet right there with Dad, David and I can relax for an evening. We make love for the first time in two weeks, and the lovemaking overflows with emotion, tenderness, and the need for closeness. Our passion turns into an urgent coupling that embraces the gift of our life together.

Afterward we hold tightly to each other throughout the night. We are fulfilled, we are relieved, we are exhausted; as a result, we find some much-needed peace that allows a long and refreshing slumber.

I wake up after eight A.M. in a panic. Nick needs to go out, and I have to see what, if any, changes have occurred in Dad overnight. David is still asleep, so I don't bother to turn on the light to get dressed. I grab a warm robe and step into my Uggs in anticipation of taking Nick out.

When I get downstairs, I hear music playing and I smell coffee, plus something comforting baking—cinnamon rolls?

Janet has taken charge and taken over the apartment kitchenette. She pours herself a cup of coffee and offers me one. "No thanks. I have to take Nick out before he has a major accident."

She smiles and tells me she already took him out.

"Oh, Janet, that's not part of your job. I'm so sorry you had to do that. We just slept late this morning. I don't even remember if we set the alarm, but we're usually up by six to take him out."

"Not a problem. I'm glad you got some sleep. I have a Great Dane who's ten years old, and he has the same hip dysplasia as Nick. I have the same kind of harness for him."

I sigh with relief. "Thank you so much."

"You're welcome. Want to say good morning to your dad?"

"How is he?"

"About the same."

And he is. He's sleeping, but he's been shaved and has on a clean pair of pajamas. Nick is on the mat next to him and struggles to get up. I hold up my hand. "Just a minute, big boy." Grabbing the large towel we use to put under him, I hoist him up.

After he's on his feet, he buries his head in between my legs. He's a study in misery and need. I bend down and kiss his face all over. I rub his head, then push my head against his for our game of push back. He yips softly and participates as well as he can. He swabs my face with a long stroke of his tongue. I kiss the graying, tender part of his soft cheek in return.

When I turn to Dad, his eyes are open and he's watching us. "So much love." He's muttering, but I hear and understand his words.

"So much love for you, too, Dad."

I don't want his eyes to close again, because it could be hours before he wakes up. "How about a cup of coffee, Dad?"

He looks interested for about two seconds but then closes his eyes. I'm deflated. I wanted more of him this morning. I want more of him for every minute he's alive.

Nick emits a low whine, and I pet his head while watching Dad for signs of revival. Unlikely. Very unlikely.

"How about you, Nickaroo? Are you hungry? Do you want your breakfast?" He knows that word, of course, but he doesn't react. At all.

*Oh, my God, what's happening here?*

When Janet comes in I tell her about the sequence of events that just unfolded with both Dad and Nick.

Her eyes hold mine. "They're both passing, Rachel. Many of the same symptoms that affect a person at the end of life also affect an animal."

I nod. "It's remarkable, isn't it? The similarities?"

"It is. I've seen it a few times in my life, and it never fails to amaze me. Sometimes I've thought the person and the dog develop the same symptoms out of a sympathy of sorts. Does that sound crazy?"

"No, it doesn't sound crazy. I've thought the exact same thing." I take Dad's hand. My other hand reaches for Nick. He's still standing, and now I see the discomfort in his eyes.

"You want to lie back down, Nick?"

He shifts from foot to foot, slowly and painfully, telling me that's what he wants. I support him with the towel as he eases back down on the mat.

"You're so good with both of them," Janet tells me.

"I love them both so much."

"That's evident."

Dad and Nick have their eyes closed, and it looks as if they're in for a long nap. "I'm going upstairs to wake David, and then shower." My voice sounds hollowed out.

"Take your time. I've got everything covered."

I nod and mumble some sort of statement about being grateful, then head out of Dad's room and up the steps with a heavy, labored tread.

---

Hospice has called to say two nurses will be here at ten to get Dad evaluated for the end-of-life care he's going to need.

I join David as he answers the door, and we introduce ourselves to Dorothy and Betty. Both hand David a business card. Dorothy encourages us to keep it nearby in case there's any reason to call.

"What reasons?" I ask.

"That's what we're here to talk about, among many other things," Betty answers.

Over the next two hours, they dose us with reality, and break our hearts.

# 53

I do the same to Kathy and Cindy when I call to tell them Dad is dying, and according to hospice, has perhaps only a week to live. I ask them to come as soon as possible.

Cindy says she'll clear some things up at work and be on a plane early Friday morning, which is two days from now. She'll rent a car so we don't have to leave Dad to pick her up at the airport.

Kathy says she'll get in her car first thing Friday and drive up. It's a long drive, nine hours, so I suggest she take a flight and rent a car. She resists that idea, and I don't argue. When I ask her to contact Laura and Sarah about coming, she agrees, but tells me not to expect her daughters to come on such short notice. *Sheesh.* As if I have any control over the timing.

As our conversation continues, David hears me defending my decisions, answering her questions and expressing my apologies for not calling sooner. "It's just like he turned a sharp corner, Kathy. It's been so quick."

David motions for me to hand him the phone. I do, and he says to Kathy, "This conversation is over. You get your ass up here if you want to, but you do not ask my wife for one more explanation or apology. Got it?"

He listens for a moment and says, "Good. Now good night." He hangs up the phone, looks at me, and shrugs. I smile.

I've asked Janet to give me the entire night with my dad. As she settles into the guest room, she thanks me, then elicits a promise I'll call her if I need her.

David takes Nick out for the last time tonight, then gets him settled on the mat next to Dad. He kisses the top of my head. "I'll be back in a minute."

Dad's arm flops off the bed and his hand opens. Nick licks his hand and then lowers his weary head. I pick up Dad's arm and tuck it under the covers before moving to the lift chair. David returns with a bottle of wine and two glasses. He pulls up a chair and sets it next to mine. I gratefully accept the wine.

Although Dad seems to be deep in sleep, we know he may be able to hear us, so we talk about happy things, mostly about good times spent with Dad and Mother.

After about an hour, I tell David to go on up to bed. He kisses me and tells me he loves me. He puts a hand on Dad's shoulder. "I love you, too, Joe."

I'm alone with my thoughts now.

---

Many wonder if we'll see our loved ones in the next life, whatever that life is. I don't wonder. I had a glimpse of it when we went to Rome two months after Mother passed.

Our plane took off from Leonardo Da Vinci International Airport for an overnight flight. The sun sets later in Rome in May, around eight-thirty P.M., and as our plane ascended, I was captivated by the sunset outside my window. I kept the shade up and was turned in my seat, fascinated by the glow that emanated from the sky. There were bands of colors ranging from a deep blue-purple, to pink, to salmon, to deep orange. I continued watching as the sun dipped below the horizon, the colors of that spectrum disappearing one at a time.

As the sun winked out, a brilliant flash of green, lasting no more than a second, took my breath away. It wasn't just the startling magnificence of the celestial dynamic that left me breathless; it was also the profession of love from Mother.

Mother's eyes were a brilliant and unique shade of green, and throughout her life, so many had said to her, "You have the most beautiful eyes." As beautiful as she was, her eyes were her most striking feature.

They were the same shade of green that I had just witnessed in the green flash. I told David, "Mother just winked at me. It was her loving farewell." That's what I felt in my soul, and it was something I could share with my soulmate, knowing he would hear in my voice the certainty of it, the veracity of it, and accept it. The gentle pressure of his hand and the look in his eyes confirmed that he did.

"Goodbye, Mother. I love you," I'd whispered to the heavens above. In that moment, all the sorrow I had felt from her loss, all the guilt-riddled questions I had asked myself regarding "Was it enough?" in terms of caring for her, evaporated.

I understood then that I had given all I had to give—every single drop—in caring for her to her last breath, and she knew it. I was lying beside her when she took that last breath. I had reached out and touched her face and said, "Oh, Mother."

Now I would watch over my father until he took his last breath. I don't know why or what purpose there is in being the child who watches both parents pass out of this life, but I am deeply grateful for the privilege, even though it comes at a very steep price.

# 54

"I called everybody on the list," Marcy comes in and tells me. I'm still in my pajamas and robe, finishing the cup of coffee David brought me a few minutes ago.

Marcy was supposed to take this day off. Before I can ask her what she's doing here, Janet comes in. She's carrying a diaper and fresh pajamas. I worry Marcy will get territorial, but instead, she introduces herself and says, "Let me help you with that."

Nick is where he usually is, beside Dad's bed, so he's really in the way. But the two women work quickly and efficiently around him while I go up to get more coffee.

When I return, I almost run into Marcy. She sets down a load of laundry and tells me, "Joe's gonna have a lot of company today."

"What do you mean?"

"Every one of them that I called is coming to see him today."

"Marcy, I know you mean well, but that might be too much for Dad."

Marcy emits a deep sigh. "Miss Rachel, one thing I believe for sure. The more love around somebody who's passing, the more comfort there is in it. I saw it with my grandma when all her kids and grandkids came in. She knew they was there, and she took in every bit of love they had to give."

I think about what she's saying. Besides Dad and Emmaline, our live-in helper, only Cindy and I were with Mother on her last day. Kathy, Tom, Laura and Sarah had been there the day before, as had David. But

I remember the lack of warmth and family love in the house on the day that turned out to be Mother's last.

Even if all of Dad's daughters and granddaughters can't be here, at least he'll be surrounded by many others who love him.

"You were supposed to have today off, Marcy. Are you here because you think this may be Dad's last day? Is that why you called everyone?"

"Ain't up to me to say what his last day is. But either way, he needs people around him."

I hug Marcy and thank her for her thoughtfulness. "Well, if we're having company, I better get in the shower."

People appear throughout the day. There's no formality, no knocking, no embarrassment at joining the others in the midst of whatever is happening. I ask only two things of them: First, anything they say to Dad or anything they say to anyone else in the room can't be sad. Second, if they want to cry, please leave the room—though I excused Anna earlier for her soft crying as she sat on the bed next to Dad and held his hand and kissed his head and face.

As is often true when people gather under such circumstances, they become social in an attempt to diminish the painful effect of what's happening before their eyes. There's laughter and tale-telling, and references to things Dad said or did that endeared him to them. Some start taking pictures of others as they sit beside him on his bed, expressing their love. I don't mind. I only hope they share them with me.

When Debra walks in, a soul-bending sorrow passes between us. She's been like a daughter to Dad and a sister to me throughout this entire time, and no one understands what is happening quite like she does.

Charles comes in and pauses at the profundity that hangs between Debra and me. I envelope her in a hug that goes on and on. We step out of the room and then hold each other again as we cry.

"Go," I tell her. "Go see Uncle Joe." She nods, dries her eyes, and then heads into Dad's room.

A vision appears at the top of the steps. A fair-haired angel named Jennie, a mighty guardian angel named Adam, and a baby angel named Lucas are there, and I open my arms wide, beckoning them.

"Thank you so much for coming, and thank you for bringing Lucas."

They're as sad as anyone I've ever seen, but they offer hugs and words of comfort. I ask them if I can hold Lucas, and as he is put into my arms, I am strengthened by the miracle of life anew.

We all walk into Dad's room together. Hugs are given and received. Nick, who is getting a great deal of loving attention himself, tries to rise to greet the Reynolds family. Marcy grabs the towel and helps him up. He sways a bit, then carefully, slowly, steps off the pad and comes around the bed. He's fixated on the bundle in my arms.

I go to my knees to show him the baby I hold. He gently, oh so gently, sniffs tiny Lucas from head to toe. Adam and Jennie speak sweetly and softly to Nick, encouraging him.

I hand the baby to Jennie, and she walks to Dad's bed and lays Lucas in the crook of his arm. Dad hasn't woken up today, and I wonder if he's in that final sleep from which he won't awaken. But when he feels the gentle spirit of the baby who is lying close to him, he speaks. It's totally unintelligible, and far too soft to hear, but Lucas coos and gurgles in answer.

Nick, with Adam's help, comes to stand by the bed. Again, he sniffs the sweet being that is Lucas, and then he sniffs Dad.

Nick lets out a low and mournful moan that, to my ears, expresses love, longing, and loss. I'm not alone in what I've heard. Everyone in the room looks at each other, all of us wide-eyed as we silently acknowledge the sorrow Nick has so poignantly expressed.

Most flee then, adhering to the no-crying-in-the-room request. Debra, Jennie, Adam, David, and I stay. And, of course, Lucas.

I watch the rise and fall of the chest of the new life, and that of the departing life, and see their short breaths are in tandem. "Do you see that?" I ask everyone present, and they all nod reverentially. The beginning of life, and the end of life. How similar they are in content and character.

The shallow breaths that are taken. Diapers that are changed. Liquids given for hydration and nourishment. A safe bed to sleep in. Lucas and Dad, at opposite ends of the span of life, share the inability to talk or walk. They are totally dependent on others to take care of their every need.

Though that care comes from the same source, love, the outcomes will diverge. The new one will grow strong, but the old one will continue to weaken.

Because it is such a powerful moment, I want to remember it. I take my phone out of my pocket and take a picture of Lucas sleeping in the crook of Dad's arm. I ask Adam and Jennie to join Lucas and Dad on his bed for a picture.

When Dorothy from hospice was here a couple of hours ago, she evaluated Dad and then asked David and me to join her upstairs. She asked if we had a minister we would like to call in. We don't belong to a church, so I told her a hospice chaplain would be most welcome. Dad is a man of deep faith, and I want him to have prayers of comfort as he lets go of this life he loves to join Mother in a peaceful afterlife.

"But isn't it too soon?" I had asked her. She and Betty had, after initially assessing Dad, told us he might be with us another week, or even longer; but they also counseled us that every person is different, and much of it had to do with the person's will to either stay or to move on.

No, it wasn't too soon, she had said. Her earnest look said as much as her words. We hadn't shared her assessment with anyone else after she'd left, but now I'm anxious for the chaplain to arrive. Just then, Marcy comes through the door, followed by a distinguished man in a robe and a collar.

*Ask and ye shall receive.* "Mr. and Mrs. Morgan?" he asks as he extends his hand.

"Please, Rachel and David," I tell him. He introduces himself as Ned Parks, and then we introduce him to Debra, Charles, Adam and Jennie.

"I'll go get everybody," Marcy says. While we wait, we talk about the kind of service we want for Dad. It takes a few minutes because guests were scattered about the house, but now everyone is here. We join hands and bow our heads, and, along with Dad, receive the words of comfort that the chaplain pours forth so generously, so graciously.

My no-tears edict no longer applies. Every one of us is crying when the chaplain leaves. As each person acknowledges that this will be the last time he or she will see Dad, each wants to say goodbye to him personally.

One by one, in no particular order, they sit on Dad's bed. Each says words I can't hear, but I'm enveloped by the love that pours from their hearts and passes their lips. Some tenderly stroke his head, while others hold his hand; and every one of them leans down to kiss him. There's a reverence for the process that's happening in this place where Dad has dwelled for only ten months.

Though all of us remain in the room throughout the goodbyes, no one is embarrassed to cry or show deep emotions in front of the others. We are bound together by our capacity to love this good man and yet relinquish our earthly ties to him.

Nick never leaves Dad's bedside. Even though everyone has to maneuver around him to sit on Dad's bed, each person offers a petting and a kind word to him. The thick mat has been removed so that everyone can access the bed with less effort. Despite having no pad and no bed to give ease to his aged and painful body, Nick stays where he is, never once seeking a more comfortable place. For more than an hour, he shares Dad with the others. He seems to be listening attentively to each person's words, and now and then he lets out a low whine. His sorrow and pain are almost too much for me to bear on top of everyone else's, and my own.

David is by my side, holding my hand, offering me comfort and sharing my sorrow. We're both crying, and I wish with all my heart my sisters were here. I'm hoping Dad will be alive to receive the loving parting words his daughters will want to say, but I'm not optimistic.

But Dad's demise is looming, and he's moving on his own timetable that won't be taking into consideration any travel schedules. I think I should call them and tell them this, but I'm not sure what that would accomplish since I can't say with any certainty he will pass away before they get here. Why dash their hopes, or cause anguish that may not be warranted? I have no say in what will happen with Dad from this moment on. No prayers or actions will alter God's plan for him.

By seven P.M., everyone has left except Marcy and Janet. They work together to get Dad cleaned up and comfortable for the night. He has slept through the entire day, except for those few seconds when he uttered some forever-unknown words when Lucas was laid into the crook of his arm. I accept that I may never look into his beautiful blue eyes again or hear the loving goodbye I long for. We've shared plenty of words of love for each other over our lifetimes, and I'm just glad to have so many beautiful words to recall when I need comfort.

David fields the calls from Kathy and Cindy that evening, telling them what we agreed on—that Dad is still hanging on and we're looking forward to seeing them tomorrow, but if anything changes, we'll call.

Meanwhile, I stay downstairs, keeping a vigil for Dad. Nick has been taken out and now looks more than ready to settle in for some rest after such a taxing day. I've put his bed on top of the mat so he can be as comfortable as possible.

David comes down and sits with us for a couple of hours before I tell him to go to bed. I love having him next to me, but it's getting late and I want to be alone with Dad.

He hugs me and tells me to come and get him if I need him. I promise I will.

The light on the nightstand next to Dad's bed softly illuminates his face, which is sunken and ashen. I watch him take several rapid breaths, followed by a period of no breathing. It happens several times, and each time I hold my own breath until I see his chest rise slightly again with the next breath he takes. From all I've learned from hospice, I know for certain now that he has only a short time left.

I close my eyes as I pray for him to go peacefully. I began giving him morphine earlier this evening when he started expelling loud rasping breaths, followed by quiet breathing. Until then, there had been no need for morphine. Dorothy had agreed with my assessment but reminded me what signs to look for, specifically near the end, when morphine would be a necessary kindness. I could have asked that Dorothy or another hospice nurse be here to do it, but I had given Mother the last drops she would ever need less than an hour before she passed.

It's time for another dose to further ease the discomfort of his shortness of breath. When I retrieve it from the nightstand, Nick whines. I soothe him with gentle strokes up and down his body, along with reassuring words of love. After suctioning the prescribed dosage, I turn toward Dad to put it under his tongue. I'm startled to see him looking right at me, without seeing me. It is as if he's seeing through me and beyond me. His eyes flicker, as if fending off a bright light.

I turn to see what he is looking at. There's nothing and no one there. I look back at him and see that in the instant I looked away, his blue eyes have become transparent. I had seen the same change in Mother's eyes.

I put the morphine back onto the nightstand and take Dad's hand. He's only moments from joining Mother, so there's no need for it now.

I softly recite the words from a stanza of a Walt Whitman poem. They come to me, beckoned from memory; words that seem especially relevant because Mother is right here with us.

*With a slow and noiseless footstep*
*Comes that messenger divine,*
*Takes the vacant chair beside me,*
*Lays her gentle hand in mine.*

*And she sits and gazes at me*
*With those deep and tender eyes,*
*Like the stars, so still and saint-like,*
*Looking downward from the skies.*

I've watched Dad as I've said the words, watched as his eyes have stayed fixed on that point beyond me. Now they shift and focus—on me. My heart speeds up, then slows down again as I feel a shift in the air around me. I am being comforted. I don't let my eyes leave Dad's. I'm looking for something, though I don't know what it is. And then I hear it.

"I love you. Thank you." Though not spoken aloud, his words reach deep into me and ignite a long-forgotten memory. Dad is young and strong and his smile is so big and bright. He's so handsome! He's swinging me around and around, laughing with me, and though I'm getting dizzy, I don't want the ride to end. In his sure grip I am safe and loved, and I know he'll never drop me, or let me go, not until he's set me back on my feet and made sure I'm steady.

I have only seconds to answer, and I say aloud, "I love you, too, Dad. Thank *you*."

Dad closes his eyes and exhales one last shuddering breath. He is gone.

Nick lets out a low-pitched moan, followed by a deep chuff. He crawls off his bed and across the mat until he's close enough to raise his head and put his nose right next to Dad's face. He takes a final sniff, then licks Dad's face for the last time. He puts his chin on the bed and closes his eyes.

I leave them there because I suddenly know that I have to be somewhere else. I run up the stairs, being pulled along to my destination by a compelling force. I have to hurry. I fling open the door to the deck and rush out into the chilly night to look up into the star-filled sky. I know there's something else, something awaiting me, though I don't know exactly what it is.

And there it is. Mother takes Dad's hand, and they turn together and walk away from me, from the bonds of Earth that no longer have any hold on them. They are together now. The light that shines on them so I can witness this celestial wonder fades away, and they are gone.

A warm tongue on my hand brings me back to my earthly state. I'm surprised to see Nick is standing next to me. How in the world did he get up the steps to come out here and join me? He hasn't climbed steps in weeks, and yet here he is.

I sink to the deck and throw my arms around him, then bury my face in his soft fur. I cry, yes I cry, but I also rejoice.

This is the second such heavenly miracle I've seen in my lifetime.

I hope I never lose my memory of either.

# EPILOGUE

"Tucker! Bring that back!"

Our black Lab puppy runs out of the garage and across the driveway with one of my favorite house slippers. He flies across the yard and goes down the steep bank. I'll never see that slipper again. He's chewed up everything he can get his sharp little teeth on, so I have no hope my slipper will meet a kinder fate.

David drives up and sees me standing there with my hands on my hips, exasperation written all over my face.

But I smile when he gets out of the car and puts his arm around my shoulder and reminds me I deliberately chose the feistiest puppy from the litter.

I had no idea what I was getting into. All of our dogs were already past puppyhood when we brought them home, but I had always said I wanted to raise a puppy into a dog.

We brought Tucker home when he was only eight weeks old. What a precious bundle of fur he was. Nick didn't get to spend very much time with Tucker, though it was our intention to bring him in to revive Nick's spirits.

When Dad passed, we were afraid Nick would go immediately after because he seemed to have just given up on life. Marcy stayed with Nick for the five days it took us to go to Florida and bury Dad next to Mother. I had stood by the gravesite with my family and listened to the soloist sing the beautiful hymn, "I'll Fly Away," which was Dad's favorite. I had smiled throughout the song. Others were in tears, but mine were already shed, and I allowed that Dad had indeed flown away and was where he belonged for eternity—with Mother.

While we were gone, I worried every day that Marcy would call and tell me Dr. Froman was coming over to put him to sleep. Marcy had been instructed to call the vet's office each day to give her an update on his status so that Dr. Froman would know when it was time to ease Nick out of our world.

I was filled with guilt and a different kind of grief to think he would pass away without David and me at his side. But I trusted that the talk I'd had with Nick the night before we left assured him we would be coming back to him. I asked him to wait for us. I believed with all my heart he understood because he was indeed waiting for us when we returned. I ran into Dad's apartment as soon as we pulled into the garage and was beyond happy to see him lying on his bed with a welcoming smile and wagging tail.

I'd nestled with him and poured out words of love until he fell asleep.

The day after we had returned from Florida, I got a call from the shelter manager, Angie, telling me someone had just dropped off a litter of four black Lab puppies. Was I interested in adopting one?

I was and I wasn't, but I had read somewhere that if you want to keep an old dog young, get a puppy. We adopted one of the puppies that very afternoon.

Though Nick's afflictions plagued him, he perked up when puppy Tucker pounced on him and started chewing on his ears as he lay on his bed in Dad's apartment. Nick spent all of his time there now. He seemed to find solace in that space.

He was an old dog to be teaching our new puppy any manners, but it didn't take long for him to establish a few rules, via a sharp bark, when puppy Tucker got too rough, chewed on something he shouldn't, or had an accident on the carpet.

Two short weeks after Tucker joined our family, we had to say goodbye to Nick. Dr. Froman came to our home in the early evening. We gathered in Dad's apartment, where Tucker joined us for a sweet but terribly sad love fest before she administered the two shots that put Nick to sleep and took him away from us forever. David and I held Nick, and we wept tears of profound loss for the second time in a month as we watched the light in his eyes go dark. David gently laid him on Dad's bed, wrapped in Dad's comforter, which had become Nick's after Dad was gone.

On many days throughout the summer, we hiked with Tucker up to Nick's favorite place, the creek. Just as we had with Rocky, we'd scattered his ashes in the shallow pools and deep wells of the creek, which feeds into the beautiful Swannanoa River. Tucker splashed around with unfettered joy, and each and every time I pictured our big boy doing the same. As I often did with Nick, I joined Tucker in the creek and allowed myself to be soaked from head to toe from his splashing and shaking.

It's now early September, and those harbingers of autumn—the cooler breezes and chillier nights—are upon us.

I call Tucker, but he doesn't respond to my calls other than to let out a yip from down in the valley now and then. David and I settle into the chairs on the bank with a glass of wine, anticipating the sunset and Tucker's return.

My mind goes back to this time last year . . .

David interrupts my reminiscing when he says, "There he is." Tucker's head comes into view as he climbs the steep bank to join us.

"What does he have in his mouth?" I ask David.

"I can't tell." David verbally encourages Tucker as he pulls his strong, young body the rest of the way up the bank to join us and proudly show us what he has found.

It's Dad's 82nd Airborne cap, the one that had blown off his head last autumn and seemingly disappeared. It's covered in dirt and grass stains, and I wonder how it survived the winter weather and the gusty spring winds.

I reach for it, but Tucker dances away from me, taunting me. David laughs and says, "I'll get it from him."

As he reaches out to snag it from Tucker, I put my hand on his arm to stop him. He looks at me quizzically as I smile and shake my head.

"I think Dad would want him to have it, don't you?"

THE END

# AUTHOR'S NOTE

Thank you so much for reading *My Dad My Dog*, which is based on my dad, Joe and my dog, Nick. To have changed their names would have diminished their value in inspiring this story.

If you would like to learn more about these two inspirational characters, please visit my website at www.rebeccajwarner.com.

If you can find a moment to leave a review for *My Dad My Dog*, I would be most appreciative. I would love to hear from you if you have any comments or questions. You can email me at rebeccawarnerauthor@gmail.com.

Being a health care surrogate to both my parents for fourteen years involved not only making medical decisions on their behalf, but also providing loving emotional support. In their lifetimes, they faced many medical challenges that required being in hospitals, surgical units, assisted living facilities, and nursing homes for rehabilitation. I spent thousands of days in those facilities, always striving to ensure their best care.

Then there was the other sweet being under my care—Nick, my big black Lab. After many years of hiking and swimming and chasing balls, Nick began to slow down. But his valiant heart and love of being with his people and his canine brothers and sisters kept him relatively active. Then Nick began showing signs of decline remarkably similar to Dad's, especially in the last year of their lives.

These experiences and events laid the foundation for *My Dad My Dog*.

Dad lived in a wonderful facility much like Crestview, and he received excellent care from the staff. I loved visiting with him almost every day when I wasn't traveling or snowed in. After he passed away, I began to imagine how different my life would have been if, as is true with many caregivers, I had tended to him in my home, without a staff of CNAs to facilitate his personal care. To broaden my perspective about what in-home care would entail, I reached out to <u>MemoryCare of Asheville</u>, a community-based, charitable organization uniquely focused on serving the whole family—caregivers and patients.

Everyone who has provided care for a loved one with dementia has had a very personal and distinctive journey. While there are medical absolutes about the disease itself, there is no cure. While there are guidelines for care, none are etched in stone since each patient's level of dementia results in diverse behaviors. Each caregiver's experience is unique to their perspectives and experiences they draw upon in dealing with this debilitating disease.

But what is a certainty is the eventual loss of our loved ones. It is the entire life journey we've taken with them that imprints upon our memories. Memories can be a gift, allowing us to hold on to feelings for the people, places and events that shaped our lives. When those with dementia lose their memories, then caregivers, family members and friends must carry those memories forward and honor their loved ones for the difficult and frightening journey they took as their precious memories slipped away. This is what I wished to do in writing *My Dad My Dog*.

My hope is that we as a society and a nation empower caregivers by making every tool and service available, including compensation, to help make their difficult endeavors as bearable as possible for them and their loved ones.

# ACKNOWLEDGMENTS

First and foremost, I want to thank my husband, Jason, a loving and giving partner through the ups and downs I experienced during those years of striving to fulfill my parents' medical and emotional needs. His selfless understanding and acceptance of our spending more time apart than either of us wanted, and his love of and generosity toward my parents, made me love him even more.

My heartfelt thanks to my dear friend, author Rochelle B. Weinstein, for showering me with the generosity of her "pay it forward" philosophy. As she has done for others, she pushed me in the right direction and prodded me to keep going. Most of all, she believed in me and never let me forget it.

My thanks to author Jill Cox Vogt, whose friendship, writing and editing skills I called upon throughout the process. Thank you, Dee Dee Evans of The Write Stuff Editing Services, for sharpening and polishing my manuscript until I felt it was ready to present to the publishing world. Thanks to author and editor Nan Reinhardt for her valuable input.

I'm grateful to those caregivers who shared with me their personal experiences in caring for their loved ones at home. Your opening up to a writer doing research was generous and courageous. All of you inspired me! Special thanks to Bill Carson and Becky Anderson for sharing insightful details of the journeys they've taken with their Alzheimer's-afflicted spouses.

Writing a book can be a lonely pursuit, but there are dear friends and family members who kept me company even when I wasn't in their physical presence. These wonderful women include my sister Sandy Rogers, my niece Stacy Neiman, friends Julie Patterson, Laura

Stapleton, Fran Strawn, Patti Grosh, Terri Fitch, Cathy Pyles, Janie DeVos, and Carole Klein.

Thank you to my publisher, Black Rose Writing, for welcoming me to its family of authors. Its credo is "We publish only one genre...our genre." In that regard, I found a perfect fit.

Finally, I want to thank the many wonderful CNAs who gave my dad exceptional care, not only out of a sense of duty but also out of love. CNAs are hard-working, underpaid but invaluable members of the medical community who provide their patients with dignity and comfort under the most difficult circumstances. We owe them our appreciation and respect.

# NOTE FROM THE AUTHOR

Word-of-mouth is crucial for any author to succeed. If you enjoyed *My Dad My Dog*, please leave a review online—anywhere you are able.

Thanks!
Rebecca

# ABOUT THE AUTHOR

Rebecca Warner is the author of the two-time award-winning thriller, *Moral Infidelity*, as well as *Doubling Back To Love* and *He's Just A Man*. She has been a newspaper columnist and a blogger for *HuffPost*.

As health care surrogate for her parents, Rebecca navigated the caregiver and healthcare labyrinth for fourteen years. Her experiences inspired her to write *My Dad My Dog*.

Rebecca and her husband Jason live in Asheville with their rescue dog, Chance.

Thank you so much for reading one of our **Women's Fiction** novels.
If you enjoyed the experience, please check out our recommendation
for your next great read!

*City in a Forest* by Ginger Pinholster

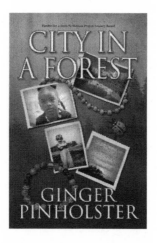

Finalist for a *Santa Fe Writers Project Literary Award*

"Ginger Pinholster, a master of significant detail, weaves her
struggling characters' pasts, present, and futures into a
breathtaking, beautiful novel in *City in a Forest*.
*–IndieReader Approved*

View other Black Rose Writing titles at
www.blackrosewriting.com/books and use promo code
PRINT to receive a **20% discount** when purchasing.

Made in the USA
Middletown, DE
17 June 2021